WORD ASSOCIATION PUBLISHERS

www.wordassociation.com
1.800.827.7903
TARENTUM, PENNSYLVANIA

ISBN: 978-1-63385-430-7

Designed and published by
Word Association Publishers
205 Fifth Avenue
Tarentum, Pennsylvania 15084

www.wordassociation.com

1.800.827.7903

SLIPPERY SLOPE

REVENGE, RUSE AND ROBBERY

RONALD O. KAISER

DEDICATION

For My mother Rosalie LaValle Kaiser
who planted the writing seed in my mind.
As Ladybird, she was the first storyteller
in our family and mesmerized us all with
her wonderful stories.

AUTHOR'S NOTE

A SPECIAL THANKS TO THOSE OF YOU WHO TOOK THE TIME TO READ this book and offer helpful advice and suggestions. A special thanks to award winning poet and writer Leslie McIlroy for her suggestions, and to Sue Murphy for her editing contributions.

I'd also like to acknowledge the invaluable advice and guidance my dear friend Bob Colville gave me for both this book and my life. He had so much more to offer when his untimely death took away one of the finest human beings I have ever known. Bob carved out a successful career as a marine in Korea, football coach, homicide detective, Police Chief, District Attorney, and a Judge in Pennsylvania's judicial system.

He walked the tightrope of life with grace and balance, a street-smart man with a commonsense outlook and a great sense of humor.

Thanks to my family, my children, grandchildren, and great grandchildren. You are the reason I'm still alive.

Ronald O. Kaiser
Pittsburgh, PA.
June 17, 2021

For more information about Ron Kaiser and his books, or to contact him, go to Ronkaiser.net.

If you enjoy true crime thrillers, you'll want to read The Whiz Kid due for release later in 2021. Read how 25 year old Pitt student, Earl Belle, wowed the business world with his financial genius and then skipped to South America with everybody's money, a flashy blonde and 27 suitcases.

Herbert's War, Ron's first book, is the true story of his childhood friend Lt. Col. Anthony B. Herbert, a celebrated war hero who dared to speak out against war crimes and the Vietnam War as the powers that be, from the Nixon White House and the Pentagon to CBS and 60 Minutes conspired to stop him. Available on Amazon and Herbertswar. com

PROLOGUE

EVERY TIME SHE THOUGHT SHE WOULD DO IT, SHE RETHOUGHT IT and the doubts crept back in. She wasn't sure what would happen if she failed, but she knew it wouldn't be good. What she was going to do was complicated. Many things had to happen exactly right.

She thought about her mother in Schwabenland, an ingenuous region in southwestern Germany.

"Land is like a child," her mother told her, "and you must cultivate it, love it, and give it good health and it will return much to you."

But now she was in America, and things were different. She was nothing but another immigrant with no money or standing, but now there was an opportunity. The question was, should she chance it? Could she do it?

That was what she was trying to sort out.

The first time she saw the land she wanted it. There was no doubt. She shuddered with excitement and for a moment she wanted to scream out her joy, but she was too controlled for that. The adrenalin rush that had swept through her body was tempered by reality. There was no way she could get it. No possible way. She felt the drain as her hands went limp.

As she stood on the bluff, some 2100 feet above sea level—the same sea that she crossed to get here—she gazed across the lush highlands, a medley of brilliant green slopes and hillocks undulating over bedrock and then disappearing into a distant ridgeline. The air was sky blue clear as she drew in its freshness while aromas of pine, spruce and fir edged with heather, laurel, and rhododendron filled her senses. This land was for her. She had to own a part of it.

She remembered the old Swabian proverb that her mother constantly pounded into her head.

Mr hots net Light, aber Light hots min.

"Things don't come easy, but easily one misses them."

She wasn't going to miss this one.

GRETA KASSER

GRETA KASSER, AN 18-YEAR-OLD BLONDE, OCEAN-EYED BEAUTY, squared into Germanic sturdiness with a will to match, had come a long way. At sixteen, Greta Wilhelm chose Augustus Kasser to be her husband, a hard-working obedient boy and one who had saved up some money. For the next two years, they scrimped and sacrificed, finally making it to America only to find the curtain going up on the Great Depression.

Discouraged, but determined, they rented a room in Deutschtown, Pittsburgh's German neighborhood on the city's north side. It was across the river, a few bridges up from today's photogenic Golden Triangle, the point where the Allegheny and Monongahela Rivers converge to form the Ohio.

Once a pie-slice of virtuous land, the triangle had been pillaged by the plutocrats and in 1931, it was an inky clutter of soot, smoke, and clanging metal. Ominous, dirty smokestacks replaced the stately trees and railroad tracks and coal cinders trampled the former Indian trace while heavy black smoke screened the sky.

Within walking distance from their cheap boarding house walk-up was Ridge Avenue, known as Millionaire's Row, where the iron and coal barons lived. It was on a bluff across from the confluence of rivers, far enough away to avoid the smoke and noise, but close enough to monitor their erupting smokestacks.

Greta knew if she wanted money, she had to dig where the gold was, so she stalked Ridge Avenue, finally landing a job as a scullery maid in the 20-room Jacob Kimberly mansion. Kimberly owned the very prosperous JK Steel Company. When one of the more favored maids came down with a fever, Greta manipulated her way into the line of sight of the head butler and he sent her, along with the others, to the Kimberly mountain estate to prepare the lodge for the family's annual visit. That's when she saw the land.

When she returned to Pittsburgh, she obsessed over the lush land, and that's when the plan germinated and then sprouted. Her obsessive work ethic and adroit manipulation resulted in a promotion to drawing room maid where she had more access to the master. Greta did her homework and was fully aware that her portly employer, a lustful man arrogant with his power and money, also had the sexual proclivities of a serial rapist.

A well-fed man, Jacob Kimberly had a generous appetite for the hired female help, and Greta made certain she presented herself as a desirable dish. Dodging Jacob, yet staying within reach, Greta finagled a job for her husband Augie as a chauffeur, but she knew that her time was short. Jacob wasted no time in foreplay. When he wanted a woman, he expected to have her, and Greta knew she had to choreograph her moves with precision. She dangled just enough promise to keep his lust stimulated. Jacob Kimberly was a wham-bam predator who disposed of his sexual conquests shortly after ejaculation. Greta did a lot of planning and timing was everything. With all her scheming, she still wasn't sure her plan would be successful. There were a lot of "ifs" that were needed to make it work, but she pressed on.

Greta didn't see life with the soft margins of prudence. That was for the dreamers. To her, life was land; to grow the food and harbor the shelter; and then to nurture it into wealth and power. Greta was Teutonic strong, dispassionate, callous, and determined. To her, America was the "money country." Currency was the fuel that fired the furnaces of life in America, and she intended to stay damn warm. She might never get this close to big money again, and although risky, she had to make her move.

Mrs. Kimberly, a tall, thin, bony woman with sagging, rouged skin hanging on to her weedy face, came from a wealthy Mainline

Philadelphia family. Childless, her only interest was her social life. She didn't care who or what Jacob did. She tossed in her embroidered Turkish towel on their marriage years ago, and now her husband was only a monetary convenience.

Everybody was happily unhappy.

Jacob was a coarse man, distasteful in his arrogance, and when he encountered Greta alone in the ornate mansion, he would harshly grope at her firm, young breasts with his clownish hands, but she was able to escape his clumsy clutches. She made certain she left him wanting more.

She gave him just enough resistance to increase his carnality. She knew that once he got what he wanted, his desire would dissipate as quickly as his erection, and he would fire her and Augie.

Greta heard all the stories about the selfish pig.

She was as ambitious as Jacob Kimberly was lecherous, and she manipulated his salacity with the skill of a harpist. She hated that fat old bastard, but he was her chance for a better life, and she was taking it. Greta had no round edges. She was an impenitent, detached woman that some said had the soul of a rock. When she set her sights on something, nothing deterred her, and she had her frosty, ocean-blues on a chunk of land in the Pennsylvania mountains.

As more smokestacks rose, defining Pittsburgh's skyline, the soot and smut leached across the river to Millionaire's Row, forcing the industrialists to find new havens. They moved nine miles downriver to Sewickley, which in native American meant Sweetwater. There, on the banks of the magnificent Ohio River, they built larger and more opulent chateaus among the rolling hills that were sheltered by stately sycamores and elms.

Jacob Kimberly hadn't made the move yet, preferring to spend more time at his summer estate in the highlands, although he was tiring of the long drive. For Greta Kasser, the trip to the mountains was heaven sent. Her city pale was replaced with a rosy freshness and she could feel the energy of the land flowing into her body.

Now, in the spring of 1931, Greta Kasser stood on a hillside in the Alleghenies, breathing in the freedom of fresh mountain air and enjoying the luxury of lush alpine greenery.

The time was right to make her move.

Jacob would get what he wanted, and she would get what she wanted.

THE MANSION ON RIDGE AVENUE

GRETA HAD A PLAN. SHE HAD BEEN MAKING THE ARRANGEMENTS for weeks. Today she would implement it. Earlier she had seen Jacob Kimberly go into his library. He rarely spent much time there, and she was getting more nervous by the minute because he was staying in there so long. She dallied in the hallway outside of the library, polishing and re-polishing the walnut panels.

Finally, she heard the latch engage and the heavy wooden door opened.

Jacob Kimberly saw her immediately. For weeks he lusted after her like a panting hound dog on scent. What he didn't know was that she was more of a sly fox than a frightened prey.

"I have something that needs to be cleaned," he said, smiling to himself, thinking about his crafty comment.

"Yes sir," she said obediently, following him into the library. It was a masculine room with heavy baroque furniture, a glass-backed bar area, and a lot of polished wood. Rows of leather-bound volumes, which the master had never read, filled the dark cherry shelves. A white limestone fireplace and two leopard skin wing chairs, angled appropriately, made up the unused reading area.

"And what is it, sir, you would like me to clean?" Greta asked innocently.

She looked at his blubbery face. He reminded her of the disgraced actor Fatty Arbuckle. His downcast lips shined with saliva as he leered at her.

He moved towards her and she feigned fear. Gossip had informed her he liked frightened women.

"I'll show you what to clean," he said, grabbing her by the arm and pushing her up against the enormous mahogany desk. He grunted as he struggled to get the layers of regulation dress up so he could penetrate her. He didn't notice that she was subtly helping him as he finally reached her cotton bloomers, pulled them down and invaded her with ferocity. She struggled, which he liked, and he thrust himself into her. For a moment Greta hated herself as she cried out in pain and guilt, Kimberly mistaking it for intense pleasure. The rape was over in about a minute. For Jacob, repudiation followed ejaculation, and he ordered Greta to "clean up and make yourself presentable."

The episode shook Greta. She was already regretting what she did. All she wanted to do was run and hide, but she knew she couldn't stop now. She struggled to regain her composure and settle her senses. The few moments Jacob Kimberly took to check out his appearance and straighten out his clothing helped her get back on course.

He turned to leave the room when Greta, in her best breathy voice, stopped him.

"Oh, my sir, you are so strong and (pause) large," she purred, "and I have something special for you."

He turned and looked at her. She was fixing her disheveled hair and smoothing out her black uniform. She reached into her apron pocket and pulled out an envelope.

"This is for you, sir," she said, holding the envelope in her outstretched hand.

Jacob Kimberly was momentarily bemused. Employees didn't hand him envelopes, especially ones he just screwed, but his arrogance overcame his caution. She slowly approached him and put the envelope in his hand.

"Please read it, sir. It is very important," she said, her voice now firm.

He glanced back and forth between her and the envelope as he opened it. He unfolded the buff-colored paper.

The letterhead skyrocketed off the page. It was the name of a barrister in Deutschtown, one Bernard Mueller, a German lawyer known for his defense of the less fortunate, and somebody Jacob Kimberly had encountered before. Mueller was one of those "union boys" who caused Jacob much distress by inciting JK Steel employees to organize. There was no love lost between the two men. Jacob's expression slimed into a sneer and every face muscle tightened as he read the document.

1682 Pennsylvania Laws Against Adultery, Incest, Rape, & Polygamy

LAW AGAINST RAPE.

Chapter 10. And be it: That whosoever Shall be Convicted of Rape or Ravishment, that is, forcing a Maid, Widow or Wife, Shall forfeit One third part of his Estate to the parent of the said Maid & for want of a parent to the said Maid, And if a Widow to the said Widow, And if a Wife to the husband of the said wife & the Said party be whist, & Suffer a year's imprisonment in the house of Correction at hard Labor, And for the second offence imprisonment in Manner aforesaid during Life.

Jacob read no farther, crumbling up the document and throwing it in Greta's face, hitting her on the right cheek. Jacob's first instinct was to slap the satisfaction off this pretentious woman's face. He glared at Greta, but her unwavering return gaze caused him to hesitate. He continued to scowl as he tried to understand the motivations of this foolish whore. She was obviously after his money.

Who did this bootlicking Hun peasant think she was?

He measured his words carefully, pausing for effect, his eyes riveted into hers.

"Do you really think that any Judge in Allegheny County or any other county in this Commonwealth," he said, "men that I personally know, would believe you over me?" he said looking at her with scorn.

"Oh, have no doubt, Mr. Kimberly, we know of your standing," she said with a strong, steady voice, feeling encouraged and more determined, "but I, too, know some people—good people who will uphold the law—people like your former employee, Pete Walsh, that's Peter Paul Walsh, our courageous Chief of Police. I'm sure you remember Chief Walsh. He worked in one of your mills, and you know his brother, the one they call Happy, you know him, the reporter over at the Gazette? I believe he's written some stories about your company. Well, these two good boys have assured my lawyer, that they will see that I receive justice, and you know they aren't afraid to do what they believe is right."

"Woman, that ancient law is as worthless as the paper it is written on. You have made a huge mistake. I want you out of here immediately. You're fired." Kimberly encountered money-grabbing women before. He dispatched them quickly.

"With respect, sir. Mr. Mueller has assured me that should I have a problem, I am to come to him, and he will see that justice is done. Chief Walsh has said the same. It is not what I want to do, and if anything should happen to me, I have instructed certain friends as to what they should do."

As calm as Greta appeared, fear and emotion were coursing through her body like a raging river flooding its banks.

Jacob Kimberly was seething but restrained himself from beating the impertinence out of this crazy woman. One look at her face told him she was not to be trifled with. He didn't want to act impulsively, and he measured the situation carefully. He was sure he could handle the judges. He could have Everett over at the newspaper fire the reporter and nothing worked better with cops than cash. That would take care of Walsh. It was Mueller that concerned Kimberly.

The man was a pit viper who was trying to make a name for himself as a man of the people, a union man, and Jacob bumped heads with him before, but he too could be quieted with enough cash.

Kimberly didn't care who found out that he screwed the German whore. That was what women were for, and his cronies at the club would cheer him on for utilizing the best asset of a female.

No, that wasn't his problem. His problem was Henry Ford. He was about to close a deal with the puritanical automobile mogul, and he couldn't afford to let this ignorant shrew ruin it.

"You're crazy, woman. I will have you drawn and quartered and shipped back to Germany in a barrel of sauerkraut," he said as he moved towards her.

"You lay one hand on me," she said in a firm voice, "and you sir will end up in the Allegheny County jail. I have warned them about you and told them I feared for my safety. They await my call to hear that I am safe."

Greta was nervous, and she stuffed her hands into her apron pockets so as not to let Kimberly see they were shaking. She had no idea what she would do if he didn't back down.

They stood there for a moment, each firm in their position, their stares fixed. Greta made her fallback move. If he interpreted her offer as a sign of weakness, the guttersnipe that he was would rip the flesh from her body and have her discarded in the local dump.

"Mr. Kimberly," she said firmly, dropping her voice an octave, "I believe there is a way for both of us to avoid the public ugliness that will be heaped upon both you and me. We can "vork" this out," she said, angry with herself for slipping back into her accent she had worked hard to eliminate.

Whatever happened next has been muddled by time and distorted by gossip.

As careful as Greta thought she was about the incident, it became fodder for the house staff as they sat in the back pantry sipping their morning coffee and engaging in aimless chatter.

Like the soot particles that floated through Pittsburgh's air, rumors soon fluttered through the gossipy atmosphere of afternoon teas and the story gained traction. It wasn't so much about Jacob's indiscretion—

everybody knew he was an insatiable boor—but the talk was more about a proposed business deal that was in the works. Word was that Jacob Kimberly was in negotiations with Ford Motor Company to become their primary steel source, and he was worried that his sexual adventures would get back to the prudish Henry Ford, who gave no quarter to adulterous heathens. Nobody is sure whether Greta knew about the Ford deal, but what is known is that Greta left the mansion about a month later.

Augie chauffeured for a few more months and he also left.

The dowagers tuned in to the NBC Blue Radio Network to listen to Clara, Lu and Em, which seemed to satisfy their need for afternoon tea chatter.

As it was with most Kimberly stories, this one also drifted into obscurity.

Everybody thought it was over.

STONY CREEK

A YEAR LATER, IN 1932, THE RECORDER OF DEEDS TRANSFERRED 50 acres of land in the foothills of the Allegheny Mountains from the KI Corporation, one of the many shell companies of Jacob Kimberly, to Greta and August Kasser for the price of $1.

That transaction sparked the gossip committee of the mountain club circuit. Some matrons were convinced that Greta received the land as a payoff to keep Jacob's well-known voracious sexual proclivities hidden from his spouse. Other's poo-poohed it, saying that Mrs. Kimberly didn't give a damn if the blowhard "screwed every chorus girl in a Busby Berkeley movie," while there were those who speculated that the Henry Ford deal had something to do with it.

Eventually, the silver spoon set tired of Jacob's clamorous shenanigans and abolished him from their conversations. In late 1932, Augie and Greta opened a single ski slope they called Stony Creek, naming it for one of the streams that Greta saw on a Pennsylvania map. She didn't realize that Stony Creek was one of the devils in the horrific Johnstown flood of 1899, or she might have made another choice. They built a two-room cabin, Augie doing most of the work, and waited for the skiers to come, but unlike the Europeans, there wasn't much interest.

Skiers were as rare as clear skies in Pittsburgh, and the Kasser's were struggling until an inventor by the name of David Dodd built the first rope tow on a hillside pasture in Vermont.

Greta, hearing about the rope tow, had Augie jury-rig one using an old truck engine and soon, more and more affluent people were skiing, especially since they didn't have to climb their way back to the top.

It began as an "in thing" among the rich sons and daughters of Pittsburgh's old money, a small group who traveled to Europe and experimented with the European sport. Their experiences with alpine and Nordic skiing led them to Stony Creek, and soon their summer retreats became winter lodges.

The Kassers saw cash flow. Greta recognized the small, hard-core group of moneyed skiers as her ticket to bigger things and she searched for other ways to get her hands on more.

At the base of their single ski slope, Augie built a small hut, kind of a maintenance shed for the rope tow, with a coal stove, an old wooden table and a couple of chairs. Augie stored his tools and gear there, along with a bottle of Old Crow whiskey to take the chill off. It wasn't long before Augie was sharing his whiskey with skiers, who thought it "quite tolerant to do a little shack-slumming" with Augie. Occasionally they would sit down to a game of penny-ante poker. Augie didn't think Greta knew about his gaming forays, but of course, she did, and that gave her an idea.

Augie, with the help of locals, built another cabin, this time much bigger, with a large central room, and three smaller rooms. Greta called it the Three Lions Lodge after the Duchy of Swabia, which by the winter of 1936, quickly became the place for a drink, a card game, and an occasional sleep-over for those who may have had one too many.

Although prohibition was over, Greta chose not to pay for a liquor license as was required by the new laws. She knew she would eventually have to get into the system, but the longer she could stay out of the bureaucracy, the faster her business would grow. She had a few well-placed bureaucrats or what she called her "OT boys" (On The Take). For a little cash, they kept her informed. She also set up a warning system in case the OT boys screwed up. Since her operation was tucked into the mountainous terrain and there was only one narrow dirt road in and out of Stony Creek, she built a guard booth at the entrance. That was her early warning system.

She remained cautious. She remembered how cops in another state raided a gambling club that was protected by a lake. The cops swooped in on water skis. Stony Creek employees had flare guns and were to fire them if they saw anything suspicious, such as cops trying to ski their way in or maybe riding in on horseback.

It didn't matter to her rich customers since they were more titillated by slumming in her mountain speakeasy rather than passing judgment on her business practices. The card games grew bigger and soon Greta was raking in a healthy skim for her services. The cash rolled in, all of it tax free.

Greta recognized the advantages of an all-cash business and through the years, she fought friend and foe to keep it that way. Credit required bookkeeping, and that meant paper, and paper left a trail. Cash got things done easily and fast.

The Pennsylvania Liquor Control Board tried to infiltrate the operation and sent in undercover agents, but they could never catch them in the act. After many failed attempts they concluded their resources would be better spent on bigger fish and they backed off. They also knew that Greta was friendly with such names like Mellon, Frick, and Laughlin, so it was easier to look the other way.

The great depression begat bread lines and hobos and some mountain money dried up, but plenty continued to flow. Greta kept finding novel ways to buck up their income, renting and selling skis and other accessories, but it was the tax-free cash from the card games and the booze that was building a substantial cache for them. Despite her intense work ethic, she needed heirs, birthing two children, Otto born in 1936 and Rosamunde in 1938.

In 1939, Hitler's jackbooted armies stomped their way into Poland and World War Two began. Two years later, after the sneak attack on Pearl Harbor, America officially joined the Allies to fight the Krauts and the Japs.

It was an avid skier and founder of the National Ski Patrol System, C. Minot "Minnie" Dole, who convinced President Roosevelt and Army Chief of Staff General George C. Marshall to form a special division that would learn how to fight in the mountains of Europe. Dole was chosen to recruit the new troops, and he contacted every major winter resort and ski school in the country. He enlisted expert skiers, including many of the finest European skiers who fled the Nazis, and converted them into a new fighting force. The 10th Mountain Division, based in the mountains of Colorado, was one of the most heroic and victorious units in the war. General Mark Clark called the 10th "the greatest unit to ever fight in Italy."

The World War slowed Greta's ambitions, but she stashed enough cash away to weather those years. The income from the booze and card games continued. When the war was ending, Greta moved quickly and expanded the resort by adding a small hotel and restaurant. She finally decided it was wiser to go legit and got all the proper licensing.

The big war ended, the boys came home, and America's economy flourished. People had more money than ever before and began pursuing all types of leisure activities. It was the vets from the 10th Mountain Division, who created the boom in post-war skiing in America.

As these men were discharged from their base in Leadville, they brought their skiing skills to the nearby mountains of Aspen and Vail, where they helped establish ski resorts. Soon such national magazines as *Life* were doing major features on the skiing surge.

More people were skiing, and Stony Creek was finally in the right place at the right time. The hard driving Greta seized the opportunity and Stony Creek continued to grow, adding extra features every year. It was becoming a year-round resort and Greta was becoming a rich and powerful woman.

The Kassers built themselves a spacious mountain mansion using local wood and stone. The rambling modern structure, architecturally inspired by Frank Lloyd Wright, was on a secluded knoll embraced by rocky wooded ridges and nestled among a stand of maple, walnut, and spruce trees. Over the years, acidic rain had seeped through the water-soluble carbonate rocks, causing holes and fractures, creating cavities, resulting in a variety of caves throughout the area.

Greta loved spring when the mountain air was filled with singing birds. Nuthatches and grosbeaks chattered as hawks and falcons circled overhead. She even overcame her fear of the tiny pipistrelle bat and named her homestead Pipa's.

Greta brought a cousin over from the old country to help with the children, and it was she who really raised Otto and Rosie while Greta focused her attention on the expanding resort.

Because the nearest school was twenty hard miles away, Greta arranged for a retired local teacher to home-school the children, although their learning time was limited because their chores at the resort were more important. Greta believed that their future was in the resort, and although Augie didn't always agree, he knew it was better to keep his mouth shut. Augie taught the twins about the land and they grew up as "mountain kids." Augie took them hunting, fishing, and hiking. They went out target shooting weekly and learned a lot about guns, and although they never took a liking to firearms or the hunting, they loved their time with Grandpa Augie.

By the turbulent sixties, Stony Creek had grown, both in acreage and facilities, and it was now a prodigious, year-round resort with swimming pools, tennis courts and an 18-hole golf course. One thing that didn't change was the card games, now a high-stakes enterprise. Although some family members wanted to drop the games, claiming they could ruin the resort, Greta and her son Otto refused. Greta reasoned that her rich clients expected it, and the tax-free cash gave her a lot of play around money that was untraceable. That kind of cash quieted a lot of squeaky wheels.

They played the games in various hotel rooms, but neither the players nor Greta was happy with that setup. She understood the rich, and they liked convenience and luxury. After a lot of discussion, she reluctantly converted her beloved mansion into Pipa's, a very exclusive member's only club.

Besides the bar, restaurant, and specially designed card rooms, Greta converted two bedrooms into a VIP suite, and turned three more into luxuriously appointed sleeping rooms. The conversion to a private club was a smart move, and soon it was the mountain society's "in place," adding even more income for the Kassers. Greta kept the memberships exclusive and personally chose who got in, and soon, anybody who was somebody wanted to join.

In 1964, her son Otto gave her a grandson, Heinrich, and nine years later Rosie added twin girls, Hedy and Heidi. At first, Greta seemed overjoyed with the births, fawning over the babies, and showering them with gifts. She left most of their growing up needs to the nannies she hired so that Otto and Rosie could continue their work at the resort.

Mountain gossip claimed that the only reason Greta wanted grandchildren was to insure the family's chain of command.

"She didn't give a damn who her kids married as long as they had a penis filled with healthy sperm," one mountain matron said summing up what most of the old money thought.

Rosie's husband Paul Hunt, a sous chef at the resort, was killed in a car accident as he sped down a back-mountain road. The twins were only two years old when their father died. Rumors of alcohol echoed throughout the valley, but they were quickly snuffed, and the official file was sealed. Rosie never took Paul Hunt's name, convincing him that the Kasser name had more influence and the twins grew up as Kassers, much to Greta's satisfaction. Otto's wife, "a Polock pig" as Greta described her, ran away with a Norwegian ski instructor who worked at the resort. None of the grandchildren were married, much to the dismay of Greta and Rosie. Otto wasn't as concerned. Unlike his mother and Rosie, he wasn't looking for any more heirs. He wasn't happy with the one he had.

In 1992, Augie died. He had a heart attack as he tended a fireplace in one of the five restaurants. Greta almost made it to the turn of the century, expiring in the winter of 1999, which would have angered her because it interfered with the shank of the skiing season. Old mountaineers said that Greta didn't "go easy."

"She'd kick God in the balls and slap the shit outta all his angels before she'd give in," they said. She was 89.

By the new millennium, Stony Creek Resort was one of the biggest of its kind in the eastern mountains, covering some 2500 acres. With 100 rooms in the Old Lodge and 500 in the new wings, plus the condos and chalets, Stony Creek had become a fabulous mountain playground. Everything you could ever want was nestled into a valley of unlimited consumables surrounded by picturesque alpine beauty. Greta had accomplished what she had set out to do. She was a rich and powerful landowner, and she loved every moment.

She groomed her son Otto to take over the resort. He was much like her, bullheaded, power-hungry, and with an excess of ambition, but at 64 he was tiring. Rosie, more of a controlled dissenter than an outright rebel, clashed with Greta and Otto but rarely stood her ground. She usually sided with her mother. She ran the office, mostly shuffling papers, leaving the operations to Otto. She had a life outside the resort, hobnobbing with the wealthy Sewickley crowd and attending highly visible charitable events that usually made the society section of local newspapers.

On the advice of her attorney, Greta cautiously gave equal voting shares to all her heirs, but she ruled with an iron fist. As she aged, she reluctantly gave up more and more control to Otto, and soon he was making most of the decisions. It was Otto's firm hand that kept Stony Creek an all-cash resort. The rest of the family was convinced that they had to accept credit cards. Greta abhorred credit cards, believing the system was a corruption of independence and a plot to control her business and the economy. It was also a hindrance to Greta's bookkeeping system, which defied modern accounting practices. But the "all cash" system was changing, and soon "limited" Stony Creek credit cards were being issued to more and more carefully selected customers daily.

Otto's son Heinrich, usually called Henry by everybody except Greta, was a bit of a wimp and wasn't that interested in the family business. Otto blamed his ex-wife for bearing a weak-willed son, saying that "the Polock's national flag should be a white sheet." Henry wasn't happy working at Stony Creek, but the money was good, so he handled all the minor concessions.

The twins, Hedy, and Heidi inherited the cool Germanic beauty of their grandmother and then some. They were stunning blondes who turned heads. Their striking aquamarine eyes seemed to alternate between a deep ocean blue and a flashing green, sometimes blending into a mesmerizing combination.

Somebody once said they had "chameleon eyes."

Their father spent little time with them, mostly because Grandma Greta kept him out of their lives as much as she could. His heavy drinking didn't help, so they had a relatively fatherless childhood. It seemed to affect Heidi the most. Unlike Hedy, who armed herself with emotional barriers that were hard to crack, Heidi was more acquiescent and naïve. Hedy, the more dominant twin, was also the oldest by a few minutes. She was smart, tenacious, and more outgoing than her much more docile sister. She was very protective of her twin sister, although there were times, she became frustrated with Heidi's naiveté.

Against Greta's wishes, the twins attended the University of Pennsylvania. Greta believed that "experience was the only real education." Hedy earned a business degree while Heidi took a different route, majoring in Art History.

Heidi didn't want to work at the resort, but she wasn't about to bump heads with Grandma Greta, so she settled for running the sporting facilities such as the tennis courts, swimming pools, game rooms and less complicated operations.

Much to the dismay of her Uncle Otto, Hedy went for anything and everything. She settled for handling the restaurants, bars, front desk, and the especially important Pipa's. Although she didn't have the title, the family recognized her as the number two person in command. Privately, Hedy made no bones about it—she wanted Otto's job and felt she earned it.

Even though the winter holidays were the busiest, Greta scheduled the annual family meeting for noon on New Year's Day. It was her way of punishing those who believed drinking heavily on New Year's Eve was a good idea.

When Greta died, the family canceled the 2001 meeting, blaming the Y2K scare, so 2002 would be the first meeting without the matriarch. Because New Year's Day fell on a Tuesday, they expected sizeable crowds for the extra-long weekend. The family agreed to reschedule to Wednesday, the day after the holiday. This meeting was more important than most. The credit card issue was on the agenda, but the big item was a proposal from a large European company. They wanted to buy Stony Creek.

Without Greta ruling the roost, there were mixed feelings in the family about selling.

The Christmas/New Year holiday was their major moneymaker, and the long weekend would make it their biggest yet. Christmas was already a record breaker, and the New Year's weekend was expected to be even better. There was a substantial snow base on the slopes, the temps were below freezing, and the party mood was in full swing. The resort was sold out for the entire holiday period. That meant that a lot of cash would be flowing.

In Room 420, in the new wing overlooking the slopes, Joe Ducci, aka Joe Duck, watched the skiers. As he stood on his balcony, he thought they looked like black ants zigzagging across a sheet of white paper. Joe Duck knew that every one of those scampering ants meant cash money and he was going to get some of it.

Hopefully, a lot of it.

JOE DUCK

JOE DUCK WAS A SCUMBAG. HE REALLY HAD NO CHOICE, HAVING been created by a pair of defective couplers. Genetically, Joe didn't have a chance. He was callously excreted from the womb while his mother was drunk, abandoned almost immediately and thrust into society to nibble, rat-like, at unsuspecting innocents. He wasn't tough, not even scary. He was just a greasy, petty thief weaseling his way through life. He was a cruddy guy who was called a dirt-bag, sleaze, and slimebucket, yet he somehow crawled out of his hole occasionally to pass himself off as a harmless weirdo. People who knew him said he was a dumber and sleazier Ratso Rizzo, but with a smaller nose and a pock-marked face.

Joe trolled the back streets of Pittsburgh's East End, mostly up and down Penn Avenue, shoplifting, hustling, and committing petty break-ins. After many foster homes and juvenile incarcerations, eighteen-year-old Joe "Duck" Ducci landed a job at Stony Creek. Positioned as a homeless boy by a sympathetic social worker, he was hired, not so much out of empathy, but because it was hard to find somebody to do the crap jobs like cleaning grease traps, hauling garbage, and other scuzzy tasks. He lasted a few months before he was nabbed pilfering food and was immediately fired.

Joe didn't treat life very well, and it reciprocated. When he was 28, he contracted a rare facial neuroma, and a botched surgery left him with a somewhat disfigured face. It didn't bother Joe as much as it did the people who had to look at him. Joe thought it made him look meaner and tougher, which paired well with his perverted personality.

Bar talk and street corner bullshit convinced Joe that his faulty face might be his fortune.

When a former jailhouse lawyer told him he had an ironclad case against the doctor and the hospital, and that he couldn't lose, dollar signs addled Joe's distorted vision. He sued. He had an excellent case and the few legitimate attorneys he talked to were willing to take him on for their usual share, but Joe wasn't about to let these shysters run over him. Too many whiskeys convinced Joe that he had a "big bucks" case and once the word was out, all those TV lawyers would soon fight to get a piece of the action. Many saw the possibilities, but they wanted 40%, and Joe wasn't about to give those ambulance chasers that big of a piece. Joe wasn't stupid like "one of them Spic fence jumpers who didn't know shit from Shinola." Joe says it was the hand of God who stepped up to the plate and hit it out of the park for him.

Dino's used to be a neighborhood family tavern, especially on those nights when they served their famous Flying Saucers. Everybody loved the pizza-like discs, which were fried bread dough instead of baked. Dino shaped his homemade dough into flat rounds and sizzled them in olive oil and butter. They were coated generously with a choice of red sauces and the usual pizza toppings, and if you asked, he'd fry up some and sprinkle them with powdered sugar for the kids.

Dino died around the same time the neighborhood deteriorated and the place slid into the gutter, becoming a "bucket of blood." Soon punks and drunks colonized the place, fighting each other over nothing but their own frustrations. There were two shootings, and the cops targeted the rundown saloon, now called Red's, as a nuisance bar.

It was at Red's where Joe met the lawyer. It was just after 10 AM when Joe entered the dark bar. Red covered the windows and kept the place almost pitch black, other than for the weird glow of the neon beer signs, which cast more light than the few ceiling fixtures that were still working. Red was scraping the bottom of the barrel for a couple more bucks before he sold the liquor license, which was worth more than anything else in the joint.

Joe downed a shot of Kessler's, grimaced, and quickly chased it with a gulp of beer. He ordered another when a white-haired old man sidled up next to him and ordered the same thing. That somehow made them compadres, and soon they were chatting each other up, talking about nothing, and enjoying every minute of it. Joe couldn't remember the guy's name, but he looked like the old movie star Spencer Tracy. He was a short stocky man with a mane of white hair and blue eyes and Joe began calling him Spence, which didn't seem to bother the amiable old fellow. When Joe learned he was a lawyer, it was a match that could only be made in a joint like Red's.

Joe told him about his surgery. Spence said he had an excellent case. Joe said maybe he should sue. Spence said he should. Joe said he wasn't paying 40%. Spence said 15% would work. They sealed the deal with a handshake and at least six more Kessler's chased with beers.

The two new buddies, arm in arm, staggered out of Red's, sure they were on the road to riches when they fell. Spence tumbled on top of Joe, knocking the wind out of him, Joe screaming that his lungs were broken. Joe would say later that the fall was a sign that God wanted them together.

They were both lost souls who needed each other, and they sugared their friendship with the toppings of the riches that were sure to come. At one time, Spence was a decent lawyer until martinis after work turned into screwdrivers for breakfast.

With alcoholic courage inspiring them, a case was cobbled together, and a lawsuit was filed.

The hospital and doctors were represented by one of the biggest law firms in Pittsburgh, and they buried Spence in more legalese than was found in the world's largest law library. With the help of a callow law student and a few sober moments, Spence muddled through and they finally went to trial.

Judge Cashmore was a pinched-nose, upper class snob who believed that God had chosen him to be a judge so he could rid this world of the detritus that seemed to inhabit it. When he looked at Joe and Spence, he was sure that God had a purpose in putting these two pathetic souls in front of him.

The judge was aware of Spence's shortcomings and was surprised that he had a decent case, one that could be won by a competent attorney. One definition of "travesty of justice" was Judge Cashmore's decision to allow the trial to continue with Spence as counsel. The judge should have dismissed Spence as unfit. He went on with the case because he was "the best judge to handle the situation fairly and for the greater good of our decent citizens." In civil cases, judges are given a generous amount of leeway, and Judge Cashmore used up his entire allotment.

Judge Cashmore carefully swayed a shaky Spence to consider a non-jury trial. Spence, his confidence reinforced by vodka, loudly exclaimed that it was exactly what he had planned on doing, proudly sitting next to Joe and saying, "The judge and I are on the same page. I think we got this one." Joe Duck was thrilled and began looking at car ads.

Spence dried himself out for a day and made a good opening statement, but that effort drained whatever will power he had, and soon he was "calming down" with whiskey shooters. Judge Cashmore was careful in his rulings in the event a reliable attorney got the case on appeal, which he doubted would ever happen.

Joe and Spence were beside themselves. Joe looked at a new Ford 150 pickup and was grabbing drink tabs, certain he'd be clubbing it up with the big boys soon.

The judge had an election coming up, and the deep-pocketed defense team was a potential asset but Judge Cashmore would never let that influence him, would he? After all, he was a man of the law, and it was his duty to uphold it. It was also his duty to render judgments that would protect society and to rule in favor of Joe Duck would certainly be harmful to all the respectable citizens of Pittsburgh.

The Judge was convinced that "you cannot arm a man like Joe Duck with a briefcase full of money and thrust him back on to the streets where he will reap havoc upon innocent citizens with it." The judge was certain that a win for Duck "would be like giving a set of Ginzu knives to Jack the Ripper."

On a rainy Tuesday morning, on the seventh floor of the City-County building in downtown Pittsburgh, the Honorable Judge Corbin Z. Cashmore did the right thing for the people of Pennsylvania and ruled against Joe Duck.

Joe was stunned. Spence's *Inherit the Wind* moment was gone, and within minutes they were downing shots in the nearest bar where they were surrounded by courthouse regulars. It didn't take long before Spence was loudly re-arguing his final closing statement about the injustice of justice, and they were both escorted out.

They drank until their money ran out, Joe going back to the streets, and Spence leaving because Joe Duck accused him of throwing the case. Joe tried to find a lawyer to sue Spence, but none would take the case explaining to Joe that "a stone has no blood."

People like Joe don't have highs and lows. They have lows and lowers, and one October night Joe was at his lowest, vacantly watching a snowy TV screen. He illegally tapped into a cable line but didn't get it quite right. His picture wriggled around the screen like a reflection in a funhouse mirror, but through it all he recognized the man on TV.

He could make out fat Otto Kasser inviting everybody to come to Stony Creek for the holidays. There he was, full screen, ready to take everybody's cash, and that's when the money idea of a lifetime hit Joe.

Holy fuck. That's it.

The more he thought about it the more he liked it.

He knew the drill at Stony Creek, and if things hadn't changed, he also knew what they did with all that cash. A lot of time had passed but that old bitch and her son who ran the place were too cheap to change anything. The more Joe thought about it the better it was looking.

Joe Duck was going to rob Stony Creek.

It was still early, so Joe figured he could get a room for the holidays, but when he called he was told they had nothing left. Joe convinced the operator he was dying of cancer and wanted to spend his last New Year's Eve at a place he loved as a boy. The operator agreed to put him at the top of the cancellation wait list, and he got lucky. Now he had to find the money to pay for it. He went back to the street and came up with enough for the room, and then some.

The extra money convinced him that God was on his side. Joe Duck's life was so dreary that it was easy to reach out to God. Hell, why wouldn't he? Nothing else worked. A lot of rich people said they got money because of God, so maybe they knew something. When he scored the money on the street, he was sure it was a message from the big man himself.

Flush with the extra cash Joe, invested it in planning. He wasn't going to screw this one up. On a chilly November day, he took a ride up to Stony Creek to check the place out. It pissed him off that he had to pay just to get into the place.

He was surprised at how big it had become. There was no way he was going to get around and see everything, so he headed for the old lobby. When he worked there everybody knew that all the daily cash ended up in a room off the old lobby. He hung around there for a while but didn't notice anything different. Actually, he didn't notice anything and that worried him a bit. He wondered if they changed the system when he saw a middle-aged woman come out of the old sales office. He could feel the rush. She could be coming from the money room. She had to be coming out of the money room. The more he thought about it, the more he was certain.

They were keeping the money in the same place.

After his day trip, Joe spent a lot of time, more than he ever did before, putting his plan together. Joe wasn't going to make a stupid mistake. Whatever doubts he had about the money room still being used were quickly erased by what he wanted to believe. This time Joe Duck was going to pull off the big enchilada.

With all his planning, Joe left one part of his operation open-ended. He hadn't figured out exactly when he would make his move. He decided not to decide until he checked the lay of the land. His choices were New Year's Eve, New Year's Day, or New Year's Day night.

There would be more money if he waited until New Year's Day night, but the holiday exodus would be a problem. Traffic might be heavy exiting the resort as the official holiday ended.

New Year's Day had its advantages, but daylight was not one of them. Joe liked robbing in the dark. It was more natural. That left New Year's Eve and the more he thought about it the more he liked it. The trouble was he wouldn't have a lot of time. He couldn't check in until 11 AM on Monday, December 31st.

He had to decide when to rob the money room and the clock was ticking towards Auld Lang Syne. Joe still favored New Year's Eve, but he wanted to take another "look-see" before he made his final decision.

Joe traveled light. He had the Nike gym bag, where he put most of the stuff except for the empty backpack, which he stuffed into an old surplus army duffle. Those he would use to carry the cash.

In his room, he unzipped the Nike bag and began removing the contents, being careful to set the items needed for the robbery in a separate pile. He wanted to make sure he had everything, but he knew he did. He pulled out the red and blue ski mask, a large fanny pack—the biggest one he could find—duct tape, plastic ties, latex gloves, a couple of garbage bags, ski gloves, bleach, which he poured into a small plastic bottle, and a ratty pair of ski goggles. Other than the clothes he had on, Joe brought nothing. Between his reversible Goodwill ski jacket, sweater, shirt, and tee shirt, he had enough combinations.

The last thing he pulled out of the bag was the small 22 Colt pistol. He knew it wasn't a powerful weapon, but it would be enough. Besides, that's all he had.

He was sure there weren't armed guards, let alone any weapons in the money room, but things could have changed. He'd check it out. He gripped the pistol. He imagined himself gunning somebody down as he aimed it at the wall. Nobody better fuck with Joe Duck. He smiled at his rhyme.

Maybe that'll be my new slogan.

He repeated it aloud and then made a slight change. *Don't fuck with the Duck.* It rolled off the tongue easier. He liked it. "That's good."

He said to himself out loud, "really good." He decided he should write it down. He grabbed a small Stony Creek notepad and scribbled out the slogan, folded it and stuffed it into a slot in his thin, stained blue denim wallet.

Don't fuck with the Duck.

He put everything back into the Nike bag and stuffed it and the empty backpack into the surplus duffle and secured it with a combination luggage lock. He put the duffle in the mirrored closet and set a tiny piece of torn paper on top of the duffle. If anybody moved it, Joe would know. He got that idea from a movie, but he couldn't remember which one.

While most of the tourists went to the new bars and restaurants in the resort, the long-time regulars usually hung out at Augie's. It was a small bar, just off the original lobby, part of the old wing where the first hotel rooms were built right after WW2. The Old Lodge, as it's called today, was still in use. The original hotel doors had been painted many times but were still the original dark mustard colored wood with black wrought iron room numbers. Although they had been updated with new furniture, they lacked the size and decor of the more recent builds. The old hotel rooms were usually discounted to ski clubs and thriftier guests.

Joe Duck decided it was time to find out if anybody would recognize him. He was sure they wouldn't. Hell, he didn't even know who he was when he looked in the mirror, although the pockmarks were still there. As sleazy as Joe was, he wasn't a killer. The sight of blood made him nauseous. Joe's toughness was in his fantasies.

Stony Creek would be his biggest caper and his first armed robbery. He was moving into the big time. It also meant more jail time, but if he had this right, it wasn't going to be that hard. He heard all the stories when he worked there. The old Grandma ran the place like a warden. They did things her way, and as far as he knew, still did. He remembered what one bartender said about Otto.

"He has one of the most advanced minds of the tenth century," he said, although Joe wasn't sure exactly what he meant, but he was sure it wasn't good because that guy really hated the Kassers.

Joe didn't think anybody would recognize him. Besides his marred face, he had grown a beard. He tested the water by going to Augie's. If anybody were going to recognize him, it would be there.

The bar was busy, and Joe Duck was surprised to see that he knew the bartender. Dave started at Stony Creek a few months before Joe, and although they weren't friends, they had some bar conversations back in the day. Dave was looking much older; his thick black, greasy hair now gray and his angular face was fuller with a lot more wrinkles. Joe Duck didn't get to know many people in his short time at Stony Creek, but if anybody could make him, Dave would.

"What can I get you?" Dave asked as Joe Duck settled on a vinyl stool at the end of the bar, keeping his head down, nervous that he'd be recognized.

"Lemme have an Iron. Make it a bottle," he mumbled. Dave didn't react, hardly looking at Joe, saying nothing, reaching into the cooler to get the beer.

Joe Duck looked around the U-shaped bar to see if he recognized anybody else. Nobody looked familiar.

"This snow should really make the skiing good," Dave said, as he put down a bottle of Iron City Beer, the unexpected comment causing Joe Duck's heart to jump.

"Ah, yeah, yeah, it sure will," Joe Duck said, wondering if Dave might recognize his voice. He avoided eye contact by looking out of the bar's window wall facing the slopes.

"Well, enjoy," Dave said as he turned to take care of another customer.

Joe sat there for a good fifteen minutes. Nobody recognized him, and other than Dave, he didn't see anybody he knew.

Joe finished his beer and left a generous tip. Well, generous for Joe.

"Thanks a lot, buddy," Dave said as Joe got up and left. Joe wondered if Dave was being sarcastic about the tip.

So far, so good, Joe Duck thought. He stepped into the hallway and looked across at Stony Creek's first hotel room, except it wasn't Number One, but Number Three.

The scuttlebutt was that Grandma Greta, for some superstitious reason, didn't want a room numbered one or two, so the first guest room on the left, off the old lobby, was three. Because Room 3 was directly across from the usually noisy bar, it was one of the least desirable rooms, but not to Joe Duck. It was why he was here.

Joe Duck meandered back into the old lobby. Its original stone floor laid by Augie was worn but still looked good after years of ski boot traffic. The old lobby got little action anymore, and it was usually quiet, but New Year's Eve was different. A lot of the people who came through the old lobby came from the upper parking lot, which was used mostly by the locals. It was one of the original buildings and was constructed on the upper end of a slope. When they remodeled, they added a new lobby on the lower end of the slope, which put it down about four levels from the original. Access was by elevator.

Joe stood in the old lobby scanning the area and didn't see any signs of guards or undercover types. He paid particular attention to the old office, which was on the left side closer to the outside door.

"Can I help you?" a voice said, coming from Joe Duck's left rear.

"You look like you're lost," the voice added.

At first Joe didn't recognize Otto. On a second look, he did. It was Otto, although he was fatter and balder.

His stomach did a spin as he tried to stay cool. He turned to walk away, thought better of it, stopped, and then started again, but Otto stepped in front of him. Joe had no choice and mumbled out a "No."

They were face to face. Joe kept his head down slightly, but not so much that he would look suspicious. Otto personally fired Joe just to let the staff know he was on top of things. Although it had been twenty years ago, Joe was nervous and unconsciously rubbed his nose, something he always did when he was anxious.

"You looked like you were trying to find something," Otto said, staring at this asshole picking his nose right in front of him.

Joe Duck was sure that Otto was looking at him in a way that said, "Don't I know you?"

"Ah, no, just lost in thought," Joe Duck blurted, turning, and walking away. Otto shrugged and went about his business.

Jesus Christ. I almost crapped my pants. That was close, too close.

Joe Duck made his decision. When you get a signal from the man upstairs, you take it. He was robbing Stony Creek that night. As he hurried back to his room, he settled on 8 PM.

THE CHIEF

CARL BAYER WILL QUICKLY TELL YOU HE WASN'T BORN BUT WAS "cleared."

"On all charges," he'd add with a quick smile.

Carl Bayer had a flippant tongue, animal instincts, and a street-smart mind.

When you have to steal to eat and then somebody steals what you stole, you learn quickly that the only person you can trust is staring back at you in the mirror. Carl "Chief" Bayer learned quickly how to get what he needed when he was roaming through the cat alleys on Pittsburgh's notorious Northside as a kid.

The untamed Manchester area, just across the river from downtown Pittsburgh, was the last stand for the underserved. It was a "no-man's-land" for the angry poor, herded into a conglomeration of decaying structures and left alone to fend for themselves. The cops stayed away, and despite its rowdy reputation, the locals took care of their own when outsiders dared step across the line. The local pols understood, but the people in the White House were too far away from their life to understand.

It's where Carl, a kid with a calculating mind that was deft with numbers, became a gambler. He started out penny tossing, graduated to craps and cards, and by the time he hit puberty, he was a cunning gamester with a nervy style.

His mother, a tough, wiry woman, had to get her kid out of the angry alleys and into a legitimate job. He wasn't just heading down the wrong road; the kid was speeding down the superhighway to hell, and she had to stop him.

For years she had been trying to claw her way out of the poverty that mired her family in the muck, but it was a hard slog. She saw a sliver of light in the local ward chairman, a pompous hack who loved the pounds of praise she heaped on him every chance she got. She built a small political base that gave her some currency, and she spent it to get her son a job.

"The only job I can get him is as a cop or a fireman," the hack said finally relenting to the incessant pleas of the desperate woman.

Six weeks later, Carl Bayer was walking a beat on the feral back streets of East Liberty. His mother had chosen to make him a cop, hoping that working on the side of law would properly influence her larcenous leaning son.

It did. He quickly learned that being a lawman was immensely more lucrative, and Carl Bayer capitalized on it immediately. It didn't take long for him to key in on illegal gambling operations, including bookie joints and the juicy numbers racket.

It was like giving a pig a free pass to an all-you-can-eat restaurant.

His knowledge of gambling and his talent for numbers made him an asset to the blue bloods, the commanders and deputies who ran the department. Soon Carl Bayer was carrying back bags of cash and distributing it to the men who could serve him best. Carl's unique ability enabled him to case an illegal gambling operation quickly, compute their take, and tell the crooks how much he needed to keep the police off their backs. That put him on the fast track to money and promotions. The blue bloods liked him because he increased their take, and he was good with the gamblers because he understood their businesses. Most important, he wasn't greedy. He understood that greed was a one-way ticket for a cruise down the river in a cement bucket.

Flush with cash, the young cop was feeling the surge, and some of that energy found its way into the vagina of a sweet, young teenager who Carl had to marry in her third month. They moved in with the girl's parents, but Carl only lasted into the seventh month when he left and moved in with a police buddy.

A son was born. Looking for help from God, Carl's angry wife named him Christian. Carl looked at the kid, shook his head, and left. It would be a long time before he ever saw his son again.

Promotions came fast and Detective Carl Bayer knew how to keep the machines of the ruling class well oiled, spreading his form of congeniality throughout the political community and the police department.

Some people get opportunities and don't see them. Carl Bayer saw them before they became opportunities.

His entrepreneurial spirit caught the attention of some powerful Pittsburgh people such as Mafia boss Frank Amato and his underboss John LaRocca, who would later become the Godfather. He also hooked up with Pittsburgh Steelers owner Art Rooney, who once had his own gambling operation in the city, establishing the Chief as the go-to cop for those little favors. Doors that were closed to almost everybody else were opened for the ambitious cop, and he walked through them— always bringing a little something for his hosts.

He became a very "connected" man and his orbit expanded to other cities. When the Mayor of Chicago needed a highly skilled undercover cop that the local gamblers wouldn't recognize, Pittsburgh's Mayor quickly suggested Carl Bayer.

It didn't take Carl long to build a national network of connections that served him well. He was like the Yellow Pages. Whatever you needed, he could get it. Not only was he the bagman, but he was also the fixer, and many of the rich and powerful found a use for his talents. He took care of those "messy little details" so they didn't have to get dirt on their hands.

Those were the salad days, the heyday of his police career, and everybody was happy—except the feds. Carl Bayer's ambitious work was noticed by a few zealous young lawyers working for the U.S. Attorney's Office. Always on the lookout for ways to further their careers, there was no better jumping off place than indicting the corrupters in local government.

Carl Bayer caught their eager eyes. They opened a file on him.

The feds started sniffing and Carl quickly picked up their scent, thanks to important people in high places, and he ducked, dodged and zig-zagged to keep them off his trail. As hard as they tried, they couldn't catch him with anything that would stick in court.

He spent over twenty years making his appointed rounds, picking up the bags of cash, skimming more off the top each year, and then distributing the agreed upon allocations. He became the top vice dick, and that's where he got the "Chief" moniker.

Each newly appointed U.S. Attorney meant ambitious new lawyers looking to make a name for themselves. At the top of their "most wanted" list was the very elusive Chief, Carl Bayer.

"I did more Houdini's than the man himself," the Chief told cronies, "and invented some the magic man never thought of."

His bag-packing skills landed him a deal in the Allegheny County D.A.'s office. Working for the District Attorney was even more lucrative. He was still a bagman but disguised the money as political donations, and his skim increased. So did his power.

The D.A. was in a potent position. He was the person who decided who gets prosecuted and who doesn't. The Chief found the end of the rainbow in the D.A.'s ear and began digging backyard holes and burying treasure chests.

The Chief also enjoyed being the right-hand man to politicians. Most were insecure because their job was so temporary. Instead of running their offices they were constantly running for their political lives which left day-to-day operations to men like the Chief. While they were out shaking hands and kissing asses, the Chief appropriated their powers to make rewarding transactions for himself.

That's when the feds went all out. They activated old files and the Chief climbed to the top of the list again. One ambitious new agent, eager to make a name for himself, wanted to bring the Chief in for questioning. The old vets knew it was a futile exercise. They encouraged the young rookie to go for it, and he took the bait. He brought in the Chief for an interview.

The greenhorn began the questioning and got nothing but smart-ass answers. Then the Chief caught everybody off guard.

"You want some names? I'm ready to give them all to you."

Even the old vets stiffened up a bit, but were still wary while the new kid went all in. Pad and pencil ready, the Chief said he was ready to talk some "real shit." The seasoned agents were skeptical but attentive, just in case.

"Dicky Mellon," the Chief said as the newbie scribbled down the name.

"Ed Thompson." The rookie wrote. The vets relaxed. "Hank Frick." The kid stopped writing. He looked up at the Chief. "Here's a good one," the Chief said, eyeballing the freshman.

"Andy Carnegie. That's C-A-R-N." The new agent threw down his pencil and took his ass back as the other agents, not wanting to laugh, got up quickly so they could let loose in the hall.

The Chief decided it was time to jump ship and get out of the city, but he didn't go far. He got himself a gig as the top cop in a small municipality about thirty miles outside of Pittsburgh. He didn't enjoy being so far away from the fertile fields that bore him such copious crops of currency, but the move softened the erection the feds had for him. Of course, he continued his ways, but the pickings were limited and the payoffs slimmer.

That's when he met Otto Kasser and the two hit it off. Otto enjoyed the Chief's quick wit, but it was his knowledge of gambling that got his attention. His experience in law enforcement and his connections were bonuses and Otto brought him on board. Otto was a bit leery of the shady spots in the Chief's past but was sure he could keep him in line. The trick to keeping a guy like the Chief happy was to always keep him off balance. Don't give him a pattern or a stationary target to zero in on. Keep moving, keep changing, and keep mixing it up. Otto was sure he could handle him.

Otto offered him the job as the Security Chief for Stony Creek with a generous starting salary and sweetened the pot with a lot of tax-free perks. At first the Chief wasn't sure he wanted to bury his career in the mountains where profitable opportunities would be limited, but after doing his research, he saw that there was a lot of serious cash moving through Stony Creek.

He also liked Otto, mostly because the guy thought he knew what he was doing. The Chief liked people like that. They were easier to handle.

He took the job.

STONY CREEK

SKI RESORTS LOVE SNOW, BUT TOO MUCH OF IT CAUSES PROBLEMS, and it looked like this storm was going to dump more white stuff than was needed.

The operations people were concerned and beefed-up staff. By late afternoon, phones were ringing around the mountain as the day shift called home to cancel New Year's Eve plans. Word had come down that anybody who wanted to keep working would go on double-time, and for most of them the offer was too good to pass up.

The Chief was in Otto's dingy office where they were meeting on another matter. Otto was such a schlump. He decorated his office in crappy old furniture, usually discarded from other offices, so his employees would see how simple and practical he was, except no one bought into the charade.

"Leaving the Pipa's bag in the money room wasn't your best move, Chief," Otto said, sitting behind a pathetic old walnut desk that had been retrieved from the trash.

"What didja want me to do? A couple of cough drops started sparring in the old lobby and I was the only one there to break it up," the Chief said looking around the shoddy office wondering why Otto thought his poor-mouthing worked. Otto caught the "only one" inference. The Chief had been laying the groundwork for more security for weeks.

"That bag should be over at Pipa's," Otto said. "I don't like the people in the money room knowing anything about the card games, Chief. We have to be careful."

"Otto, them two woofers in there couldn't find the sky if you told them to look up, which reminds me that you gotta do something with that setup. That fuckin' money room is only an abacus away from disaster."

Otto was aware of what the Chief was trying to do. He wanted to bring on his son as a security consultant. Otto knew he had security leaks that needed plugged but bringing on somebody close to the Chief was iffy. Otto checked him out and he had excellent credentials, but Otto was still leery.

"Just get the money over to Pipa's."

"Otto, if you think them two squirrels, and every other wetback in this place, don't know about the card games you're living in Mickey's house."

"Chief, just get the money over to Pipa's, puh-leez," Otto said. "There's over two hundred grand in there, and that's the most we ever had for the games."

"Well, if it wasn't for the Wallman brothers, we wouldn't need so much cash, but you know those two ass wipes. They play like it was monopoly money. For rich guys, they ain't got much going on upstairs. Lemme tell ya, anybody that wants to repeal Roe versus Wade will change their minds after they meet them two cough drops."

Otto smiled and put his hand over his mouth to cover it. He got a kick out of the Chief's colorful descriptions.

Otto knew that the Chief was skimming the skim and the Chief knew that Otto was on to him. It was kind of an unspoken understanding between them. The Chief wasn't being greedy, and Otto had people in place to make sure he didn't.

What Otto didn't know was that the Chief was tipped about every move Otto made. It was part of the game. The Chief knew not to be greedy because that's when you got your ass in a sling. When there's a lot of cash involved, a little here and there is considered the cost of doing business. The Chief prided himself on being reasonable. He never stole from poor people. He only robbed the robbers, kind of like Robin Hood, except he didn't give to the poor. They had to get off their rears and make their own way. He did lay some green on the church from time to time, but that was nothing more than an insurance payment. God always had his hand out.

The Chief was an important asset to Otto. He was well connected and moved around in important circles. The crooks knew him; old money used him to clean up their family spills; and his political due bills were plentiful. In fact, it was the Chief who swung the deal to make Stony Creek its own political sub-division. Making Stony Creek its own town allowed the Kasser's to establish their own police force and Mayor, levy and control taxes, and ensure that Stony Creek would get all the government perks that benefitted the Kasser family.

The Chief became the top cop in Stony Creek.

He spent most of his time overseeing the card games at Pipa's, leaving the detail work of running the force to assistants. Otto gave the Chief plenty of leeway. He was generating a lot of cash and modernizing the gambling operation. He used special ceramic holographic chips and cash was never used. Controls and safeguards. were tight with monitors everywhere. The Chief understood that you can't piss anybody off because they'd go running to the authorities and squeal, but he had insurance. He kept them in check by building a personal file on every one of them, and he made sure that they knew he had the dirty and he'd use it if they stepped out of line. He learned that trick from J. Edgar Hoover.

The Chief had some problems with the rake, the amount the house skims from each pot. Because the games were high stakes, some pots getting into the six-figure range, the 3% rake was bothering some players, so the Chief set up a sliding scale which ended up being more profitable for Otto.

In Vegas, the high rollers are called Whales. The Chief had his own label for the big bettors calling them Mountain Climbers.

"Them rich people will climb over a hungry puppy to get to the top. They think fair means an albino's butt."

The Chief believed that the cops, robbers, and the rich all wanted the same thing—money and power. They rarely made emotional decisions. Show them the money—give them the power—and they were in. That meant a lot of extra handling charges for the Chief. To him, the rich were nothing more than thieves who dressed well. In fact, they were worse than street degenerates because they had weird little perversions that they believed were privileges.

Otto didn't care how the Chief saw things. The cash he generated took care of a lot of warts.

The Chief left Otto's office and made his way through a maze of shortcuts, down hallways and back stairs exiting out of an unmarked door in the back office to the main lobby.

"You still holding that suite for my kid, right?" he said to the junior clerk, dressed in Stony Creek green, who snapped to attention as the Chief approached.

"Yessir, Chief. It's one of the VIP suites and I did everything you told me to do," the clerk said eagerly.

"Good man," the Chief said, as he walked away. He'd slip him a coin or two later.

The Chief's son was bringing his girlfriend to Stony Creek for the holidays. The Chief called in some favors to make certain everything was first class. If he could get the kid on Otto's payroll, they'd all pocket some nice change.

The Chief fancied himself as the model for the Kenny Rogers's song. He knew when to hold 'em and knew when to fold 'em, and you had to be careful who you let into the game. Win or lose, you never show your cards, and you let nobody into the game unless you got something from them. You do for me and I'll do for you.

Everything had a "I do" bill. No matter how insignificant, when the Chief did a favor, he expected a return. He never gave unless he got.

As the Chief walked through the lobby, he was thinking about the Wallman Brothers. They were rich and more trouble than nymphomaniacs on a banana farm. When they played cards, they were like turds in a tornado. Shit would be flying everywhere. He hitched up his pants as he tried to hold in his stomach. His damn gut was creeping over his wide leather belt like the Blob. At 57, his once-chiseled face had gotten a little doughy, but his clear blue eyes were sharp as he scanned the room.

He headed for Pipa's.

CHRISTIAN FOLEY

THE AIR WAS THICK WITH EXHAUST FUMES SWIRLING AROUND THE caravan of blinking red taillights as holiday travelers lined up to get on to the Pennsylvania turnpike. Foley felt a little schadenfreude as he headed for the E-Z Pass Lanes and breezed right through. He realized it was silly to feel so smug about such a little thing, but he hated waiting in line.

He took a brief sideway glimpse at her as a chain of shadows fluttered across her face. He was thinking about the first time they met. She caught his glance but pretended not to notice.

Foley wasn't certain that he was in love with her—at least not like the books and movies portrayed love—but then, he wasn't sure he was capable of that kind of love. He wanted to love and be loved, but something held him back. A college friend, who became a psychologist, suggested that he may have a fear of rejection, but Foley dug no deeper into it, although the comment jumped into his mind from time to time.

Linda Nexton was different. From the moment she first sat across the desk from him, he felt the pull between them. Call it chemistry or instant attraction—whatever it was, it had a lot of energy—and they both felt it. But there were some roadblocks in their relationship, and even though the trip to Stony Creek was primarily business, Foley had other plans.

His business was growing, and Linda was the biggest reason. It was amazing how in-sync they were on both a personal and business level, and yet he was feeling some discomfort. He was hoping this trip to Stony Creek would help relieve that feeling.

Things were going well, and he wanted to keep it that way.

Foley, everybody called him by his last name, a habit that started when he was in the Marines, had come a long way since his troublesome teen days in Buffalo. After his birth in Pittsburgh his father, Carl Bayer, abandoned him, and his mother took him as far away from the bastard as she could, which turned out to be Buffalo.

She met James Foley, a millwright who worked in one of Buffalo's auto parts factories. He was a nice man, stable, hard-working, and he fell in love with her. She finally agreed to marry him if he legally adopted her son, which he did without hesitation.

Christian Bayer became Christian Foley, and his mother breathed a sigh of relief. She wasn't sure a name change was enough, but it was a vital step. Things stayed relatively quiet, but her son was running with bad kids and although she was leery of sending him anywhere near his birth father, desperation set in and she shipped him off to Aunt Mary in Pittsburgh.

Foley loved his Aunt Mary. Compared to his overly protective mother, his Aunt Mary was freedom personified and summers found him running the same back alleys of Manchester on Pittsburgh's Northside that his birth father ran, but that was as close as he got to him.

Foley's mother was an unswerving Catholic who believed that whatever words were uttered by the church or their priests was the absolute word of God. There were no ifs, ands, or buts when it came to the church and she expected the same of her son.

Although she tried to impale her religious fervor into him, she was unsuccessful. Foley did all the Catholic things he was supposed to do, but with little enthusiasm. He just wanted to keep his overprotective mother off his back.

Foley entered his teen years as a muddle-headed juvenile who wasn't sure whether he was afraid of life or life was afraid of him. He had his pious moments to please his mother but the streets didn't take kindly to holy boys. He had his share of fights; stole when he could; managed to slide through school; and the church and God made little sense to him. He had little interest in his birth father, although he had curious moments, which he quickly dropped.

Then he met Father Gretz. Father Jamie was a guy's guy, a big strapping six-footer, built like a bull, with the blackest hair Foley had ever seen, and man o' man could he throw a ball. Whether it was a scorching fast ball or a perfect spiral, Father Jamie could heave a strike every time. Foley was sixteen when he discovered him on one of his summer visits to Pittsburgh. Father Jamie once pitched in the Double A League and had the chance to go to the bigs but turned it down to go to the seminary.

There were no playgrounds or ball fields in Manchester, so Father Jamie, one of the assistants at St. Joseph, would block off Fulton Street at both ends with sawhorses every day at noon for an hour so the kids could play.

Foley joined a bunch of the boys in a touch football game. They had no football, so they made one by taking a bunch of old newspapers, winding them up tightly, shaping it as best they could, and tying it with a string to hold it together. They'd wet it down in the center to give it some weight. Father Jamie could fire that paper football like a rocket, throwing it from the corner of Liverpool to the next corner which was Franklin.

A cabbie on his way to pick up a fare was blocked by the sawhorses, and that pissed him off. He jumped out of his cab, uttering every expletive he knew, and threw the sawhorses off to the side.

"Hey, you ain't allowed to do that," one of the nervier kids yelled at the cabbie, who was a stocky guy with a two-day beard which didn't make him look too friendly.

"Fuck you, asshole," the cabbie said, getting back into his cab just as Father Jamie came out of the church.

The angry cabbie revved up his motor to let the boys know they better get out of his way. He put the car into gear when Father Jamie stepped in front of the cab.

"Git your ass outta my way or I'll fuckin' run you down," the cabbie yelled out of the driver's side window.

Father Jamie was in his game playing outfit, black pants, and a white tee shirt.

"I think we can settle this peacefully," Father Jamie said softly as he casually walked around the front, his hand gliding along the hood, to the driver's side of the yellow cab.

The cabbie was about to tell the asshole to fuck off when Father Jamie, in one seamless move, opened the cab door, quickly reached in and hooked his hands around the cabbie's shirt, pulled him out, pushed him to the ground, and put his size twelve shoe on the cabbie's neck.

"You shouldn't use that kind of language in front of young boys," Father Jamie said as the cabbie's face turned crimson, "and I'm sure you're sorry about that," he said pushing down a little harder on the cabbie's neck who quickly bawled out a shaky "yes, (louder) I'm sorry, I'm really sorry."

"Apology accepted," Father Jamie said, removing his shoe from the cabbie's neck and helping the poor slob up, brushing off some street dirt from the cabby's shirt.

As the cabby hurriedly got back into his vehicle, Father Jamie said, "You should know that those barriers are authorized by the Pittsburgh Police and you would be wise not to anger them if you come back this way in the future."

"Yeah," the cabby mumbled, backing up slowly, as Father Jamie walked alongside.

That incident made a huge impression on young Chris Foley. Every chance he got, he hung around St. Joseph's and soon became the catcher to Father Jamie's fast balls that left Foley's hand raw and burning, but he loved every moment. They talked about a lot of things during those baseball sessions, and Foley found some direction.

A year later, with the approval of Father Jamie, he joined the Marines.

"The Marines saved my ass," he'd say, "and without them I would've ended up in jail like a lot of my friends. The Corps squeezed the bullshit out of me."

He won a Bronze Star in a skirmish in Mogadishu, but downplayed the award saying he was trying to save his own ass.

Foley explains.

"We were on patrol when we got ambushed and me and Joey Confalone were pinned down. He had been hit, and I knew if I stayed where I was, I'd take a bullet sooner or later, so I had to get out. What was I supposed to do? Run for it and leave my wounded buddy there? I'd have been drummed out of the Corps. I had to take the guy with me, so I threw him over my shoulder and ran my ass off, and that's what I got the medal for—running my ass off."

When his African tour was over, Foley clerked in a NCIS (Naval Criminal Investigation Service) office stateside. That brief assignment got him interested in law and when he was discharged, he explored going to college on the G.I. Bill.

That thrilled his mother until he told her he wanted to go to Pitt. He assured her he'd stay clear of the Chief, and he meant it. He liked Pittsburgh, and he liked his Aunt Mary. Father Gretz was also there. Still, some thought he was looking to meet up with his birth father.

"No way. I have no connection or feelings about him. Nah, that isn't why I like Pittsburgh. I have friends there, plus Pitt is an excellent school."

Foley believed what he said and didn't contact his father when he started at Pitt. Over the years, his mother had pumped enough negatives about his father into him so he had a healthy fear of the old bastard. He grudgingly admits he had some interest, especially when his Aunt Mary would tell him he looked like his father.

When he first started at Pitt, he stayed with Aunt Mary. For years he thought she was his real Aunt and didn't find out until he came back from the service that Mary Eileen Hogan was his mother's best friend. Foley slapped himself for not seeing the obvious, but it was something he just didn't think about.

Although Mary Eileen thought Carl Bayer was a con man, she disagreed with her best friend and gently pushed Foley to meet up with his birth father. She believed every kid had the right to know his real parents. It wasn't until Foley was in law school that Mary Eileen made contact.

To the surprise of some family members, Carl Bayer agreed to meet his son.

"Why not?" he said.

It wasn't a ringing endorsement for the idea, but it was more than most expected.

A meeting was arranged. The Chief named the place and time. The Rosa Villa was a neighborhood joint on Pittsburgh's Northside. Unbeknownst to Foley it was owned by relatives of former Mafia Godfather John LaRocca.

Foley didn't want to be too early for the 3 PM meeting, so when he got there at 2:50 he stood out front for a few minutes, but that seemed stupid, so he went in.

Coming in from the bright sunshine, it took him a moment to adjust to the dim light. When he focused, he saw that the large rectangular bar was empty. There wasn't even a bartender in sight. For most restaurant bars, 3 PM is the dead zone except for the cheaters. That's rendezvous time for wayward spouses.

Foley stood there for a moment and then took a seat on one of the red vinyl padded chrome stools. He was thinking about calling out when he heard voices getting louder as two men walked in from another room.

The short, dark-skinned, squat-necked guy, built like a fireplug, looked like he just stepped out of a Godfather movie set.

"You must be Chris Foley. Meet your old man," he said, gesturing to the taller, gray haired man behind him, and then let out a quick laugh that sounded more like a growl.

Foley pushed the stool back and stood as squat-neck went behind the bar. "Beers okay for both of you?" he said as he reached into the cooler.

The Chief walked up to Foley and extended his right hand. "Good to see ya, kid. You been here long?"

Foley wasn't sure what to do next.

"Everybody calls me, Foley," he blurted out nervously. Foley was wondering what in the hell he was going to call the man in front of him. One thing was certain-it wasn't going to be Dad or anything like that.

"Well, you can call me whatever you want and I'm sure your mother gave you some suggestions," he said extending his hand. It was an awkward moment for Foley.

"Most people call me Chief," he added. Foley was a bit relieved but stayed away from the name thing. He'd deal with it later.

He wished he were somewhere else, but he wasn't, so he gave it his best shot. He grasped his father's hand with a firm grip, which wasn't returned. His father's hand felt like a glob of flabby flesh and just as Foley was pulling his hand back, Carl Bayer applied some major league pressure, tightly squeezing his son's hand and then quickly ending the handshake. It was as if his father was letting him know who was boss. Foley wasn't into that kind of game playing.

The Chief asked Foley where he was living and that got things rolling. Foley studied his father's face as they talked. He was trying to see the resemblance. Their eyes were the same blue, but the shape of their face was different. The Chief had a rounder face while Foley picked up some of his mother's features. His jaw line leaned square, and his complexion was darker.

Squat-Neck set two Iron City Beers down on the scarred wooden bar. Foley took a slow sip, stalling for time when his father asked about his plans. When he mentioned he was attending Pitt law school, his father brightened.

"Smart move. Them shysters make the big coin," he said. "They're like metal detectors—they can find coin no matter how deep it's buried," he added with a quick smile, "especially if it's in your pocket."

"So, how's the Virgin Mary?" his father asked.

The question flustered Foley.

"Oh, ah she's… everybody's fine," he said, wanting to get off that subject.

As they depleted the small talk, the Chief ended the conversation by giving Foley his phone number and telling him to keep in touch.

"If ya need anything, give me a call."

Foley winced a few times during the conversation, but overall, he was glad he met the old man.

They parted company, Foley promising to keep in touch. He was satisfied with their first meeting, certain there would be others. He kind of liked the old man. He was a throwback, a Runyonesque—like a character that acted like he stepped out of Central Casting.

The one problem facing Foley was what to call him. After thinking about it, he settled on CB, the old man's initials. Along with the initials he also referred to the Chief as the old man, usually to friends and family.

While he went to Pitt, he landed a job as a night clerk at a motel out by the airport. That gave him some much-needed money and the chance to study while he tended the front desk. CB slid him a few bucks during their sporadic meetings, usually at a local bar.

At one of the get-togethers, he asked Foley if he wanted to become a cop. The Chief said he could get him on the force in Pittsburgh and a schedule that would accommodate his college studies. Foley jumped at the opportunity. Being a cop sounded good to Foley. He could use the money and it put him into the criminal justice system.

Foley became a patrolman with the Pittsburgh Police Department. He was greeted warmly by fellow officers, especially when they found out his connection to the Chief, although he got a few sideway glances from some of them. What Foley found interesting was that they never mentioned his father's name again, not even an occasional "How's your old man?" inquiry.

Foley worked hard at both his studies and police work. It was a grueling schedule, but it was paying off. They promoted Foley to the homicide department as a detective. His street smarts combined with his intellect, his military experience, and law school, soon had Foley moving up the ranks. During that time, he wondered whether CB had a role in any of his promotions, something that would always nag at him even when he thought the old man had nothing to do with it.

It was a stroke of luck that changed Foley's life, although he wasn't sure it was luck. He suspected the Chief's long arm may have reached in again and nudged his career.

In an upset victory, a new Mayor took office. He ran as a reformer. The current police chief openly campaigned against the mayor and had to be replaced. The new mayor met Foley only once. Staffers said he was impressed with the young officer.

The mayor's advertising messages claimed he would get rid of the old, entrenched political machine and clean up the corruption. His billboards saturated the city. "Don't get run over by a machine" they proclaimed, showing huge tire tracks running over a flattened cartoon character that represented the voter.

When the new Mayor quickly booted out the old police chief, he didn't have a replacement in mind. His aides combed through the possibilities, and Foley's name popped up.

It surprised everybody, including Foley, when the mayor chose the young homicide detective to be Pittsburgh's police chief. For Foley, who was in his last year of law school, it meant a lot of scheduling logistics, but he made it work. The biggest problems he faced stemmed from the new mayor's campaign promises.

It was Foley's job to clean up the police department, something most insiders said was impossible. The corruption was well entrenched at the highest levels. Foley also had to lug the baggage of his birth father's reputation. Although the Chief was never convicted, the insiders knew he was a bagman. They watched closely to see how far the apple fell from the tree.

Foley wasn't a goody-two shoes, nor was he a dirty cop. He was a common-sense kind of guy who broke a minor rule here and there, but he was careful. A lot of important eyes were watching to see what he would do with the police force. In a strong union town like Pittsburgh, you didn't fire a well-entrenched cop, even if you could prove corruption, which Foley couldn't.

The new mayor had idealistic ambitions, but he was still a neophyte, and there were many people in powerful positions who didn't like their friends in the department being fucked over. Foley knew that removing even one embedded commander would be like stealing an ice cream cone from a poor kid. There would be a lot of hysterical screaming that would make too much noise to be ignored.

What Foley pulled off even boggled the minds of the inner circle.

He swept the department clean without raising a particle of dust. There was no blowback from the police union, not a murmur from the politicos, and the public didn't give a damn. The media had no place to go with it other than some silent praise from those reporters in the know.

Nobody knew how he did it. Enter the Chief. He had the book on every key cop in the department, and on the politicians and crucial money players. He opened it for Foley. The information was invaluable. Once Foley understood each of the players, what they liked, who they screwed, and who they owed, he used it to ease the bad guys out; for those eligible he suggested early retirement was their smartest move if they wanted to protect their pensions; for others, he directed them to potential new jobs. It was surgically clean, with nobody losing a drop of blood. His reputation soared.

The Chief suddenly became the proud father and began bragging about his son. Despite Foley's warnings, the Chief was hanging around police headquarters like he was back on the force. Foley understood the old man's game and kept him at bay.

Foley had a good run as police chief but felt his new law degree was worth more in the private sector. He left and was offered jobs in some of the biggest law firms in the city. He declined those offers, choosing to open his own business. He considered opening his own law firm but became more intrigued by the security business.

His experience in the military and law enforcement helped decide for him. Pittsburgh lacked a full-service security company. There were several rent-a-cop firms, but none engaged in the more sophisticated aspects of business security, and Foley jumped into that niche.

Rejecting investor offers, he opened The Security Agency with his own money. It was tough going, but the business was growing. He was looking for an assistant when Linda Nexton applied for the job.

As sharp a cop as Foley was, with ability to size up people fast, the chink in his armor was women. It was as if every instinct that he honed to be razor sharp went dull with female relationships.

Sitting next to him was a major fracture in his relationship instincts.

She'd change everything.

LINDA NEXTON

LINDA NEXTON GREW UP RELATIVELY POOR. SHE DIDN'T LIVE IN the lap of poverty, but she was cradled in its arms. She lived with her parents in their two-bedroom wood frame house on the backside of what used to be called Coal Hill, now elevated to Mt. Washington, both figuratively and literally.

The area had a split personality. The front side of Mt. Washington rises some 500 feet above the Golden Triangle with a view to kill for. Along its scenic edge are rows of luxury condos and high-end restaurants. On the backside were the old wooden frame company houses built by the coal mines during the depression. Linda and her family lived in one of them. It was a neat neighborhood, and the people did their best to keep their small, cookie-stamped homes livable.

Linda loved her family, and she intended to move herself and them out of there as soon as it was financially viable. She would not be like her mother. Marge Nexton let it be known she didn't like the life she was living, and she wouldn't let that happen to her daughter. She taught Linda that money and power were partners, but they always didn't show themselves the same way. Money usually exposed itself in things such as houses, cars, and clothes. It was harder to hide money, but power was different. It could hide, and it had exceptionally long tentacles that could reach out from all directions. Money was the show-off; power was a quiet killer.

To make her point, Marge came up with her "plug-in" analogy and taught it to her daughter early and often.

One afternoon, while Linda was watching one of her favorite programs, Marge pulled the plug on the TV.

"Maauumm. What are you doing?"

"Teaching you a lesson."

"I didn't do anything bad."

"What is this?" Marge said, holding the plug close to Linda's face.

"What? A plug?"

"Right, so when I take this plug and find the power and I plug it in," she said inserting it into the outlet," the TV set goes on."

"Sooo?" Linda said.

"So, when you find the power, you can watch whatever you want, whenever you want," she said removing the plug again.

"C'mon Mom, what are you doing?"

"Like I said, teaching you a lesson and you'll like this one. Okay, now it's your turn. You find the power," Marge said as Linda grimaced with a loud groan.

"This is silly," Linda said angrily grabbing the cord. She got up and went towards the outlet when Marge stopped her.

"Now what are you doing?"

"You're going the wrong way."

"I am not. The thingy is right there on the wall."

"I said find the power."

"This is crazy, Mom. The power is right there and…"

"It's not the outlet. It's me. I have the power because I am controlling this plug. I am the power and I want you to listen carefully—and if you do—I'll get you that dress we saw in Macy's."

Linda sat back down.

"Always make sure you know where the actual power is. When you grow up and get a job, the power could be your boss, but maybe not. It might be his wife. On the street, a police officer is powerful, but the

Mayor is more powerful and people with a lot of money have power, some more than others, so choose wisely. Make sure you know where the real power is, and when you find the real power, plug into it and soon you'll have your own."

Linda nodded.

"And Linda," Marge said, moving her face directly in front of Linda's, "Once you get the power, don't ever let anybody take it from you."

Her mother reminded her daughter frequently about plugging in. Fortunately, Linda was born with the tools to do it. She was exceptionally smart, her IQ hitting 130, and she was attractive—on the male chauvinist scale, a ten—and she was adept at manipulating people and situations.

For a world that had been dominated by men for much too long, a beautiful woman with brains and ambition was a powerful combination. Add a spoonful of feminine sweetness and it helps a lot of things go down.

Her talent, drive and hard work landed her a full scholarship, and she graduated from Duquesne University Summa Cum Laude. She was a much sought-after job candidate and had already interviewed with a few major corporations, but she had her eyes on a high-visibility job. She wanted to get into television.

Her plan was to get a position in the news department doing whatever she had to do. Next step was to work her way to the front of the camera, establish herself as a credible on-air journalist, and then make a move to the executive suite.

She knew that breaking through the glass ceiling was a formidable task, but she knew how to use her assets to get what she wanted. She wasn't chippy about it, but women in the workplace didn't get equal treatment from men, and Linda saw nothing wrong in using whatever resources she had to break through.

During college, she hooked up with the son of an affluent businessman which gave her a leg up into the moneyed class.

Her mother wasn't thrilled when she took the job with the cop. That wasn't in her workbook, and Marge shortened the leash.

So, why did Linda respond to Foley's ad for an executive assistant in a small security company?

She's asked herself that question many times.

Running a self-analysis check, which she did frequently, she thinks it was his self-deprecating humor, charm and free-wheeling attitude about life, something that differed from her rigid, set-in-stone disposition.

She also saw a quick growth opportunity. She would be his assistant. That would give her access to him, his contacts, and inside company information. Those, along with his political connections, were attractive, which made the road to power in his company a shorter trip.

Foley liked her immediately. He recognized her smarts and would be a liar if he didn't admit that he was taken by her physical attributes.

He essentially said the job was hers if she wanted it. She promised to get back to him. Only a few days had gone by when Foley called her. She explained she had a few more interviews and she would get back to him once they were completed.

What Foley didn't know was that she had already decided to accept the job. Now she was angling for more money..

She also had her eyes on the TV show Foley created which was running on one of the local channels. He developed a half-hour show on security and featured segments on home, business, and travel security; demonstrated new security products; and warned people about current scams and neighborhood crimes. He didn't use fear, but a "neighbors helping neighbors" approach, and his police background and contacts gave him credibility and sponsors.

It was doing well, and Linda had her sights set on becoming the co-host of the show.

As they drove through the toll booths, Linda was thinking of ways to avoid too much conversation with Foley. She wasn't sure she could hold back what she had to say, so she feigned a headache, closed her eyes, and lay her head on the neck rest.

This would not be a pleasant trip.

THE SHERIFF

WILLIAM JAMES HOGG WAS THE SHERIFF IN FAYETTE COUNTY. HE
lived in Uniontown, the county seat. It was a community of some 7300,
50 miles southeast of Pittsburgh, and another fifty or so back road miles
from Stony Creek.

How Hogg ended up in Fayette County is still a matter of speculation
and rumor. It depended on what and who you believed. As a young
detective in Cleveland, Bill Hogg solved a high-profile case which
launched his career. He was a hard-nosed ex-marine who knew how to
work both sides of the street, and he parlayed one big case into a very
profitable career. The media liked the ruggedly handsome man who
gave them what they wanted—a no nonsense, tell-it-like-it-is tough cop
who was always good for a great sound bite.

Hogg knew how to play to the cameras. What nobody knew was
that he had hired an acting coach from Carnegie-Mellon in Pittsburgh
to teach him all the tricks.

Money was at the core of everything Bill Hogg did. To him, life
was simple. You get whatever you want with enough cash, and word on
the street was that Hogg had connections with the "boys." One rumor
claimed that Hogg was close to Tony "Lib" Liberatore, a crime boss who
was high on the FBI's family tree, and another claimed he had an angel
in the powerful IATSE labor union, but it was side-street gossip.

Wherever he got the money, he invested a substantial amount of it
back into his business, which was establishing one of the best informer
networks in the nation. Hogg paid big bucks for information to those in

both low-and high-level positions and manipulated them with generous compensation which kept him in every loop in the area. He gave them what they wanted—money and protection—and they fed him what he needed. His network of CI's (Confidential Informants) also enabled him to make some major busts enriching his reputation as a tough cop.

He was Cleveland's version of "Dirty Harry", and he milked it for everything it was worth—and it was worth a lot. He always got the high-profile cases, which sated his image-building, while he kept a list of good-paying clients safe from any interference by law enforcement. Because of his popularity, both inside and outside the force, Hogg had a free hand until an ambitious assistant U.S. Attorney showed interest in him.

Hogg found out that the feds were on his trail just a few days after they officially opened a file on him, courtesy of Annie Durbin, an insecure mousy young lady who worked in the U.S. Attorney's office. Annie was the poster girl for the lonely-hearts club.

Hogg took part in many joint operations with the office and got to know Annie. He quickly saw the opportunity a lonely female offered. He wined and dined her and plied her with the attention she desperately needed, convincing her, he would if he could, divorce his wife and marry her. It was the church that was stopping him. After all, he was a good Catholic, and divorce was not an option. That was his "take it or leave it" deal.

Annie Durbin took it.

She innocently became his inside source of information. Whenever she told him something, he pretended he already knew it. He manipulated Annie into thinking she really wasn't doing anything wrong. It was nothing more than shop talk between two people in the same business.

At first, Hogg wasn't concerned about the feds. They opened files on a lot of local officials, so it was no big deal. When Annie told him that the feds had a mole inside the mob, Hogg's antenna shot up. Annie knew no more than that, but it was enough for Hogg.

At 49, he logged in 28 years and planned to cash out at 30, but with the feds looking to make headlines, Hogg wasn't about to hang around. As much as it pissed him off (he was going to lose some additional pension money), Hogg made his announcement, saying he was tired of the grind, and was going fishing in the mountains.

Although Fayette County is in Pennsylvania, their attitudes come from across the border. It is "West By God Virginia" and Hootie all the way. It's a no bullshit, gun-totin', country roads kind of Wild West, fortified by moonshine and mountain mommas. It's also where the French and English drew first blood and George Washington fought his initial battle. With the Youghiogheny and Monongahela Rivers cutting through the Laurel Summit, nobody with brains messes with the Fayette County way of life. When the power brokers heard Hogg was coming their way, they immediately made contact. He was their kind of man. Fayette County had their own version of the electoral process; they called it "say-so's."

"Who we gonna put up for Sheriff?"

"Hogg."

"Why?"

"Because I say so."

Fayette County became Hogg's stomping grounds, and that's when he met Otto.

The story that seems most accurate is that Bill Hogg did some unidentified "favors" for Otto. In return, Otto cut him a deal on a nice lot in Stony Creek. He introduced him to the right people, and Hogg established himself in the area.

Hogg was proud of his Scottish heritage, regaling anybody within hearing distance of his bloodlines. The name Hogg bothered him, but he never let on that it did. To overcome it, he would launch into the rich history of the name, explaining that it came from the Old English word *hoga*, which means prudent. He claimed he was a descendant of James Hogg, who was Governor of Texas in the 1890s and that he had some connection to Alexander Wilson Hogg, who was a Member of Parliament in New Zealand, although nobody ever cared enough to check.

Sometimes Hogg considered changing his name to Hoga, but he thought it sounded too Italian. It might have been helpful in his extracurricular dealings, but the made guys would start asking what part of Italy his family came from and crap like that, so he dropped the idea.

Whether his bloodlines were real or embellished, Hogg had masterful political skills and he used them effectively, mostly for his own personal enrichment.

Hogg's mountain house can be described in three words: wood, stone, and plaid. It was a bastardized Cape Cod/A Frame exterior, compact, but without all the picture windows usually found on mountain homes. Hogg liked his privacy. His room, he called it the den, had the obligatory stone fireplace, a tartan plaid carpet, and walls of cedar and pine, mostly tongue-in-groove paneling. A locked gun cabinet harbored six weapons and on the other wall was a large portrait of the Robin Hood of Scotland, Rob Roy MacGregor, the famous Scottish folk hero who was a legendary swordsman, outlaw, and cattleman. In the corner stood bagpipes that Hogg never played.

Hogg spent a lot of time at Stony Creek, usually at Augie's bar in the old lodge where he held court regularly. He was an unofficial advisor to Otto, mostly on political matters, and even though the Sheriff was an Ohio transplant, his Pennsylvania connections were well cultivated and solid. Otto was not above a little skullduggery himself, and he found Hogg and his contacts useful.

For his advice and counsel, Otto gave Hogg certain privileges at the resort, such as a free membership to Pipa's, which he rarely used. He preferred to hang out with what he termed "the real people," the regulars at Augie's Bar. As he did in Cleveland, Hogg considered himself a "man of the people" because that image served him well. He also cultivated a following among the elite, doing them "small favors," like getting their kids out of scrapes and burying drug problems and sexual indiscretions. He was also available for bigger issues and the "Mountain Climbers" were generous when they needed him, so he made periodic appearances at Pipa's just to remind them he was around. He also met the Chief, and they became "business" friends, each wary of the other, but always ready to collaborate if there was enough cash involved.

It was dusk as Bill Hogg drove the back route from Uniontown to Stony Creek. Snow edged the two-lane asphalt road, but the Sheriff didn't slow down, his foot heavy as the big black Yukon Denali roared up the deserted mountain road.

He was pissed.

He decided to stay home over New Year's, hoping to keep his wife happy and her mouth shut, but all she did was bitch. He didn't want to be at Stony Creek during the crowded holiday weekend, but his wife's whining finally ended up in a fierce argument and he stormed out of the house.

No matter how hard he tried to be peaceful she wanted war. She bitched that he was always at Stony Creek, and yet when he stayed home, she made his life miserable. He'd dump her if he could, but divorce could be costly. He threatened it many times, hoping to back her off, but it didn't work.

In one fierce argument she fired off a warning round. "If you ever try to screw over me, I'll hang out more dirty laundry than the National Football League does after a muddy Sunday."

He never told her much, and he wasn't sure what she overheard, but as careful as he was, he couldn't risk it, so he had to live with the bitch for now.

As the skies darkened and the snowflakes multiplied, Bill Hogg wondered if that little redheaded bartender was working this weekend. If she wasn't, there was always the twin.

He was going to have a good New Year no matter what.

HEDY

HEDY ACCIDENTLY LEARNED ABOUT IT TWO MONTHS AGO, AND since then, her mind was like a blender, spinning and chopping her thoughts into a million pieces. Every time she believed she had a handle on it, it spun out of control again. She prided herself on her cool restraint, and keeping her emotions in check, but Heidi's stupidity had her seething. She wanted to hug and protect her sister while kicking her ass at the same time.

She tried to find a logical explanation for Heidi's actions, but she knew she was just kidding herself. Logic rarely applies to emotionally driven decisions.

She found out about it because her mindless sister never locked the door to her condo. Hedy stopped by for a quick visit, let herself in, and was about to announce her arrival when she heard Heidi talking on the upstairs phone. Hedy went over to the bottom of the stairs and was about to yell out when she heard something that stopped her.

Did she hear right?

She cupped her hand around her ear and listened. She could tell Heidi was walking around her bedroom, chatting away. As Heidi passed her open door, the words leaked out again and Hedy heard them clearly. She was stunned, suppressing a gasp, shaking her head as if that would somehow change what she heard. Then she heard more. Any doubts she had were gone. She felt like she had been stabbed through the heart with an icicle, the searing heat of pain alternating with the icy cold of reality. She had to get out of there. She left immediately. She sat in her car for the longest time, trying to sort out the agitation she felt.

Totally crazy.

She couldn't believe her beautiful twin sister, a sister she loved so much, was having an affair with the same bastard who savagely raped Hedy seven years earlier.

How does this happen?

It was more than a shock; it was a sharp thunderbolt that hit her right between the eyes and split her head wide open. How could Heidi get involved with a bastard like Bill Hogg? Of course, Heidi didn't know what Hogg had done to Hedy, but he was such a conspicuous degenerate. How could she not see it? She knew Heidi was a trusting soul, who saw everybody as cute and fun, but Hogg? It made Hedy physically ill every time his name crossed her mind.

For seven years, Hedy had been trying to find the right time and place to make him suffer like she did. Over the years, her hate grew. She couldn't expel him from her memory, his cruel face jumping in and out of her mind regularly, taking energy away from the positive things in her life.

Intellectually, she knew that the shrinks said hate was unnatural and she should move on, but Hedy didn't let it consume her or misguide her—she channeled it into positive energy—and nothing could be more satisfying than seeing Hogg suffer like she did.

She took a novel approach. Since the pervert forced himself into her life, she was going to make him her inspiration. She was going to find a way to make him the example of what no man should ever do to a woman. For years, she had been trying to find a foolproof way to avenge what he had done to her. Now that she found it, her twin goes and screws it all up.

Her sister, her beautiful twin whom she loved dearly, let that sicko touch her with his venomous hands, pawing away at her innocent body. She shuddered at the thought. An acid shower would be less painful.

Not a day went by that Hedy didn't think about that horrible night in 1994.

She returned home after graduating from college and she and Heidi were spending time together, using one of the VIP chalets for a little sisterly bonding. They didn't see each other much in college, each going their own way, so they were looking forward to hanging out.

Otto had a small party that evening to introduce Sheriff Hogg, who had just moved to Stony Creek. On a whim, Hedy stopped in, Heidi was already there, and Otto introduced them to Hogg. Hedy found him interesting, and a relatively handsome man and they had a short conversation. He referred to them as "the beautiful Bobbsy twins" which Hedy thought was a bit cheesy, and Heidi found cute. It was a brief encounter.

It was the second encounter that would haunt Hedy for seven long, agonizing years. God, it was hard to believe that it had been that long. It seemed like the whole ugly thing just happened.

It was a typical summer night in the mountains. The sky was coal black, gilded with an overlay of shimmering silvery stars as the gelid air cut through her thin silk blouse, raising goose bumps. Hedy left the party early and was making her way through a small stand of trees, a shortcut to her chalet, when she heard noises behind her. She quickly turned to see a dark figure, back lit by the lights seeping through the leafy trees from the building she just left. At first, she didn't recognize the voice, but relaxed a bit when she heard a male call out, "Hey you, Bobbsey twin, wait up."

She paused, and within a few seconds she saw it was the Sheriff. He must have left right behind her.

"Hey, Sheriff. Your party over already?" she said.

"I hope not," he said. "I don't know which Bobbsey twin you are, but my vote says you're the prettiest one," he said with a slight slur. She noticed it immediately and resumed walking towards the chalets. She was about twenty or thirty yards away as she made her way down the narrow dirt path. He stayed with her.

"I hope you enjoyed your party," she said, seeing the twinkling lights of the chalets through the trees.

"I'm enjoying this a lot more," he said without losing a beat.

Warning signals went off in her head. She could feel her muscles tighten, but she had no reason for alarm. Still, she didn't like the feeling she had. She scanned the area quickly, looking for an escape route. Her only choice was the narrow dirt path that she was on. She picked up the pace, not so much that he would notice, but enough to shorten her walk time.

"How nice of you to say that," she said, staying cool as she continued walking.

"Hey, pretty lady, slow down," he said jogging up and grabbing her arm causing her to tense up, "I have a question."

Hedy always kept a healthy dose of paranoia for situations like this, and it kicked in. She assembled a defense. Her first move was verbal. Let him know she's not pleased and hope that will chill him down.

"What's your question, Sheriff Hogg?" she said firmly, with a cool edge to her voice, hoping to create some verbal distance between them.

"I can tell you're a little mad," he said, sounding drunker, "but join me for a drink at my place and we'll make up," he said. "Just a quick drink, nothing else," he said, his hand encircling her upper arm.

She didn't like his gestures. She gently tried to move her arm away from him, making it look as natural as possible, but she felt his grip tighten. That was a red flag, and she went into escape mode.

"I just wanna talk," he said, holding her one arm and grabbing her other, a weird smile on his face.

Don't panic. Stay in control.

But one look at his eyes and she knew. They were glazed and empty, staring past her at some faraway object, as if she weren't there, yet he was only inches from her face. She could feel his hands tighten around her arms. She quickly surveyed her surroundings, looking for something— anything—that would help.

A draft of warm alcohol breath hit her, and she turned her head as he moved his face closer. She felt her stomach knotting. This had gone too far, and she was about to scream.

Hogg could see the fear in her eyes and hurried. He grabbed her ponytail and yanked her head back as he smothered her mouth with his. She kept her lips compressed as he roughly tried to jam his tongue into her mouth. She struggled and attempted to knee him, just missing, hitting his thigh.

"You fuckin' cunt," he said, squeezing her upper arms and pushing her to the ground, his body falling on top of her, squashing the air from her lungs and causing her to gasp. She wanted to scream, but she couldn't.

Trying to get a breath, she felt the prickly brush ripping into her back and his erection grating against her vagina. For a moment she stopped struggling and lay still, hoping that would stall him as she tried to think her way out. She was sure she couldn't hold him off physically. Maybe she could talk her way out.

"Ah, if you'll just give me a minute," was all she got out before he started tearing at her panties, getting his fingers on the lip of her vagina as she clamped her legs together trying to fight him off. She let out a scream which he quickly muffled, clasping his hand over her mouth as he kept grinding his erection against her.

"I know what you want, cunt, and I'm gonna give it to you," he said, his hand still smothering her mouth as he unzipped his pants.

Using all her strength, she attempted to break away, twisting and turning, but he was too strong. Exhausted, she went limp again, hoping it would cause him to slacken, but in that moment he tore the rest of her panties off her upper leg, the fabric cutting into her skin, and brutally thrust himself into her.

"Take it bitch, take all of it," he panted, plunging hard into her. "This is what you wanted, and I'm giving it to you," he said, attacking her with barbaric ferocity. She let it happen. She shut her eyes and bit her lower lip as he spewed his venom into her, and then she felt his body deflate.

He jumped up, brushed himself off, and in a controlled voice said," Just remember, you told me to meet you here and I did. You wanted me to go with you to your chalet, but I hesitated, and you started kissing me. This was consensual sex, and that's it."

She laid there, her body stained with his filth, keeping her eyes closed, breathing hard, but not moving although every part of her was burning. She was confused and scared. She wasn't sure that what happened had happened as she tried to herd her thoughts into something that made sense, but she couldn't box them in.

"I know you enjoyed that, so maybe we can get together again," he said.

What was he saying?

Her eyes still closed, she slowly replayed what happened. One moment it was clear and vivid, the pain raw and piercing; in the next it was shadowy and vague. Everything was blurred into a montage of images as stars, trees, flesh, eyes, hair, and hands swirled helplessly in and out of her consciousness. She felt his heavy body crushing her into the thorny brush. She heard his angry voice, his lustful grunts; she felt barbs digging into her back; the awful smell of stale whisky, the greasy sweat. God, the greasy sweat.

Afraid to move, she lay there, listening for any sound, but all she heard was lonely silence. She didn't want to open her eyes. She knew that when she did, the horror of it all would become real. After what seemed like a long time she moved sideways slowly, and then suddenly stopped, thinking she heard something. She lay still again, not moving a muscle, trying to blend her body into the brush. She waited. Again, she moved, just a little, and then stiffened and listened before she moved again. She slowly opened her eyes, seeing an out-of-focus starlit sky. She lay still for another moment or two and then slowly got to her feet. Her body felt swollen and grimy.

Her mind was a tangle of thoughts, but it was the smell. She couldn't eliminate his smell, a mixture of sweat, alcohol, tobacco, and something like sour milk. She fell back down to her knees, the smell nauseating her. She shook her head, trying to shake the foul odor loose, but it was embedded deep inside her nose and throat. She gagged, tried to hold it back, but her stomach contracted, she choked, and felt the burn in her throat as she vomited followed by a series of dry heaves. She stayed on her hands and knees, trying to think, but she was riveted with fear and confusion. She couldn't seem to get one clear thought from the unruly mob of them that rumbled through her brain.

Finally, she struggled to her feet. Like frightened prey, she looked around to see if anybody had seen her, as if she had done something wrong. Her eyes darted back and forth, as she brushed off her dress, and found her torn panties. She desperately made her way back to the chalet.

She tried to scrub his filth off her body but couldn't. No matter how hot she made the water, or how much soap she used, she smelled his stench. She tried to sleep, but it wouldn't come.

One moment she was going to go to the police and the next she vowed never to tell anybody. After a nightmarish night, she was sure that if she reported it, they would throw her into a cauldron of character assassination. He was a cop, a connected cop, with contacts at every level, and they would rip open her life in court.

The law was not a safe place for women who claimed rape. His lawyers would bring up every sexual encounter she ever had, and many that she didn't, wrenching away the layers of her life and slicing them into raw chunks of bloody meat and throwing them to a hungry media mob.

She couldn't let that happen, and that angered her even more. She felt like a trapped animal in a cold, dark cave with no way out.

She hated herself for not reporting it, and her anger grew to an explosive point. Although she would never admit it, it was the suppressed resentment that was pushing her hate to the breaking point. It was consuming her, and that wasn't healthy. She needed to take the passion from her anger and turn it into a plan. College taught her how to do it. She would establish a strategy, set goals, and implement the tactics to achieve those goals. She even gave the project an unwritten title, "Hogg's Head." She was intent on inflicting the same pain on him that he inflicted on her.

A surgical cold replaced her bitter heat, and she planned her revenge. She had to be patient, dispassionate, and one day, when the time was right, she would make a calculated strike.

She fantasized constantly about ways to hurt him, never wanting to kill him, but to scar him in some way so he would have to live with it for the rest of his life. She wanted to cause him terminal pain and shame, the same things she felt every day for the past seven years.

Patiently she researched revenge crimes. The one constant was that most were acts of uncontrolled passion. That was one of the first things cops investigated. She had to be careful and control her hate, but it was difficult. Her hatred of Hogg had no boundaries and she set out to violate him as she had been violated.

She spent months trying to find a way to hurt Hogg and not put herself in jeopardy. She had no doubt that he was an evil man who had no redeeming value for civilization, and she spent months finding a way to exact her revenge. She would not rest until she saw Hogg voided.

She found many ideas but none as befitting as the one she rejected. She thought it extreme but then was a brutal rape moderate? What can be more extreme than invading a person's body against everything they hold sacred? Isn't shattering the soul of a person not a devastating act? No human has the right to invade another's body. That is war.

Hedy decided. She knew what she was going to do. Now she had to see how she could do it without endangering herself or her family.

Thank God for the internet. It had everything she needed. She devised a plan, and the things necessary to do it, but she hadn't settled on a when.

Unfortunately, it came unexpectedly. The time had to be now. Heidi's stupidity had changed everything. She had to act immediately.

What she had to do repulsed her, but the thought poured adrenalin through her body triggering goosebumps and a new kind of strength.

Hogg was a scourge on society.

LINDA & FOLEY

WHEN LINDA WENT TO WORK AT THE SECURITY AGENCY, FOLEY didn't assign her a title. All he told the employees was that she would work directly with him on most issues concerning the company. That didn't sit well with George Hoffman, who considered himself the number two person in the company.

After managing a police department, Foley tired of operational duties. He was happier creating and innovating, especially on his TV show, so Hoffman took on some of those tasks, but he wasn't good at it. Internal operations in the company were weak. Linda quickly saw an opportunity.

It was like unleashing a genius in a roomful of idiots.

She set up systems and procedures, taking on projects that others in the company ignored. One moment she was working on the bookkeeping system, the next setting up a job tracking system.

Before long, she knew more about the business than anybody else. The employees embraced Linda's efforts except for Hoffman. Six weeks after she started, he resigned.

Although Linda expressed dismay at George's resignation, she was pleased. She no longer had any hurdles, and she continued to reshape the company. Three additional people were hired, and they were all Linda's choices.

Foley was pleased with her performance. He knew he found a gem. She quickly became the operations manager, sans title, and there was little or no resistance from the other employees. The future of his company never looked better.

Linda set the tone, which was contrary to Foley's casual approach to business. While he dressed informally, Linda's wardrobe was business conservative. She never fraternized with her co-workers, while Foley had lunch and drinks with them frequently. But Foley's passion and creativity appealed to Linda, and she was a good fit for him, offsetting his operational weaknesses.

Foley was attracted to Linda, and she found him engaging, but their relationship was all business. Foley knew Linda had a boyfriend, but she never mentioned him. Linda discussed nothing about her personal life.

It went that way for six months until one October evening. Linda surprised everybody by agreeing to join Foley and two other employees for a drink. She left after only one cocktail.

A few nights later, she joined them again, and this time, she stayed longer. Everybody left, leaving Foley and Linda, who decided they would have one more and then call it a night. They got engaged in a business issue and went back to the office to resolve it. Finding the paperwork that proved her point, she was jokingly waving it back and forth when Foley gently took her wrist. Linda was chuckling, Foley was smiling, and then they stopped, their faces going serious. Foley let go of her wrist, his hand sliding up her arm, their eyes saying everything that had to be said, and they kissed. It was gentle at first and then intensified. Linda abruptly pulled back.

"I'm ... No, I'm sorry. This can't happen," she said, composing herself. "I have to go," she mumbled, leaving quickly before Foley had a chance to say anything except "I understand."

Foley was a little apprehensive the next morning, but Linda arrived and went about her business as if nothing happened. Things seemed normal, but there was a new tension. Simple glances and inadvertent touches were charged with latent energy.

One summer evening, a new business opportunity kept the entire staff working late as they scrambled to get a presentation finished.

Everybody was on a work high and it was almost 11 PM when they finally wrapped things up, high fiving each other.

Since Foley and Linda were the primary presenters, they were in his office going over their scripts. They weren't aware that everybody left. They finished up and Linda went back to her office. A few minutes later, Foley came to her office looking for a document. She got up from behind her desk and retrieved it from a file cabinet. They were standing face-to-face. They both looked at each other. They kissed, slow and gentle, and this time instead of breaking away she embraced him, hesitantly at first, and then more firmly.

They had sex on the brown suede sofa in her office. Their lovemaking was reserved, with surges of intensity, and when it was over, there were a few uncomfortable moments as they sheepishly untangled themselves and parted.

From that night on, things changed. Although Linda maintained her cool daytime demeanor, when evening came, she let go. It was as if everything she restrained in her life was set free in her lovemaking.

At work she was still distant and reserved, but their eyes were constantly hooking up in knowing glances.

Soon they were working late frequently. They thought they were taking great care to keep their romance a secret, but like most office affairs it didn't escape the scrutiny of other employees, especially another female. Carly, the office assistant, noticed it within days and passed her suspicions on to the others.

Linda's late-night work also caught the attention of her mother. Her daughter had both beauty and brains and that made her a high value catch. Bobby Wagner fit the bill. He came from a wealthy family with an established business that would provide her daughter with opportunities and security. What Marge Nexton liked most about the relationship was her daughter's absolute control over Bobby Wagner. It was the icing on a very promising cake.

Everything was going as Marge hoped until Linda took the job with the security company. Now her daughter had lost her way, but Marge Nexton would get her back on the right road. Linda picked up on her mother's subtle questioning, which became more direct and demanding. Linda kept insisting that nothing was going on.

Marge Nexton wasn't fooled.

Linda and Foley's time together was spent in lovemaking with little discussion about their bourgeoning relationship. Their focus was physical and when there was conversation it was usually about work and both knew that there were other issues that would have to be addressed at some point. Foley knew that she was practically engaged to some guy she went to college with, but Linda never mentioned his name or anything about him to anybody. Foley wanted to discuss it but felt it was up to Linda to initiate that conversation.

When it finally came up, it came at an unexpected time. Foley was still trying to catch his breath after an intense lovemaking session when Linda sat up and began dressing.

"My family's not too happy with what's been going on between you and me," she said.

Family? What in the hell?

"Your family's unhappy?" Foley repeated, stalling for time, "What do they have to do with it?"

"My mother says you're too old for me," Linda said.

"Or maybe you're just not old enough for me," Foley said with a smile.

"I doubt that," Linda said.

"Well, I guess we both have issues," Foley said, hoping to bring her boyfriend into the conversation.

Linda didn't respond.

"So, why are you telling me this? Is there something I should do?

"Nope. Just wanted you to know," and with that Linda gathered up her coat and briefcase and headed for the door.

"It's late. I have to go. See you tomorrow," she said and left.

Realizing that she wouldn't get a confession from her daughter, Marge decided she needed hard evidence and convinced her brother-in-law to spy on Linda. He always fantasized about being a private eye and almost bought one of those internet licenses and badges, but he was afraid his wife would find out, so he jumped at the chance to show off his investigative skills and began planning his stakeout.

The problem was that he couldn't get near their office. It was on the sixteenth floor of a mixed-use residential building, and Foley had taken a three-bedroom unit and converted it into offices. The would-be Sam Spade decided his best move to see anything was in the parking garage. Using his keen sense of deduction, he deduced that they probably left together and if he could get into the indoor parking garage, he might get the evidence he needed.

The problem was that the garage was for residents only, and the regulars used a garage door opener to gain entrance.

Undeterred, he bought a fake mustache, sunglasses, and began wearing a hat. Taking his cue from one of the many cop shows he watched, he waited until a regular opened the large steel door and he walked in behind the vehicle. He found Linda's car and shadowed himself a few spaces away. He knew she would go home that evening because of a family function.

When Linda and Foley came into the garage, they walked over to her car where they engaged in a passionate embrace and a series of kisses that left no doubts. Mission accomplished.

Once Marge had confirmation, she nibbled at Linda's lies, taking little bites at first, slowly chipping away at her psyche. She peppered Linda's mind with doubts about Foley. Nothing substantial or dramatic, just fragments of possibilities that when fed and watered grew bigger and stronger.

When she thought Linda was sufficiently weakened, she made her move. Without telling Linda, she called Foley. She started the conversation calmly, telling Foley she worried about her daughter's health. The long hours and intense work were stressing Linda out, and she was concerned.

Foley was surprised. Even though Linda had warned him about her mother, he never expected this kind of reaction. He tried to reassure

Marge that he was equally concerned and would do anything he could to ease the pressure on her. That's when Marge Nexton tore into him, blaming him for taking advantage of a sweet, young, innocent girl and ruining her life. No matter what Foley said, Marge Nexton was not to be denied. Like a lioness protecting her cub, Marge didn't hear a word Foley was saying, lashing out at him with threats and public exposure that the former police chief was preying on a young virtuous woman.

Although Foley wasn't concerned about Marge Nexton's threats, it was a problem that could escalate. As a police officer, he knew that domestic issues quickly turned into chaotic situations and they shouldn't be ignored.

He told Linda about the call. She brushed it off, saying her mother could get a bit overprotective and that it wouldn't happen again. Foley was skeptical, but there wasn't much he could do. He and Linda continued their relationship and anytime he brought her family up, she cut it short by telling him everything was fine.

But Marge Nexton was not fine with the situation. She had to back off for fear of pushing Linda and Foley even closer together but that wouldn't stop her from protecting her daughter.

She wasn't going to surrender her daughter's future to somebody like Foley.

Linda was far too good for the likes of him.

LINDA NEXTON

THE SNOW WAS GETTING A GRIP, BUT THE PENNSYLVANIA TURNPIKE was one of the more efficient snow removal roadways in the state. They touted their record of rarely shutting down because of weather. A legion of big, powerful orange Mack trucks, armed with monstrous plows, patrolled the four-lane road with military precision.

Linda stared at the snowflakes doubling on the windshield, some melting, while many accumulated outside the range of the monotonous wipers. She was deep in thought about her relationship with Foley.

She was attracted to him, maybe even more than she liked to admit.

She knew he was smitten with her, maybe actually in love, but she also knew his reputation. He was much more of a free spirit than she liked, a risk taker, and he certainly had a way with the ladies. She was more Catholic than she acted, politically liberal, yet socially conservative, and she chose her men. They didn't choose her. Until Foley, her life had been well organized. Yet here she was involved with somebody that didn't fit into her plan.

There were things she loved about Foley and things about him that frightened her. She really liked her job and was getting the chance to do things she'd never get a chance to do in another company. She was learning a lot. She was feeling positive about her job, but her emotions were a mess. It was bad enough that she had two lovers, but with the family pressure and her own uncertainty, she was walking on a high wire without a net.

Then came the day that she lost it. Her head exploded and everything went haywire. Everything has been crazy since then. That's why she was on this trip.

She had to tell him but how do you explain something to somebody when you can't explain it to yourself.

What in the hell did I do?

Her once well-organized world had become cluttered. She stared straight ahead, watching the wipers slide back and forth. Back and forth. Back and forth. That was her life now.

"You're pretty quiet," Foley said.

"Just thinking," she said.

"Can I ask about what?"

"You can."

"But you're not going to tell me, right?"

"Not unless you want to hear about a billing mistake that was made," she said knowing that Foley wouldn't want to discuss it.

"Don't tell me."

"I won't."

She was relieved that Foley took the hint.

She went back to her thoughts. They weren't pretty.

HOGG'S MOUNTAIN RETREAT

BY THE TIME BILL HOGG GOT TO STONY CREEK, THE STORM HAD brushed a fresh veneer of clean white snow over the alpine terrain. It was a Christmas card scene.

Hogg's mountain house was near the entrance to Stony Creek. It was nestled on a large half-acre lot surrounded by hemlocks and pines, providing Hogg with the privacy he needed. He kept it low key because he understood that ostentation led to investigation and that was the last thing he needed.

It was easy to spot the pimps and drug dealers. They stood out like flashes of lightening in a dark sky. The assholes were walking jewelry stores, cock-strutting down ghetto streets lit up with bling like a July Fourth sparkler, making it easy for the cops to target them. When Hogg built his house, he was conservative. He didn't want one that looked like a neon sign screaming "check me out."

It was a modest, two-bedroom home without a lot of gingerbread. It didn't have a basement, but it did have a crawl space for piping. The contractor pushed for a basement, but Hogg declined claiming they were nothing but junk collectors. Hogg wanted an insulated attic where he could store a few things and keep the house warm. The contractor figured it was a money issue and let it go.

He splurged by adding a small, railed balcony off the master suite on the second floor. He liked to sit out there, weather permitting, sipping a nightcap, and enjoying the peaceful sounds of the mountains.

Hogg just arrived at his Stony Creek house when the phone rang.

"Yeah," he said, grabbing it on the fourth ring, right before voicemail kicked in.

"I'm surprised you're there," said a soft, female voice. "You said you weren't coming up, but I took a chance and damned if you…"

"Call me back in ten minutes. I just walked in the door."

"Okay."

He turned up the thermostat, poured a Johnny Walker Black and topped it off with a layer of buttermilk. He had a stomach ulcer and believed that thick, tangy buttermilk added a protective coat that neutralized the alcohol on his inflamed tissue.

He downed three generous portions of scotch at home, minus the buttermilk, trying to drown out his wife's incessant bitching, and his stomach was burning. He switched on the TV, but muted the sound, and settled into the oversized leather armchair. He deserved this peace and quiet. He looked around the room and thought that he had done a pretty damn good job of decorating. He was pleased with his abilities.

The decor was a mixture of plaid and early Americana with a lot of wood and little evidence of any feminine touch. Hogg jokingly called his two-bedroom mountain retreat his "plaid palace" and he was proud of it.

He was well into his second scotch and buttermilk when the phone rang again.

"I said ten minutes," he said brusquely, without waiting for a "hello," sure it was the twin.

"Sorry. We had a problem in one of the concessions. I'm only two minutes late," she said, "Do you have some time for me?"

"Only if you're here in the next thirty minutes." He enjoyed pushing this bitch.

"I can't get all nice and pretty for you in thirty minutes. Can we make it...?"

"I said thirty minutes."

"Please. Give me an extra fifteen."

"That's your New Year's present. Be here in 45 minutes. Period."

"You are so cruel," she said.

"That's the way you like it, baby," he said, feeling a little stirring in his loins, "fifteen minutes or I'm gone."

"I'll be there," she said.

He hung up, a satisfied smirk on his face.

He was a little tired of her needy ways, but she was a good-looking woman who appreciated his dick. She was a grateful fuck who thanked him for slamming one into her. He liked them a little friskier than she was, but now was not the time to dump her.

He finished his drink and poured another. He wanted to be a little drunk when she got there because it made the sex better. He figured he'd bang her and then head over to Augie's. It could be a double-header night.

Hogg knew he was handsome and being a cop didn't hurt. Women liked cops, well most women, except for the ugly bitches who were usually fema-Nazis, as Rush called them. Real women liked strong men, especially good-looking men who carried guns.

Hogg understood their need and he gave it to them. He couldn't understand why in the hell he ever got married. Well, he did know. He wanted an heir, but his wife wasn't conceiving, so he quit wasting his time on that worthless bitch. He had to find a way to get rid of her.

If that little redhead wasn't working at Augie's tonight, he'd find something else. He always did, and besides, he could use some new ass. He had to keep his dick happy.

He smiled at the thought.

HEIDI'S CONDO

As she expected, the door to Heidi's condo was unlocked. She was angry as she let herself in. Since she learned about her sister's affair with that piece of shit Hogg, she made it a point to enter Heidi's condo quietly, hoping she might overhear her talking to him on the phone again.

She tiptoed to the stairs and damned if she didn't hear Heidi talking on the upstairs phone. She couldn't make out everything and she debated about creeping up the steps a little but thought better of it.

She made out something about "thirty minutes" but little else. She heard Heidi close a door, probably her closet, so she scurried back to the entryway and yelled out.

"Heidi, it's me. Are you here?"

"Upstairs. Be down in a sec."

Heidi came down the stairs, looking schoolgirl cute in her Uggs, green knee highs and a plaid miniskirt with a white filmy blouse. She looked like Lolita going to meet the professor.

She's meeting Hogg.

"What's on your agenda this evening?" Hedy asked innocently as she could.

"I'm meeting Sarah at the Rolling Rock club for an early New Year's Eve drink."

Does she really think I'm that dumb?

"The Rolling Rock Club?" Hedy said.

The Rolling Rock Club was the exclusive country club founded by the Mellon family on some 10,000 lush acres in the Loyalhanna Valley, which was a tedious drive from Stony Creek, especially on a snowy night. Club dress was old money conservative, and the schoolgirl look was hardly appropriate.

Although she was prepared, Hedy didn't like being rushed, but she had no choice. She was ready and if tonight had to be the night, so be it. The problem was keeping Heidi out of it but now that wasn't possible. When Hedy left her condo, she had a hunch it might come down to this, so she put together most of what she needed. Walking to Heidi's condo was a mistake. She could rectify it but the first thing she had to do was get Heidi out of the way.

"Oh, ah, I'm in the mood for a glass of champagne," she said, walking over to the fridge, "Have one with me before you leave."

"Well, I'm kind of in a ..."

"C'mon, we'll make it fast," Hedy said cheerfully, retrieving a bottle of Charles Krug, and popping the cork like a seasoned sommelier.

"Well, okay, but it has to be fast," Heidi said looking at her watch.

"Let's go into the living room," Hedy said, "You go ahead and sit down. I'll pour and bring it in. I'm kind of in a New Year's state of mind."

Heidi grumbled under her breath, but she obliged. She reluctantly went into the living room and sat down on the plush white sofa like a little girl being punished.

Heidi decorated her condo to fit her personality. It was totally white, sprinkled with glistening silver touches, much like a fresh snowfall. It wasn't sterile but teddy bear soft with lush silvery white carpeting and plush soft pillows and drapes. Hedy mused it was fit for a snow queen, but one drop of red wine would stand out like a neon sign.

Keeping her back to her sister, Hedy slipped a small glassine bag from her purse and emptied the contents into the flute, quickly adding the champagne. She watched the tiny bubbles rise to the top as the white powder dissolved into the amber liquid. She gave it a finger swirl just to make sure there was no residue and then poured herself champagne.

As Hedy walked into the living room, she said a brief prayer, asking God to "please make everything work," and even though she wasn't religious it was worth a try.

She needed every bit of help she could get.

She wasn't going to let Hogg destroy her sister like he destroyed Hedy's life.

Before this evening was over, that monster Hogg was going to rue the day he met the Kasser twins.

Hogg was finally going to get the short end of the stick, literally and figuratively.

PIPA'S

THE CHIEF UTTERED QUICK HELLOS AND NEW YEAR'S WISHES, shaking a hand here, nodding there, and muttering that he would be back shortly as he pushed himself through the crowded bar at Pipa's. Most people like knowing a cop. It was excellent insurance.

Converting the Kasser home into Pipa's was a relatively simple transition. When Greta built her home, she wanted to bring the outside in, so she insisted on large, airy spaces using local wood, stone, and greenery with few solid walls as possible. Instead, she separated the rooms with dividers of vertically louvered local woods interspersed with natural plant life.

Remaking the home into a club, Greta used wood such as black cherry, red oak, black walnut, and local stone like Sandstone and quartzite. The primary room became an outdoor panorama. Under a crystal and wood ceiling it became part atrium, part boardroom, and part greenhouse. The décor harmoniously blended into the outside environment as water trickled down a cobblestone wall and live greenery was in abundance. Yet as open and airy as Pipa's was it had a warm, intimate feel with soft lighting and luxurious cushioned seating.

Unlike the larger main room, the rest of the house had more dimly lit nooks and crannies than a Transylvanian castle.

The Chief wove his way through the crowd to a veiled door that was blended to look like the adjacent wall. It took him down a long hallway into what used to be the mechanic's office for the six-car garage. Augie loved to tinker with cars, and tinker was mostly what he did, using Stony Creek mechanics for the more complicated jobs. It was now the control center, with a bank of television monitors that covered all of Pipa's public areas. A man sat in front of the monitors. This function had been sub-contracted to an outside security firm, but The Chief had changes in mind. Otto opposed spending the money, but the Chief reminded him what pains in the ass rich people could be, especially the mountain climbers, and video evidence oiled the squeakers.

"Chief," said the man monitoring the video wall.

"How's it going, Nick? The boys in the back room happy?" he said, looking at the screens.

Card games were in full swing in all three rooms. Usually, they started later, but since it was New Year's Eve, they were trying to pack in as much card time before the bewitching hour. The Chief was sure that some would keep the game going past midnight. That would piss off a lot of wives and girlfriends.

Getting into the high stake's games wasn't easy. The vetting process was extensive, and once admitted, you had to sign a document that said the games were for entertainment only, and the small print explained how Stony Creek wasn't liable for anything. Even though Otto knew it would never hold up in court, the Chief insisted on it because "You always want to keep them mountain climbers on the edge of the cliff so they think a little shove will end it for them."

The private jet crowd knew about the games. Many flew in causing an overload at those nearby airports that could accommodate the equipment. Otto built a small strip on one of the flatter peaks, but it couldn't accommodate the jets, and mountain weather was always a problem.

The Chief ran the card rooms, each one secured by impenetrable doors, electronic key cards, and roving plain-clothes guards. It was an expensive operation, but the tax-free take made up for it and then some. The card rooms were in a separate area with only one entrance, which was well secured, making it difficult, if not impossible, for any unwanted guests to get in. What most people didn't know was that there was a secret exit in every room hidden behind a movable wall that connected to a narrow corridor which led to stairs and then to another short hallway that snaked its way to an outside exit. They could clear the rooms in less than a minute. Otto, via the Chief, Hogg and other well-placed contacts kept Stony Creek safe from outside police interference.

There was a time Otto wanted to dispense with the lucrative card games, but greed and the pressure from the Mountain Climbers changed his mind. Some who knew Otto claimed he never seriously considered dropping the games and that he was only setting up the players for an increase in the skim.

The Mountain Climbers received first class treatment, eating, and drinking nothing but top shelf, and the well-appointed private bedrooms upstairs were theirs for the asking. They also represented some of the oldest and wealthiest families in Pennsylvania, powerful names with a lot of money and influence. Otto wanted to be one of them, but he didn't realize that it would never happen. Old money traveled with old money and Otto's riches were relatively new, plus there was that rumor about how his mother acquired the property.

The Chief ran a tight ship and although all the players were millionaires, many of them were penny-wise and pound-foolish. They would spend lavishly on silly extravagances and argue for hours over a quarter. There were some that even believed that they were privileged enough to cheat, but the Chief kept them in line. Before the Chief came on board, Otto was taking a one-point skim. Now the rake was a healthy five points on each no-limit pot, and Otto was accumulating bags of tax-free cash that the Chief delivered to him personally. The Chief was still a very efficient bagman.

It was a substantial profit center for Otto, although he continually bitched about the expense it took to run the play. The high stakes games required upwards of a half million dollars in cash to be available for the players on big nights. Legend has it that one pot hit over one hundred thousand dollars, but nobody will confirm that. As more and more players wanted to get into the games, Otto faced a dilemma—to expand or not to expand. He was very reluctant to do so, as was most of the family, and he knew the day would come when they would have to end the illicit gambling.

Because of the long holiday weekend, Otto stocked up on cash. Stony Creek didn't accept credit cards and the banks would be closed so the resort would be cash heavy exactly what Joe Duck was counting on.

Cash was king for the games, although markers were accepted with the Chief's okay, which he kept to a minimum, but it helped build what he called his library. He kept a book on just about every wealthy family in western Pennsylvania, which came in handy when he had to quiet down any noisy voices.

After watching the Climbers on the monitors for a few minutes, the Chief went into his small office just off the operations room. He'd hide out there for a while and then call Foley. Maybe they could have a drink together. Before he left, he noticed something on the monitor covering the bar area that people he was paying to watch missed. That was another chip he'd use to get his son a deal with Stony Creek.

He saw a bartender palm money.

He didn't want to deal with it.

He'd tell Hedy and she could handle it.

JR LEON

ONE NEW FACE THE CHIEF MISSED AT PIPA'S WAS THE MAN WHO sat in the shadows in the far corner of the busy dining room, his back to the sandstone wall, as he quietly people watched. An attractive fortyish blonde, looking disinterested, sat next to him. Sitting quietly at the next table, trying to look like they belonged, were two younger men wearing the obligatory ear buds and dark suits that signaled they were bodyguards.

JR Leon was an enigma to the silver-spoon crowd. His recent arrival in Pittsburgh had their tongues wagging. Little was known about him except that he was extraordinarily rich and had South American ties. That information spilled out from their banking connections and was enough to get the mountain matriarchs prattling about him.

"I understand he lives on a boat. If he has all that money, why live on a boat?"

"I never heard of the Leon's."

"I was told he was born in South America to an American who owned half of Brazil," echoed another.

Everything about JR Leon was shaded with mystery. His personality and features matched the shadows that seemed to surround him. He was low key, speaking slowly with an almost whispery intonation through thin lips. His dark eyes and dyed black hair added to the mystery. But he had fair skin hidden by a perpetual tan, some saying he used a bronzer. His chiseled features suggested some middle European or

Nordic ethnicity. Age wise, the guesstimates were in the fifties, but he was sixty-eight.

He was selfish with personal information, and over the years, his ability to pay cash for just about everything left no paper trail. He had a small, tight-lipped staff that was well paid and legally secured. JR shared little with them. He retained three different legal companies and never gave any one of them enough business so they could see the entire picture. He kept a personal log on every project that only he could access. He was considered paranoid but to JR prudence was the smart road to riches. He was willing to take risks but only after all the boxes were checked. Then it became a question of odds.

As a child, he was taught the need for secrecy. He was raised by nannies and home schooled on a secluded estate that had few visitors. He learned how to take care of himself. To him, seclusion and secrecy were normal. JR stayed out of the public eye. Quiet money was always more effective than those who liked to flaunt their wealth.

Those whose egos took over couldn't see past themselves and needed to continually feed their addiction.

Narcissism was their God, and adulation was their drug of choice.

They worshipped the spotlight as camera's flashed and oversized bodyguards cleared a path for them. It was the magic elixir for their drugged personalities.

It was indeed the breakfast of egomaniacal champions.

JR tried to avoid doing business with the publicity hounds. He didn't want to be dragged into their world. When he had no choice, he found them easy to control and manipulate. Treat them like royalty, shower them with flattery, and blind them with glitter, and the rest was easy.

Like many wealthy people, JR believed God chose him to be rich. He took that responsibility seriously and handled it appropriately.

Of course, he defined what was appropriate.

When he came to Pittsburgh, he didn't operate as quietly as usual, allowing information to dribble out in a series of controlled leaks. He didn't change his style. It was part of his plan, and that's what he was thinking when he was interrupted.

"Sorry to disturb you, sir," the tuxedoed man said as he approached JR's table causing the bodyguards to execute their alert mode, "My name is Michael Barron, and I am the manager here at Pipa's."

The bodyguards pushed back their chairs, but a slight wave from the boss stopped them.

"A pleasure, Mr. Barron. What can I do for you?" JR said still seated.

"I just want to welcome you to Pipa's and present you with your electronic access membership card and to see if there is anything else you need at the moment."

"Everything is fine. Thank you," JR said taking the envelope and placing it on the beige tablecloth.

"Well then, enjoy the evening, sir, and I hope you have a very rewarding new year," Michael said as he backed away from the table, almost bowing but catching himself. As he was about to turn, JR spoke up.

"Thank you... and Michael, there is one thing."

"Sir?" Michael said, taking a step back towards the table. The bodyguards stayed in their seats but kept a watchful eye on him.

"If any member of the Kasser family is in the club, I would like to say hello."

"Yes, sir. Right now," he said turning and scanning the room, even though he knew there were no Kassers, "nobody is here but I'm certain Miss Kasser, ah, Hedy Kasser, will be stopping by and I'll relay your wish. I know she'd be pleased to personally welcome you to the club."

"Thank you," JR said.

As the manager made his way through the crowded club, JR was smiling to himself. He knew that Hedy Kasser would meet with him. He imagined the look on her face when she was informed. His blonde companion Laura interrupted his thoughts.

"You'll like Hedy Kasser," Laura said, "she's definitely your type. Young, beautiful and rich, just your kind," she added, giving him a big toothy smile.

"Now why do you say that Laura?" he said, with a mischievous tone, playing it coy, which he liked to do with women. To him they were like playful pets, somebody to toy with until he got them into bed where an urgent ruthlessness took over.

"I've only known you for what? Two months? I've seen you in action. You have an eye for beautiful women," she said.

"That's why I'm with you," he said.

"Cut the BS, JR, I'm too old for you. You like them young, sweet and firm, but I am enjoying the ride, even if it will be a short one."

"There you go again, Laura," he said with a quick smile that looked more like a twitch, "always making me out to be a bad boy. You are such a cute little kitty," he said, almost lapsing into baby talk. Most women found it annoying, but for some his money inspired tolerance.

"A kitty with sharp claws," she said, "Remember, I'm a banker."

JR gave her a warning look and then smiled.

"Yes, you are."

When JR came to Pittsburgh, word seeped out that he was looking for a banking connection. She was a Senior VP at a large chain and was surprised that she got in to see him so quickly. She dressed businesslike but showed enough cleavage and curves to let him know she could also be part of his financial package.

Laura Emery was an attractive woman. When necessary, she used her God-given looks to further her ambitions. She had a model's face, high cheekbones, narrowing to a nicely formed chin, with generous, but not thick lips, and large oblong brown eyes. She kept her blonde hair short, perfectly coiffed in a pixie cut that suited her narrow face. Wrinkles were emerging, but she covered them as best she could. She lacked a model's height, and her child-bearing hips were pronounced, although she had never given birth, being married once to a former bank president.

She became JR's banker, or at least one of them. She knew no more about him than anybody else. His background check yielded little. He did mention that he spent most of his time on his yacht. She was certain he had other residences, but with the money he deposited, she didn't care if he lived in a cave.

What she didn't know was that it wasn't her sales ability that landed the Leon business; JR chose her. One of his assistants provided him with photos and bios of all the key female bankers in the area, and he picked out Laura.

He never mentioned the name of his yacht or she would have checked it out in the registry, but she didn't much care. With his money, she didn't need to know everything.

Wealthy people expected special treatment, and she was an excellent provider.

SUITE 417

LINDA WAS NERVOUS AS SHE WANDERED AROUND THE SUITE chatting aimlessly about inane things like the décor and wall color.

She was acting like a visiting General reviewing the troops. "I like this detail," she said, running her hand lightly over the ornate brass floor lamp. "Very nice."

She continued her inspection tour, stopping for a moment to sip her champagne, glancing at Foley, and then moving on. Foley wondered why she was so restless. He decided to talk business. That always got her attention.

"Any thoughts about what kind of fee we should ask for?" he said.

She stopped and gave him a puzzled look.

"I mean about handling the security up here." That was the reason he gave Linda when he was trying to entice her to come to Stony Creek.

"Oh, ah, no. I think you'll have to play it by ear depending on what services they want," she said, taking another sip.

"I should be ready with something."

"Any idea of budget?" she said, coming over to the sofa.

"No, but hopefully CB will fill me in when we meet."

She was about to sit on the armchair but changed her mind. She didn't want to seem like she was trying to stay away from him, which she was, but she didn't want to be so obvious.

She sat down on the sofa and he reached for her champagne flute.

"No more for me, thanks."

"C'mon, it's New Year's Eve," he said, taking the glass from her hand and refilling it. She didn't resist.

They sat for what seemed a long moment, both sipping their champagne, Foley finally breaking the silence.

"Are you okay?"

"Yeah, no, well, I'm feeling a little off."

"Can I get you something? I have some aspirin in…."

"Ah, no. Maybe it's that time of the month coming on. I don't know. I'm just…."

"Come here," he said, "Let me give you a hug." He put his arm around her. He felt some resistance, but then she relaxed.

They sat quietly, looking at the flames swirling around in the fireplace.

She felt his fingers playing with her hair. Occasionally his hand would rub her neck. It felt good.

This wasn't in her plan. Actually, she didn't have a plan. She wasn't sure when she'd tell him.

She was thinking about her next move when she felt him snuggle closer. Maybe she should just let it happen. After all, she owed him that.

My God. Am I about to give him a mercy fuck?

She shuddered ever so slightly. She never used that word, not even in her mind.

"Chilly?" he said, pulling her even closer. She turned and looked at him. It was a turn that told them both what was about to happen.

He kissed her, gently and then harder and deeper. She responded and soon his hands were moving on her body. Helping each other, they quickly removed their clothing. Somehow, he turned the light off and their nude bodies felt good against each other. They rubbed, skin to skin, feeling their cravings bubbling up, and then he was inside her. It was quick and intense, bursting into muffled grunts and gasps, and then it was over.

They were both spent, but he still lay on top of her. She wiggled her way out from under him and he quickly rolled off and stood up.

For a moment she felt strangely removed. As she lay there, she felt a canopy of cold air waft over her, chilling her back to reality.

Suddenly she jumped up. "Nature calls," she said as she half ran into the bathroom.

The mess was getting messier.

HEDY'S REVENGE

HEDY WAITED A LONG TIME FOR THIS MOMENT, AND NOW THAT IT was here, she was anxious and excited at the same time. She felt like she did when she went on her first "rolly" coaster ride. Rosie took the nine-year-old twins to Kennywood Park in Pittsburgh when they were big enough to ride the Thunderbolt for the first time.

Heidi was having none of it and refused to get on the ride. Hedy was uneasy, but she suppressed her fear and applied her "let go" theory, although at that young age she hadn't developed it into a full-scale rationale. The first time she crystallized it into a reality was when she did her first parachute jump at eighteen.

She was nervous as she kneeled in the doorway, looking down at rectangles of green countryside from 13,000 feet, the noise from plane engines and the wind rushing into her ears.

"Okay, you ready?" yelled the instructor into her ear as they prepared to make the tandem jump.

The instructor told her that if she wanted to abort, all she had to do was yell it out. She didn't think she was facing death but there was a chance. The thought crossed her mind, but if she was going to live life fearing death that wasn't living. Every nerve in her body was firing, but she couldn't let fear win.

"Ready," she yelled.

The tremendous blast of air hitting her face startled her. She hadn't expected the rush to be so powerful and noisy. For a moment, she forgot to bend her legs upward and quickly did so, getting a shoulder tap of approval from her instructor. On TV sky divers looked so silently graceful and serene, but when you're hurtling earthward at 120 miles per hour, there's nothing quiet about it. She just let go, handing her life over to destiny, and she felt free. When the chute opened, the severe stream of air against her face changed to gentle breezes and she gently floated earthward. As she peacefully drifted down through the warm air, she felt exhilarated and happy.

Later she would say that "fear is one of the weakest links in the chain of life. Once it takes over, you've lost and fall under its control. Worse, when the enemy knows your fears, they own you."

Hedy wasn't a crazy risk taker, impulsive and reckless. She always did her homework and calculated her odds before she engaged in anything that was dangerous or dicey.

Yet she had doubts. Was she doing the right thing? She fought with herself for seven years over what to do. Seven years. Long, agonizing years. Hedy could not erase that horrible night. She tried. She spent a lot of hours undergoing counseling, but Hogg's rape was an indelible stain on her body that couldn't be scrubbed off. It was as if a blistering hot branding iron had been seared deep into her skin. Rape disfigures women. Rape invades, insults, and invalidates the soul of women. It is not erasable. She didn't want to get even—*she had to get even.* But she questioned her decision. Was it the right thing to do? The worst a rapist suffers is jail where they get three meals, hot showers, and a roof over their heads. For the woman it is a life sentence of mental hell. And now Hogg had his slimy hands on her sweet sister. Hedy had to do something, anything, but something. She wouldn't be free until Hogg felt her pain.

Tonight was the night.

She had to get back to her suite, stop at Pipa's, God I hope the Chief's there, get her car, no, maybe… damn she had to think straight.

Even though she planned for this moment, her decision to do it tonight changed things. She was headed for the gondolas when she saw Max Barron sitting on his snowmobile. He was the brother of Pipa's manager, Michael, and a group leader on the groundkeeper's team.

"Max, I need a ride. Can you take me down?"

"No problem, Miss Kasser. Hop on," he said, revving up the snowmobile, thinking who wouldn't like to have a woman like Hedy Kasser pushing her boobs up against you?

"I'm in a hurry, Max."

"Hang on."

Max Barron knew the trails well, and he zipped down the mountain quickly, sliding to a stop in front of her door in just under five minutes.

"I need to go to Pipa's. Can you wait a few minutes and take me back up?" she said, hopping off quickly.

"You got it, Miss Kasser."

I hope she has a lot of places to go tonight.

He couldn't ask for better duty than squiring around the boss lady. She had a reputation for being a little tough, but she was always good to him. No matter how tough anybody thought she was, one thing was certain—every red-blooded male in the place wanted to get into her pants, including some red-blooded females. There were those who thought they really could, but it never happened. She dated, but nobody local or on staff, and there was no gossip about anybody serious.

The snowfall was thickening, and it looked like a good old-fashioned nor'easter. Max wiped his wet visor with the small hand towel that he kept in his forest green Stony Creek issue jacket. He looked up at the dark, flake filled sky and bet himself that this storm was going to drop at least a foot, maybe more.

Hedy rushed into her suite and headed for the utility closet. Digging into the corner, she pulled out a locked suitcase. She turned the combination to the desired numbers on the aluminum case and it clicked open. She was relieved. Every little step was important.

Inside the hardback was a large soft calfskin Prada shoulder bag she prepared for this moment. She removed it, shoved the suitcase back into the closet, and flung the Prada over her shoulder. She stopped for a moment and gave herself the once-over in the full-length mirror in the entry hall. As she inspected herself, she continued to re-run every detail over and over in her mind.

Damn, she didn't look nervous.

She wore tapered black fleece pants with a white cashmere turtleneck and a navy-blue ski jacket. She didn't like the white top; it wasn't the best color for what she was about to do, but she didn't have time to change. Besides the Prada, she put a pair of navy-blue slacks, a powder blue cashmere sweater, knee highs, bra, panties, a pair of black Louboutin's, her toiletries, and a couple of garbage bags into a canvas tote, took another look in the mirror, and then hurried back outside.

"Let's head up to Pipa's," she said to Max, hopping on the snowmobile.

He threw the Yamaha into gear and roared up the trail leading to the club. The proliferating snow slapped at their face masks and it was getting more difficult to see.

As the snowmobile slashed through the floury snow, the huge flakes zipping by their faces, Hedy finally got her mind to slow down and she felt calm. She ran through the checklist one more time.

She stiffened her body and tightened her jaw. She had to get the deed done early.

She was ready to let go.

JOE DUCK

JOE DUCK WAS STARING OUT OF THE LARGE PANORAMIC WINDOW in his hotel room as skiers crisscrossed their way down the slippery slopes, but he didn't see them. What he was seeing was snow. The tall, powerful slope lights lit up the countless snowflakes tumbling out of the black sky and splashed the milky run with gray-blue shadows.

More snow was good news and bad news for Joe.

His plan was simple. Rob the money room and get out of Stoney Creek fast. The cops would expect him to head for the turnpike, which is always maintained during a snowstorm, but Joe would outsmart them. He'd take the back roads. He hoped his SUV could handle it.

He registered as Jim Scarcini and paid cash. He had a fake ID that a guy fixed up for him. It wasn't particularly good, so he was glad he didn't have to use it. He met Scarcini years ago in Augie's when Joe worked at the resort. It was casual bar chat, but Scarcini made an impression on Joe. He didn't brush him off like most people did. Joe never forgot it and when he needed an alias Scarcini was perfect. Joe remembered Scarcini said he was from Herminie, a small coal town a few hours' drive from the resort.

As far as Joe knew, the money room had no security of any kind. The Kassers didn't think people even knew about the money room, so why call attention to it with security guards? Joe knew that family members picked up the cash from the various entities a few times a day, but the schedule was intentionally irregular. That didn't matter to Joe, mostly because he couldn't do anything about it. He was going to get a lot of cash no matter when he robbed the money room.

His biggest problem was getting off the property before they sealed off the entrance. There was only one road out. He timed it. Once he had the cash, it would take him three to five minutes to get to the car. The drive to the gate would take another five minutes, and Joe added five more for cushion. Fifteen minutes was the most it would take him, and probably less. The entrance had five toll booths coming in and two unrestricted lanes for leaving.

Joe worried he wouldn't make it. One radio call and they'd seal off the exit within minutes. This was the big hitch in his plan. He thought he could scare the money room people enough so they wouldn't alert anybody for maybe fifteen minutes, but there was no guarantee.

He thought about options. It didn't take long for him to realize that he had few or none. It was make a run for it with the money or hide it somewhere on Stony Creek and then come back for it.

Joe racked his brain, an overwhelming effort that netted few results. Every place he could think of was unsafe, even the caves. The problem with the caves was "them see-plunkers" or whatever they were called. They were in Stony Creek just about every day, rummaging around. The other problem was the snow. Getting to the caves was hard enough, but carrying big bags of money? It was too risky. Besides, with the heavy snow, he'd leave a trail that a blind man could follow.

And then he remembered.

The retention pond.

It was down in a little valley just below one of the housing developments. The pond was fenced in with a small brick shed just outside the locked gate.

Otto put in a computerized aeration system that was monitored in the operations center, so employees rarely needed to go into that area. The pond was maintained by an outside company. As far as Joe knew, they came two or three times a year. It was doubtful they'd show up over the New Year holiday.

It could be a good place to stash the money until after the holidays. There was no reason for anybody to be in that area, and the narrow road leading there dead ended. Driving down that rarely used road would leave tracks, but if the snowfall kept up, there was a good chance any tracks would be covered. Nobody paid attention to that road.

Then he had to find a place at the pond to hide the money. He assumed the brick shed was still there. Maybe a spot around or near the shed? The smart thing to do was to case the area to make certain. Maybe he'd do that.

He dug out his jar of Georgia Moon. The label said it was legal corn liquor. It tasted like shit, but it only cost him ten bucks and it did the job. He didn't like the stupid pickle jar they put it in. He took a hearty swig. He felt the stream of heat leaving a trail down his throat.

He looked around the room. He didn't bring many clothes, so there wasn't much to pack, and… wait, maybe he could fake out the maid into thinking he was still there after the job. How'd he miss that?

What if he went to the little shopping mall just off the main lobby and bought some clothes, left them hanging in the closet, and scattered some around the room, along with his half-used Georgia Moon? That way the maid would think somebody was still using the room, which would give him a head start.

Things were shaping up, and he had to get a move on.

Finally, Joe Duck was going to make a buck.

He smiled at his little rhyme. He was pumped.

This time, he wasn't going to make any dumb mistakes.

HEDY

HEDY WAS METICULOUS IN HER PLANNING. OVER THE YEARS, she re-examined it many times. It was well thought out, but she wasn't happy about having to move so fast. She had to establish an alibi. She'd use Pipa's, but she preferred some backup. She didn't want to involve her sister, or any member of her family, but that might not be possible now. One idea that struck her was to use the Chief. He was a cop. Even though he was a bit questionable, his colleagues would believe him if the Chief believed it.

One advantage New Year's Eve provided was alcohol. Pipa's patrons would consume a lot, causing clouds to move into their brains and shade their memories.

Normally she used Pipa's rear entrance, but tonight she wanted to be seen even though it would absorb valuable time getting through the early dinner crowd.

As soon as she came through the front door, it started.

"Just the person I was looking for." a heavily made-up middle-aged woman in a bulky mink said grabbing Hedy by the arm.

"I'm sorry, Trish, but I have a business emergency. Can we talk later?" Hedy said as she pulled away.

"Hedy, good to see you. Are you available next Thursday for…"?

"Hedy, did you get a chance to…?"

"Hey, Hedy, are you coming to the…?"

Her response became repetitive. "Sorry, I'm really late for a meeting. I'll be back later." She kept twisting and pushing her way through the crowd.

Just when she thought she had made it through, Mike Barron, the club manager, stopped her.

"Hedy, JR Leon is here. He's the businessman from South America that we talked about at the last meeting. He wants to meet you."

Damn, what's wrong with him?

"Ah, I'm really jammed right now," she said, and was about to keep going when she rethought it.

"I'll meet him, but only for a minute. Where is he?"

"Follow me," Mike said as Hedy fell in behind him. She used him as a shield as they snaked their way through the lively dining area. She quickly brushed off anybody trying to talk with her, invoking the "meeting" line. She wondered why in the hell Leon had asked for her. She didn't need this right now.

Christ, why does he have to be at the other end of the room?

As they neared his table, Mike stepped to one side to allow Hedy to move to the front. Mike made the introduction.

"Mr. Leon, Miss Kasser."

"Miss Kasser, good to see you again," JR said, moving his chair back, rising, as he extended his hand.

"JR, nice seeing you. Please stay seated. Thank you," Hedy said, shaking his hand.

"Oh, you two know each other," Mike said, "I thought..."

"Thanks, Mike," Hedy interrupted, and Mike knew he was excused.

"Say hello to Laura Williams," JR. said.

"Laura, nice to meet you," Hedy said, extending her hand as Laura rose from her seat.

"Nice seeing you again. We met a few years ago at the Clubhouse when my bank sponsored an event there," she said. When Hedy looked puzzled, she added, "Our Clubhouse, the Pittsburgh organization down in the Strip that works with people with cancer. It used to be Gilda's Club and..."

"Ah, yes, the Clubhouse. They do such wonderful work. I do remember you now. Nice seeing you again," Hedy said, smiling generously.

JR glanced at Laura. "Excuse me, I need to go to the Ladies' room," Laura said getting up.

He waved his open hand to a chair, but Hedy nodded a quick "No."

They both remained standing. Hedy, smiling, said under her breath, "Do you think this is really a good idea?"

"I don't think it hurts."

"I thought we were going to keep a low profile. This BS about wanting to meet me..."

"I said a Kasser. It doesn't matter. Please, have a seat and I'll get you a drink."

"I can't. I have another meeting. I'll stop back later and if you're here, I'll have that drink with you," Hedy said, anxious to leave. She also knew that a lot of the Pipa's crowd had their eyes on them. She wasn't sure whether that was good, so she wanted to keep it short.

"A meeting on New Year's Eve? Sounds suspicious to me," JR said playfully, thinking that Hedy was naïve if she thought she could play him. He was certain she didn't have another meeting. That made him wary.

"See you later," Hedy said as she hurried to an exit from the main room. She rushed down the hallway that separated the kitchen from the dry food storage area, and then through a series of corridors, and up some dimly lit stairs to the Chief's office.

She banged on his door.

"Yeah?"

"Chief, it's Hedy. Do you have a moment?"

Hedy knew the Chief kept his office door locked, even when he was in it. She anxiously waited until she heard the click of the deadbolt.

"What's up?" the Chief said casually, turning to go back to his desk. He liked Hedy, but it was important for him not to act like the brown-nosers who were always scraping and bowing when a Kasser entered the room.

"I need a favor, Chief."

"Tell me what it is, and I'll tell you if I can do it."

"Oh, it's not a big thing. Do you have some time to run up to Heidi's condo and check on her? She wasn't feeling well, and I left her on the sofa sound asleep. I need to freshen up and get back downstairs. I just want to make sure she's okay. You have a master key so you can let yourself in, if necessary, and the way she sleeps it might be necessary. I'd really appreciate it."

The Chief gave Hedy a "I don't do piddling errands," look but said, "As a favor to you I'll run up and check on her," with a "now you owe me," tone.

"Thanks, Chief. I'm going to take the green room, number 3, and use it to shower. Let Mike know, will you?" she said and with a twirl, turned and left. The Chief didn't like being ordered around, but she was gone before he could give her a dirty look or a sarcastic response.

Hedy knew the Chief was annoyed, which was good because it would sharpen his memory. Every step was critical, leaving little room for error, but Hedy was sure that if she got through these first steps with no problems, she was going to get through all of them.

Once inside the green room, she moved fast. She turned down the bedspread, threw herself on the bed and messed it up so it looked used, unpacked, hung up her slacks and cashmere top in the closet, dropped her shoes on the floor near the bed and went into the bathroom. She put the bathmat on the floor and turned on the shower. She closed the frosted glass door and dropped a pair of panties and bra on the tile floor. She took a fast look around and closed the bathroom door behind her.

When she was certain she had everything the way she wanted it, she went to the door and peeked into the hall. She was pleased that it was deserted. She took another quick look around the room and left, locking the door. She walked rapidly down the stairs, hoping she wouldn't bump into anybody.

As she made her way through another short hallway, a thought suddenly struck her. How could she have missed it? Two snowmobiles were always kept at Pipa's. One in the garage and one at the ready just outside. What if the outside snowmobile was being used? She'd have to use the inside one which was on a trailer and it was a bitch to move around.

She entered the code and went into the garage. She saw the one snowmobile under the security light. She hoped the other was outside the side door, ready to go.

It was, and she hurriedly removed the cover and fired up the engine, saying a quiet "thank you" when it started on the first try. She started out slowly, not wanting to be noisy, and headed down the wooded back trail.

She was tense and doubt kept snipping at her confidence. As she accelerated and picked up speed, she revved up her courage. She could feel her adrenaline kicking in.

Thinking about what she was going to do gave her a nervous smile for a moment. What she was about to do was deadly serious. It would certainly be life changing for Hogg, which conjured up many funny images in her mind causing her to laugh out loud. She also recognized it as a cover-up for her nerves.

One thing was certain.

The sick son-of-a-bitch would never live this down.

THE CHIEF

"CHRIS, YOU SETTLED IN?" THE CHIEF SAID ON THE PHONE, "everything okay?"

"Yeah, It's good. Really nice. Thanks."

The Chief wasn't buying. The kid sounded like he lost his dog.

"You okay?"

"Fine. What's up?"

"Listen, why don't you and your, ah, friend meet me in Augie's for a New Year's drink. I need to discuss this security thing with you. Otto's ready to pop."

"Ah, well, she's napping and…"

"Take your time. I have an errand to run. Can you make it at seven?

Chris looked at his watch. That gave Linda 20 minutes to get ready, if she wanted to go, which he doubted.

"Okay, we'll be there."

The Chief hung up, grabbed his coat, and headed for the monitor room.

"The Wallman brothers show up yet?" The Chief asked as he walked into the room, the TV monitors casting a shadowy glow on the man watching the bank of screens.

"Not yet, Chief. Maybe they got hung up in the snow."

"That would be a break. Call me on the radio if they show."

"Will do."

The Chief left, taking a back route to avoid the bar crowd. He drove his Jeep to Heidi's condo, muttering to himself that he wasn't a goddamn errand boy, but happy to get out.

This snow is looking serious.

The snow blowers were already out, clearing the walkways and parking lots around the condos. The Chief had to give it to the ground crew. They cleared the flakes when they hit the ground.

He maneuvered his way around the two orange-jacketed men as they expertly pushed their blowers so that the snow coming out of the side chutes arced out of the parking area. The two men, seeing the Chief, nodded as he made his way past them to Heidi's condo. He was about to knock on the door when his radio crackled.

"Come in, Chief."

"Yeah, what's up? The Wallman brothers get there?"

"No, Chief, they're not coming tonight. They'll be here tomorrow night."

"So, why are ya calling me?"

"To let you know they're not coming."

"I only needed to know if they were coming."

"Right, Chief. Over and out."

That asshole got his brains on sale at the Dollar store.

The Chief shook his head as he knocked on Heidi's door.

No answer.

He knocked louder.

No answer.

He rang the doorbell. He knew it was working because he could hear the rhythmic ding-dong inside the condo.

Still no answer.

Heidi said she was sleeping. He stood there for a moment debating whether he should bang on the door, but he didn't want to scare her. He took out his master key, gently turned it in the lock, and slowly pushed the door open while calling out Heidi's name.

"Heidi," he called out, somewhat softly, as he gingerly stepped farther into the condo.

"Heidi," now a little louder but still no response as he looked around the room.

Then he saw her. She was lying in the fetal position on the white sofa, covered with a white crocheted throw. She was sound asleep.

This place is whiter than an albino's ass. God forbid she runs out of Kotex at the wrong time.

The Chief chuckled at his thought as he walked over to the sofa and saw there was plenty of color in Heidi's face and her breathing was steady. He gently nudged her as he whispered her name. She gave a soft moan, curled her legs up a little tighter, and didn't open her eyes.

She was really zonked out. When he saw the half full tulip glass on the coffee table, the once bubbly liquid looking lifeless, he figured she had a little too much. He stood there for a moment and looked around the room.

He spotted another tulip glass setting on the kitchen counter. Somebody had a drink with her. The champagne cork lay on the silver flecked granite counter. He checked out the fridge. He saw the left-over champagne, probably expensive, corked with a fancy stopper, and a couple of bottles of unopened white wine. Heidi didn't keep much. There were some salad fixings, the usual condiments, orange juice, Perrier, and milk.

He did a quick check of the place, just so big sister Hedy wouldn't find something to bitch about, but he was sure everything was kosher.

He checked the two guest bedrooms, each of them hotel ready for visitors. There was no mistaking Heidi's room. Once again, white on white on white dominated. White furniture, silver trim, a thick white carpet, even a white desk, and if it were possible, he was sure the screen on the Apple laptop would have been white. The white satin cover on the bed was disturbed by a multi-colored flowered dress laying on it, a radical element in this ocean of vanilla.

He went through the entire condo and saw nothing unusual except Heidi's obsession with white.

It looks like a terminal virgin lives here.

The Chief thought Heidi was mousy compared to Hedy. She was just as beautiful, but her personality was subdued, almost little girl like. Heidi's life was monotone compared to Hedy's surround sound. On a chart it was a straight line with very few peaks and valleys. She lived in the shadow of her sister. The Chief thought it was odd for identical twins to be that different, but then he wasn't about to spend any time worrying about it.

He glanced at his watch. It was getting close to seven, so he picked up the pace.

He went back downstairs and checked on Heidi again. She hadn't moved.

He turned off the overheads, leaving the stove light on, and locked the door behind him.

He was happy to get out of Heidi's obsessive white out. He couldn't understand how she could live that way. A couple specks of dust would turn the place into a coal mine. He looked at his watch. He hurried past the rumbling blowers as they continued hurling snow into the night air. By the looks of it, they were losing ground to the dense mass of flakes gyrating through the dark sky.

It looked like this could be a big one. He had ten minutes to get down the mountain to meet Foley.

But he wasn't concerned about that. He was thinking about the container of milk in Heidi's refrigerator.

FOLEY

THE CROWD FROM AUGIE'S FLOODED INTO THE HALLWAY AND spilled into the old lobby. Foley was in no mood to deal with it. In fact, he was in no mood to deal with anything. He was relieved to get out of the suite. Clear his addled head. Every thought caused a quiet grunt and head shake. If he hadn't been there, he'd never believe it. His training told him to stay steady and think it out slowly, but this one was for the books.

Meeting CB would temporarily divert him and give him some cool down time. For a moment he wondered if he should say something to CB, but quickly shook that out of his system.

Augie's was bulging with bodies, pressing, shoving, pushing, and going nowhere. Daylight skiers came in from the slopes for Happy Hour adding to the crowd. Those who got a drink were doing everything possible to protect their jiggling glasses.

He spotted a relatively quiet corner in the old lobby and headed for it. He leaned up against the wall and waited for CB, but he couldn't get the last hour out of his mind.

He kept repeating it, trying to make sense out of the craziest thing he ever heard. It was like he was in a bad soap opera. No, this wouldn't be believable even in a stupid soap opera.

He wasn't sure who to be pissed off at himself or Linda—probably both.

He rewound and thought it through again.

He saw that Linda was a bit edgy, but nothing serious. The sex was okay, maybe a little restrained, but that wasn't unusual. Linda had her moods. After they were finished, she made a dash for the bedroom to lie down. He thought she might not be feeling well, so he watched TV. When it was time for his meeting with CB, he peeked in and she was sound asleep. He debated about waking her. He knew she didn't want to go to the meeting. She wasn't a big fan of the old man, but he wanted her to hear what CB had to say about the Stony Creek business.

She was curled up under the covers and he gently tapped her shoulder. She mumbled and turned over.

"We have to meet CB," he said, giving her shoulder another jiggle.

"I can't go," she mumbled, pulling the cover over her head.

"It will be a short. No longer than fifteen to twenty minutes and then we can go somewhere or just come back here and have a nice quiet dinner," he said.

She lay there thinking. She wasn't as groggy as she made herself out to be. She had to tell him and waiting to find the right time was nothing more than a stall because there would never be a right time. She hated springing this on him right before he was going into a meeting, but that's the way the cookie crumbles.

"Chris, I have to talk to you." Foley caught the name switch. Like everybody else, she usually called him Foley.

Before her sentence was finished, Foley knew something bad was coming down.

He went to sit on the side of the bed, but she stopped him.

"No, I want to get up," she said as she got out of bed. Other than her shoes, she was still dressed.

"Ah, you want to talk here or go…"

"The living room. Go ahead, I'm coming," she said, heading to the bathroom as she fluffed her hair. "I'll only be a minute."

Foley looked at his watch. He had a brief window before his CB meeting, but knowing Linda she would primp and preen and that would take time. She was a perfectionist. Everything had to be just the way she wanted it. She always ran late.

"Lin, I don't have much time. Should I cancel? It'll be no problem," he said, hoping she'd hear him through the closed bathroom door.

"I'll be out in a minute."

Her minutes were interminable.

He called the Chief and told him he'd be about fifteen minutes late.

He went into the living room and sat on the sofa, wondering what was coming down. His first thought was that she was going to leave the company. That wouldn't be good. He prepared a rebuttal.

She surprised him by coming out of the bathroom after only a few minutes.

"Okay. Sounds like you have something serious to say," he said wanting her to know that he was aware.

She stared at him for a moment, her blue eyes filling with things he didn't understand, and then she shook her head.

"I can't do this anymore," she said, standing on the other side of the coffee table.

"Do what?" he said.

"Everything. All of this. You, my parents, all of it. It's tearing me apart."

Realizing this could take some time, Foley said, "You stay here and rest. I'll go and meet CB for a fast one, and when I come back, we'll order some food and talk."

She looked at him, sadly annoyed, and shook her head.

"Chris, you just don't understand. Our relationship is causing problems, big problems. My entire family, even my aunts and uncles are preaching away at me to end it, that you're using me, and you want me just for sex and…"

"I'm sorry. You know that isn't why I'm with you."

"I don't know why you're with me. I thought I did, but I just don't know," she said, standing and waving her hands in frustration.

Foley started to stand, but she came over and collapsed onto the sofa, exasperated, and then slipped down to the floor, her back leaning up against the front of the dark green fabric. He got up, moved the coffee table aside and sat in front of her.

"Chris, I'm not sure this is right anymore."

"I understand what you're saying and I'm sure we can find…"

"No," she said, interrupting him.

Alarms went off. One look at her face told him he had a problem—a big one. He had to diffuse it. She was about to say something when he put his finger to his lips in a "don't say another word" gesture. It momentarily threw her off, and she paused.

"Marry me."

The words that passed through his lips were unplanned. Later, when Foley replayed it in his mind, he didn't know what prompted him to say what he did. Panic? Fear? Time? Or maybe it was his truth.

What followed was the kind of silence you can hear, the kind that makes weird noises in your head.

Linda looked at him. They were sitting on the floor, face to face. She was beautiful, the most beautiful woman he had ever been with.

Her eyes filled with tears and her lips quivered.

He said it again, this time quietly, more confident.

"Marry me. I mean it." He realized he meant it.

She had the strangest look on her face. It was her eyes. They seemed vacant, as if she weren't even seeing him. She reached for his hand, pulled back, and clutched them on her lap.

Her silence had Foley concerned.

"I can't," she said shaking her head ever so slightly from side to side, not looking up at him. Before he could get his "why" out, and with her eyes fixed on her hands that were clutched on her lap, she whispered. "I'm already married."

There are moments in our lives when the words we clearly hear can't be right. We immediately try to diminish their effect because we don't want them to be true.

"What do you mean?" he said.

"I'm married," she said again, still staring at her hands as she clasped and unclasped them.

"You? When did you...?"

"I'm sorry, Chris. I really am married. For a couple of weeks now and..."

"What do you mean you're married? For a couple of weeks?" he repeated.

What do you think she means, asshole?

She dropped her head, and with movie-like little girl guilt, mumbled out, "I'm really married, Chris."

"You're really married?"

"Yes," she said her eyes glistening with tears.

"You're serious. To who?" He knew he sounded stupid, but now everything was stupid.

He could barely hear her when she murmured, "Bobby."

At that moment, he knew she was telling the truth.

"Why?"

She just looked at him, her face expressionless. "I don't know why?"

Who doesn't know why they got married?

"I really don't understand," he said, "Is this what you wanted?"

"I don't know."

Foley's mind quickly filled with questions.

Her family forced her into it.

She didn't love him.

This is what she wanted.

She chose money over love.

She's pregnant. By him? Or me?

This is not her. She wouldn't do this… or would she?

She dumped you. Get over it.

He'd been in some crazy situations, but this one was something else. None of his military or police training included anything like this. His first instinct should have been to get all the facts, evaluate them and then act, but he was off balance.

He needed to think all of it out, but in that moment, he made his first mistake. He asked her when she got married instead of "why?"

"When I went on vacation," she said, now ready to give him the details. She needed to get it all out and done with.

"To Miami?"

"Yes."

"You got married in Miami? That took some planning."

"No, I got married in Pittsburgh. I was afraid you'd find out because it was in the newspaper, and…"

"It was in the newspaper?"

"No, not like that. You know, in that section where they list marriage applications?"

"What difference does it make? I don't understand how you did this."

"I don't either."

"What does that mean?" he said with a little disgust, now coming out of shock and moving into anger.

"I don't know what any of it means," she said, tears making her large, marbled eyes look glassy.

"You better know what it means. You did it."

"I know. I'm sorry."

"About what?"

"It's not what I wanted to do."

"Then why'd you do it?"

"I don't know. I panicked, I think. I did it to stop everybody from yelling at me. I had a severe panic attack, I don't know, I don't know."

She was sobbing heavily, her body slumping forward, her face in her hands.

She had a history of panic attacks. That made sense, and he needed something that made sense. He grabbed on to the panic attack possibility. At least that was something he might be able to deal with. But did panic attacks last long enough to plan a wedding and get married? He doubted it.

He saw she was in genuine pain and began soothing her, sitting down in front of her, putting his arms around her and holding her, somewhat uncomfortably because they were both sitting on the floor facing each other. It was awkward, and he tried to move into a better position, but she pulled away and stood up.

"I made a mistake. I'm sorry. I'll get it annulled." She was walking around the room, her head down, thinking, becoming more animated.

Is she putting on some kind of act?

"I think I had some sort of weird panic attack," she said. "Look, you have to meet your father. Go ahead, I'm sorry about all of this. We'll get it worked out, we'll… we'll figure it out," she muttered as she walked towards the door.

He wasn't ready to leave, but he thought it might be best. Give her some space and time.

He followed. She opened the door.

"You're going to be late," she said. "Go. When you come back, we'll talk more."

She closed the door and leaned up against it.

What just happened!

LINDA

LINDA WAS RELIEVED THAT FOLEY WAS GONE. SHE COULDN'T HAVE handled another minute. She wasn't certain what she was feeling, but it wasn't good. Waves of nausea kept lapping around in her stomach, and the dull ache in her head was getting worse.

She was standing motionless, her hand still gripping the heavy metal door handle.

She was in an emotional tug-of-war—first with herself, and then with two men in her life. She just wanted to crawl under the covers and hide. She turned and saw herself in the large closet door mirror.

God, her hair was a mess.

She stared at herself for a second and then began to primp, her focus shifting quickly to her hair and face. She needed a makeover. Maybe she should make an appointment at the resort beauty shop, go for the whole shebang, and get put back together again.

She didn't know what to do. She should leave. Go home. Maybe her sister would come and get her. She walked into the living room and when she saw the champagne bucket, another wave of nausea crawled across her stomach.

She sat on the sofa. Got up and turned on the TV. People were cheering in Times Square. Freezing their asses off to watch a stupid ball drop. She turned down the sound. She remembered she saw an extra blanket in the hall closet. She curled up on the sofa and covered herself with the blanket. She couldn't get under it deep enough, but it felt better.

But only for a moment. And then everything came crashing in on her again. She wanted to run. She pulled the blanket tighter and then the buzzing in her head stopped.

Her body was numb. She wasn't even in it. Where was she? She felt so far away from everything. She tried to think it out, make sense of it, but her thoughts were being buffeted by a tornado of talking heads screaming out a profusion of ugly words.

It began that night when her aunt and uncle stopped by. They barely settled in when her mother brought up her affair with Chris, and soon everybody was harping away at her. Back and forth, back and forth, incessantly, over and over, they kept pounding away at her. Her mind was breaking, being eaten away by all these voices coming at her, and when her sister, who had always been on her side, joined the chorus of dissent, she snapped.

She could feel her heart thumping, her palms damp, her skin hot and her body shaking. She had to stop it. She had to hide, get out, run, but she couldn't move. She was overwhelmed, everything was closing in on her, and everybody was yapping at her, yelling, accusing her, stripping away the skin from her body. She had to stop it.

"Do you want me to marry, Bobby?" she shrieked. "Is that what you all want?"

Linda's outburst surprised them. Nobody said a word. Linda started walking around the room.

"Tell me," she shouted. "Is that what you want?"

The silence continued as Linda stood there and then her mother broke the silence.

"It would be better than what you're doing," Marge said.

"You want me to just go off and marry Bobby?" Linda said angry at her mother for saying it.

"Well, not just go off. You could have a nice wedding, maybe at ..." Linda just shut it all out as her mother talked wedding plans and soon everybody in the room was chattering about it as if she weren't there.

She was in an emotional fog. It was like a screen had been pulled over her eyes, and then a strange calm came over her.

It was surreal. She was floating above the fray, feeling nothing. They were talking about somebody else. She didn't care.

If that's what they wanted, she'd give it to them.

Her mother took over and Linda robotically followed, doing what had to be done with little or no emotion. Bobby was surprised that she finally accepted his previous proposals; his father gave him a plum job in the Philadelphia office as a wedding present; Linda said she needed a month to finish out her job at the Security Agency; she'd join Bobby in Philadelphia later; he was okay with that; no big country club wedding; no fancy dresses; small, family only; no European honeymoon or cruise.

Everything click-clacked along and Linda followed. They went to Miami for a week. It was fine. Linda told the office staff that it was a vacation with friends. She came back to work at the Security Agency and said nothing.

She kept planning to tell Foley she was leaving, but she didn't. Maybe she was making excuses to herself, but she had projects to finish. She couldn't just leave in a lurch.

She went into an emotional tug of war with herself. The back and forth was inside of her. She had to escape from herself. She created an illusory world and moved into it, trying to seesaw herself back to some reality.

Unable to make a decision she made none, waffling between her husband and her lover.

She felt chilled and curled the blanket tighter around her.

Why did I tell him I would get it annulled? Do I want it annulled?

What was she going to do when Chris came back to the room? She had no answers. It was all so strange.

When all else fails, do nothing. She got up and decided a hot shower and some fresh makeup might make her feel better. At least she'd look better.

And then what?

JOE DUCK

AS HE RODE THE ELEVATOR TO THE OLD LOBBY, JOE WAS LOSING IT.
It felt like his blood was shooting through his veins like a backed-up horse taking a much-needed piss. His hands felt weak and shaky. He knew the signs. It was like the time he broke into the church and hit some switch or button and the stupid organ started playing. He about broke his heart running out of there so fast. Hell, he must've run two miles without stopping, collapsing against a brick wall in an alley off Penn Avenue.

He had to get off this damn elevator. It was packed with people and Joe couldn't catch his breath. As soon as the doors opened, he pushed his way out quickly, getting his fanny pack caught on a girl's ski jacket. She untangled them as Joe kept mumbling out "sorry," his stomach feeling like he swallowed a rock, and his legs wobbling, but he stumbled out of everybody's way and sucked in big gulps of air.

He had to get his act together. Breathing hard, he talked himself down from the edge and then slowly made his way through the busy hallway. He was sure people were looking at him. He was acting guilty, and he hadn't done a damn thing.

As he shuffled down the hallway, staying close to the wall, he kept trying to control his urge to get in his car and go home. He could see the old lobby ahead. There were more people than usual moving around the place. Just as he entered the lobby area, he was almost run down by drunken assholes rushing to get nowhere. He scrambled to the side and stood there staring at the office on the far side of the lobby.

The old office, formerly a souvenir shop, was fronted by a large plate-glass window. The venetian blinds that had been installed when it was converted, hung open as Joe tried to see through the slats, but the lobby lights caused reflections to bounce off the glass.

Joe robot-walked towards the office, jiggling his head back and forth as he tried to see through the constantly moving images that reflected off the large window, but he couldn't tell if there was anybody in there or not.

If the people crisscrossing the lobby weren't so busy with their own thoughts and destinations, they would have noted the strange little fellow stutter-stepping his way across the stone floor.

Somebody else bumped into him and Joe almost dropped a turd. He pulled himself together and hurried towards the oversized exit door.

He had to get to his car. Once he stepped outside, the cold, blowing snow snapped at him like one of those little rat dogs. The parking lot was crammed with vehicles, some illegally parked, and the few flimsy lights that Otto erected hardly did the job. Dark shadows crisscrossed the rows of snow-covered cars. It took Joe a few moments to realize that the poor lighting was a good thing.

He had a rough idea where his car was parked, but he wasn't sure. That triggered another thought. He had to do a count, so he'd know exactly where his car was when he came out with the money.

He counted the rows from the resort's front door, losing count once, and starting over. He finally found his car. It was eleven rows down, seven cars in. To Joe that was a lucky sign.

Seven eleven... no. eleven seven. Eleven-seven. Eleven-seven.

When he got to his car, he was undecided what to do about the snow that covered it. Wipe it off now or wait. The way it was snowing, it would just get covered again. Because it was so cold, the snow was dry and fluffy. It would come off easy. He'd clean it right before the robbery. Joe was shivering like a naked Eskimo. He opened the back door to get rid of the bags, causing a clump of snow to fall on his head.

Bitching, he grabbed the Dollar Store plastic bag from the back seat.

Inside were a flathead and Phillips's screwdriver, WD40, and pliers.

He only had to tramp through the snow one row down before he found the right car.

It looked to be a '99 Jeep Cherokee. What appealed to Joe were the empty ski racks. He took a quick look around, bent down and began removing the license plate. Fortunately, it came off easily. He replaced it with a plate he stole in Pittsburgh. He went back to his car, screwed on the stolen plate, stuck his in the visor and hurried back to the lodge.

Once inside, he headed for the shops in the mini-mall and found the men's store. He bought a pair of the cheapest jeans they had, a Stony Creek tee, a three pack of boxers and a pair of wool socks.

Fucking Otto is a rip-off. This stuff cost twice as much as the stuff at K-Mart, and its crap. Almost a hunnert bucks and it was probably made by Gooks?

Back in his room, he removed the tags, chewing through the plastic ties to get them off. He almost threw the tags into the wastebasket, but his quick thinking saved that mistake. He stuffed them into his pocket.

Smart move.

The new jeans were stiff, so he had to crumple them up a couple of times to make them look worn. He finally rolled them into a ball and threw them on the floor near the chair. He did the same thing with the boxers, leaving them on the bathroom floor, and dropped a pair of socks near the bed. He threw the tee over the back of the forest green chair, stepped back to the center of the room, and surveyed his handiwork. The jeans didn't look right, so he messed them up a little more.

He stuffed the duct tape, plastic bags and ties into the fanny-pack and hooked it onto his belt. He put on his reversible Goodwill jacket, the black side out, and his ski mask, but he didn't pull it down over his face. He had trouble getting the thin latex gloves on, almost tearing them, but he brought extras, which he stuffed into his jacket pocket.

He was ready to go. He glanced at the ladies' Timex he stole from a drunk hooker.

What the hell did he care it was a chick watch, just as long as it worked?

It was 7:45PM. He removed a couple of sheets from the stack of paper towels he had in his jacket pocket, grabbed the bottle of Clorox, and cleaned everything he might have touched.

He was praising himself for bringing the Clorox, except the room reeked of it.

He'd dump the Clorox in one of the fancy garbage containers that looked like Stony Creek Beer cans. They were all over the place. Otto never missed a trick. The brewery probably picked up the tab for them.

He closed the drapes, taking one last look at the busy slopes. The snow was falling in droves, and that could be a problem.

He left the floor lamp on, walked to the door, took one last quick look around, put the ski gloves on over the latex gloves and left.

It would take him five to seven minutes, depending on the elevators, to get to the old lobby. First, he'd get his car "getaway ready" and then he'd rob the bastards clean.

Joe Duck was about to pull off the biggest score of his life.

HEDY

SHE KEPT THE SNOWMOBILE AT A STEADY SPEED, AVOIDING gunning the engine, staying on the back trails until she had to move to the main road. She saw the lights of the upper parking lot. Slowing down she carefully traversed down a small slope, through a gully, and then back up on to the plowed road. It was still covered with a thick layer of snow.

Just ahead, on her right and below her, was the upper parking lot. Once she was past it, she'd be in the dark again.

As she watched the headlight reflect off the fresh snow, seven years of thoughts scrambled through her brain like ants swarming over a sugar cube.

She was smart enough to know that things go wrong quickly, no matter how careful her planning and that kept her on edge. There were times she thought she was crazy trying to pull this off, but then she'd remember the reoccurring nightmare.

One night she dreamed Hogg grabbed her heart in his hands, and he was squeezing it. It was so vivid. She could see ribbons of her heart sliding through his fingers like ground meat. She'd wake up sweating, clutching her chest.

She pulled that nasty image back up. She needed it to remind her of what she had to do. She stayed on the right side of the road, one of her skis riding the berm. The parking lot was to the right and below her. She saw the lights pouring out of the windows and thought about all the people inside, drinking, talking, laughing—no one aware of what she was about to do. It gave her an eerie feeling.

It was a roar and a flash, like thunder and lightning suddenly smashing into her face. She was momentarily blinded. Instinctively she veered to the right, her Yamaha ski hitting a groove of crusted snow that stopped the machine from going over the hill as she rode the brow of the berm. She hung on to the snowmobile's quivering handles as a huge Stony Creek snowplow roared by.

Her heart was thumping so loud she thought it was going to break out of her chest as she eased her machine back onto the road.

Whoever drove that truck was going to get a new asshole. She'd track down that stupid ass and fire him. She had to settle down. She had bigger problems.

Using the snowmobile to go to Hogg's could be a mistake. Heidi would never do that, but Hedy had that covered. She'd use the retention pond road, which was just below his house.

As she neared the turnoff, she inventoried her... things? Tools? Weapons?

Two 5-inch stainless steel scalpels, Z fold combat gauze, duct tape, the drugs including liquid morphine, sleeping pills, alcohol, Celox granules, bleach, gauze pads, latex surgical gloves, a couple of different sized baggies and the burdizzo.

Damn, the burdizzo? I shouldn't have brought it.

The burdizzo fascinated her. She had never heard of the damn thing until she found it on the internet. She even asked a couple of doctors if they knew what it was, and they all drew blanks. It triggered a lot of thoughts. One day she'd do something with it. Maybe make it into a symbol for assholes like Hogg.

She was getting close to the retention pond road, so she leaned forward and squinted through the blowing snow as she tried to spot the old gray weathered post that once held an arrow shaped sign that said, "Employees Only."

Her headlight picked it up. She made a mental note to get rid of the old sign when this was over. She slowed and turned left on to the narrow road.

She went about ten yards, gave the engine a quick spurt, and climbed up into the woody brush off to her right. She went in just far enough to hide the snowmobile behind a large snow-covered mountain laurel bush.

Through the ghostly trees, their spider like black branches bordered in snow, she could see the lights in Hogg's house. She was nervous and kept re-running details through her mind.

I've got to stop over-thinking this.

For a moment, she hesitated about which door to use and decided on the back. If it were a bad choice, she'd ad lib her way out of it.

She was shaky, but she imagined the times she went deer hunting with her grandfather, and not only shot the deer, but gutted it as well. She could do this. She kept thinking about what Hogg had done to her and what he was doing to her sister.

She stood at the door, holding her Prada bag close to her side, and debated.

To knock or not to knock? What would Heidi do?

She straightened up, took another deep breath, brushed the snow off her hat, looked at her watch and reminded herself that she had 30 minutes to get the whole thing done.

She caught herself clenching her teeth, took a breath and tried to relax as much as one could relax when you're about to change a man's life forever.

She decided not to knock, opened the storm door, and turned the doorknob slowly. It opened, much to her relief. Puffing up her confidence, she pushed the door open and in her best cutesy voice yelled out, "I'm heeere."

JOE DUCK

AS THE CLOCK TICKED CLOSER TO THE ROBBERY, JOE BECAME more agitated. Break-ins and shoplifting were his specialties, along with petty scams and hustles, but he wasn't an armed robber. He didn't have the balls for it. It was risky and involved guns, and Joe Duck was scared shitless of getting shot. Robbing Stony Creek was different. It wasn't like he was robbing a stranger.

What's the worst that can happen?

He was standing just outside the main door when he felt something cold on his feet. He looked down at his Redwing work shoes and realized he was standing in a pool of crappy brown slush. The beat-up shoes were taking on water.

Christ, I can't even afford a decent pair of shoes.

Even if he gets nabbed for the robbery, what in the hell does he lose? At least he gets three squares a day and a roof over his head. Hell, with luck he could land in the new county jail in Pittsburgh.

Who in the hell builds a jail on prime waterfront property?

Joe smirked at the thought. He knew that there were a lot of bags of cash being passed around on that deal.

Screw it. It was his time to get his hands on a bagful of cash.

He hiked up his collar, hunched his shoulders, and leaned into the stiff wind, the blowing flakes hitting his face like shotgun pellets, and began the trek to his car.

Seven-elev... no, eleven-seven, eleven-seven...

He found his snow-covered car, scowling at how much had piled up on it. He almost opened the door before brushing off the snow around the door. He put his gym bag in the back along with the backpack and duffle and then got into the front seat.

He sat in the car for a moment when another jolt of panic shot through his body.

What if the car doesn't start?

For a moment, the apprehension sickened him, but so what? If the stupid car didn't start, it was all over. Nothing would happen.

He turned the key, heard the starter whirr, and then the motor kicked in. It sounded good. He relaxed, but when he turned the wipers on, they didn't move. They were frozen. He fumbled for the heater dial, turned it to defrost, and got out of the car.

Goddamn, why didn't I bring one of them snow scrapers?

Using a screwdriver, he carefully chipped away at the ice around the wipers when they broke loose, startling Joe. He staggered back, almost fell, caught himself, and then slipped again, falling on his ass. It was a bitch getting back up, but he made it, brushed himself off and looked around to see if anybody was watching him. He didn't see anybody, but then why was he worrying about that? He had to quit acting like he was a crook. This was his car, and he had every right to be there. He had to act natural.

Since he didn't have a broom or one of them snow things, he used his hands and arms to clean all the windows and scrape off the heavy layer of new snow that accumulated on the hood. He didn't want that crap flying back and blinding him when he made his getaway.

Freezing, he jumped back into the car. As he sat there, warming up, he mentally ran through his robbery checklist. A bead of snot that was hanging on the edge of his nostril was about to fall, and he quickly wiped his nose with his sleeve. He was thinking that he should leave his car running while he robbed the money room, but a second thought convinced him it was a bad idea. Somebody might report it, and then he'd be up the creek.

He sat there for another moment, the ice-covered wipers loudly scraping back and forth, his teeth clenched, and his jaw rigid. It was now or never. Suddenly he slammed the side of the steering wheel with his gloved hand.

Let's do it.

He pulled the ski mask down over his face, put on a pair of goggles, and patted his right pocket to make sure he had his gun. The bulky ski gloves bothered him. As he opened the door and exited the car, his fanny-pack snagged on to the steering wheel. Grunting, Joe used his body to undo the snagged fanny-pack. It broke loose and Joe went tumbling out of his vehicle, his left hand hanging on to the door which caused him to twist and he had to let go. He tumbled into the soft snow, feeling the cold, hard asphalt beneath as his left butt cheek took the brunt and his arm felt like he pulled it out of the socket.

Jeesuz fuckin' Christ.

He sat there for a moment as the pain in his shoulder subsided. He struggled to a standing position, thinking he may have broken his ass. Brushing himself off, he retrieved his backpack and duffle, slung them over his shoulder, causing another bump of pain. He took a breather and the arm pain settled. He was about to lock the SUV when he thought better of it.

The locks could freeze.

With all the shit he was carrying, he felt like a handicapped stuffed rag doll as he slogged through the snow. The parking lot was quiet, and he didn't see anybody, which bolstered his flagging courage. He had to be tough, and he willed himself forward, stifling his desire to turn around and get the hell out of there. When he pushed open the swinging door to the lobby, it was his point of no return.

The place seemed less crowded, but he wasn't sure. He reminded himself that he looked just like every other skier, but he was sure that everybody was staring at him. Just as he stepped inside, he was forced to stop quickly, and the heavy swinging door hit his back knocking him forward, but he caught himself. He felt somebody rushing by him, which gave him another palpitation. He saw a figure go by mumbling something about "sorry."

He threw up his hands halfway in a "why me?" surrender, but quickly dropped them when he saw the door to the old office just a few feet away.

That was the way into the money room.

He moved closer to the big plate-glass window and glanced in. He didn't see anybody, but the light was on. That was good, or was it?

He took a deep breath and hesitantly walked the length of the large window, taking quick looks inside as he moved closer to the entry. The place was empty. He was almost to the office door when everything went foggy. He couldn't see a damn thing. He stopped dead in his tracks.

What the fuck?

His heart hopped and his stomach rumbled. It took him a moment to realize what happened. His ski goggles had fogged up. He was sweating under the face mask as he yanked the goggles up on to his forehead. He went to rub his eyes, but he still had his ski gloves on.

Everything's going wrong.

The old office was the cover for the money room. Otto had cut a new door from the old office into one of the hotel rooms. (Room 3) The old doorway for guests was permanently locked. In the event Joe encountered anybody in the old office, he would pretend he was a drunk looking for the men's room. He intended to use the drunk routine when he got into the money room, hoping that would keep everybody off guard until he got control.

He sidled over to the office door, took another peek in, and seeing nobody tried to turn the doorknob.

At first, he couldn't get the door open, and his stomach did a back flip until he realized that his bulky ski gloves were the problem. He was about to take off one glove when he realized he had latex gloves underneath. He looked around the lobby. Nobody was paying attention to him. Using his body as a shield, he took off the ski glove and turned the knob. The door opened. Relieved, he quickly stepped inside the office and moved off to the side, flattening himself up against the wall. He was breathing hard.

He was scrunched up against the cheap walnut paneling, scanning the room, his eyes locking on the door to his right. It was the money room, and it was closed. He could feel rivulets of sweat crawling down his back. He tried to shrug the tickle off, but it didn't work. He rubbed his back up against the wall. He got rid of the bulky ski gloves, shoving them into his left jacket pocket.

He crept closer to the money room door. It was a cheap, hollow wooden door. Joe figured the door would be locked. He had a plan. He'd knock, yell out emergency and hope they'd open it. If they refused, he'd get his ass out of there pronto. If they opened it, he'd pretend he was a drunk looking for the rest room and force his way in.

He patted his pocket to make sure his gun was still there. He slunk over to the door and put his ear up against it. He didn't hear a thing. He expected the door to be locked but it was flimsy. Should be easy to force open. Joe's plan was to plant his left shoulder up against the door with his hand on the knob. He'd use all his weight to power the door open.

Joe clenched his jaw, took a step back, and threw his shoulder against the door while turning the knob. He about dropped a load when the door flew open easily. Joe went flying into the room at full run, staggering, stumbling, and finally falling. The two women in the room were so stunned they just locked into position behind a long wooden table.

Joe was on the floor, his back to the women, staring at an empty pale green wall. As he struggled to his feet he turned and saw the women which almost caused him to lose it again. He frantically searched his pocket for his gun.

The women watched as this crazy, little man with twisted canvas bags swinging around his neck might be a joke gone wrong. They never thought about a robbery.

He tried to get the gun out of his jacket pocket, but it was hung up on something. He couldn't get the damn thing out, and then he remembered he was supposed to be drunk.

He began to stagger and started singing.

"Oh, what a bee-u-ti-ful morning, oh what a bee-u-ti-full day."

It was the only song he could think of.

The two matronly women moved their chairs back to get up, but everything was happening so fast and when the short, little man started singing they stayed put.

Joe stopped singing and looked at the women. They looked back. Nobody said a word. Joe realized he had to do something.

"Is sis sa men's sroom," he said exaggerating his slurs as the skinny woman stood up, remembering that she forgot to lock the door. She had to get this idiot out of here before she got into trouble. The chubby blonde woman, sitting to her left, never moved as skinny tried to maneuver around her to get the drunken asshole out of there.

Seeing the skinny woman trying to get around the blonde's chair, Joe went for his pistol again, but he still couldn't break it free. It felt like a bunch of threads were tangled around the gun. He looked back at the open door he had just come through. He didn't see anybody.

Oh, what a bee-u-ti-ful day.

The skinny woman was still trying to squeeze herself between Chubby's chair and the wall, when she said, "Sir, I think you're in the wrong room. The rest room is out in the lobby."

I got this bee-u-ti-ful feelin'.

Joe saw the money on the table. Piles of it.

"Don't move, this is a stickup," Joe shouted, shoving his pistol pocket forward, hoping they would believe that he had a gun.

Skinny's first thought was that this idiot was really plastered, and she had to get him out of there fast or her ass was in trouble. She struggled to get the blonde out of the way, smiling at Joe and talking in a calm, measured voice.

"Everything's okay, sir. I'll take you to the men's room and everything will be fine," Skinny said as she worked her way around her co-worker who appeared to have gone catatonic.

The stupid idiots don't believe me.

Still battling to get his pistol out of his pocket, Joe finally wrenched it free.

"Goddam it, I said this is a holdup," he said waving his pistol at them.

Skinny froze. At first, she thought it was a joke, but now she wasn't so sure. The short roly-poly guy waving a gun at her looked like he was stuffed into his clothes. He looked like a barrel with arms and legs.

My God, we're being robbed by Danny DeVito.

From the moment Joe crashed through the door, the chubby blonde had been comatose. She couldn't move or talk, and when she saw the gun she lost it.

"Don't shoot. I have a puppy… a little puppy. Please don't shoot. I'm a mother and… and…" Chubby sobbed breathing heavily between moans.

Joe was trying to figure out what to do next, and the fat bitch was blubbering, fouling up his brain.

Shit, is there a dog in here?

He looked around rapidly, jerking his head in quick movements, and then re-focused on the women.

"Oh my God," Chubby said loudly, her plump rosy face going white and her eyes widening to owl size. Her pupils looked like big dark purple grapes. For a moment there was silence, everybody wondering what was coming next, including Joe.

"Quiet 'n do what I say, 'n nobody'll git hurt," Joe said getting into his Bogart mode. "You," he said to Skinny, "sit your ass back down." She quickly complied.

He attempted to shrug the duffle off his shoulder. He seemed to be doing a weird dance as he jumped and jerked, trying to dump the damn thing off. Finally, it slowly slid down his right arm, coming to rest on the wrist of his pistol hand. Joe tried to ignore it, his eyes glued on the women, and theirs on the dangling duffle and pistol.

Skinny just stared, wondering if all of this was real. Maybe this was one of those hidden camera shows. Maybe the idiot robber was Danny

DeVito. She took a quick look around the room for cameras. She didn't see any, but the pros knew how to hide them.

"Don't worry, Dan, ah sir, we will do whatever you tell us to do," she said with a knowing smile

"Ah, don't move," Joe said nervously.

"Whatever you say, sir," she said primping her hair, still looking for cameras.

"That's right," Joe said, wondering why he said that. He added another "Don't move" as he worked the duffle over his gun hand and let it fall to the floor. He moved the gun quickly to his left hand, wriggled the backpack off his right shoulder and slid it down his arm to the floor.

Skinny reconsidered her hidden camera idea. Maybe this was a real robbery. If it was, the short, fat butterball robber waving his pistol all over the place was a real asshole. She looked around the room again for cameras now wishing that Otto had installed them. One of those stupidest robber TV shows would have paid big money for this one.

Chubby felt a dribble of warm pee tickle down her leg.

Joe's mind was whirling like a buzz saw as he tried to figure out what to do next. The women were behind the table, the wall at their backs, and he wanted them to stay that way. Besides, there was no way Skinny could get around Chubby, who looked like Porky Pig caught in the headlights.

Realizing they were afraid of him, Joe's confidence took a leap upwards. He was the man with the gun.

The first thing was to get that damn door closed. Anybody that came into the office could see them.

"Stay still and nobody gits hurt," he said as he shuffled sideways over to the door, keeping his pistol pointed at the women. He pulled the door shut and pushed the button on the knob, locking it, thinking any asshole could break into this room.

He walked back and picked up the duffle and backpack. He put them on the table and saw that his pistol hand was shaking like a fat lady's ass on one of them gym machines. The women never took their eyes off the pistol. They bobbed and weaved, following the pistol, as Joe kept waving it.

Each woman had a money counting machine and two or three brown paper bags next to each of them. Stacks of banded bills were piled up on either side. At the end of the table, against the far wall, were a half dozen liquor boxes stacked up. The way they were stacked they looked empty, but Joe wasn't sure. He could see a box on the floor between the two women and figured that's where they were dumping the cash.

"You," Joe said to the chubby woman, his voice deeper, "get that box, the one under there," he said as he gestured with the pistol, "and put it on the table."

She just sat there stone faced.

"I told you lady, git that box," Joe said waving his pistol at her. He hoped she'd obey because he didn't have a follow-up. She slowly struggled to get out of the chair, her weight giving her a hard time. She was close to 200 pounds, a lot for her five-foot five frame. Grunting as she tried to push the chair back and get her substantial legs out from under the table, she finally struggled to a half-standing position. Her right elbow embedded itself into Skinny's 34A breast.

"Ouch," yelled the skinny brunette as she grabbed for her breast. Skinny was hawk-faced, her nose sharp and beaky, with close-set eyes and a chin that could impale you. Joe sensed she was the dangerous one.

"You, quiet," Joe said, pointing the pistol at Skinny as Chubby finally grunted herself to an upright position. Chubby's eyes were bulging and her mouth was wide open as if she were trying to suck all the air out of the room. Joe wasn't sure what to do about this beast of a woman. She was like a sack of Jell-O.

What in the hell does the skinny bitch do if she has to take a leak?

"Jist get the fuckin' box and put it on the table," Joe said.

Chubby gave him a helpless look. There was no way she could bend down, wedged between the wall and table, and pick up the box.

Joe signaled her with his gun to get the box.

She bent down, her ass flattening up against the wall, when Joe stopped her. She could knock the damn wall down.

"You," Joe said, pointing the gun at Skinny, who instinctively ducked, startling Joe, who also ducked. Realizing what happened, he quickly recovered, "You git that box up here on the table, and you," he said waving the gun at Chubby who tried to duck but couldn't, "jist stand still."

Skinny got the box on the table and waited for her next instruction, a disgusted look on her face.

Joe looked at the stack of liquor boxes against the wall and saw one by itself, a Seagram's Gin box. It was setting on the floor to the left of the tall stack.

"Git me that box and put it on the table," Joe said to Chubby, hoping she could do it. He had no choice. She had Skinny wedged in. "Git your ass moving," Joe said, flapping the pistol around.

Chubby sidled sideways, her back to the wall, her eyes frozen on the gun. She felt her legs weakening, and she went to lean on the banquet table for support. She put her hands on the edge causing the table to slide towards Joe, slowly at first, and then with a zzzssshoost.

Chubby, and the table, went skidding forward, one of the counting machines clanging to the floor, as Skinny froze against the wall. Chubby hit the floor with a huge whuuummpf and all the air she sucked in came exploding out.

The panic Joe had been suppressing came rushing out of his body as the table came sliding towards him. It went so fast he wasn't sure what was happening.

Joe panicked. He backed up and then made a run for the door. He tried to turn the knob, but it wouldn't move. He was trapped. He was about to piss himself. Hell, maybe he did. He could feel the bullets that were sure to come ripping into his back. He braced his back against the door and pushed when he looked up and saw the women.

Skinny was like wallpaper, her thin body plastered against the pale green wall while Chubby lay on the floor, her one hand still hanging on to the table that was now in the middle of the room.

Joe's hands were shaking as he tried to regain control of his bodily functions.

Jesus Christ. This is turning into a nightmare.

Joe stood by the door, catching his breath, and then limped back into the room. He yelled at Chubby to get up, using his gun to signal Skinny to help her. Skinny pressed herself against the wall even harder, sure the asshole's gun was going to go off and hit somebody.

"I said help her up or I'll blow your brains out," Joe yelled.

He watched the two women struggle as he tried to get control of himself. He was really shaking, breathing hard, and all he wanted to do was grab some cash and get the hell out of there.

He was going to order the women to pick up all the stuff that had fallen off the table, but he was afraid that would turn into another circus. He told them to pick up all the cash as he pushed the table back using the front of his pudgy body.

"Now I want you to take that box," Joe said, indicating the lone Seagram Gin box, "and put it on the table." Joe was certain it was filled with cash. Chubby complied.

"Now empty that box into the duffle," he said slowly. He was feeling the control.

Chubby looked at him for a moment and was trying to say something, her mouth moving, but nothing came out.

"Goddamn it, lady. I said empty the box, so do it now."

Chubby's mouth was still moving, but whatever she was trying to say was stuck in her quivering throat.

"It's empty," Skinny said with disgust.

"I know it's empty," Joe said, shoving the duffle towards the box with his non-pistol hand, "Now, fill it with the money from that Seagram's box."

Skinny, statue-like, because she wasn't sure what the asshole would do, replied in a bored monotone voice. She didn't suffer fools easily.

"The Seagram's box is empty. There's nothing in it. Empty," she said, tilting it towards Joe.

Joe was confused. He looked at the box and Chubby lifted the cardboard lid to show him it was empty.

What the fu...

"Where's the goddamn money?" Joe said.

Chubby couldn't unfreeze her mouth. Skinny pointed to the box on the table, "It's in there," she said.

"That's it, only one box?"

Both women nodded profusely.

Jesus Christ. Only one box?

"Put the money in the duffle," Joe said, waving his pistol, causing both Skinny and Chubby to duck.

Chubby gently removed the thousand-dollar packets, one by one, carefully placing them into the large duffle, as if she were handling fine china.

What the fuck is this broad doing?

"Jist dump the whole box into the duffle," he said, "and you help her," he added, using his gun again as an extension of his hand. Skinny ducked, and then grabbed the bag and held it open, nodding to Chubby to dump the box into it.

Chubby nervously followed orders, some packets missing their target. Joe would've been at his wit's end if he had any wit, but instead, he felt like a wet paper bag. He was sweating like a junkie needing a fix.

That's when he saw the large green Stony Creek canvas bag behind the chair where Skinny had been sitting.

"What's in that?" Joe said, waving his pistol in the bag's direction. Chubby had the liquor box on its side and was frantically sliding out the remaining packets of bills into the duffle.

"What's in what?" Skinny repeated.

Joe pointed his gun at Chubby and said louder, "You, what's in that bag?"

Chubby, her voice quivering like she was talking under water, blurted out, "Pipa's. It's for Pipa's"

She could feel shit wanting to come out and she squeezed her sphincter.

"I didn't ask what it was for. What's in it?"

"What's in it?" she echoed because she didn't know what else to do. Skinny stayed out of it.

"Lady, I'm going to stick this gun in your fuckin' mouth and pull the trigger," he said.

Chubby was rigid, unable to function, her blubbery body going stiff. Joe lost it. He wanted to put the gun in her mouth like he seen in the movies, but she was on the other side of the table. He wigged out. Furious and frustrated, he threw himself on top of the table, his gun arm outstretched, trying to get to the fat one, when he realized what he was doing. He tried to wiggle his way back off the table, his legs and arms flailing.

Skinny stood there thinking that nobody would believe her when she told this story.

Joe finally snaked himself off the table and back to a standing position, his eyes darting around the room, waving the gun, and yelling, "Don't nobody move." Skinny wondered how she could move any less.

"Money, there's money in there, for Pipa's," she said, realizing she was the only one that seemed to have any control.

"Get it, NOW."

Skinny was struggling to get the Stony Creek bag up on to the table.

"C'mon, lady, get that bag up here."

She tried to swing it up on to the table, but it hit the edge. The flimsy table slid forward again. Joe's heart jumped, and so did he, yelling, "Freeze."

Chubby unfroze and went ballistic.

"Oh my God, oh my God, please don't kill me," she yelled.

Joe was yelping for her to shut up, his heart about to beat itself loose from his chest.

"Shut up now or you're dead. You," he said, pointing the pistol at Chubby, "Sit down and be quiet." The sweat was unbearable, and he knew he had to hurry before he melted or got caught.

Chubby was afraid to turn her head to look for her chair, so she kept her eyes on Joe as she grabbed at air trying to find it. Skinny wasn't about to move to help her. The asshole said not to move, and so she wasn't moving. She could see his pistol hand was really shaking, and the damn thing could go off.

Chubby finally found the chair and tried to maneuver her bountiful body into it. Keeping her eyes pinned on the pistol, she finally found the chair arms and grasped them for support. As she began to lower herself, her weight was too much for her knees and she almost fell, the chair sliding away from her and hitting the wall.

"FREEZE. Everybody just freeze." He was having trouble breathing under the hot ski mask.

Skinny shivered, hoping that would signal the gunman she was freezing, while Chubby stood statue-like, afraid she was going to wet her pants again. In fact, she was peeing as she felt dribbles of warm liquid meander down her leg. Fortunately, she was wearing long pants.

"Okay, both of you," Joe said his breath coming out in gasps, I want you to go over there and sit down on the floor, your backs against that wall," he said, gesturing with his .22 pistol.

They moved simultaneously.

"STOP," Joe yelled, "You," he said to Skinny, "you go first, and then you," he said to Chubby, waving his gun at her as she snapped her head back and forth trying to avoid the gun.

Because the table had been pushed out, Skinny worked her way around the blonde and was on the floor with her back up against the wall in a matter of seconds. Chubby grunted, wheezed and wriggled her way over and leaned her back up against the wall. She slowly began to slide down the wall, when her legs gave out and she zipped down like a slippery pig going down a greased pole. She hit the floor with a loud thump.

Joe tensed. He was sure somebody heard the jolly green giant crash to the floor.

"Quiet," he said. He listened for any sounds but heard nothing.

"If you sit there quiet, you won't get hurt," he said, stuffing the gun in his pocket, shoving the money that was still on the table into the duffle and zipping it up. He went around the table, picked up the heavy Stony Creek bag and wrestled it up to the table. He unzipped it part of the way and peeked in. He saw nothing but shrink-wrapped fifties and hundreds. He had no idea how much was in there, but he knew he found the mother lode.

He saw where the phone cord went into the wall. He reached down and tore it out. He noticed their purses on the floor and thought about checking them out, but he didn't have time to screw around.

The women didn't move as Joe took the gun from his pocket and put it on the table. He kept his eyes on them as he strapped on the empty backpack and hoisted the duffle on to his left shoulder. He picked up the gun and pointed it at them.

The women sat still with their backs against the wall and their legs sprawled out in front of them. Chubby was hurting. She was sure she broke her tailbone.

He pulled the Stony Creek bag across the table with his left hand. He slid it off the edge, and it fell to the floor. Joe was flustered.

"Don't move," he said, exasperated as he brandished his pistol. The women hadn't moved a muscle.

"Okay. Like I said, I ain't gonna hurt yunz if you listen. Now I'm gonna leave. On the other side of that door is my confederate. (Joe really liked the word "confederate.") He's gonna stay there for fifteen minutes while I get the money outta here 'n then he's gonna disappear into the crowd out there. So, if you don't move nobody gits hurt. Don't risk your lives for Otto. I'm sure he has insurance, so everybody's happy."

Damn. Why did I say Otto's name?

The bags were heavier than Joe's compact frame could handle. The women watched as Danny DeVito struggled to get the empty backpack on and the heavier duffle over his shoulder while keeping his gun on them. Skinny was sure there was going to be a misfire and was looking for a place to dive. Once Joe had the duffle secured, he battled to lift the heavy Pipa's bag. He struggled, almost toppled, and finally got it up. Still holding the pistol, he backed towards the door. He was grunting and sweating profusely.

He reached the door, dropped the Pipa's bag, kept his pistol trained on the women, and turned the knob with his free hand but it wouldn't move. He hurriedly stuffed the pistol in his pocket and used both hands to turn the knob but no go. He remembered that he locked the door earlier. He released the lock button and the door opened. The women were still statue stiff.

He went through the drill again, finally getting all his bags positioned.

"Stay here for fifteen minutes," he said to his imaginary confederate. He looked back at the women.

They hadn't moved a muscle. They had their backs pushed hard against the wall, their teeth clenched, and their jaws tight.. They weren't about to do a thing, even when that crazy little man almost fell trying to get through the door.

Joe's original plan was to close the door, wait a few seconds and then partially open the door so they couldn't see him, and in a disguised voice pretend he was the confederate, but it was taking all his strength just to stay upright. He closed the door and grunted his way to the exit door.

Thank God the office was still empty.

Joe hurried through the office, the bags weighing him down, the one strap cutting into his neck. He took a fast glance through the window. Everything looked normal. He was about to open the door when he remembered the latex gloves. He dropped the Pipa's bag and peeled them off his sweaty hands and pushed the door open. Lifting the Pipa's bag was about to break his back, but he finally got it up. He was in a hurry to get out of there and as he battled his way through the doorway the duffle caught yanking Joe back and he dropped the Pipa's bag.

As Joe struggled to untangle the duffle, he saw a man heading his way. Thinking it could be security, Joe frantically bent over to get the Pipa's bag, the duffle sliding over his head. Joe was bent in half, the duffle pulling him forward while he held on to the Pipa's bag for balance. He felt like he was about to take a header.

Joe saw a pair of men's boots as he felt the duffle being lifted. He'd surrender if he could move his arms.

"You need some help, buddy?" the voice said.

Joe didn't know whether to shit or get off the pot. He realized he couldn't get off the pot. He was bogged down. The strap of the duffle around Joe's neck prevented the voice from getting the bag off, so he grabbed Joe's arm to help him up.

"Looks like you could use a hand," the big guy said.

"Ah, no... I jist, well..." Joe muttered as he struggled to a standing position, the duffle moving back onto his shoulder.

"Here, let me get this bag," he said, reaching for the Pipa's bag.

"No, ah... I can get it," Joe said as he reached for the bag again, but the big guy picked it up like it was empty and moved it out of the doorway.

"Thank you, sir," Joe said. "I can take it from here. Thanks. Thanks a lot. Just set it down there."

"You sure you're okay?" the big man said, wondering why this little guy was still wearing his ski mask.

"Yeah, it was just getting through the door, but I got it now. Thanks again."

"Okay, man. Happy New Year," he said as he walked away.

Joe took a deep breath. He had to get out of that lobby fast.

"Yeah, same to you," Joe said, not realizing the man was out of earshot.

Fortunately, the door to the outside was only steps away, but Joe was having trouble navigating his way through when another skier held the big door open for him.

The cold air hooked up with his hot sweat and Joe was sure ice crystals were forming on his body as he struggled through the ever-deepening snow towards his SUV.

The fucking bags were heavy. Eleven down, seven across.

A rotund guy carrying an assortment of mismatched bags that were swinging every which way as he tried to maneuver his tired, short legs through deep snow was not destined to be successful.

Joe fell on his ass. He didn't care if anybody saw him or not. He slid the bag off his shoulders and sat there, trying to catch his breath.

He struggled to a standing position, his legs shaky, and looked around. The ski mask had slid to the side, and he had trouble seeing. He pulled it up over his head and felt the sharp sting as the cold air hit his sweaty face. He adjusted the empty backpack, hoisted the duffle over his shoulder and grappled with the Pipa's bag, took a few steps, and realized it wasn't going to work.

He unraveled the duffle from his shoulder and slid the bags through the snow. Counting the rows with grunts, he finally made it and with a last burst of energy threw the bags into the rear of the SUV. He hurried around the side, brushing off the windows as he did, jumped in, some snow blowing into the driver's seat, and started it up. When he heard the motor, he let out a deep breath.

With the heater cranked up, and the wipers doing their job, he gently pulled out feeling the snow crunch beneath his wheels. He was sure his trusty four-wheeler would get him out of there.

He looked in his rear-view mirror for any sign of activity. He saw nothing. No cars, no headlights, no anything. He pressed down on the accelerator and made his way out of the parking lot as the fluffy snow flew off his car.

Now he had to hide the money and get the hell out of Stony Creek.

Joe Duck was close to pulling off the biggest score of his life.

THE CHIEF

THE CHIEF DIDN'T EXPECT THE MOB AT AUGIE'S. THE OVERFLOW flooded out into the hallway as they tried to balance their drinks while jabbering away. He was sure Foley didn't break through that horde. He took a quick look around and spotted him standing in a corner of the lobby. He didn't look happy.

"Looks like Augie's is a bit crowded," he said.

"You're really observant," Foley fired back.

"You noticed? Look, we can go over to the old office," he said, gesturing with a nod of his head, "or we could go downstairs to one of the meeting rooms. It's quieter, and I'll get us a couple of drinks."

"Look, CB, I'm really pressed for time and …"

"No skin off my teeth," CB said, "Excuse me for trying to make you some coin."

"I'm sorry. Just having a bad day."

"Where's the little lady?"

"She's back at the room. She's tired."

"Of me or you?

"Not now, CB."

"Look, let's go downstairs. I'll fill you in on the details and you'll be outta there fast."

"Okay," Foley said.

CB stopped at The Swabian Lounge on the lower level and told the waitress to bring their drinks to the Alpine Room. CB used his master key to get in. It had the usual meeting room accouterments. The customary polished veneer table; chalkboard and easel; and twelve high back upholstered chairs. CB signaled Foley to sit.

Foley was about to say something when the door opened. The waitress maneuvered a tray full of drinks through the door and started putting them on the table.

"Put 'em on my tab," CB said. He had double-ordered, an old "busy server" trick. He handed the waitress a twenty-dollar bill. The Chief was a generous tipper, especially with restaurant employees. They were excellent sources of information.

"You sure you ordered enough?" Foley said.

"Helps with the pussy problems."

"I don't have pussy problems, so drop it."

"Okay, but you can't fool an old snatch grabber like me. I can smell pussy problems a mile away if you'll excuse the pun."

Foley gave him a dirty look

"Look, CB I have to…"

"Got it," CB interrupted, "so let me get to it."

He explained the need for an overall security plan for Stony Creek and that he had been "greasing" Otto for weeks prepping him for Foley.

"You can make a nice buck if you play this thing right," CB said.

"Any idea of how much?"

"That's up to you but make it good. We need enough to go around."

Foley knew exactly what the old man meant.

"What kind of numbers are we talking about?"

"No big deal. I'll work with you. I'll set up a meeting with Otto, maybe tomorrow."

"No good. I have to leave."

"You're kidding."

"No, I'm not. Have work to do."

"I'm sure New Year's Day is a busy time," CB said with a knowing glance. "Tell you what. Let me try to get Otto for coffee tomorrow morning. Does that work for you?"

"Earlier the better," Foley said. "Call me when you get it resolved." Foley stood up and headed for the door. He stopped and turned.

"Enjoy the drinks."

"Don't worry, I will."

The Chief sat there. He worried about Foley. He was a smart kid, but he didn't have his eye on the ball right now. The Chief was certain it was the female that was the cause. A hard dick had a way of softening the brain.

He picked up one of the drinks, leaned back in the chair, and took a big swig. For bar scotch, it wasn't bad.

Anytime you let your willy do the talking, there ain't going to be much of a conversation.

HEDY

"I TOLD YOU FIFTEEN MINUTES. YOU'RE LUCKY I'M STILL HERE," Hogg said from the other room, not even turning around to greet her, as she cautiously followed his voice. She was never in his house and that was a weak spot in her plan.

"I'm sorry but I ..." she muttered, tiptoeing into the dimly lit den.

The only light came from the muted TV and the fireplace, which cast nervous shadows around the room. The dim light would help. He was sitting in a mahogany leather chair watching TV without the sound. To the left of his chair was a small end table with a phone and his drink. Next to the end table was a matching leather sofa.

"I didn't hear your car," he said without turning around. She was off to his left, a few steps behind the end table. She decided to hold her position.

Damn, she hadn't thought of that.

"Oh, I parked down on the old retention pond road and cut up through the back," she said, now standing behind him as he sat in the oversized leather recliner, still staring at the TV in front of him.

"Why?"

"Why what?"

"Don't fuck with me. I'm not in a good mood. Why'd you park there?" he chided, keeping his eyes on the silent TV, letting her know she wasn't as important as what he was watching.

What a flaming asshole.

She didn't answer right away, not sure what Heidi's usual routine with Hogg was when he yelled out, "I ASKED YOU WHY YOU PARKED THERE!"

Reflexively she ducked, her hands going up towards her face. She fought off the impulse to get out of there.

"I didn't want anybody to see," she quickly said, her voice a little squeaky. She paused, wondering if she should say she came by snowmobile, but canceled that thought, "and with all the plows out I was afraid that…"

"You never did that before," he said.

"So, there's always a first time for everything and…"

"You're right, baby, there's always a first time, but this isn't your first time. I pulled my car in so you'd have room and goddamn it you go and…"

"I need a drink," she interrupted, not wanting this conversation to continue, "and let me freshen up yours and we'll start all over again," she said, moving to the side of the chair and reaching down to take the glass from his hand. At first, she thought he was going to let it go, but as she went to lift it, he tightened his grip, holding it for a long moment, making her tug it out of his hand. She couldn't believe that the bastard still hadn't looked at her, which was good, but his macho man routine was pissing her off. She could see how he was treating her sister—like some sort of willing sex slave. Her stomach churned again.

She walked into the kitchen, put his drink on the counter, and realized she didn't know what he drank. What he left in his glass was some sort of milky brown concoction.

A Black Russian?

Hogg wouldn't drink something like that, or would he? She took off her jacket and hung it on the back of a chair. She left her knit cap on, her hair tucked up underneath it. She didn't want to take it off, afraid she would leave hairs, but she doubted she'd get away with it. Still, it was worth a try. She did her homework, and she knew the cops needed the roots to determine DNA. Because she was a twin, her DNA would be the same as Heidi's, but a few scientists said that there were rare instances that some twins had different DNA, so she was taking no chances.

Damn, what does he drink?

She saw a Dewar's bottle on the counter, so she figured it was scotch mixed with what? Baily's? Not macho enough for Hogg. She smelled the milky fluid. She couldn't tell what it was, so she tasted it. Yuk. Sour milk? She looked in the fridge and saw two cartons of buttermilk. One had been opened. She checked to see if there was any other kind of milk. There wasn't, and she took a deep breath and lip whispered, "Thank you."

Scotch and buttermilk. What a douche.

She looked at his half-full buttermilk/scotch drink, added more scotch, concerned that it was getting too brown, and added another splash of buttermilk. She didn't want to dilute it too much.

She stopped for a moment and listened but didn't hear him moving around. She quickly reached into her Prada bag that she hung on the kitchen chair. She was nervous and kept glancing at the doorway to the den.

Before she could do anything, she had to get the drugs into Hogg. Once she decided what she was going to do to Hogg, getting the materials was a lot of work and research. The internet was invaluable. What she couldn't get on the internet, she learned how to get it in Mexico.

Although possession of illegal drugs in Mexico is a crime, small amounts are not. Even opium and cocaine are legal if they are under the required maximums.

Hedy made two trips to Mexico, where she found both doctors and pharmacists willing to help. Although she didn't need it, her cover story was that she was an author looking for medical information to use in her next book. In fact, she found an obscure book on Amazon and, said she was the author. She even autographed it for the doctors and pharmacists as a gift for their cooperation. They never asked her for any ID.

She consulted with two Mexican doctors about the drugs that were used to sedate and numb a person. Both doctors agreed on GHB which is an anesthetic and would work best for the victim in her story. Some valium was also added to the mix. That would be the drug she'd put in his drink so he would lose consciousness and not experience pain. To be safe, she asked if there was a way to numb the area where the cutting would take place and they recommended a local anesthetic of 2% Xylocaine and adrenalin using a 5cc syringe. Hedy asked them how somebody who wasn't a doctor would learn how to inject drugs and the one doctor suggested that they could practice injecting water into a banana with a 25-gauge needle. She had trouble suppressing a laugh.

Once she had the information, she asked the doctors for a written prescription. She told them she wanted one so she could take it to an American pharmacy and see if she could get it filled. It was all part of the story she was writing. Her generosity eliminated any doubt the doctors may have had.

Getting drugs out of Mexico wasn't a problem. She had valid prescriptions, and even if she were stopped, the doses were small enough to pass through customs. She passed through easily.

Now the moment of truth was here. She was nervous as she poured the pre-measured mixture into Hogg's drink and stirred it. It looked normal. The doctors told her it would knock him out in ten minutes or less.

She had a moment of doubt thinking she was crazy to do this, but then she remembered the rape and Hogg's brutality. The man didn't know what the word remorse meant.

She took a deep breath, put a smile on her face and walked back into the room.

"Here you go," she said, standing behind him and putting the drink on the end table between the chair and sofa, "enjoy, while I make me a drink."

In the kitchen she grabbed the scotch bottle and almost began to pour herself one when she stopped. Heidi usually drank white wine, but was it possible she drank scotch just to keep the asshole happy? Hedy played it safe and went with the wine. She found an open bottle of white in the fridge and poured herself a glass.

She took a few healthy swigs and refilled the glass. She needed it. Her next step was the big step. She could still call it off. He'd just have a good, long sleep. She took another sip of the wine. It was cheap crap. Typical Hogg. He was such a lowlife. She hated him. He'd destroy Heidi. She felt her anger rise.

She took another gulp of wine, refilled, grabbed her Prada bag, and went into the den.

She threw her shoulders back, walked around the sofa and sat on the ottoman directly in front of him. This was her either or moment.

He didn't move, and his expression didn't change. He just stared as if he was looking right through her. She noticed his eyelids flutter, but he continued to pretend she wasn't there. She was worried that he might be studying her face, but his eyes had a distant look. So far, so good.

She leaned into him and let her hand drop on his leg, pausing for a moment to allow him to react, but he didn't move nor did he make eye contact.

He was really one sick bastard.

She rubbed his leg softly but couldn't get any closer without changing positions.

"How's your drink?" she said, thinking that was a safe question.

He didn't respond.

"Do you want me to freshen it up?" she said nervously, sorry she asked so soon.

Finally, he looked at her. He locked his eyes on to hers and stared. It was a long, hard stare and Hedy felt the panic that she had been suppressing dribble out.

"What's with you, bitch?" he said loudly, causing her stomach to jump.

She quickly pulled her hand off his leg as if it were a hot stove.

"I'm sorry. I didn't mean…" she said, not finishing the sentence, wondering if he was on to her.

She began to think of escape when he got up from the chair. She started to stand as he shoved the ottoman back with his foot, causing her to fall to the floor.

"And get this fucking hat off," he said, grabbing the knit cap from her head and throwing it on the floor. She was frightened. She was just about to roll over and run for it when he grabbed his crotch.

"You want this, baby?" he said.

She said nothing, afraid any words would be wrong.

"I asked you a question. Do you want this, bitch?"

He seemed to stagger. "Yes, baby. I want it," she said, hoping that would work. He was fumbling with his zipper as she got back up to a standing position when he staggered again, this time almost falling.

"Christ," he said, shaking his head. He tried to get back to his chair.

Hedy jumped up quickly and helped him sit down. He slumped into the chair, trying to focus on her, wondering why the scotch was hitting him so hard.

"Take a drink. That'll help," she said, feeling a little better about the situation, reaching over and putting the glass in his hand. He used both hands to hold it and took a long swallow, almost dropping the glass, but Hedy grabbed it and set it back down.

The booze was hitting him faster than usual. He liked the buzz, but the wooziness he was feeling was bothering him. He had trouble focusing and his tongue felt thick. He couldn't get any words out of his mouth. Something wasn't right.

"Ah, I'm telling… ah, you better…" he mumbled, his neck loose and his head rolling around.

Hedy watched him, noting his heavy-lidded eyes closing from time to time. The drugs were working.

Suddenly his entire body lurched forward, and he yelled, scaring Hedy, causing her to rear back.

"You bitch," he said clearly but then his words lost their strength, and he began to mutter and ramble, "you, you, I… the family meeting… n' you better … you …" his voice now just above a whisper.

She saw his shoulders collapse, his chin falling to his chest and his right arm dangling over the side of the chair as his entire body slumped.

For a moment she thought she misunderstood. Did she hear him say "family meeting?" She reran the moment in her mind. He did say "family meeting."

What in the hell did that mean?

Without thinking, she grabbed Hogg's upper arm and shook him.

"What are you talking about, family meeting?? What did you mean, Hogg?" she said loudly, forgetting that she was supposed to be Heidi.

He didn't respond. His body was like a wet dishcloth.

"Hogg, you bastard. Wake up. What did you mean?" She was about to shake him again when she realized what she was doing.

She pulled back and sat for a moment, trying to collect her thoughts. She almost blew it.

She didn't like his "family meeting" reference. She had no idea what Heidi might have told him. Right now, she didn't have time to deal with it. She picked up her hat and put it back on. For a moment she thought she should check the floor for hairs but dismissed it as futile.

She stood and grabbed her Prada bag that was on the sofa. She used the ottoman as her workstation. She slid the ottoman off to her right and kneeled in front of Hogg.

She removed a pair of sterile latex surgical gloves and put them on. She glanced over at Hogg and he hadn't moved, so she continued. She removed a small white cotton towel, unfolded it, and spread it on the leather ottoman.

She placed the filled hypodermic needle, two five-inch surgical scalpels on the towel, the handles facing her. Then the gauze pads, Celox granules, Z-Fold Combat Gauze, white duct tape, surgical tape, and small plastic bottles of hydrogen peroxide, alcohol, and oxygen bleach,

each marked with a P, A, and B in black magic marker. The plastic bottles wouldn't stand on the tufted leather, so she double-checked their lids and lay them flat on the ottoman. She finished by putting a few baggies next to the tape.

She stood up, reached over, and squeezed one of his cheeks as hard as she could. He didn't move.

She began to get his pants off. She pulled hard at the large silver buckle, finally releasing the prong, and unbuttoned his denim jeans. Holding tightly to the top of the jeans, she unzipped his fly and then began tugging and pulling off his jeans until she had them down to his ankles. She did the same with his boxers.

Jesus Christ, they're plaid too.

Hogg, his face showing no sign of life other than his breathing, lie sprawled back in his chair, his bare legs spread open, and his limp penis looking like a small round of ring baloney nesting in a beehive of curly auburn hair.

It was a strange moment. The quivering light from the TV and the fireplace cast dancing shadows across the lifeless Hogg, the pale skin of his legs an eerie white.

God, am I really going to do this?

A weak moan from Hogg jarred her back to reality. Time was wasting. She clenched her teeth and grimaced. It was now or never, and she was going with now.

Any uncertainty drained from her body, replaced by an icy determination. She had to disable the sack of shit lying in front of her so he could never damage another woman.

Her years of planning kicked in and she knew exactly what to do. She kneeled in front of Hogg and checked her Prada bag to make sure she removed everything. She saw the burdizzo, the tong-like instrument, lying in the bottom of her bag. There was something about this little-known instrument that fascinated her.

Enough burdizzo. I have to get moving.

She picked up two large gauze squares, rolled them into a ball, grabbed the duct tape, and stood up. She set the tape on the chair arm, and using both of her hands, opened Hogg's mouth, and stuffed it with gauze, Hogg making a moaning sound. She tore off a pre-cut piece of the duct tape and stuck it over his mouth. She peeled off a longer strip, placed it over the smaller piece, lifted Hogg's head, and wrapped the tape tightly around the back of his neck. She repeated the procedure, thinking she hadn't planned this part out as well as she should have because the tape was hard to work with. It was taking more time than she liked. She made sure his nose was clear so he could breathe.

She cut another four strips of duct tape from the roll and stuck them on the right side of the chair where she could quickly reach them.

She kneeled, positioning herself between Hogg's legs, and slowly reached in and then quickly pulled back. There wasn't enough light. She turned on the end table lamp. She took a quick look to make sure the scalpel was where she put it, and then with her gloved forefinger and thumb delicately lifted Hogg's penis up and tried to see where it was connected to his balls. She felt like she was holding a dead night crawler. She was leaning back as far as her outstretched arm would permit, keeping it as far away from her as possible, as if the thing might attack.

One of the Mexican doctors suggested using a rubber band tourniquet that could be placed at the base of the penis, but she decided against it because of time and hoped she had that problem covered.

Still holding his outstretched penis and gritting her teeth, her jaw as tight as a drum, she injected the anesthetic into the base of his shaft. Hogg gave a little jerk, which scared the shit out of her, and she almost got up and ran but regained control and settled herself. Other than a moan here and there Hogg was disabled.

Over the years she had seen a lot of penises on the internet. She saw drawings, cross-sections, and even got a medical tape of a penis removal. It was tough to watch, but the close-up shots gave her a good idea of what she had to do. Of course, she wasn't going to be as neat and patient as the dick doctors as they sliced layers away like they were dissecting a sausage. She practiced on a hot sausage and a kielbasa.

Based on anatomical drawings she knew there were arteries and spider veins that ran through the shaft which made bleeding her biggest concern. She hoped she had that covered with the Celox granules and combat gauze. She also read about men who cut their own penis off and survived, something she couldn't imagine. Then there was the Bobbitt woman who sliced off her husband's penis with a kitchen knife.

Even though she wore surgical gloves, touching Hogg's penis was repulsive to her. She realized she was leaning too far back. As much as it disgusted her, she had to get closer.

She saw veins running down the shaft, and for a moment thought it might be easier to cut it from underneath. The videos she viewed showed them cutting across the top, but they were doctors who knew what they were doing. One doctor removed all the skin first. It looked like a butchered chicken neck. She just wanted to get the damn thing off fast.

She dropped his penis back into his pubic hair, leaned back and took a deep breath. This was harder than she thought it would be. She was worried about blood spurting out and getting all over her.

Damn, she should have brought one of those cheap plastic rain ponchos.

She couldn't over think this anymore. The sicko deserved it. The night he raped her flashed through her mind and she clenched her teeth. Hogg's dick was an evil weapon and it had to be disabled.

He called us the Bobbsy twins that night. Well, this Bobbsy is going to make you a Bobbitt.

She picked up the scalpel with her right hand, his penis with her left, and stretched it upwards. She felt her nerves buzzing, her hand shaking, the thought of what she was about to do nauseating her. She thought how silly she must look, holding a sleeping man's floppy penis with her finger and thumb like it was a slimy dead snake.

She had to get a better grip on his penis. She grabbed it firmly around the shaft and pulled it towards her. She was surprised how much give there was. She stretched it even farther, looked at his face for any signs, took a deep breath, and using her knees, moved her body in closer.

Holding the scalpel tightly, her elbow bent at a right angle, she held the blade over the spot where the top of his penis met his pubic hair and stretched it out as far as she could pull it with her left hand.

From the video she knew she had to saw rather than push down and she had to be patient, although her instinct was to slice the damn thing off in one fast motion.

Jesus, was he getting a hard on?

The more she stretched it the thinner it seemed to get. She could feel her heart pumping and her adrenaline kicking in as her body's system rose to meet the challenges surging through her mind. She could do this.

She gripped the scalpel tightly. She was sure it would take two cuts. She studied the spot where she thought she would cut on top of his penis, seeing strands of pubic hair overlapping the shaft, a thin blue vein visible through the parchment-like skin.

Here's looking at you, kid.

She clenched her teeth and with a swift slicing motion the razor-sharp surgical blade cut across and into the shaft. She made another quick short slice, and it was off. She dropped the scalpel and severed penis on the towel on the ottoman and immediately covered, pressed, and pushed against the wound with gauze.

Hogg grunted and gave a quick jerk and then settled down. She grabbed the peroxide, poured it on the bloody wound and then did the same with the alcohol. She quickly sprinkled the wound with the Celox, which was supposed to stop any bleeding immediately, and then placed the Z Fold Combat Gauze tightly against the bloody area. The Z Fold was used by the military to stop bleeding instantly from major wounds. She paid fifty-three bucks for it on the internet and was praying she would get her money's worth.

Hogg moaned as she held the Z Fold against his body, pressing hard as she fumbled for the strips of duct tape. She used the strips to tape the Z Fold tightly to his body. Hogg seemed to settle, then jerk, and settle again. She had dosed him heavily and was afraid he might die from the drugs, but so far he was still alive. There was a folded blanket on the floor near the chair, yeah it was plaid, and she threw it over Hogg's midsection.

She had to hurry. She dropped the penis into a baggie. She gathered up the rest of the stuff on the ottoman, keeping the remaining alcohol and small plastic container of bleach out, and put everything into one of the larger baggies, and then into the Prada.

She stood there for a moment and surveyed the room. She had to clean up everything she touched. She poured a lot of alcohol on the wound earlier, and she hoped that would erase any DNA that might have leaked through her latex gloves. To be safe, she removed the blanket, and wiped around his scrotum and pubic hair with alcohol. She threw the blanket back over his legs, smoothed it out so it looked neat, and began her clean-up.

She retraced her steps, cleaning everything she touched with the oxygen bleach including their drink glasses, the scotch bottle, the buttermilk carton, and the wine bottle. Using the kitchen light, she checked herself closely for any blood splatters and was happy not to see any although she'd get rid of what she had on just to be certain. She bleached every hard surface that she may have touched, rechecked the place for the second time, took another look in her bag, and satisfied that she had covered everything, checked Hogg. He was quiet, and she was worried. She leaned over to see if he was breathing, relieved that he was, and straightened out the blanket again. When she was sure everything was like it was when she first came in, she removed the duct tape and gauze from Hogg's mouth, hoping a scream wouldn't come out of it.

Hogg only moaned and groaned but hadn't moved from the chair. She had been there for almost thirty minutes and she had to get a move on. She left the way she came in, wiping down the doorknobs and making her way through the woods to the snowmobile. She started it up, slowly worked her way through the cluster of rhododendron bushes and drove out.

The snow was still coming down as she roared down the road, hurrying to the back trail that would take her to Pipa's.

Under the plastic face mask, she took a deep breath and smiled.

Whoever said revenge was sweet was right on.

THE GREEN ROOM

SHE LEANED AGAINST THE DOOR, TAKING DEEP BREATHS, TRYING to calm down. It was hard to believe that she did what she did. She thought it went better than expected, but she had to be careful. There was no room for overconfidence. That always led to mistakes.

She forgot it was New Year's Eve. Thinking about it made her smile. What better way for a rapist to begin the New Year than to be without the vile instrument that enabled him to execute his loathsome acts?

The thought of a barbaric savage like Hogg without his spear was such a delicious thought. It dripped with the sugary succulence of pleasurable irony.

She felt a trickle of sweat run down the back of her ear as she surveyed the room. Nobody had been here. The shower was still running. She opened the door and a blast of steam greeted her. She turned off the shower, picked up her underthings from the damp tile floor and put them on the bed. She quickly changed clothes, being careful to put what she wore to Hogg's into a separate plastic bag. She'd burn them.

New Year's Eve at Pipa's was a major "seen" event, and some mountain fashionistas pulled out all the stops. There were those who thought they were walking the runway in Milan while others stayed out of the fashion show, going casual. The one thing they had in common was that everything they wore was expensively uncommon.

Hedy kept it simple. She put on a pair of knee highs, a suede stretch legging, shearling ankle boots, and a Cuccinelli cashmere turtleneck with simple gray piping.

She brushed out her hair and twirled it into a ponytail which was fast and simple. The mirror confirmed she was looking good. The ponytail gave her that schoolgirl look, and tonight she needed to look as innocent as the kids in The Sound of Music.

As she dressed, she tried to get into Hogg's mind. She didn't think he'd report it. His ego was too big. If he does, he'll blame Heidi. All Heidi has to do is tell the truth and offer to take a lie detector test. She'll pass.

In addition, the Chief will confirm that she was asleep in her condo at the time. That should be enough to eliminate her as a suspect. But Heidi was a problem, and she'd buckle immediately if pressured. Keeping her upright and steady was going to require a lot of intensive maneuvering.

Hogg was a smart cop. He might pick up on the twin switch but proving it would be tough. Hedy will say she was at the club, and many will confirm that she was. They'd also have to come up with a motive. Nobody knew about the rape and Hogg wouldn't bring it up, but she had to be careful.

If Hogg goes to the hospital, it will be reported. She couldn't see Hogg taking that chance unless he was desperate. If he did, he might try to use his connections to get the hospital to squash it. At worst, the cops question him, and he keeps quiet. Case closed.

She had some concern about DNA. If Hogg squeals, they'll have to prove whose DNA it was. Because they were monozygotic twins, developed from a single egg/sperm, their genetic makeup was the same and their DNA was identical. If she had to, Heidi could admit to an affair with Hogg, and that's why her DNA was there. Again, the lie detector would prove she didn't do it.

One thing was certain. Hogg would come for them. Right now, he'd be too preoccupied with his lost penis. That gave Hedy a little time, but not much. They could go away for a while, but that was a temporary fix. Her best hope was that the son-of-a-bitch would go crazy because he didn't have a penis but that was a longshot. There could come a point when she might have to deal with him, but she hoped his being dickless would take up all his time and energy.

She had to cover her tracks. She had to get rid of his penis and the tools she used to cut the damn thing off. Her original plan was to get rid of it using the commercial disposal in Pipa's kitchen but finding a time to use it presented problems.

She thought about discarding it in the food dumpster. Local farmers picked up the discarded food every other day and fed it to their pigs.

She learned that the farmers were careful about what they fed their pigs and monitored the stuff they gave them. The Stony Creek food was removed by the bucket and spot checked. Even though Hogg's penis could pass for a shriveled-up chicken neck, she didn't want to take the chance. The thought gave her a chill.

Maybe she was overthinking it. She would just dump the hardware and software in different trash cans around the resort.

For some silly reason, she didn't want to get rid of the burdizzo. Even though she hadn't used it, she thought it was an instrument with powerful symbolism.

She stumbled across the burdizzo on the internet. It was a tool used by veterinarians to castrate animals, and when she dug further, she found that some mentally ill men used the tool to castrate themselves. One copywriter, with a sense of humor, probably a woman, wrote this descriptive piece about the burdizzo on their web site.

"Our burdizzos are of the highest quality with excellent crushing power. It's great for cracking all kinds of nuts, and after it's done the task it was designed for, it is especially useful for taking on hard shell nuts such as the black walnut.

It is also a beautiful crimping tool, creating a lovely pattern on your pierogis, raviolis, or any other filled delicacy.

Hedy was amused by the writer's ingenuity although she was repulsed at the thought of using it on an innocent animal.

Even though she didn't think she could use it, she spent the $49.95 and bought it. In fact, she got most of the stuff on the internet, except for the drugs she bought in Mexico. The computer she used was long gone.

What nagged at her was whether Hogg was alive.

She had to find out.

JOE DUCK

JOE WAS HUNCHED OVER THE STEERING WHEEL, LEANING AS CLOSE to the windshield as he could, trying to spot the retention pond road through the snowflakes. The light from the dashboard dusted his face with a cool green glow as the warm air from the noisy heater bounced off the windshield.

Finally, he made out the old sign through the teeming flakes and he let out a deep breath. He no sooner made the left turn on to the pond road when he saw them. He felt the sweat turn cold on his forehead and his heart started beating faster.

Ski tracks? Who in the hell would ski here?

He stopped. His first instinct was to back out, make a run for the front gate, and crash through if necessary. He took another look at the tracks. Although they were already partially covered, they looked too far apart to be ski tracks unless there were two one legged skiers. Maybe a snowmobile? From what he could see, they didn't track all the way down the road.

Joe drove down a few feet and stopped. He couldn't see the edges of the road. Too much snow. He felt a leap of hope when he saw the tracks veered off to the right into the woods. He knew there were houses on the other side of the narrow-wooded area.

He slowly drove his SUV to where the tracks turned off the road and exited his vehicle. Maybe somebody visited one of the houses at the top of the small grade using a snowmobile? He looked around and couldn't see any snowmobile although the tracks said they probably left.

The retention pond was another fifty yards down the road. By the looks of it the road hadn't been cleared since winter began and he could get stuck. Going on foot was out of the question.

Joe was trapped. He had a small fortune with no place to go. He looked up at the house on the other side of the woods and could see a dim, flickering light through the tangle of bare limbs. Could be a night light or a TV.

He was standing there trying to figure out what to do when he realized his SUV lights were still on. He jumped into his vehicle but couldn't see the markings to turn them off manually. He turned the motor off, but the automatic delay kept them on.

I might as well send up a signal flare and surrender.

Desperate, he followed the snowmobile tracks into the wooded area. Somebody walked up and back. Looked like one person but he wasn't sure. He took another look at the house when a light switched off.

Joe dove behind the big bush and burrowed himself deep into the snow. He lay there motionless, the side of his face buried in the icy snow. He was trying to control his heavy breathing, but he couldn't. He lay there for a moment and then slowly lifted his head to look around when he realized what happened.

It was his automatic headlights turning off.

He struggled to his feet, brushing off snow and bitching at himself. He looked back up at the house.

Joe was out of options. He had to get rid of the money and get the hell out of Stony Creek.

He tried to think. By now the cops had the main gate blocked. He couldn't go back to his hotel room. Not with the money. He looked down the road again. No way he could pull that off. Maybe hide the money in the woods, under the snow? Snow melts. Tracks?

He was up the creek without one of them rowing things.

He looked back up at the house. Other than the one window that had a dim glow, maybe a night light, the place looked deserted. He was running out of time and had to do something fast.

Maybe he could find a place around the house to hide the money.

A holiday weekend? There had to be people up there. No way would it work. But what were his options? Zero and zero.

Whatever he was going to do, he had to do it now. He followed the tracks up a slight grade to the edge of the tree line. The deep snow made it hard going for a guy with short legs. He was puffing his lungs out, but he finally made it. There was a window to the right of the back door. Hunching over, he scrambled on to the snow-covered patio and past the door, ducking under the window and plastering his back against the side of the house.

He stayed that way for a moment and then cautiously turned and glance through the kitchen window. He saw nothing except the stove light.

It didn't look like anybody was home. With his back against the side of the house, Joe closed his eyes and tried to think. He felt the snowflakes melting on his face as he tried to figure out his next move.

Maybe he should just go back to his hotel room. Leave the money in his car and hope they didn't find it. But what happens when he leaves? He didn't like the idea of hanging around. Knowing Otto, they'd go through Stony Creek with a strainer or something.

He took another look in the house. Still quiet, and then it hit him. Maybe he could hide it in the house—in the basement, in some corner filled with junk where nobody would notice it. Most of the people didn't live up here year-round. Once the holidays were over, the ski clubs come rolling in and most of the people who own homes just came up on weekends. Joe could come back up during the week, break in—he was good at that—and get the money out of there.

A plan was forming in his mind.

It could work with some luck.

He looked around the far side of the house. It was only a few feet away.

He peered around the corner and jumped back immediately, pressing his back up against the house.

There' a car there.

He took another look. The car had a lot of snow on it, so it was there for a while. Maybe they left on the snowmobile? He looked again. To the right of the car was a small hill. To the left, a slope that dropped down to the house. There was a window on the side of the house, just below the car. It was a little high, but he thought he could reach it. It looked dark, but his angle was bad. He had to get closer. He saw a flickering light coming through the window. Could be a TV. Some people left their TV's on for security. That never fooled Joe.

Look for the flicker's, fuckers.

With his back against the house, he carefully sidestepped his way to the window. He was directly below it when he thought he heard something. He stiffened his back against the side of the house, his eyes darting back and forth, feeling like he was a target at a shooting range. His nerves were so shot that maybe he imagined he was hearing something.

He took a couple of steps towards the window, stopped, listened, and took one last look around. He thought he could reach the windowsill with his hands and pull himself up, and he could if he was Wilt the Stilt. No way. He remembered seeing some boxes piled up on the back patio. He hurried back, goose stepping through the snow, and breathed a sigh of relief when he found one of those plastic crates that supermarkets used. He made his way back to the window with the plastic crate.

He hurriedly tamped down the snow to create a level spot and stepped up on to the crate. Close, but no cigar. He reset the crate on its side, positioning it vertically for more height, and climbed aboard. Grabbing the windowsill with his hands for support, and standing on his tiptoes, he stretched to take a quick look in when a light flashed. He almost lost his balance but held on and froze in position. He thought the light might be a TV. Not good. After waiting, and nobody came, he looked in again. It was the TV. Worse, somebody was sitting in a chair watching. He dropped back down. There was no way he was going to hide the money in this house. He looked around. When he worked here, they were building these houses, but he couldn't go traipsing around the area trying to find an empty house, especially on New Year's Eve.

He took one more look. Gasping, he pulled himself up and focused on the person sitting in the chair. It looked like a man. He wasn't moving. Joe's arms were hurting, and he couldn't hold on, slipping, his hand slapping against the window. He fell to the ground. He was sure they heard it at Augie's.

He didn't get up. He rolled and plastered himself up against the house hoping that whoever came to the window to check wouldn't see him.

He lay there for a long time, huddled up against the house, the cold snow melting on his exposed neck. After what seemed like hours, he slowly lifted his head and looked around and then sat up with his back pressed against the house. A dead man would have heard him bang on that window, and yet nobody reacted. He'd take another look.

The person in the chair hadn't moved. Joe dropped back down from the window. He thought it was a man. As Joe stood there, he realized he was out of choices. By now cops would be swarming around Stony Creek like bees at a picnic.

And then a thunderbolt came flashing out of the sky and hit him right between his eyes. The house, the man, everything fired into his brain like he was hit over the head with a hammer.

He might know the man in the chair, and if it's who he thinks it is, he's up shit creek without a boat. He took another look. It was hard to make out in the dim light, but Joe's churning stomach told him he was right. He knew the Fayette County Sheriff bought a house in Stony Creek. He even seen him a couple times in Augies. Everybody knew Hogg. Hell, his picture was in the newspaper more times than Britney Spears-and he ain't no Britney. If that was Hogg zonked out in that chair he was fucked. He's got bags full of cash and no place to stash them. He thought about stuffing his pockets and making a run for it, but he was sure they'd nab him.

He wracked his brain for an answer, but none came. A deaf man would've heard him bang on that window unless…unless the guy is already dead, or maybe he's blasted…on booze…or maybe drugs. Shit, that could be it. Hogg on drugs? Them cops are into all kind of shit.

What if he knocked on the door? If somebody answered he'd pretend he was drunk, looking for the Stony Creek exit. Hell, there's a bad storm out there. Anybody could get lost. If it was Hogg, he'd thank him and just leave. The drunk act worked good at the robbery.

If nobody answers…well, he'd just have to wait and see. All that cash was worth it.

He stumbled along the side of the house, staying in its shadows, going back to the kitchen door. He tapped the pistol in his belt to make sure it was still there. He took a deep breath and knocked. His knock was restrained, not much more than a tap. Joe's stomach was rumbling.

No response to his first knock, so he knocked a little harder.

Nothing.

Whoever's in there is drunk or dead.

The next time he banged hard on the door. If they didn't hear that, they wouldn't hear anything.

Joe straightened up, ready for somebody to answer, running his "lost drunk" story over in his mind, and waited… and waited. After at least a minute, it felt more like ten, there was still no answer. Joe stepped to the side and looked through the kitchen window. Everything looked cool.

His heart was pumping double time and his stomach had that funny feeling. He had bump keys, which some said could open any lock, and a set of picks. He'd try the bump keys first. He opened the storm door and tried to get a good look at the lock as he put his hand on the doorknob. He turned it and couldn't believe his luck. The door opened.

He stopped and listened and then pushed it open all the way. The only light came from the stove.

"Anybody home?" he said in a subdued voice, forgetting that he was supposed to be drunk.

No answer, but then even an alert person wouldn't have heard him, so he went for it.

"ANYBODY HOME," he yelled, knocking on the open kitchen door as loud as he could.

Nothing.

He was about to close the door but left it ajar, just in case. He crouched down and crept towards the room with the flickering light. Just inside the doorway he called out again. No response.

"Is," he said, and then remembering he was supposed to be drunk, began again. "Ish anybody shere?" he said in a puny attempt as a drunk. "I'se knocked and… and… your door opened and…"

He peered into the room, keeping his body to the left of the arched entry. The TV was the flickering light, but no sound was on, and the person in the leather chair wasn't moving. He crept up closer, stopping every foot or so. He took a few more steps and when he was almost behind the chair, he moved to his left, towards the sofa, to get a better view of the person's face. He thought it might be Hogg but he wasn't certain. He took a closer look.

Holy crap. It is Hogg.

He straightened up and took a step back. This was not good. Hogg still hadn't moved. Joe leaned down and looked at his face. It was Hogg, and he was out. Maybe the booze. He saw the glass on the end table. It didn't look like booze. It looked like shitty milk. Joe thought he saw a bottle of whiskey on the counter in the kitchen, but his mind was in such a jumble he wasn't sure. Joe also saw the phone, and for a moment he debated about moving it, or even hiding it, but let it alone. Hogg would shoot first and then call, so why rock the train?

Hogg had a blanket across his legs. Maybe the fucker was sick.

What to do? What to do?

Joe studied Hogg. It sure and hell looked like the guy was out. Maybe his best move was to wake him up and use his drunk act. Maybe he should just get out of there now. And go where?

He reached over to shake Hogg's shoulder but pulled back. He had to think this out a little more. He didn't see any gun lying around, but Hogg could have one under that blanket. He wouldn't put it past him.

He slowly reached out again and gently put his hand on Hogg's shoulder and shook it gently. Hogg didn't move. Joe shook harder. Nothing. Joe really gave him a solid shake, and Hogg didn't even moan.

Jesus. The bastard is doping'.

For a moment, Joe thought he might be a goner, but he saw his chest contracting. Hogg suddenly grunted and Joe almost went down for the count. He went into a crouch, trying to get his gun out of his belt, but couldn't reach it under the ski jacket. He imagined Hogg leaping up, a 357 in his hand, pumping a clip of bullets into his chest.

He waited and then slowly crept back up and took a close look at Hogg. The guy was totally out. It must be drugs.

Maybe I can pull this off.

The first thing he had to do was make sure there was nobody else in the house. With all the noise he made, he doubted anybody else was there but he'd check. If there was somebody he'd go into his drunk/lost act claiming the Sheriff was sick or something and he was looking for help.

He crept through a short hallway and came to the stairs. The room to his left, probably the living room, was empty. He was about to make his way up the stairs when a light went on. With no place to hide, Joe fell to his knees and hugged the first three steps when he realized it was a night light.

He took a deep breath and told himself to settle down. He went back and checked Hogg. He still looked like he was in la-la land.

"Sheriff, you okay?" Joe whispered, and then shook his arm harder while talking louder.

"Sheriff, you..." Joe said, stopping and stepping back.

He realized he was calling him "Sheriff."

Hogg moaned again, but Joe stayed cool this time, thinking Hogg might be a junky. When they shot up too much, they wouldn't hear a freight train if they were in it. Fuck, Hogg a junky. That was a blast.

What better place to hide the money than in the Sheriff's house? Hogg probably had to be at work after the holidays. That's when he'd come back and get the money.

Joe was excited. He'd hide it somewhere in the basement. Hogg must have stuff piled up somewhere, and he'd bury it under that stuff. The question was whether he should look for the hiding place now or get the money into the house first? He decided to get the money in. Hogg could come out of his stupor.

He moved swiftly, chugging through the deep snow like a short sumo wrestler on a broken pogo stick, hopping one moment and tripping the next. After vaulting and falling many times, he got both the duffle and the Pipa's bag into the house.

Breathing hard, he stood between the two bags on the kitchen floor. The snow on his clothes was melting, forming small puddles on the gray-white tile floor as Joe tried to catch his breath.

He went into the den and checked Hogg again. He had to find the cellar door. It was usually in the kitchen, but he didn't remember seeing it. He checked out the first floor. Nothing. Back to the kitchen. There was no cellar door.

Who the fuck builds a house without a cellar?

He opened every door he saw, dashing from one to the other, and didn't find a safe place for the money. He went upstairs and checked out the bedrooms. Nothing. He thought about putting it under the bed, but that wouldn't work.

He stood in the short hallway between the two bedrooms, breathing hard, realizing he made a mistake hauling all that money into the house.

Exasperated, he rubbed his hands over his face. Maybe he should take as much cash as he could hide on himself and get out. He looked heavenward for help and rubbed his face again.

Wait, did I just see what I thought I saw?

He rubbed his eyes and took another look. He did see something.

Directly above him was a miracle. It was a rectangular door with a black metal handle. It must be the attic. The handle was too high for him to reach. He rushed into the bedroom, frantically searching for something to stand on, when he saw the vanity bench. He carried it back to the hall, climbed on it, and pulled the black handle.

It didn't give, and Joe yanked harder. It broke loose, and Joe almost fell off the bench but regained his balance. The inside of the door had a small ladder, and the entire rig was controlled by heavy springs. Joe hung on to the handle as he yanked the resistant ladder down, almost falling again. He finally unhooked the ladder, slid it to the floor and locked it into position.

He climbed up the ladder. His body was halfway into the dark attic, but he couldn't see anything. As he tried to adjust his eyes, he felt something crawling on his face. Joe slapped at it wildly, lost his balance and fell, grasping at the ladder as he slid down a couple of rungs, scraping his hand and bumping his knees.

Joe was tired of falling, and he was having a hard time moving around in the tight ski jacket. He stood quietly for a moment, listening for any sounds from Hogg. He heard nothing.

He couldn't believe his luck. That bitch, Ruby Begonia, would say it was all part of God's plan. To her, everything was part of God's plan. Like if you hit the lottery it was God's plan and if you shit yourself, that was his plan, too. So, if God's pulling the strings, why worry about anything?

But Joe was worried. He went over to the top of the stairs and listened again. No sounds from downstairs. No lights. The clock was ticking. He went back and climbed up the ladder, fearful of spiders, or whatever crawled on his face, when he saw a string hanging down. That's what bumped his face. He pulled it and a bare bulb popped on. He saw junk piled everywhere. Perfect.

Joe switched into high gear. He hurried downstairs, gave Hogg a quick glance, and went back into the kitchen to get the bags. It was a bitch getting them up the stairs and worse getting them up the ladder. Joe pulled, grunted, snorted, and finally got all the money into the attic.

Earlier he saw two boxes marked "XMAS". He opened the top box. It was filled with ornaments and other decorations. He looked in the other box. It was filled with the same stuff. If Hogg was going to use the Christmas shit, he would have already done it.

He looked around and noticed a U-Haul moving box. Inside were about a half-dozen hardback books. He removed them and hid them behind some other boxes. Taking the empty U-Haul box, he transferred the contents from the Christmas boxes into it.

He put the money into the empty "XMAS" boxes. His heart was pounding as he loaded packet after packet of one thousand dollars, and some five thousand. He couldn't believe how much there was. He stuffed his pockets with as much as they would hold.

Once all the money was in the boxes, he stuffed the empty Pipa's bag into one box and the duffle in the other and flattened them on top of the cash. He covered the bags with a bunch of gold and silver garlands, put the lid on, and stacked the boxes under the U-Haul box. He stood and studied his handiwork. Everything looked cool.

He climbed down the ladder and unhooked the release. He pushed the ladder up and locked it, but the damn door got away from him, its heavy springs slamming shut, making enough noise to wake up the dead. Joe ran into the bedroom, tried to crawl under the bed, but didn't fit. He scrambled to the other side of the bed and lay down, breathing hard.

After a nervous wait, he slowly lifted his head and looked around. He couldn't believe that Hogg didn't hear him. Something was wrong with that man. He slowly made his way down the stairs, creeping cautiously into the room, and saw Hogg still conked out in his chair.

The son-of-a-bitch hadn't moved. Joe mumbled a "thank you" and got his ass out of there.

He labored his way through the snow to his car. He held his breath as he turned the key. The bitch started. Joe was elated. He threw the car into gear and backed out. He headed for the main gate.

In a few minutes, Joe would know whether he was going to get away.

What he didn't know was that a small paper matchstick fell to the floor when he opened the attic door.

THE CHIEF

AFTER FOLEY LEFT, THE CHIEF TRIED TO FINISH THE DRINKS BUT couldn't do it. He hated leaving unfinished drinks. He said it was a sin, what with all the thirsty people in Bangladesh. He went back to his office to hide out for a while.

The hissing buzz from his police radio interrupted his nap.

"10-1, come in. Chief, come in," the voice on the radio crackled.

"Yeah, this is the Chief, What's up?"

"We have a thirty-seven oh one," Chief.

What the fuck was a thirty-seven-oh-one?

What's the problem, Wheeler?" the Chief said.

"We got a thirty-seven oh-one, Chief."

"Cut the number stuff and just tell me what happened."

"Robbery, Chief, a big one."

The first thought that entered the Chief's mind was a card game robbery. That would be messy.

"What happened?" the Chief asked.

"We're on radio, Chief."

"I know we're on the fuckin' radio. Give me the info, NOW."

"Ah, the money room."

"I'm in my office. I'm leaving now," the Chief said somewhat relieved but still looking at a mess.

The women in the money room waited the fifteen minutes, as they were instructed. They weren't about to give up their lives for Otto's money. Edith, the thin woman, used her cell phone to call for help. The first officer to arrive was an overweight, aging cop, who had retired from the Bedford police force after 25 years. Officer Kress was weary of police work, but he needed money and the Stony Creek job looked like an easy ride. He hardly needed a robbery to screw up the holiday.

"Ladies stay here in the office and don't touch a thing," he instructed them as he went into the money room. Kress took a cursory look around. He saw nothing unusual. Besides, it wasn't his job. He wasn't going to sweat it.

When the Chief arrived, he yelled to Kress who had his back to him.

"What happened?"

"Christ, Chief, you scared me," Kress said jumping back, "I don't know. Been waiting for you."

Meanwhile, every cop on duty was converging on the money room.

"Has Otto been notified?" the Chief said.

"Like I said, Chief, I was waiting and ..."

The Chief picked up the phone and dialed Otto's number.

"Otto, it's the Chief. We have a problem and I need you to come to the old lobby office as quick as you can."

"What's the problem?"

"We were robbed."

"You're kidding."

"Yes, I am Otto. I think this is one of my funniest gags."

"Alright, Chief, cut the crap. I'm on my way."

"Were you two in the money room?" the Chief said to the two women huddled at one end of the office.

They nodded.

"Stay there and don't talk to anyone until I talk to you," the Chief ordered, looking around to see that the place was filling up with cops and onlookers.

"Rhett," he said yelling over to a young, cherubic faced cop, "Come here."

Rhett was a big kid, a former high school football star with an engaging personality who was enthusiastic, but inexperienced.

"Clear this room of everybody except you and Wheeler. Send Williams and LaVella out to the front gate. Tell them to search every vehicle leaving. No exceptions. They're to check every driver's license and write down their driver's license number and their plate number and state of issue. Do you understand?"

Rhett nodded enthusiastically.

"Be careful. Your head might fall off. Now, if they need help, and I can't see why they would since there won't be many people, if any, leaving tonight," the Chief said.

"Repeat back to me what I just told you."

"There won't be many people leaving tonight because there won't be... ah... many... ah..."

"About the searching, the license number and plate, Rhett," the Chief said with a frustrated calm.

It was close enough for government work. Rhett forgot about recording the plate's state, but it was good enough for Rhett. The Chief liked the kid. He had one of those faces that looked like it was in a state of perpetual bliss. The Chief wondered why anybody would name their kid Rhett. Somebody had the hots for Gable, or maybe his mother's name was Scarlett.

"One thing, Chief. You said they should search every car?"

"Right."

"For what?"

The Chief gave jolly face a long look. "Money, Rhett. Cash. A lot of it. Remember the robbery? Hang on for a second."

The Chief yelled over to the money room women who stood stiffly against the wall.

"What did he put the money in?" the Chief asked.

They both started to talk at once.

"You, ah, it's Edith, isn't it?" The Chief said to the thin, bony woman, not waiting for a reply, although she nodded in the affirmative, "What did he put the money in?"

"He had a duffle bag, like the army kind, greenish color, and a red backpack," she said, calmly, "a short guy. He was an asshole."

"Okay, Rhett, you heard her. That's what we're looking for, a red backpack, a greenish army duffle and a short asshole."

"Got it, Chief."

"He also took the Stony Creek bag," Edith added while her partner stood there, glad nobody was asking her anything. Her mind was blank, and she didn't think she could talk.

"What Stony Creek bag?" the Chief said, momentarily forgetting that he had dropped the bag off.

"The one for Pipa's."

Holy Christ, they got away with the gambling money. Otto will go batshit.

"They got that?"

"Yessir, took bag 'n all. I hope it wasn't anything important."

The Chief checked her expression. He wasn't sure whether this broad was really dumb or was playing dumb. His bet was the latter. He'd have to keep an eye on that one.

"You got that Rhett? Stop and search every car leaving, and look for a red backpack, army duffel, a Stony Creek bag, and a short asshole."

"Will do, Chief. What if somebody refuses and asks if we have a warrant or something?"

"Rhett, I don't give a fuck if they're a goddamn Supreme Court Judge, search every vehicle. Now get those other two out to the gate."

"Okay, you two stay close. The states will be here, and they'll take more detailed statements from you," the Chief said eager to get out of there when the thin women spoke.

"He seemed to know that the money was in the liquor boxes and he mentioned Otto's name," she said.

Most people knew who Otto was, but the liquor boxes?

Maybe it was one of ours.

He had to get the state cops on this. He had no interest in investigating the robbery. He was the "cash 'n carry" guy—find the cash and carry it out. He'd leave the Dick Tracy stuff to the states. Better yet, this was perfect for Foley. He jumps in and makes a nice buck, and the Chief picks up a little scratch, and Otto gets his crime solved. Hell, it's drinks on the house for everybody.

Before he turned it over to the state cops, he had to stop the card games, brief Otto so he could deal with the gambling money and see that everybody leaving Stony Creek is checked.

Some people in the lobby were curious about the police activity in the office, but most didn't even notice, as Otto pushed his way through.

"What happened?" Otto said to the Chief, trying to catch his breath, "and no smart mouth crap."

"Somebody cleaned us out, including the gambling money," the Chief said.

"Don't tell me that."

"Okay, they didn't get the Pipa's money."

"Goddamn it, Chief, this isn't funny."

"You're telling me?"

"Anybody have a total count on how much they got?" Otto said, trying to calm his insides.

"Well, two hundred big ones for sure. Didn't get to the rest. You better call Jonsey and get him and his people over here to do an accounting."

Otto winced on the "two hundred." "Okay, yeah. Did you call the states?"

"No, I was waiting for you. We need to get our stories straight about the Pipa's money."

"Yeah, that makes for a lot of cash that we'll have to explain," Otto said his face wrinkled in thought.

Otto was thinking about the insurance. They were covered, but to include the gambling money they had to do some creative bookkeeping fast. It was tricky stuff and could open a Pandora's Box, but letting over two hundred grand go down the tubes wasn't in Otto's company manual.

"Do you have the last number on how much money you already counted?" Otto asked Esther, thinking that she needed to lose some weight. He almost didn't recognize her.

She just stared at him, her Betty Boop eyes big, black, and round.

"Esther, did you hear me? What was the last count you had on the money?" he said louder. Esther just stood there staring at him when Edith intervened.

"She's in a little shock," Edith interrupted. "We have it on the money machine, and we record it after each count. I think it was $287,223, but I'll confirm."

"What about the bag for Pipa's?" Otto asked, watching Edith's face closely for any reaction.

"Yeah, like I told the Chief, he took that. I don't think the guy was too smart. He was just grabbing everything. I hope there wasn't anything valuable in the bag," she said, looking as naïve as she could.

Esther turned her head sharply and looked at Edith. She had seen Edith zip open the bag and take a quick peek. She knew what was in there. Esther felt like she was going to throw up.

"Ah, look, you two go over and sit down. You've been through enough. I'm sure the state police will question you so stay close, okay?" Otto said as both women nodded.

Otto pulled the Chief aside and in a low, whispery voice said, "I think the skinny one knows what was in the Pipa's bag."

"No shit, Otto. You'll be hard pressed to find somebody that didn't know."

"I don't think it's as rampant as you think, Chief, and the way Edith's playing it dumb means she's wants to stay out of it."

"I think you're right on that, Otto. The skinny broad ain't going to say a word, and the fat one looks like she swallowed her tongue and looking at her maybe a side of beef. But if I was you, I'd cover my ass."

"Our asses, Chief. Cover our asses. But let's not get excited. Only you and I know how much was in the bag. If one of the money room people tells the cops there was cash in the bag, we'll just say that it was income from a busy week."

"So, why are we shipping it up to Pipa's?

"As a safety precaution. We never keep all of our cash in one place," Otto said, brightening up, thinking that was a reasonable answer that made sense.

"I don't know. When somebody sits down and starts adding up things, they're going to wonder where we got all the cash, and the books ain't going to show it," the Chief said.

"Yeah, there's no paper trail," Otto said with a worried look on his face. "I have to work on that."

While Otto was trying to save the gambling money, the Chief was thinking about how he could cash in on the robbery. Foley could be the key, but with all his pussy problems, he could screw up the whole deal. He had to get the kid's head straight. They both could make a nice piece of change.

There was no better time to cut a deal with Otto than right now.

He was on the ropes in more ways than one.

When there's a lot of money involved, there's lot of money to be made.

HEDY

NEW YEAR'S EVE WAS IN FULL SWING AT PIPA'S. EVEN MIKE BARRON was bussing tables when he spotted Hedy. He needed to talk with her. He tried to get her attention, but she was busy chatting with guests. As he made his way through the crowd, he caught her eye and signaled her. She was glad to get away and excused herself.

"My manager needs me," she said to one comely matron who was displaying more diamonds than Harry Winston.

"Hedy, I need to talk with you. Can we go back to my office?" Mike said as he led Hedy towards the kitchen.

"I could use the break, Mike. I've been down here for the last few hours trying to sit down and have a drink," she said, happy to get the chance to establish her alibi.

"I didn't see you."

"Well, I saw you, but this crowd doesn't make it easy. Anyhow, let's go to your office, but you must make it quick," she said.

"So, what's up, Mike?" Hedy said once they were inside his small office, just off the kitchen. She didn't sit down, so neither did he. Even with the door closed, the clanging of pots and pans and clinking of dishes on the metal work tables, along with cooks and servers yelling, made it difficult to talk.

"I hate to bother you with this now but it's a continuing problem, and I wanted to talk with you when it was happening," Mike said, "and one look out there shows it's happening. We need more help."

Things were falling into place better than she thought.

"You're right, Mike. I got here, early, maybe six-thirty or thereabouts and I understand exactly what you're saying."

"I'm sorry. The noise. Did you say six-thirty?"

Hedy signaled him to move to the far corner of the tiny, cluttered room.

"I said," cupping her hand around her mouth, "I've been here since six-thirty," Hedy said louder, glad she could pound that timeline into his head, "and I saw how busy you've been."

"It's not only the holidays. Our numbers have been increasing but our staffing hasn't kept pace. I need to get more people on board and have them trained so when I need to bring more in I can."

"I've seen how you and your people have been working your tails off all evening and I congratulate you. I agree. You need more people. Let's do this. As soon as we get past the holidays let's meet and you tell me what you need in budgeting and I'll push it through. Does that work for you?"

"Thanks. I really appreciate it."

"Now I've got to get back out there and so do you, and Mike?" she said, stopping and turning to look at him directly, the kitchen noise subsiding for a moment, "I think we need to take care of you, too, and I'll make sure that we do," she added, and left. Hedy was pleased. That conversation couldn't have come at a better time.

She saw JR Leon, still sitting in the corner with the blonde from the bank. Hedy suspected their relationship was more than banking but that wasn't important right now. She was feeling good about the way things were falling into place. She braced herself for a flurry of inane BS and moved into the boisterous room.

Seeing all those people seeing her was perfect. If she ever needed an alibi, she had one.

JOE DUCK

JOE DUCK WAS FACING HIS LAST BIG HURDLE. HE HAD TO GET through the exit. He was nervous about the money he stuffed into his pockets, but he'd refuse to be searched if it came to that. He doubted that it would. He didn't know how much he had, but he'd claim he won it gambling in Pittsburgh.

He eased up on the gas pedal. Now that the money is stashed maybe he doesn't leave. Problem is that Stoney Creek will be crawling with cops and they'll be sniffing everything out. If he stays, the cops could get to him.

No, he's getting his ass out while the getting's good.

He had to be cool. Stay calm. He'd tell them he had to leave because of a family emergency. He hoped they didn't ask for ID. They might spot it as a fake. If they did, he'd make a fuss, like he was rich and had lawyers, and then he'd really throw them off by telling them to search his car.

He was practicing some of the lines in his head. He'd bring up illegal search and seizure, probable cause, and he was also trying to think of the name of that big fancy law firm in Pittsburgh. He'd say they were his lawyers. He knew there was one that began with Reed something and something, but he couldn't remember. That was the trouble with lawyers. Every fuckin' one of them wanted their name on the door.

He took a deep breath. He was just a guy leaving because of family. Ain't no law against that. He had nothing to hide, well except for the gun and the money in his pockets.

He was close, yet so far.

FOLEY

THE CHIEF CALLED IT "SLOPE-STARING." THAT'S WHAT PEOPLE did in slope-side rooms and that's what Linda was doing when Foley returned.

"I need to get back to Pittsburgh," she said, not turning around.

"I know," he said, "but we can't get out of here tonight with all this snow."

"I called my sister. She'll pick me up first thing in the morning. I'm sorry about all this."

Foley thought it better not to comment. When a man asks a woman to marry him, he should have a good idea of her marital status. It was such a bizarre situation. He felt foolish and angry, but where in the hell do you go with something like this?

"How about … ah, would you like a drink?" Foley said, hoping to relieve the tension in the room.

"No thanks," she said.

Foley checked the ice bucket. There were still cubes left. He removed a few from their watery grave, mumbling to himself but loud enough for Linda to hear.

"This is one helluva way to start the new year."

Linda ignored him.

Foley tried again, this time with more confidence.

"CB is setting up a meeting with Otto about us handling security for them," he said, hoping that business would be a good conversation starter.

She remained quiet.

Foley sipped his drink. He wished he were a little drunk. This insane situation wasn't amenable to common sense and reason. It was crazy and irrational. He tried another approach.

"Your sister shouldn't drive up here in this stuff. Look, as soon as I finish the meeting, actually you should come, and then we'll head back. By that time the roads will be cleared. Sound like a plan?"

Linda wanted to leave. She was embarrassed and confused. She needed alone time, the sooner the better.

She broke her silence. "Foley, you go to the meeting and don't worry about me. I just need time to work this out and then we can…"

The piercing ring of the phone startled them.

They glanced at each other. Neither one was expecting a call. Foley answered.

"Foley get your ass down here as fast as you can. We've had a robbery. I'm in the office, the one just off the old lobby, near Augie's. Somebody robbed the money room. Took a lot of cash. This is your chance to get on the payroll, so get moving." The Chief said.

He hung up before Foley could respond.

JOE DUCK

WHEN JOE SAW THE TOLL BOOTHS, HE STIFFENED. IT LOOKED LIKE one booth was still open. Why in the hell would Otto do that on New Year's Eve? In a snowstorm? The problem with rich people is that they don't even know when they're being assholes. Nobody has the balls to tell them.

Money shuts everybody's mouth.

It's a wonder that Otto isn't charging people to get out of Stony Creek.

The exit looked clear. Joe was thinking that maybe he was going to zip through when he saw a light bar flash. He didn't notice the police car. It was parked off to the right.

Joe's first instinct was to just drive through, not at high speed, but fast enough, as if the flashing lights weren't meant for him, but that might make things worse. He had nothing to hide. Well he did have the 22 in his belt and the money in his pockets but he wouldn't let them search him. But, what if they arrested him and…?"

A short, stocky cop jumped out of the car and waved him down.

Another cop came out of the booth. Joe stopped and put his window down.

"Yessir," Joe said. "Is there some sort of problem?"

"No problem, sir. Do you mind telling me why you're leaving on such a bad night as this?"

"Family emergency. Got a call from my sister about my Dad. She wants me to get there as fast as I can."

"Sorry about that. Where's there?"

"I'm sorry, where's what?"

"Where do you have to go?" the cop said.

"Oh, ah, I have to go to Herminie, it's down near Irwin," Joe said.

"Yeah, I know it. Never been there. Do you mind if we look in your car, Mr. (pause)?"

"Ah, Scarcini. Mike Scarcini. Go ahead. Help yourself. Can I help you with anything?"

"No, just a routine check. Had some petty thefts lately," he said, peering into the side window.

"I can get out and you can look all you want," Joe said, opening his door.

"Just stay in your vehicle, sir, this will only take a minute. Mind if I open the back door?" LaVella said, totally forgetting about the "short asshole," description.

"No, go ahead," Joe said, thinking his voice might reveal how nervous he was.

"What's in the bag?" the cop said.

Joe could feel his heart speeding up and his body felt numb.

My bag?

He wasn't sure what to do when he realized the cop was talking about his Nike bag. He coughed and cleared his throat.

"Just my clothes 'n stuff," Joe said. "You wanna look in, ya can," Joe said, almost too eagerly.

"You don't mind," the cop said, not waiting for an answer, unzipping the bag, and rooting around with his gloved hand.

The other cop was behind the Explorer. Joe could see that he was writing something on a pad, probably his license plate number, but Joe had that covered.

As the cop looked in the bag, he asked Joe, "What's the problem with your father?"

That question caught Joe off guard, and his mind raced for what he hoped would be a logical answer. His hands felt clammy, and he had to control his urge to gun the car and make a run for it.

"Ah cancer… lung cancer. He was doing okay, but I guess he had a relapse. Anyhow my sister wants me there pronto."

"That's tough, man," the cop said, zipping the bag shut. "Mind if we check your spare tire?" he said just before he closed the back door.

"No, go ahead. What's going on?"

"Hey, it pays to have a good spare on a night like this," the cop said to Joe. He used his flashlight to look under the vehicle and saw nothing unusual. He opened the rear hatch and checked under the cargo cover to see if anything was hidden in the spare tire compartment. It was clean.

The cop closed the hatch and said," Okay, Mr. Scarcini, you can go, but I'd be careful. The road to the turnpike should be plowed, but the way this snow is coming down they could have trouble keeping up with it."

"Thanks Officer," Joe said, feeling his body relax, "Appreciate the information," he said as he closed his window and slowly drove the twenty yards to the main road, watching the cops in his rear-view mirror.

Joe was so tense that if somebody ran their fingernail over his neck muscles, they'd snap faster than Ruby Begonia's bra strap.

LaVella walked back to his cruiser while Williams headed for the warmth of the tollbooth. Neither one had asked Joe for his ID.

They didn't notice that Joe turned right, heading away from the turnpike.

JR LEON

JR SAT AT HIS CORNER TABLE IN PIPA'S, GETTING MORE IRRITATED by the minute. He watched Hedy for at least twenty-five minutes. She was flitting around the place like a politician at a fundraiser. She missed nobody, giving hugs, shaking hands, and engaging with just about everybody in the place.

People didn't make JR wait.

He began his business life with ample assets left to him by his father and then parlayed them into an immense fortune. He was extremely proud of his financial acumen and would frequently point out how too many children of wealthy people blew their family's fortune.

Business wasn't for cowards. JR gave no quarter. It was his way or the highway. If JR didn't get what he wanted, he'd walk. He could afford it.

Except for this deal.

He needed Hedy more than she needed him. That was a new problem for JR. That's why he was still sitting in the corner waiting for her. Any other time he'd be long gone.

"Why the glum look?" his companion Laura said, reaching over and brushing back his hair with her hand. He reared back as if a large wasp had just landed on his forehead. He slapped her hand away with substantial force.

Laura was stunned, and the bodyguards reacted, but JR quickly quelled the situation.

"I'm sorry," he said. "I was lost in thought. Are you okay?" he said to a startled Laura.

She pulled herself together quickly. She understood the game. It was time for her to get out of the line of fire.

"I'm fine, JR. I didn't mean to catch you off guard. Listen, I need to freshen up a bit … for later, so why don't I head back to the condo. I'll wait for you there and we'll finish the evening off with a nice nightcap. Okay?" she said with a come-hither smile.

"You're sure you're okay?"

"Of course. You know a little slap here and there doesn't bother me," she said, using her eyes to make him promises.

JR gave her a knowing smile. "Roger will take you back. Wait for me."

"Of course," she said as she rose from the table. JR signaled Roger, and he was at her side in seconds.

"Roger, make sure she gets back safely and then come back here."

Never leave any of your male help alone with an attractive female.

He summoned his other bodyguard.

"Get Hedy Kasser. She's the blonde, well you know what she looks like. The last time I saw her, she was over by those big palms. Find her and bring her back here. I need to see her now. You know the drill," he said.

Hedy was busy solidifying her alibi and didn't see the buff young man come up behind her. She was saying her goodbyes to an elegantly dressed older couple. Hedy turned and almost bumped into the bodyguard.

"Well, hello … and you are?"

"Excuse me, Miss Kasser. I'm Tim Wilson, an associate of JR Leon, and he asked me to escort you to his table," he said, taking her hand and leading her through the crowd.

She didn't want to go to JR's table on his terms, but this guy was giving her no choice. She had to admit he was smooth.

JR nursed his Glenrothes, the single malt scotch that he drank. Since it was a special order at the state-run liquor stores, JR provided the club with a few bottles for his use only.

He had to keep Hedy Kasser in line. It was a delicate dance.

She was a strong-willed woman, who was not only smart, but beautiful. That could be a deadly combination, but this was one woman he was staying far away from.

He was ashamed of himself for even having the lustful thought and vowed not to let it enter his mind again.

He was staring at the amber liquid when he heard her voice slicing through his thoughts.

"Hey, if it isn't the famous businessman, Mr. JR Leon. How are you this evening, sir?" Hedy said with exaggerated perkiness.

JR disliked outward displays of emotions. He didn't like her cute cheerleader approach.

"Please sit down," JR said, glancing to see if anybody was paying attention to their exchange.

"Thank you, kind sir," she said with another flourish, annoying him even more.

"You're in a cheerful mood, aren't you?" he said.

"Well, I am, kind of," she said.

Wouldn't you be if you just disabled a rapist?

"I'm glad to hear that," he said somewhat curtly.

"Look, JR, I know you're disturbed. You have that look, but I thought you wanted to keep a low profile," she said.

"I like to keep my business dealings private, but since your family meeting is only a day away, I think it's appropriate. I just want to make sure that we're both on the same page, and there are a few things I'd like to go over with you," he said.

"Look, I apologize, but I have to leave. My sister's not feeling well, and I need to check on her. Why don't we meet tomorrow for a drink here at the club? Does noon work for you?"

He wasn't pleased but didn't want to make waves. "I'll be here. I expect we won't be disturbed."

Hedy let the dig pass. "Good seeing you, JR. I hope you... we have a happy new year," she said and stood up.

"I'm sure it will be."

Hedy swung around and made her way back through the chattering crowd as the anticipation of a new year grew.

She almost didn't hear her cell phone ringing.

"This is Hedy," she answered.

"Hedy, get down to the old office immediately. We have a problem," Otto said, not waiting for a response.

Hedy wasn't sure what was going on, but she saw an opportunity to reinforce her alibi. She told Mike Barron that there was an emergency and asked him to get somebody to take her to the old lobby.

Things were falling into place.

THE OLD LOBBY

WHEN FOLEY ARRIVED AT THE OLD OFFICE, IT WAS A BUSY PLACE.
It looked more like a cocktail party than a crime scene. He saw CB talking to a stout man whose bald head was fringed along the sides with blonde-gray hair. The way CB was paying attention to him, and nodding his head, suggested to Foley that it was Otto.

The Chief spotted Foley coming up on his right and began introductions before he got there.

"Good. I'm glad you're here. Say hello to Otto Kasser."

Foley spoke as he picked up his pace, "Mr. Kasser, pleased to meet you, sir."

"Good meeting you, ah ..."

"You can call me, Foley. Everybody does."

"Yes, ah, Foley. I'm sure your father discussed our situation with you?"

Foley glanced at the Chief, who jumped in. "I told him that you were interested in discussing a business relationship Otto, but we didn't go any deeper than that."

"I'd be glad to make a proposal on what we can ..." Foley started to explain. Otto interrupted.

"I meant about the robbery. Were you filled in?"

"No details. Just that there was a robbery and ..."

"The Chief will fill you in. Let's meet tomorrow to discuss details, but as of right now, you're on the payroll. Is that okay with you?"

"Ah, well, certainly. What ah …"

"Just keep a record of your hours. I'm sure we can work out a satisfactory fee to cover everything until we get an agreement. Meet me in the coffee shop at 8 tomorrow. Now, let's get this place under control and see what we can do about getting this guy."

"Yes sir," Foley said, "We have to clear this room and secure the robbery scene," he said, giving the Chief a nod.

"What's going on, Chief?" Hedy interrupted, ignoring Otto, who didn't seem to mind.

"Oh, Hedy. We'll fill you in, in a minute. Say hello to my son Foley. Otto just hired him to help us with security," the Chief said with a glint in his eye.

Foley uttered a quick hello. Hedy reached out, and they shook hands. "Welcome to the Stony Creek family," she said and then acknowledged Otto with a low key, "Otto."

"Were they in the money room?" she asked, nodding her head towards the two women who stood stiffly against the wall.

"Give me a minute, Hedy," the Chief said.

The Chief guided Foley off to the side. "I don't need this shit right now," he grumbled. "How do you want to handle this?"

"CB, this is your case. I'll consult, but I will not run the investigation," Foley said.

"You don't have to. I'm giving it to the state boys. They love this kind of crap. Why don't you get things organized here while I call them?" the Chief said.

"You know, you can really be a bastard when you want to be," Foley said.

"Hey, this is your shot. I'm just stepping out of the way to give it to you."

Foley knew better, but now was not the time to argue.

"Who's your best cop?"

"You're kidding, right?"

"C'mon, CB. Quit jagging. We need to secure this crime scene and I need somebody who understands crime scene investigation to work with me."

The Chief looked around the room. "All my guys are rookies or locals, and the biggest crime scene they ever worked was a bar fight."

"That won't help. Okay, I'll just grab one of your boys to work with me. If we step over any lines, let me know. Otherwise, I'll try to make some sense out of this," Foley said.

The Chief began to leave and then stopped near Otto.

"Otto, I think you should introduce Foley to the employees," the Chief said as he headed for the door to the old lobby.

"You son-of-a-bitch," Foley mumbled under his breath as Otto yelled out, "QUIET. Everybody just quiet down."

The room finally fell silent and Otto introduced Foley, saying he had joined Stony Creek and would work with the Chief. They were to give him their fullest cooperation.

"Okay, ladies and gentlemen," Foley said loudly, "I'd like everybody, other than police, to leave this office, please. Thank you."

Mumbling and shuffling as people filed out. Otto, Hedy, and another man moved into one corner and were busy talking. The money room ladies stood off to the side waiting for instructions. Foley saw a Stony Creek cop standing near the door. He waved him over. The young, rosy-cheeked man, a big, strong looking kid, voiced Foley an enthusiastic "Yessir."

"What's your name, officer?"

"Rhett, sir. Rhett Catania."

Foley thought that Rhett, with his rosy cheeks and twinkling eyes, would make a perfect Santa Claus. All he needed was the beard.

"Rhett," Foley said, wondering how a Yankee with an Italian surname ended up with a movie character's southern name and was tempted to ask, but nixed it, "Do you know whether there are any officers out at the front gate?"

"Yessir, we got two of 'em out there and the Chief told 'em to search every car leaving."

That's a bunch of lawsuits waiting to happen.

"Okay, ah …" Foley said, seeing another cop come into the office.

"Rhett," he continued, "You'll act as my liaison. That officer over there …"

"Donahue," Rhett said.

"Post him at the front office door. Nobody, and I mean nobody, comes in unless they're police or have been authorized, and nobody touches a thing. The money room is off limits. Nobody gets in. Got it, and you stand by," Foley said as he turned and went over to Otto.

"Sorry to interrupt, but is there an empty office, or maybe that Alpine Room that we could use as a command center?" Foley asked.

"Ah, yes, of course. I'll have somebody get you a key," Otto said, nodding at the man he was talking with who turned and left.

"He'll get the Alpine Room open for you and give you a key," Otto said.

"Thanks." he said glancing at Hedy. She stood stone-faced. He went back to where Rhett was standing.

"Rhett, we're going to use the Alpine Room as a command center. See that guy over there for the key. I'm going to take a quick look in the money room and then I'll be down. Tell the money room women we'll talk to them in about ten minutes. Thanks."

Foley took a quick look around the money room and then instructed Donahue to close the door and put up police tape or a sign warning people that it was a crime scene.

Otto and Hedy were finally alone when his cell phone rang.

"Yes, Chief."

Hedy watched Otto's face as he listened.

"Good. Everything cleaned up?"

Otto nodded, hung up, and spoke to Hedy.

"Let's step over here for a moment," Otto said, nodding toward an empty corner.

They walked over, and as they did, Otto, never looking at Hedy, said in a low matter-of-fact voice, "The games are closed, and everything is clean."

"Good."

"But we have a problem. They got the Pipa's money," he said as they stopped and faced each other.

"How did...?"

"I'll explain later. Right now, I'm going to tell the cops that the money was ordered in extra for the holidays and that it was being moved to Pipa's for safety reasons, just in case the money room women say anything and so..."

"Jeez, Otto," Hedy said, "they start checking and they'll know we're lying through our teeth. Hell, everybody knows about the games, including those women."

"I'm not so sure. Maybe they heard stuff, but we can deflect the rumors, so it becomes gossip against our word, and I think we have the edge, don't you?"

"Maybe. Why can't we say we had the cash to give our employees a holiday bonus?"

Otto looked at Hedy, thinking about what she just said, the frown on his face slowly turning into a smile.

"Goddamn it, Hedy. That's it. It makes sense. That's it," he said, giving her a hug, she didn't return. Historically, they didn't give bonuses, a policy his mother set, but he didn't think anybody would pick up on that, and besides, there was always a first time.

"Look, we can say that we've been accumulating cash for that purpose. They're not going to investigate the Pipa's money from the get-go, so we'll have time to fudge the books a bit, showing that we've been putting it aside for months. We'll tell them we wanted to give bonuses out in cash, which is logical. It will take a little bookkeeping work, but it's doable," Otto said, feeling relieved.

"Get the word out to the rest of the family," he said, as he turned and left.

Hedy was pleased. The robbery would be another diversion. So far it appeared that Hogg hadn't reported anything. If he had, Stony Creek police would have been informed, but that was also a worry. What if he was dead?

She had to find out.

THE ALPINE ROOM

AFTER QUESTIONING THE TWO WOMEN, FOLEY ISSUED AN OFFICIAL description. The robber was short, maybe 5'3 or 4, built like Danny DeVito, and armed with a pistol. He wore a blue ski mask with some red in it, and a black or navy-blue ski jacket and latex gloves. He was carrying an old duffle, maybe army surplus, that was a faded olive green, a red backpack, and a green Stony Creek bag.

Grabbing pads and pencils from the credenza, Foley signaled Rhett to sit as he slid a pad across the polished veneer table.

"When I say something write it down," Foley said and then looking at Rhett's eager, boyish face added, "I mean instructions and things like that, Rhett, not everything I say."

"Got it, Chief."

"Call me Foley, please."

"Yessir, ah Foley, sir."

"Rhett, does the radio signal reach the front gate?"

"Yessir, it covers all of Stony Creek and then some."

"Good. Call the two guys who are out there and see what's going on."

"Yessir." Rhett pulled out a laminated 3" x 5" card from his shirt pocket and found what he was looking for as Foley watched.

"Looking for the call number," Rhett said sheepishly and then took care of the business at hand. "Fourteen, come in. This is ten, come in fourteen."

The radio crackled, but nothing happened. "Fourteen, this is ten, please come in. I'm with the chief ... ah, the chief investigator. Important you respond."

"This is Nine. I think Fourteen's out at the main gate."

"We know Nine. We're trying to reach him."

"I can try," the nasal-like voice sizzled.

Rhett's face flushed as he saw Foley watching him.

"Negative Nine. Keep the radio clear," Rhett said, standing and pacing around the small meeting room. "Fourteen, come in, please. I'm with Able One, important you respond."

Foley wondered when he became Able One.

"Just heard the call. This is Seven. I'm down by the tennis courts. Can I help?"

Rhett's rosy cheeks were getting redder as he saw the expression on Foley's face go from curiosity to a frown. Foley signaled Rhett to shut it down. Rhett put his hand up in a "just give me a minute" gesture.

"Everybody stays off the radio except for LaVella or Williams," Rhett yelled into the receiver.

He looked at Foley.

"Sorry, sir... ah, Foley, it's just that everybody wants to help. We never had anything this big before."

"I understand. Go ahead, try again," Foley said in a calm, low voice, hoping to relax Rhett.

Rhett went over to the corner of the room, hoping a location change would help. He called Fourteen again.

Rhett jumped back when Fourteen answered, crackling through the static.

"This is Fourteen. Sorry, I forgot my radio in the car and..."

"Fourteen, hold on transmission. I repeat, hold on transmission. I am with Able One, ah, or Foley, the guy who Otto put in charge of the investigation. He wants to talk to you," Rhett blurted, handing the radio to Foley, showing him the button to push.

Foley leaned back, his eyes flat, looking pained as he mechanically took the radio from Rhett.

This isn't going to be easy.

He straightened up his back, pushed the button, and in a loud, authoritative voice said, "Fourteen, my name is Foley and I've been hired to handle this robbery investigation. Please listen carefully and answer my questions quickly and simply. Do you understand?"

A burst of static rippled across the airwaves and Fourteen answered, "Got it, sir."

"Has there been any activity out at the gate?"

"Yessir."

Foley rubbed his face. "Okay, what activity?"

"A couple of people came in and a guy went out," Fourteen said.

"Tell me about the guy who went out."

"Nice guy. His father has cancer, and he had to..."

"Fourteen. I need a name, description, and did you check out his car?"

"Got it. Yessir. We searched the car and got his license number 'n all that. He didn't have anything except his little gym bag with nothing but clothes in it. We even searched the spare tire thing and under and over and it was clean. Guy said he had to go to Herminie, that's just down the road an hour or so, because his father was dying from cancer. Over."

"Can you describe him physically? Tall, short, facial features ...?"

"I think he had a beard ... (Off mic) He had a beard didn't he Larry?" Yeah, he had a beard. Over"

"How tall was he and what was he wearing?"

Nothing but static. Foley looked at Rhett for help with the radio when it sputtered, "My guess, average height, sir. He didn't exit the vehicle. Over."

"What was he wearing?"

Silence. "Fourteen, what was he wearing?"

"Ah, we were trying to figure that out. Hold on."

After what Foley figured was too long, he called them again.

"Did you understand my last transmission? What was he wearing?"

"Yeah, we understood. We think it was dark colored clothes, but Williams says no. He thinks it was a light-colored ski jacket, but maybe not. Over."

Foley shook his head. It was illegal to conduct a search without consent. From experience he knew that most people would usually agree to a search when asked, even those who had something to hide, but if a person refused, they had every right to do so. The problem with the Stony Creek cops was that they weren't sophisticated enough to handle it and trying to train them now was out of the question. Since they were instructed to search every car, Foley let them continue until the state guys showed up. Hopefully, they won't encounter many people leaving.

"Fourteen, from now on, have everybody exit their vehicle. Check out their height, and what they are wearing. If they don't complain, search their cars carefully. Watch for a brownish-green army duffle and a red backpack, and a short guy, not much over five feet, wearing a dark blue or black ski jacket. Be careful. Our actor is armed. Report any problems back to me immediately. Over."

"What if they don't wanna be searched? Over."

"Then you can't search their vehicle. You need probable cause, and the robbery might pass muster, but it's shaky ... look, just record plate numbers and their ID. Tell them you're conducting a police investigation and would like permission to look into their vehicle," Foley said and then added, "If you're unsure as to what to do just let dispatch know and have them contact me."

"We don't have a dispatch. Over."

"Right," Foley said, "Just contact Catania and he'll follow-up. Over and out," Foley said, happy to end the conversation.

Foley scribbled a note on the pad. "Fix radio system."

Foley thought about the one guy who left. He could be the actor, but if those cops did what they say they did, and really searched the vehicle thoroughly, maybe not. One thing he was sure of was that he had his work cut out for him.

Foley decided to hold up on everything and let the state cops take over. He called his father.

"CB, things are a mess. Did you call the state cops and when will they be here?"

"They're on the way," the Chief said, avoiding the "mess" comment.

The Chief told him he shut down the card games, Foley interrupting and telling him he didn't want to know anything about them. He quickly changed the subject, suggesting that they wait for the state cops before doing anything else.

"It's your call," the Chief said, "but we have some problems we have to deal with."

"What problems?

"Well, there's a shift change at eleven, which means we'll have a lot of people coming and going, in and out."

"You don't need me for that, CB. That's operational. My advice is to beef up the personnel at the gate and determine an orderly procedure for all employees leaving, maybe alphabetically, or something like that. Every employee has to be checked out because there's a good chance one of them pulled this off."

"Good suggestion. I'll discuss with Otto. Stay close to your phone and I'll tell Otto you're on the case somewhere in the resort."

"Thanks, CB. I'm going back to my room but if you need me, call."

As soon as the Chief hung up, he called Otto and filled him in, and they agreed on a procedure. The Chief would send out two more men. They were to verify identities. Name, address, driver's license number and plate were to be recorded, along with the time they exited. If somebody protested, the cops were to get their identities and photograph them. The Chief was pleased with his idea. He had somebody go to the gift shop and collect a dozen disposable cameras for that purpose.

After talking with the Chief, Otto called in his VP of Operations and briefed him. They called in the Team Leaders (Hedy's College course concept that Otto disliked) and had them personally account for every person in their group. They were to physically see every member of their team, ask about their whereabouts for the previous two hours, record all their answers and warn them not to leave Stony Creek with any containers, bags, or suitcases of any kind. If they had a lot of stuff in their cars, they were to take it to a designated storage shed where they would be shown where to store it. Every employee's vehicle leaving Stony Creek had to be empty. The employee's contents from their vehicles would also be checked.

The heavy snow was now working to Otto's advantage. Fewer people would leave the resort. The employees had Stony Creek IDs so that would speed up the exiting process.

Foley went back to the room where he found Linda still asleep on the sofa, the once roaring fireplace now nothing but a pile of smoldering embers. He was going to wake Linda and have her take the bedroom, but he was sure she would refuse. He was too tired to go through the process, so he went in, closed the door, stripped down, and climbed into bed.

"Happy New Year," he muttered to himself, hoping he could fall asleep.

HEDY

EARLIER, JUST BEFORE FOLEY AND OTTO LEFT THE ROBBERY SCENE, Hedy announced, a little more loudly than necessary, that she was leaving to check on her sister who wasn't feeling well. She took a snowmobile to Heidi's where she found her still sleeping on the sofa. Hedy woke her and led her half-asleep, bleary-eyed sister to her bedroom. Heidi snuggled under the covers, never uttering a word other than a few pleasurable moans.

Hedy went back to Pipa's where she welcomed 2002 with the rest of the revelers. When she had the opportunity, she let people know that she had been in the club all evening. Other than for a few diehards, the alcohol eventually took its toll and things wound down around 3 AM.

She found Mike Barron back in his office.

"It's been a long evening for me, Mike. I'm just going to crash in the Green Room," she said.

"Everything okay with you," he said.

"We had a problem at the old lobby. I'm too tired to get into it right now."

"I already heard."

She shook her head wearily, excused herself and went upstairs to the Green Room where she climbed into bed and snuggled deep under the covers.

With her mission accomplished and the feathery covers making her feel warm and safe, she thought she'd fall asleep quickly, but she couldn't get the evening's events out of her mind. Some of the images she pulled up under her tightly closed eyelids made her shudder. She curled into the fetal position and tried to think of other things, hoping to crowd out the Hogg images. She replayed a wonderful evening in St. Bart's with a French writer, but the bloody mess at Hogg's trampled over every one of her pleasant thoughts. Hogg had to be neutralized.

He was an evil waiting to happen again. She understood that people would say it was extreme but was it any more extreme than taking a person's life for a crime? Hell, it's still legal to hang or shoot somebody for crimes in some states. Hogg invaded her body and scarred it forever. If any foreign country invaded the U.S. we'd go to war, bombing the living hell out of them, but when it's a woman's body we must go to court where defense lawyers tear our souls apart even more. Things have improved since she was raped so that's a good thing but she couldn't let Hogg continue to destroy women, especially her sister. No, an eye for an eye was right for a rapist like Hogg.

She'll have to live with it and Hogg will have to live without it.

It was going to be a long, sleepless night.

She was worried about Hogg. If he died, it would bring in more cops than the St. Patty's Day parade. Cop killers zipped right to the top of the Most Wanted list. She had to find a safe way to get somebody to his house and check him out.

Her original plan was more complicated, and it would have diverted any suspicion away from Heidi, but when she learned about their affair she was forced to act quickly. It changed everything. Now the entire family was in danger and she had to involve Heidi, which was a precarious proposition.

But as timid as Heidi was, there were a few rare occasions Hedy had seen another side to her. Once, when she was around 12, another girl slapped Heidi and for a moment she just stood there looking as if she was going to cry, which was her usual reaction. Instead, Heidi suddenly lashed out, slapping the girl viciously and grabbing a handful of her hair and throwing her to the ground. Hedy had to step in and stop her sister from inflicting any more damage on the surprised victim. And then, just as quickly, Heidi reverted to being herself-a frightened little girl, crying and apologizing. It was as if another personality emerged for a moment and then disappeared. It happened one other time, the last some six years ago.

Hedy knew that Hogg would be a threat, but she thought she'd find a way to handle him. As she lay there, she was thinking she miscalculated.

She stopped a rapist, but she may have unleashed a monster.

She was in for a lot of restless nights.

This was the first one.

HOGG

HOGG SLOWLY OPENED HIS EYES FOR A MOMENT AND THEN drifted off again. His mind was beginning to clear, but it was a struggle. He tried to open his eyes, but they felt heavy. He opened them again, and everything was hazy. Where in the hell was he? He finally lifted his one arm, which felt like a hundred-pound weight, and rubbed his eyes.

Fragments and flashbacks fought their way out of the murkiness that clouded his mind. He saw the flickering TV and remembered he was in Stony Creek. He sat up but felt exhausted and lay back in his chair. He wasn't certain if it was night or early morning. He dozed off again.

He awakened and sat up, trying to get his bearings. His mouth was filled with cotton and his eyes ached. He got his drink on the end table and took a sip, but it didn't help. He needed a glass of water.

As he struggled to get up, he felt a pain in his groin and something tight around his stomach. He dropped back into the chair and reached under the blanket and felt something smooth and cold around his waist.

What the hell?

He ran his fingers over the strange surface with his one hand while peeling back the blanket with the other

He couldn't see, so he pushed the blanket down and saw that his hand was touching duct tape.

Duct tape?

It couldn't be duct tape. He tried to get up but couldn't. He leaned back and closed his eyes. He wasn't sure how long he was under, but a sharp pain shook him out of it.

He remembered the duct tape.

He pulled the blanket aside. At first his mind couldn't process what he saw. He was wrapped in silver duct tape. Without any light, it was hard to make out anything else. He sat up straighter and reached for the lamp on the end table when a jabbing pain hit him. He rested for a moment and finally turned the light on.

What the fu…?

He saw spots of blood and gauze sticking out from the edges of the tape.

Christ, my stomach's bleeding. What the fuck is going on?

He was awake now. His chest felt tight, and the muscles of his neck were hard, the tendons jutting out against his skin. Beads of sweat formed on his upper lip.

He took another look. He felt a shock run through him as he looked at the duct tape which appeared to be covering a bandage.

Christ, was I shot? Duct tape?

He tried to lift the bandage and see underneath, but there was too much tape. He lay back again, closed his eyes, and tried to focus his thinking, but his mind was like a sieve, thoughts dripping out every which way.

He lay there trying to get the strength to understand what was going on. He tried to peel the tape off, but it was too sticky. As he worked the tape, he kept trying to remember what happened. He must have been shot. He knew people could get shot and not know it. He wasn't feeling a lot of pain and it didn't look like much bleeding, but that meant nothing. He had to get the tape off.

Finally, the tape loosened enough so he could lift the bandage with his thumb and index finger. He cautiously peeked under the tape. He was thinking about what he'd do if he had to call an ambulance which was a problem.

Holy fucking Christ.

He couldn't believe what he saw. His mind went bonkers. It was like loading a gun with every destructive emotion known and shooting yourself with it. Disbelief, confusion, humiliation, hate, anger, anguish, and fear caromed through his being like a runaway train.

He was sick to his stomach.

His mind kept recoiling. It was going off in every direction. Nothing made sense. He squeezed his eyes shut and tried to breathe, but he couldn't catch his breath. He was having a nightmare. He'd wake up soon.

The burning pains shooting through his groin said it was real. He looked at the bloody mess again. It hadn't changed. It just couldn't be, but it was.

His dick was gone. Somebody had cut off his dick!

His mind exploded. He squeezed his eyes shut, trying to block out what he thought he saw. It had to be a nightmare. It had to be. He opened his eyes again. He looked around the room. He pinched his cheek and then slapped himself hard. He was awake.

What in the hell happened?

He tried to fit the scattered puzzle pieces together, but nothing fit. Images fluttered in and out, flickering like an old silent movie.

He had to settle down, get control, think rationally.

He tried to remember, but his mind refused to help. He needed a drink. And then it hit him.

Where was his cock?

He tried to get up but fell back. His pants were down below his knees. Pulling them up and holding his pants, he struggled to a standing position. He checked the bandage to make certain it was affixed, buckled his belt, and tried to take a step. He felt like he had a ten-pound weight between his legs, and he moved like he did. Standing still, he looked around for his dick. Bending was a bitch, but he checked under the cushions of the chair and then the sofa.

This can't be happening.

He painfully made his way to the kitchen where he downed a huge swallow of scotch, the alcohol burning his throat, causing him to cough. That sent shivers of pain echoing through his groin. He had pain pills in the cabinet. He took a thankful breath when he saw the brown plastic tube with the Percocet. He took two chased by scotch and stood there wondering what happened, trying to think out what he had to do. He checked the wastebasket in the kitchen and even looked in the fridge and cabinets.

Somebody had cut his dick off. What in the fuck did they do with it?

He limped his way back to the chair and looked under it and the sofa again. Nothing.

He knew he had to find his dick. That's what saved that Bobbitt guy. He started searching everywhere. He couldn't make the stairs, but he convinced himself it wouldn't be up there. Maybe outside. He went back into the kitchen and opened the back door but saw nothing except a lot of snow. Then he saw the tracks. They were covered with snow, but somebody was here.

Hogg's police training kicked in, and he thought more like a cop than a guy who just lost his manhood. The percs were working, and he was feeling a little looser, so he kept looking for his penis and anything that might tell him what happened. He searched the entire downstairs, but no luck.

He needed to get help and considered the possibilities. Hospitals were out. So were doctors, except for Dr. Jim. He owed Hogg big time. He called and explained that he needed medical attention but didn't identify the problem, much to the frustration of the doctor.

"Look, Jim. I'll explain everything when I see you. I'm in Stony Creek so it'll take me a while to get there, but I need to see you," Hogg said. The doctor said he'd be waiting.

Now Hogg had to get to Uniontown. He considered driving himself, which he preferred, but he was in no shape to take on that journey. He thought about calling his wife, but that would be calling the devil for a ride to hell.

The Chief?

He trusted him about as much as a rat in a cheese factory, but the Chief would keep his mouth shut unless he found a way to make a buck on it. Hogg figured he had enough shit on him which should keep him quiet. He had no time to mess around.

He called the Chief.

He started looking for his dick again. He looked behind doors, in the freezer, and in drawers, and then a sickening thought hit him. He went into the kitchen and stuck his hand into the disposal, grimacing at the thought. He had to calm down, think this out logically. He poured more scotch, added a little buttermilk, and went back into the den. He was about to sit in his chair when he thought better of it and sat on the sofa.

He wanted to smash something. He tried to think what a person would do with somebody else's dick. It was a problem he never faced before as a cop. He closed his eyes and dozed off. It was only a few seconds when his body jumped, his head jerked, and his eyes fluttered, opening wide.

How in the hell was he going to piss?

THE CHIEF

HE WAS DREAMING THAT HIS PHONE WAS RINGING WHEN HE realized that it wasn't a dream. As he fumbled for the phone, he saw the big red numbers glowing on the bedside clock. It was 5:03. For a moment he wasn't sure if it was morning or evening.

"Bayer," he mumbled into the phone, trying to get a better grip on it.

"Carl, this is Hogg. I have a problem and need your help."

The Chief's first thought was that Hogg had been arrested. Probably for being drunk and disorderly.

"Where are you?"

"I'm at my Stony Creek house. I had… ah, an accident and I need you to get here as fast as you can."

Hogg sounded like he was in pain.

"I'll get an ambulance down there right away and…"

"No ambulance. No police. Just you. I'll explain when you get here."

"If you need medical help, let me get somebody there to…"

"Goddamn it, Carl. I said I need you here and nobody else. Just get here and then you'll understand why this has to stay between you and me."

"Okay, okay. Do you need me to bring anything?"

"Carl," Hogg said with a forced calm, his voice painfully controlled, "You owe me this. Quit your fucking around and get your ass down here. Trust me, you will understand once you get here, now goddamn it, cut the shit and hurry," Hogg said raising his voice so loudly that it startled the Chief.

"Okay, Okay, Bill. I'm on my way. Don't get your nuts in an uproar," he said as he climbed out of bed. Hogg recoiled at the thought and groaned.

"Please hurry, Carl, and don't mention this call to anybody," he said, his voice softer.

The Chief hung up. He had to be careful. With Hogg you never knew. Although he and Hogg were loosely joined at the hip over a few dubious deals, he didn't want to step into a pile of shit. They were both cops with refutable reputations, and trust was not part of their vocabulary. The Chief believed that there was more honor among thieves than there were among cops. He liked telling the story about the union guy at a Christmas party.

A Pittsburgh millionaire held a big holiday party every year for law enforcement types. The guest list included everybody from street cops to FBI, ATF, and DEA agents. Also sprinkled among the crowd were politicians, lawyers, labor, and church leaders. It was quite a soiree that drew over 300 people who feasted on gourmet treats prepared by renowned chefs. The Chief was at the party and saw the Business Agent for the local Teamsters Union sitting on a chair over in the corner. As he approached, he noticed that the man was sitting on his topcoat.

"Hey Sal. How ya doing?" the Chief said as he approached.

"Good, Chief."

"Christ, whattya sittin' on your topcoat for? Here, give it to me and I'll hang it up."

"C'mon Chief, are you shittin' me? This coat is cashmere. Cost me a small fortune. No way I'm letting this coat outta my sight-not with all these cops in here. They'll steal it faster than a dope fiend looking for a fix."

"Sorry, Sal. I musta went under ether or something. If ya wanna move around, I'll hold it for you," the Chief said.

Sal gave the Chief a "do you think I'm that dumb" look and sat silently.

"Have a good time, Sal," the Chief said and walked away.

Right now the Chief had Hogg to worry about. Something was up, but what?

As he dressed, he replayed Hogg's phone call.

He could be hurt, but why call me? He has more gofers on his payroll than a Rockefeller has bankers. Something was fishy, and he wasn't about to get the smell on him. He'd go slow and careful and have backup in place.

Hogg never did anything that didn't benefit Hogg.

HOGG'S HOUSE

THE CHIEF MADE A QUICK STOP AT THE TOLL BOOTHS ON THE WAY to Hogg's. Whatever happened to Hogg didn't sound like he was in a death rattle or he'd have wanted an ambulance. Two of his officers were milling around the exit area, and they gave him a wave. He saw one of his patrol cars parked off to the side, fumes swirling out of the exhaust. He pulled up next to it and got out.

He looked through the window and saw Williams and LaVella sound asleep. He tapped on the window and getting no response pulled open the door. LaVella almost fell out of the car, the Chief grabbing him, feeling a wave of heat blast out of the vehicle.

"What the fu… Oh, Chief, yes sir," LaVella stammered, trying to get his words into a sentence.

"It's good to know you guys are on top of things. A fucking armored division could come rumbling through here, and you two pimples wouldn't notice it."

"No sir, I mean, yes sir, we would. The toll booth people, see they're watching us right now, they promised to alert us if anybody came through, and Nick and Zoe are over there, and we did like you asked us and got their plate numbers and, you know?" LaVella said staccato-like, rubbing sleep out of his eyes.

"No, I don't know. Now get your asses up and out. I'll send relief in about an hour. Move it."

The Chief shook his head as he got back into his vehicle and drove to Hogg's. He went through the main entrance of the housing complex that Grandma Kasser named the Bavarian Village. He parked in front of Hogg's. In the past he always went in around the back, but the goddamn snow was at least eight or nine inches deep and Hogg hadn't shoveled yet, so he went up to the front door and knocked.

Nobody answered. He knocked again, louder this time, but still no response. He tried the knob, and it turned. He went in shouting out Hogg's name. He heard Hogg mumbling something from the other room and he walked down the short hallway.

"What the fuck you coming in this way for?" Hogg said, looking bleary-eyed, a scotch in his hand, the painkiller's helping but his groin sizzling, as he sat on the sofa.

"Jesus, it's barely daylight and you're sucking down booze," the Chief said, "or are you still going from last night?"

Hogg tried to stand but fell back into the sofa.

"Are you okay?" The Chief said. Hogg didn't answer.

"So, what's the emergency?" the Chief asked.

"If you want something to drink, get it yourself," Hogg said.

"I don't want anything, and you better take it easy. You ain't ever going to see Happy Hour the way you're going," the Chief said.

"Yeah, but I need this shit right now," Hogg said, taking another drink, trying to find a starting place to tell the Chief what happened. "Take a seat," he said, gesturing towards the leather chair.

The Chief ignored him and slid the ottoman over in front of Hogg and sat down.

"So, what's going on?" The Chief asked.

How in the fuck do you tell somebody you just had your dick cut off?

"Just bear with me, Carl, please. When you hear what I have to tell you, you'll understand."

"Okay, so tell me."

"It's not that easy."

"It can't be that hard."

"You're fucking right about that," Hogg said grimacing, "and it ain't ever going to be hard," he added with a painful grunt, thinking about all the jokes that were going to be made about him if this ever got out. He wasn't sure how he was going to keep this crazy mess under wraps, but he was going to try. He needed to get to Uniontown before things got worse

He didn't want to tell the Chief anything, but he had no choice.

"What I'm about to tell you has to stay between you and me, and I mean between you and me, because if you say anything, remember, I can say some things about you that I know you don't want said," Hogg said.

"It's that serious?"

"It's that serious," Hogg said, grunting from the pain that came and went. He had two more Percocet's in his pocket.

"You know I can keep my mouth shut. Is there anything in this deal where I can get a little action?" the Chief asked.

"Goddamn it Carl, this isn't about money, it's… it's something else," he said slurring his words as he struggled to get them out.

"Okay, okay. Take it easy. C'mon, Bill. you know we know how to get things taken care of and whatever the problem is we'll find a way. It's not like you lost an arm, or something."

As punchy as Hogg was, he clenched his jaw, squinted his eyes, and gave the Chief a cold death stare.

The Chief decided to keep his mouth shut. Tiny beads of sweat formed on Hogg's forehead.

He just didn't know how to explain what happened.

There isn't an easy way to tell somebody you had your dick cut off.

HEDY

HEDY HAD AN UGLY NIGHT. DISSOCIATIVE IMAGES TRAMPLED across her mind and she was certain Hogg would come crashing through the Green Room door as a series of weird nightmares kept her from getting any rest. When she thought she heard a door close, she bolted upright in her bed. It was 5:25 AM She slipped out of bed and went to the door and put her ear up against it. She heard footsteps, but they seemed to move away from her door. She waited and listened, but the footsteps faded, and things were quiet.

She was thinking about everything she had to do. No way she was going back to sleep.

She wondered if the noise she heard was the Chief. He had a room at the end of the hallway. She didn't think he was an early riser, so if it was him, what got him up?

Her first thought was they found Hogg's body and called the Chief. She felt the chill in the room and shivered. She wanted to climb back into bed, bury herself deep under the covers and never come out, but she knew better.

Trembling, she dressed quickly as she willed herself into fight mode. She wouldn't buckle because of an asshole like Hogg. She started planning out her next steps. She'd go back to her condo and start from there. She had to get rid of any incriminating evidence as fast as possible.

Damn, I still have his penis.

She gathered everything up, carefully scanned the room, and softly closed the door behind her. She checked the hallway, especially where the Chief's room was, but noticed nothing. She repeated her route down the back stairs to the garage. As she passed the kitchen she hesitated, debating whether to grind the damn thing up, but she wasn't sure she could work the food disposal. She'd dump it somewhere else. Getting back to her condo was job one right now.

Who would believe I have a man's penis in my purse?

She gunned the Yamaha to life and headed for her condo. As she powered her way over the fresh snow, the blackness shaded to a gray as dawn forced out the night.

It was going to be a long day.

HOGG

THE CHIEF WATCHED AND WAITED. SOMETHING WAS GOING ON with Hogg, probably too much booze, but the guy seemed drugged. When the Chief saw Hogg's eyes drooping, he figured he had to do something, or he was going to leave.

"Okay, Bill," the Chief said, as they sat in Hogg's plaid room, "I ain't gonna say a thing so let's get to it. You know I can zip it tighter than a gnat's pussy, so what's going on? I got shit I have to take care of, so I don't have time to fool around."

Hogg couldn't believe any of this was happening. He was hoping he'd wake up and find out it was all a bad dream. He didn't know how to tell the Chief what happened. He had been in a lot of tough spots before, but none like this one.

There was no field manual for severed penises.

"I had an accident," Hogg said haltingly, "an unusual accident."

"You look a little beat-up," the Chief said, "You were moving like somebody stuck a nightstick up your ass."

"Goddamn it Carl, let me say this my way, okay? Just listen."

"I'm listening."

"Okay. When you hear what happened, you'll understand."

The Chief nodded. He wasn't sure what was going on, but Hogg was certainly stretching it out.

He looks like he's gonna cry.

Hogg took another gulp of scotch, wiped his mouth, and let out a deep sigh.

"Okay, and I don't want you laughing or anything, thinking I'm joking. This is fuckin' serious."

"O-kay," the Chief said, stretching out the O and K, now curious.

Hogg took a deep breath and blurted it out. "My dick's been cut off!"

He stared at Hogg. He heard what he said. He wondered what was going on in that sick head of his. Was Hogg trying to pull off some weird, sick joke? He studied Hogg's face.

What in the fuck is he trying to pull off?

"What do you mean your dick's been cut off?"

Hogg frowned. He knew this would happen. He shook his head and then got pissed.

"What in the hell do you think I mean? My fucking dick, that thing between my legs, my cock, it's been cut off. Do you understand me? It's been cut OFF," Hogg yelled his head falling back against the sofa in disgust.

"Your dick, ah, your penis. It's been cut off. You sure?"

Hogg glowered at the Chief. "Am I fucking sure? No, Carl, let me look again. Maybe it came back, you know, just walked back in and hooked itself right back up."

"Well, okay, but how did it happen, I mean did somebody whack the thing off or...?"

"What the fuck does that matter right now, Carl? I need help. I don't know who cut it off. The dick is gone," Hogg said, and then thinking about it, straightened up and yelled frantically, "Damn Carl, check the house out, quick, if we can find it, we can save it like they did with that Bobbitt guy's dick."

Hogg's lost all of his marbles. He's on LSD or something.

"Take it easy, Bill. Easy. I'll find your... I'll find it for you. Just tell me what happened," the Chief said, trying to calm him down.

"I can't tell you what happened. I don't know what happened. I think I was drugged."

"Let me understand what you're telling me. You're saying that your dick's been cut off?" The Chief said loudly, enunciating each word and adding extra pauses between them just to make certain he was being crystal clear. He had to walk Hogg down from whatever was fucking up his head.

"Yes," said a tired, drunk, doped up Hogg, barely audible.

"Are you sure?"

There was a long pause. Hogg was struggling to explain. Then a dark look eclipsed his face. His eyes widened, and he leaned forward, glowering, his words coming out choppy, but clear.

"What in the fuck do you mean 'am I sure'?"

The Chief studied Hogg's face. It looked like it had been chiseled out of a ham.

"Okay, well yeah. Sure, you're sure. So, you don't have a dick," the Chief said gesturing towards Hogg's groin, "down there?"

"No, Carl, not down there, not over there, not anywhere. I don't have a fucking dick, No cock. No penis, no nothing," he said, his voice cracking.

"Well, that is… unusual," the Chief said. A plethora of funny lines looped through his mind. He shook them out.

Hogg was exhausted. He mumbled. "I gotta get to my Doctor in Uniontown."

"Sure, Bill. Not a problem. Why don't you lie down for a while and then I'll get you to your doctor where he'll make everything better again? Just lie down there on your sofa and rest for now."

He doesn't believe me.

Pulling himself to an upright sitting position, Hogg reached out his hand.

"Help me get up," he said as calmly as he could. He was woozy.

"Why don't you lie down and…"

"Help me up. Please," Hogg said, his arm tiring from holding it out.

The Chief sighed. Got up from the ottoman, took Hogg's hand and pulled him up.

"Thank you," Hogg mumbled. He wobbled a bit, and the Chief steadied him.

"Please, Carl. Please. Do me this favor. Ah, just sit back down on the ottoman, okay? I'm fine. Just sit."

The Chief shrugged and sat down.

"From this moment on, nothing leaves this room. Got it Carl?"

The Chief nodded. Best to go along with him right now.

"Fine, because if you ever say a word, I'll kill you," Hogg said his eyes seeming to clear up.

"I'll never say a word, Bill," the Chief said humoring him. "You can tell me."

The Chief thought that whatever Hogg was going to tell him could be worth something in the future.

"I'm going to trust you, Carl," he said as he undid his belt, "and if you ever say a word, you know what I can do, Carl." The Chief kept his eyes locked into Hoggs.

"You have my word," the Chief said when Hogg suddenly let his pants drop.

The Chief almost fell back off the ottoman. All he saw was a silver bandage with a bloody edge around Hogg's middle. He spun around and got up off the ottoman and backed up a step or two.

"Jeez, Bill, what in the hell happened?" the Chief asked. He still wasn't sure if Hogg was telling the truth. It could be a sick joke or some sort of setup.

"This is what happened, you dumb fuck," Hogg said. "Some son-of-a-bitch cut my dick off. Do you get it now, Carl?"

"Okay, so you're saying you don't have a dick... ah penis... ah, where it should be. Is that what you're saying?" the Chief said, still wondering if this was some sort of trick.

Hogg felt everything draining from him. He gathered up what strength he had and took a step towards the Chief who backed up a step.

"Do you want to see it? Do I have to take off this... this bandage? My dick's been cut off, Carl and I need help," Hogg said pleading now.

The Chief stayed silent.

"Carl, I want you to listen to me carefully. I am not crazy." His voice was cold and firm. "Somebody cut off my penis, the thing I fuck and piss with, that thing that hangs between men's legs. This is not a setup. I need help now, and if you don't get it for me, I'll see you rot in hell," he barked and then sat down on the sofa and closed his eyes. He was wobbly and weary and had nothing left.

The Chief looked at an exhausted Hogg.

"Whoa, Bill. Sorry. What do you want me to do?" the Chief asked now thinking the son-of-a-bitch may have had his dick cut off.

"Drive me to Uniontown," Hogg pleaded, "now,"

"Easy, Bill. Are you okay now? I mean when did this happen? Are you bleeding?"

"It happened last night, and the bleeding has stopped, but not the pain. In fact, I'm gonna take another couple a Percocet's once you say you'll get me back to Uniontown. You owe me that much, Carl."

"Okay, I'll get you there but, ah, like where is your dick? I mean is it... do you still have it... or did somebody... shit, Bill... I ain't ever been on a cock-cutting case."

Hogg's eyes went cold, and his jaw tightened. He leaned forward, locked his eyes on the Chief's, and in a very controlled voice said, "Carl, I am telling you the truth. I have a serious problem and I need your help. Now, you're either going to help me or I'm going to..." Hogg's voice broke out into a yell, "BLOW YOUR FUCKING BRAINS OUT. NOW HELP ME."

"Whoa, man. Okay. I have to ask questions. It's not every day somebody gets their cock cut off. You know what I mean?"

Hogg nodded and let out a groan of pain.

"You couldn't of picked a worst time to get your dick cut off. I can't leave. Stony Creek was robbed last night."

"I don't give a fuck if the place burned down," Hogg ranted, and then caught himself, "Stony Creek was robbed? You're bull shittin' me?"

"No, sometime after eight some guy comes in and robs the money room and gets away with a lot of cash. The states are here and more will be coming so I got a big mess on my hands."

"Goddamn it, Carl. I could die." Hogg was using every bit of his strength to stay awake, but he was losing ground.

"Let me get an ambulance and get you to the hospital. They'll take care of you," the Chief said,

"I told you I don't want anybody to know what happened. Would you want people to know you had your dick cut off? For Christ's sakes, think about that, Carl."

"You make a good point," the Chief said with a slight smile. "Okay, give me a minute. I can't do it. I got the robbery. Maybe I can get somebody." No way was the Chief going to get involved any deeper.

Hogg didn't want anybody else, but he was too tired to argue anymore.

"You don't tell them a fucking thing, Carl, not a fucking word, or I will blow your head off," Hogg said, his eyes glaring at the Chief. "We gotta hurry, Carl."

"Okay, okay, keep your nuts in your..." the Chief stopped in mid-sentence, "Let me think this out."

The Chief paced around a little, trying to come up with somebody to get Hogg to Uniontown. One thing was certain. He wasn't going to do it.

"Jesus, I didn't think about it. How are you gonna piss?" the Chief said.

Hogg's eyes narrowed; his face appeared to puff up as if he were about to explode. He tried to get up out of the sofa, but he was too wobbly. He fell back in a heap, exasperated. If eyes could sneer, Hogg's were sneering.

"Okay, Bill. I'll get you outta here. I have to make some calls,"

He called Max Barron.

"Max, Chief Bayer. Hey, I need a little help. Do you have anybody going into Uniontown in the next hour?"

"No, sorry. I don't have anybody," Barron said, not wanting to lose any staff.

"Max, this is a major emergency. It has to do with the robbery, but I can't get into detail. I need somebody to drive into Uniontown immediately. I thought you might have somebody that you could loan me."

Barron thought about it for a moment and realized he had no choice. The robbery was too big.

"I do have a kid on my crew who lives there but I really need him, what with all this snow and… look Chief, I'll do you a favor, but it's going to hurt me and …"

"Max, this is police business, and I won't forget it. The next time you need a little help you can count on me," the Chief said. "Have him come to Sheriff Hogg's house pronto. You know where that is. I'll meet him there."

The Chief hung up and looked at Hogg. Even a sick Hogg with no dick was dangerous. Maybe even more so. He was convinced that Hogg was born with some kind of evil genetic malformation that required an exorcist.

"A kid from the ground crew is on his way. Do you need help?" the Chief asked.

"Nah, I can make it. Is he coming right away?"

"Yeah, should be here in about five minutes."

"Good. I couldn't check out the place. Maybe you could look around and ..."

"No problem." The Chief went room by room downstairs and then did a fast check upstairs. Never in his life did he think that there would come a day that he'd be looking for a man's lost dick. This one is for the books. Worse yet, what if he finds the damn thing?

It wasn't a picture-perfect search, but the Chief looked in every logical place for Hogg's penis. The thing was that the place was undisturbed, so if somebody came in and chopped off his cock, they didn't leave any mess behind except for Hogg. The place was clean, so they probably took the dick with them. They could have dumped it in the woods anywhere. Hell, with a cold winter and a lot of snow the thing could stay frozen until spring. The Chief smiled at the thought of a spring dick hunt. He imagined lines of people tramping through the woods looking for a man's cock. He chuckled when he thought about what would happen when they found it.

"Sorry Bill, no luck. Any idea who the perp could be. Probably somebody you know," The Chief said. "Ain't no for-hire cock-cutters on the streets that I know."

Hogg ignored the Chief's musings.

"I appreciate it, Carl. Thanks."

The Chief wanted to say, "Just call me anytime you have your cock cut off" but refrained and muttered out "Anytime" and stuttered his way out by adding, "well, not, I mean, glad I could ... look, just get better. I'm sure they have transplants 'n stuff like that ..." the Chief said, his voice trailing off.

Hogg just stared at him with a look that confirmed the Chief's suspicion.

Fucking Hogg needs an exorcist.

HEDY

ONCE SHE WAS IN HER CONDO, HEDY RAN THROUGH HER post-surgery checklist and began the process. It took her longer than she expected because she burned everything she could in her fireplace. She'd dump the scalpels in a couple of different trash cans around the resort, and she still had to do something with the penis. Although she never used the burdizzo, she sanitized it and threw it into her utensil drawer. She could use it to crimp her home-made raviolis.

Dawn had punched its way into the first day of the New Year by the time Hedy arrived at Heidi's condo. Heidi's door was locked, which surprised her. She rang the bell and banged on the door when a sleepy-eyed Heidi finally answered as Hedy was digging through her bag for a key.

Heidi, moving around trance-like, made her way to the sofa where she curled up and closed her eyes while Hedy made a pot of coffee. She handed Heidi a steaming cup, warning her it was hot and to sip carefully, and sat down next to her.

"God, what happened last night?" Heidi said, "One minute I'm talking to you and then nothing. Everything's a blank and I have a terrible headache."

"After you drank some champagne, you got a little woozy, so I told you to lie down on the sofa. You did and zonked. You must have been pretty tired. Then I stopped back here late last night and walked you into bed. Don't you remember that?"

"I don't. Jesus, what knocked me out? I wasn't tired. I can't believe this. Did anybody call?" Heidi said rapidly. She took another sip of the coffee and put her cup on the table.

"Not while I was here."

"I can't believe I slept like that. I've got to make some calls," she said, getting up and pacing around the room.

"What calls?" Hedy asked.

"Just calls. People I was going to meet, stuff like that."

"Go ahead and make them. It's okay with me," Hedy said.

"Well, they waited this long, so they can wait longer. It's not that important, I guess?" she said as she nervously walked around in little circles.

"You look worried. I hope it's nothing serious."

"It's not, it's just that … oh, no matter."

"Go ahead, finish."

"No, that's it. It'll all work out."

"Well, maybe it will, and maybe it won't," Hedy said.

"What do you mean?"

"I know about you and Hogg."

"What about me and Hogg?"

"Heidi, cut the crap. Some things happened last night that I need to tell you about and you need to be honest with me or we'll both have serious problems."

"I don't understand what you're talking about," Heidi said, putting on her best innocent face.

"Heidi, I love you, and I'd do anything for you, so please, don't bullshit me and listen, because a lot of things happened while you were sleeping."

Heidi's face became almost childlike as she sheepishly asked her sister, "What happened?"

Hedy felt her stomach flutter. She had no idea how she was going to tell her sister she cut off her lover's penis. She wondered if anybody else ever had to do it. She doubted it.

"Please, come over here and sit next to me," Hedy said, patting a spot on the white sofa.

Heidi slid into her submissive little girl mode, something Hedy suspected she did with Hogg. They were sitting close to each other. Hedy put her arm around Heidi and pulled her close.

"I want you to listen, and wait until I'm finished," Hedy said, "before you do or say anything. Okay, honey?"

"Okay," Heidi whimpered, snuggling up to her sister.

"A long time ago, an evil man did something to me that I never told anybody about," she began, as if she were telling a bedtime story to a child.

"One night, when I was walking home, that man jumped out from the bushes, threw me to the ground, and brutally raped me. Do you understand?"

"My God, Hedy, who did this to you? Oh my God, you're joking, no you're not joking," Heidi said, sitting straight up and looking at her sister.

"I know you're going to find this hard to believe Heidi, but it was Hogg," Hedy said, tightening her arm around Heidi, who struggled out of her grasp, finally getting loose and standing.

She knew what she heard, or did she? She stood there, unbelieving, trying to process what Hedy said to her.

"It's true, Heidi. Hogg raped me. I wouldn't lie to you and you know that."

"You're just saying that," she yelled, "because you don't want me with him," hoping that was the reason but deep down she knew better. Hedy wouldn't lie about a thing like that.

Heidi started pacing around the room, rubbing her throat, squeezing her eyes shut, opening them, and shaking her head, hoping those little gestures would somehow help. She didn't know what to do or say, finally uttering, "When?" "Where?"

Hedy told Heidi about the rape. She covered it from the beginning, describing every step in detail, pausing to let the sordidness sink in, demonstrating the fear and pain she felt with gasps, tears, and grimaces.

Heidi just stood there, transfixed. When Hedy finished, she got up from the sofa and stood face-to-face with her sister, and quietly said, "He raped me, Heidi, Hogg brutally raped me!"

Tears filled Heidi's eyes as she tried to absorb the horror she was hearing. There was no way her sister would lie about something like that, but it was still hard to believe. She looked at her sister's face and saw the pain in her eyes. Poor Hedy. All these years she's been going through hell. Guilt flooded Heidi, and she reached out to her sister. They embraced, gently at first, and then tightly, almost desperately.

They stood in the middle of the white living room, hanging on to each other, both wailing and weeping. Finally, Hedy pulled back, wiped some tears away from her sister's face, and looked directly into her eyes.

"It's true, Heidi. Every word, and last night I got even for both of us. Come back to the sofa and sit down and I'll tell you what I did," Hedy said feeling more confident.

Heidi obediently followed her sister to the sofa and sat as instructed. She was searching her mind for some sort of logic. She couldn't find any.

Hedy held Heidi in her arms, letting everything sink in. She had to take her time with Heidi. Hedy cuddled with her, holding her close as her sobs turned to whimpers, occasionally brushing Heidi's hair with her hand.

When Hedy felt her relax, she said, "Everything's going to be fine, darling. You trust me, don't you?" Hedy could feel Heidi nodding under her arms.

"What I'm going to tell you will shock you, maybe even scare you, but I promise you, everything will be fine. You know I wouldn't let anything happen to you."

Hedy told her she went to Hogg's, and that he thought she was Heidi. She explained that she wanted to hurt him, to do something like he did to her, but she didn't want to kill him, just cause him pain. There was no easy way to explain that you cut off somebody's penis.

"Honey, this may sound awful, but it was necessary. I took away Hogg's weapon. I took away the one thing that the madman used to harm women like you and me. Somebody had to stop him, and I did. As horrible as this may sound, Heidi, it wasn't that bad," she said slowly.

Heidi snuggled closer to her sister, listening to her but not really hearing, her mind spinning uncontrollably, when Hedy's next words sliced through her like a razor blade.

"I cut off his penis," she blurted.

No response.

"Did you hear me, honey? I cut off his penis. He will never rape again," she said, "at least not with the one he used on me."

Hedy could feel Heidi tense and then she unraveled herself from her sister's warm, safe embrace, sat up and looked directly into Hedy's eyes.

"You did what?"

"I amputated his penis."

Heidi stared at her, trying to discern whether this was some sort of joke, but Hedy's face was dead serious.

Did she hear that right?

"You amputated…?"

"I cut off his fucking dick, Heidi," she said loudly, "He doesn't have a hickey anymore."

Heidi studied her sister's face. She shook her head from side to side and just stared trancelike at Hedy.

"Okay," Heidi said a little more firmly, running her hand thorough her hair, and pulling her shoulders back, "Let me understand. Did you say you cut off his…ah… his penis?"

"Yes, Heidi, I cut off his dick, his thing, his cock. It's gone. Kaput."

"All of it?"

"Yes, Heidi, all of it."

"With what?" Heidi said as if the instrument she used would change things.

"A scalpel."

"You cut off his penis, with a scalpel?" she repeated, looking like she might go into some sort of shock.

"Are you okay?"

"How can I be okay," she said as the reality of it sank in. She got up from the sofa.

"How can I be okay when you just told me you cut off, that you… you removed a man's penis?"

Regaining some composure, Heidi stiffened up and in a firm voice said, "Are you crazy, Hedy?"

"Calm down, honey. Come sit for a moment. It'll be alright. You'll see after I explain."

"I can't believe this. Please wake me up. Tell me this is a bad dream," Heidi said, as she paced around the room again.

Hedy let her get it all out.

"You really cut off his … hickey? You really did?"

Hedy just nodded as Heidi continued her pacing, mumbling, "Oh my God."

"Is he still alive? God, Hedy, please don't tell me you killed him."

I didn't kill him, Heidi. I just wanted to hurt him, like he did to me and like he would do to you."

"You cut off the whole thing?" she asked, still incredulous.

"Well," Hedy said, "As gross as it sounds, I cut off as much as I could. I don't think there's even a stub left. He is now dickless, cockless, hickleyless," Hedy said getting up and standing eyeball to eyeball with her sister.

They stared at each other and Heidi broke first, and in a flash they were laughing and crying at the same time, hugging each other, rocking in each other's arms.

"God, how's he going to pee?" Heidi asked, stifling a nervous laugh between tears.

"That's funny. I thought the same thing," Hedy giggled, "I guess it just dribbles out," she laughed.

"I can't believe it. Bill Hogg without a penis. That's like giving him an AR-15 without bullets," Heidi chuckled, trying to joke her way out of the moment.

"More like giving him a free lifetime pass to a whorehouse," Hedy countered with a deep laugh.

Exhausted, they both fell on to the sofa and sat there for a moment. Reality checked back in.

"Jesus, Hedy, what are we going to do?"

"It's okay, honey. It will be okay. I've covered everything."

Hedy told her only what she needed to know. The less she knew, the better.

"Hogg won't call the police, and if he does, all you have to do is tell the truth. If necessary, you'll take a lie detector test and that'll do it. I don't think it'll ever come to that."

"God, I hope you're right," Heidi said, and then thinking about it said, "Does he know you did it? "

Hedy fudged the truth. "I'm not sure, honey. He was drugged. Right now, there's nothing to worry about."

They sat on the sofa for a while, Hedy hugging Heidi, brushing her hair with her fingers, gently telling her it was all going to be good.

After a few minutes of quiet, Hedy said she had to leave.

"Will you be okay, sweetie?" Hedy said.

"I'm okay," Heidi said, slipping back into her little girl's voice.

"I'll stay if you want me to," Hedy said.

"No, really, I'm better. You go ahead and do what you have to do."

"Always remember, he had it coming," Hedy said as she walked away.

"He did, Hedy. He had it coming."

"One very important thing, darling. Do not discuss this with anybody. Nobody... and whatever you do, don't talk to Hogg. If he calls you, and I doubt he will, at least not now, do not talk with him. Call me and I'll handle it. Truly honey, there's nothing to worry about. It will be okay. Hogg's not going to do anything. He'll be too busy trying to figure out what to do without a penis," Hedy said, grabbing her coat and walking over to the fridge.

"I need a Coke or something to drink," she said, her mouth like cotton, as she opened the fridge and looked around.

"Mind if I steal this cannoli? It looks scrumptious," Hedy said, thinking something sweet would erase the foul taste in her mouth.

"No, take it. I'm not sure I can eat anything right now."

She grabbed the cannoli and a bottle of Perrier. Hedy found a Baggie, dumped the cannoli into it, took her water, and went to the door. Just before she opened it, she called over to Heidi.

"I totally forgot. Happy New Year, darling."

"Ah, yeah, thanks. Same to you."

"Oh, and one more thing, Heidi. I'd get rid of that buttermilk. You won't need it anymore," Hedy said as she went out the door.

THE CHIEF

MIKE BARRON'S GUY WAS AT THE FRONT DOOR. HOGG MUMBLED out that they were coming as the Chief helped him on with his coat. With all the drugs and booze in his system, it's a wonder that Hogg wasn't on a stretcher.

"You know where you're going?" the Chief asked, as they made their way to the front door. He held Hogg's arm to steady him.

"Yeah, I know," Hogg mumbled, "and this stays between us, right?

"Right, Bill. Don't worry, I'll lock everything up. I think it's important that you get to Uniontown as quickly as you can. Hogg tried to say something but couldn't get it out.

A skinny young kid with stringy light brown hair a pale white face and an undeveloped mustache, about 18 or 19, was standing there. Parked next to the Chief's car, the motor running, was his 1995 Jeep Wrangler soft-top.

"You old enough to drive," the Chief said.

"Yes sir, I have my driver's license right here," he said reaching for the back pocket of his skinny jeans, but the Chief stopped him with a wave of his hand.

"Get him to where he has to go and drive carefully, or I'll shove that toy car of yours up your ass."

The kid shook his head in the affirmative, taking Hogg's arm to help him. Hogg tried to shake him off but didn't have the strength. It took some doing, but the kid finally got him into the Jeep.

The Chief stood outside the front door and waited until they were out of sight. He wasn't about to let an opportunity like this pass by. He'd check out Hogg's house thoroughly. Maybe he'd find the penis, the thought causing him to cringe, and he might find something that would give him a little insurance. Hogg was pretty drugged up so maybe he got a little sloppy not locking everything up. The Chief had no idea what he was looking for. He always remembered a line an old street cop once told him, "When you don't know what you're looking for, look at everything."

The first place the Chief headed for was Hogg's chair. He wasn't sure that's where the deed took place, but it was a good bet. He turned on the overhead lights. He searched around the chair and found some blood spots. The cutter who did this, and that could be a long list of men and women, really cleaned up things. He was sure that Hogg knew the perp.

The Chief was betting it was a female. No man would slice off another man's dick unless he was a pansy or a fence sitter.

The Chief checked out the house, but he saw nothing unusual. Whoever was here left little, not even a lipstick-stained glass, which was the obvious clue. He saw an open bottle of scotch on the kitchen counter and found some glasses in the dishwasher, but they all looked as if they had been wiped clean. He smelled bleach, which said this could have been a professional hit, but who would take the job of cutting a man's dick off? No respectable hit man would take that whack job.

He looked in the fridge and saw an assortment of soft drinks, beer, champagne, and the usual stuff. There was also a carton of buttermilk, and not much food except for some eggs in a plastic bowl.

He checked the doors for any sign of forced entry, but they were intact, confirming his belief that it was somebody Hogg knew. Out back he saw a lot of footprints, mostly covered over, so he wasn't sure how old they were when he noticed that a pair went to the side of the house. He stepped outside and followed them around the corner. Somebody had been here. He plodded through the heavy snow and noticed there were signs of activity around the window. It looked like somebody rolled around in the snow and was doing something, probably looking in the window. Maybe it was the cock cutter.

The Chief wasn't sure what in the hell took place, but somebody had been there. He couldn't tell if the tracks and indentations in the snow were made by a man or woman, but somebody was peeking.

When he made his way to the back patio, he saw the plastic supermarket cases had been moved. Maybe to stand on for a better view. Looking at the height of the window and the plastic case, it could well be a woman. Whoever it was probably didn't know Hogg or wasn't welcome. Otherwise, why go through all that trouble.

He went back in and looked through all the closets and seeing nothing unusual, went back upstairs. He found a light switch that turned on an overhead at the top of the stairs. The bedrooms looked untouched, and he noticed it was colder, meaning that the thermostat was probably turned down. The place was clean.

He stood in the hallway for a moment, sure nobody had been up there, and was just about to leave when he spotted something on the floor. He leaned over and saw that it was a paper matchstick. He also noted that the carpet had indentations in it.

Jesus. This is right out of an old Humphrey Bogart movie.

He picked up the bent matchstick, squinted at it for a moment, and then looked up at the ceiling.

OTTO

OTTO WAS LIKE HIS MOTHER. HARD WORKING, SUCCESS ORIENTED, yet never satisfied with his accomplishments, and always feeling he had to do more. He was tiring of the daily grind. He thought how different his life could be without the bullshit obligations which he woke up to every day, but finding a successor was a problem. Henry, his son, wasn't interested, or capable, much to Otto's disappointment. The only person competent enough was Hedy. and Otto wasn't ready for her. Once she gained power, she'd throw him to the wolves so when the Swiss called, Otto answered.

They wanted to buy Stony Creek.

Although he felt he was ready to make a move, he resisted the Swiss overtures at first, not as a negotiating ploy, but simply because he was uncertain about selling, but the Swiss were persistent. They wanted Stony Creek and upped the ante. Otto saw it as his duty to take care of the family, and the Swiss offer would certainly do that. It was also nice of them to recognize his hard work and leadership over the years by offering him a private side deal that he certainly deserved. Of course, that would be strictly between him and the Swiss.

Otto presented the Swiss offer to the family. He said he was doing it because the rules said so but he took no position. He was casual about it, presenting a brief overview, skipping details but it didn't get past Hedy. While the others were as casual as Otto, Hedy wanted all the documents. He gave them to her, and a vote was scheduled for the annual family meeting.

Although Otto brushed off the deal, Hedy was leery.

Hedy made her position clear. Grandma Kasser would never sell out, and neither would Hedy. Hedy was sure about Heidi's and her mother's vote, and that would kill any deal. Otto needed to get Rosie on board. He planted a few seeds in Rosie's mind about the toll running Stony Creek took on their lives. It was something Rosie continually complained about. The seeds grew.

It never entered Hedy's mind that her mother would vote against her, so she paid little attention to that possibility.

"Otto, this kills me, but I can't let Hedy tie up her life in this place. I saw what it did to Mom and Dad, and to you and me, and I want her to go out and have a normal life, well, as normal as possible when you're a millionaire. She'll be angry with me, but I know it's for the better," Rosie surmised.

Otto felt comfortable that Rosie would keep her word. She honestly believed that she was doing the right thing for Hedy. With his vote, his son's, and Rosie's he had the majority.

Initially, Rosie felt certain she could get Heidi's vote. She explained to her how the resort would ruin Hedy's life, and the money they received from the sale would enable them to travel the world together on a champagne and caviar budget. At first, Heidi was receptive but over time Rosie sensed a change.

They didn't need Heidi's vote, but Rosie wanted her to be on board. It would help dilute Hedy's reaction, which was expected to be strong.

During this time Otto received news that was disturbing.

One of the resort's employees spotted Heidi going into Hogg's house. He thought little of it until he saw her doing it a few more times. The gossip reached Otto.

Otto heard talk about Hogg and Heidi but discounted it until the employee confirmed it. Otto agonized over it for a time and decided that his best course was to confront Hogg. They had a close relationship, so he didn't think it would be difficult, but Hogg was unpredictable.

"Otto, I have to be honest with you because you're my friend," Hogg said.

Otto braced himself.

"I think she had a crush on me," he said, "and she sought my advice, and I gave it to her, but Otto, when she came on to me, I explained to her in very clear terms that we could only be friends. I thought she handled it okay. The rumors started when, as her friend, and at her request, we got together and talked. She just needed somebody to talk to, like a father, and I did. That's probably what started the bullshit."

Otto wasn't sure that Hogg was being truthful, but it sounded plausible. Heidi was the clingy type, always looking for advice and guidance.

"She even asked me my thoughts on whether she should vote in favor of the sale," Hogg said.

"She told you about the sale?"

"Well, not in detail. She just said that there were people interested in buying Stony Creek, and she made sure I understood that offers came in regularly, so this was no big deal, but she just wondered what I thought about it."

"So, what did you tell her?"

"What do you think? I don't get into other people's business unless I'm invited. I told her she should do what she thought was right. I don't know what's going on Otto, but if there's any direction you want me to lead her, you know I'll do that for you."

"Yeah, I know. No, there's no reason for you to get involved."

"You sure? I'll help you any way I can."

"If I need you, I'll let you know."

With the family meeting coming up in a few hours, Otto was confident that he was about to complete his future.

He looked at his watch. He had to hurry. He had to meet Foley at 8 AM.

FOLEY

FOLEY OPENED HIS EYES, AND FOR A MOMENT, HE DIDN'T REMEMBER where he was. He looked at the bedside clock. The room was pitch black, but the glow from the bedside clock told him it was 6:00 AM. He jumped out of bed and opened the drapes. It was still dark, and the slopes were already busy with day pass skiers amortizing their entry fee.

Happy New Year, he grumbled to himself.

He thought Linda was still sleeping on the sofa because he heard no sounds. He quickly pulled on his jeans and slipped into the living room. The drapes were still closed, but he could see she left. He switched on one of the table lamps. The blanket she used was folded neatly on the sofa. That puzzled Foley. He doubted her sister drove up this early, but with the way things were going, anything was possible.

He went back into the bedroom and turned on the light. That's when he saw them.

Over in the far corner of the bedroom was her luggage, a small overnight bag and a larger traveler, the familiar green/red/green signature of Gucci. Even though she couldn't afford it, Linda's choice of designer labels was her way of elevating herself out of her modest upbringing. Her fashion tastes were expensive, but on the conservative side, staying with muted colors and tailored business-like attire. Her most casual outfit was jeans and simple tops and she rarely wore shorts, although she did a great deal of justice to a bikini. She didn't like her small breasts, but they fit her body perfectly.

Foley wasn't sure where she went, but she wouldn't leave without her luggage.

Foley showered, the steamy water feeling good. He wasn't sure when a shower became his go-to place for meditation, healing and thinking. It was as if the hot water flowing down around his body was like a heated blanket that insulated him from the outside world. It was a renewing experience that washed the debris out of his mind, cleansing his thinking, as he thought about the Linda problem.

Standing under the cascading water, he tried to rationalize the bizarre situation with her. If she wanted to end their relationship, there were easier ways to do it than run off and get married. That just wasn't a normal act. Either that or she had mental issues. She had a history of panic attacks, so it was possible that's what happened. If so, this was the mother of them all. He had to get more information on panic attacks. People do rash things when they're under a lot of pressure but going through the entire process of a wedding and honeymoon was a giant leap.

Or did she get married to protect herself from Foley? It could be a combination of all these things. There was the unthinkable. Maybe she was using him the entire time. The thought that she may have suckered him was a thought he didn't want to have, but it crept in.

The only thing Foley knew for certain was that he knew nothing. It would take an army of shrinks to clean up this mess.

The other problem was his company. She was the key employee, and a major part of the future. He could see her as the chief operating officer in a few short years, and he didn't want to lose her.

But this time a hot shower failed him because he exited the same way he went in—uncertain.

He shaved, dressed, putting on jeans and the Ralph Lauren V-neck cashmere sweater she bought him for his birthday, and headed down to the coffee shop. As he neared the elevator, the door slid open, and there was Linda.

"Imagine running into you here," he said, smiling.

"Went to get coffee," she said, holding a takeout box with two cups of coffee.

"Jesus, thanks, but I'll take a rain check. I have that meeting with Otto at 8 and I'm going to meet the old man first. Actually, you should come," he said, holding the elevator door open.

"Oh, ah, I would like to, but I need to get back to the little girl's room, plus I have some other things to do. You go ahead. You don't really need me."

He did need her, but he let it drop. It also annoyed him when people used "little girl's and little boy's" room, as if that would somehow make a normal human function less uncomfortable. What was wrong with "bathroom?" The elevator door kept trying to close, and he kept pushing it back.

"Okay, but I can wait," he said as the door made another attempt to close.

"No, please go ahead. I'll talk with you later," she said with a smile, and brushed past him. He let the door close and did what most people do on the elevator—he watched the floor lights above the door blink on and off.

She said she was going to annul the marriage, but did she really mean that or was she just saying that to keep him at bay? But then why keep him on the hook?

Foley had seen a lot in his relatively young life, but he was a rookie about love.

He felt like he was trying to swim in quicksand.

THE ALPINE ROOM

THE CHIEF WAS RUNNING LATE FOR HIS MEETING WITH FOLEY AND called to tell him he may not make it. Foley said he was already on his way and he'd be in the coffee shop.

The Chief had more important things to do. He needed to cover his visit to Hogg's.

He called one of his officers and told him he had been out checking the perimeter, including the front gate, and would be back as soon as he could. The officer told him the state police investigators arrived and wanted to meet with him. He said he'd be there shortly and to send in LaVella and Williams for questioning.

With the old man canceling, Foley had time to kill. Rather than going back to the room, he grabbed a newspaper and sat reading it in the coffee shop, waiting for Otto.

The meeting with Otto went well. They arrived at a monthly fee quickly. Otto told Foley to draw up a proposal and get it to him ASAP. Otto wrote Foley a check for the first month's fee. The meeting lasted less than twenty minutes.

When Foley got back, Linda was watching television. She turned it off and rose from the sofa.

"How was your meeting?" she asked.

"Short, but good. We got a year's contract at five a month plus expenses. We need to get a proposal to him right away."

"That's great. Congratulations."

He felt the tension. He brought up the elephant in the room.

"I guess you'll be leaving. I saw your suitcases," he said, still standing just inside the door. She hadn't moved either.

"I think it's better right now."

"Could be," Foley said, moving into the room. "I don't think I can drive you," he said, knowing that she made arrangements.

"My sister is on her way."

"Okay, so that's it, I guess."

There was a momentary pause as they stood there, both uncomfortable. Linda broke the silence.

"Foley let me work this out. I am not going to go to Philadelphia," she said, forgetting that she hadn't told Foley about Bobby's job with his father's company.

"What's with Philadelphia?"

"Ah, nothing, really. He's going to work there for his father."

"And you were supposed to go?

"We discussed it, but I'm staying here. Please, Foley, give me a little time to straighten all of this out," she said, her face soft and pleading.

Foley didn't know whether to kick her ass or hug her. From what he knew, he should tell her to go live her life without him, but he couldn't bring himself to do it. He thought it possible that she did something she didn't want to do. He wanted to leave that door open so she could correct the situation.

"Do you want to be married to Bobby? It's a simple question."

She looked at him for a moment and then bent her head, looking at her hands as she kept clasping and unclasping them.

"No," she said quietly.

"Then get it resolved," he said, feeling more in control.

"I will," she said in a subdued voice, but regained her composure and spoke louder, "I'll get it worked out."

Foley wasn't sure about anything, and the little cop's voice in his head kept saying. "Cut her loose," but he just couldn't bring himself to do it. Maybe he was more in love with her than he realized. The ringing of the phone in his pocket broke into his thoughts. Foley caught Linda's eyes, and she returned his gaze for a fraction and then turned and went into the bedroom. Foley retrieved his phone and answered. It was the Chief.

"How'd it go with Otto?" the Chief asked.

"Fine. Hey, I'm tied up right now. Can I call you back?"

"Meet me in my office in fifteen minutes?"

Foley, anxious to get off the phone, agreed and hung up. He headed for the bedroom, but Linda came out carrying her suitcases.

"Do you need help?"

"No, my sister's picking me up in the lobby. She should be here shortly, so I'll wait there."

"I can help, or get a bellboy and..."

"No, I'm good. You go ahead and do what you need to do. I'll call you. We'll get it all worked out," she said as she headed towards the door.

Foley opened the door. "I have to meet the old man, so I'll ride down the elevator with you," he said, trying to grab the bigger suitcase, but she pulled it back.

They rode down in silence, mumbled some awkward goodbyes, and parted company.

As she walked away, Foley wondered if he'd ever see her again.

THE CHIEF'S OFFICE

As Foley expected, CB was unhappy with the $5000 monthly fee chastising him for settling so quickly.

"You could of got double that," the Chief said.

"Look, it's a done deal, CB, and I can work with it."

"Yeah, you can, but I can't," the Chief said.

"Don't sweat it. I'll see that you make out."

The Chief let it ride for now. He gave Foley an update.

"The state boys are here and they're happy as hell to take the case. They have LaVella and Williams in for a debriefing. Only a couple of dozen people left the resort so far and only a few made a fuss about the search, but they all agreed. Nothing suspicious was found. We did have one guy leave last night. He claimed he had a family emergency in Herminie. That's down the road a piece. The boys at the gate were a little sloppy. They didn't have him exit the vehicle or show his ID, but he did give us a name and I checked him out. Said his name was Scarcini, and he was cooperative. My guys said they searched the vehicle thoroughly and found nothing. The never searched Scarcini. They did get a plate number and we're running it now. Them two Sherlocks couldn't find an elephant in a phone booth, so who knows? Scarcini paid cash for his room upfront and was registered in Room 420. He never checked out or asked for a credit so he may be coming back, but I'm thinking we should check out his room."

"Without a warrant?"

"Exactly. By the time the state boys go through the legal rigmarole, if this guy's our perp, he'll be laying in the sun on Cabana beach in Brazil."

"Copacabana," Foley said, thinking CB didn't hear it.

"I thought that was a nightclub, the one…"

"Forget it, CB. We can't go into that room without the proper warrant."

"Where there's a will, there's a way."

"Yeah, and your way will lose the case if this guy's the perp."

"Well, housekeeping is certainly allowed to go into the room," the Chief said.

"Not if you initiate the action. That won't fly with a judge."

"I'm not going to initiate anything. I got a report that there may be a water leak in there, and I alerted housekeeping. I asked them to go in and check, but not to touch anything. Just look at everything carefully and report what they see back to me."

"You'll never get away with it, CB. Keep me out of it."

"I have no idea what you're talking about," the Chief said with a quick smile.

Foley got up from the ratty chair he was sitting on, an old vinyl padded chrome kitchen chair probably retrieved from the trash. The Chief's office was sparse, decorated in early attic, but Foley knew the old man never did anything unless there was a benefit in it for him. CB liked the good life, but his MO was to always look poor and beleaguered. As he said, "Never give anyone a target."

Foley was startled by the knob turning back and forth, accompanied by impatient banging on the door. The Chief slowly got up from behind his small. littered desk.

"That's probably Karen Cramer, our head of housekeeping. Don't mind her smart mouth. That broad studied 'Bitch 101' in school and got all A's."

He slid the dead bolt and stepped back quickly as Karen came charging into the room.

"I don't know what you're up to, Carl," she said, not noticing Foley who had stepped back off to the side, "but I trust you about as far as I can throw that pig pen of fat hogs that you hang out with and I'll be...." Karen said stopping when she realized there was somebody else in the room, mumbling out an "I'm sorry. I didn't know you had company."

"No problem. I'm Foley, the hog farmer's son," he said smiling, and to diffuse the situation added, "and just so you know, I agree with you."

Her face was a little flushed. She was a short-haired, reddish blond, wearing dark brown horn-rimmed glasses over wide-set brown eyes. She was attractive, in a plain sort of way, with a pleasant face. Her soft sneaker like shoes said she spent a lot of time on her feet and Foley figured she was the head housekeeper.

"Look, Karen. We've had a robbery and I just..."

"I know," she said sharply. "Whoever rented that room hasn't left. There was a pair of boxers on the bathroom floor, but the towels weren't used. The soap and shampoo weren't touched. There was a pair of jeans on the floor near the bed, and in the closet another pair of jeans and a shirt. What I didn't see was the suitcase. I didn't touch anything, but there was the smell of Clorox and the maid hadn't been in the room yet. There was a ten-dollar bill on the bed. The bed was a bit mussed up, but it didn't look slept in. That's everything... oh, I didn't touch them, but the jeans on the floor looked new. That's it. I have to leave," she said, and quickly exited the room without waiting for any reactions.

"What in the hell did you do to her, CB?

"That's it. I didn't do anything. We had a little fling, and she thinks we're going steady."

"Looks like a catch to me."

"Yeah, well, she never has to worry about losing her looks. She'll be ugly all of her life."

"You're a piece of work, CB. You need to cool it with your smart mouth She's a damn good-looking woman. I hope you can trust her because if that guy is our perp, and she testifies, you're finished."

"She pisses me off, but she's a good person, and I trust her, and I'm not blind. She's smart and pretty, but she's also tough. I let her know how much I like her she'll have me for lunch. So, what do you think about what she said?"

"Doesn't sound like much. The fact that the guy hasn't used the room much doesn't mean a thing. Remember, he left early last night," Foley said.

"I guess you're right. He doesn't sound…"

Foley interrupted. "I don't get the Clorox smell. As I understood it, the room wasn't cleaned yet, so that's a little odd, but everything else seems natural.

"Well, I guess that's it."

"I don't know. Since he's the only guy that left last night, he's worth checking out. According to your boys, the guy was clean."

"Yeah, but my cops make Barney Fife look like Sherlock Holmes. They didn't even see his ID. As far as the perp, my experience with these punks is that they don't like to get separated from their loot. Let's see what the state boys think after they get done with LaVella and Williams."

HEDY

HEDY SOAKED THE TWO SCALPELS IN BLEACH AND WIPED THEM clean, checking them under a magnifying glass for any residue. She wrapped each of them in a paper towel, then covered them in plastic wrap and put them in old McDonald's bags. She threw one bag in a trash can in the hall near the kid's game room and the other in a can in the main lobby.

The last thing to get rid of was his penis. She checked the resort pickup schedules and settled on an outside trash can. She chose one near the new wing. There was an afternoon pickup, and the outside temperatures were in the freezing range.

She found the can, took out the baggie with the cannoli, and pushed it through the swinging door of the large trash container, when she heard a voice behind her.

"You shouldn't throw good food away when there are kids starving in Bangladesh," the male voice said, scaring the hell out of her.

She turned to see Foley ambling up to her with a smile on his face.

"Ah, Mr. Foley, how are you this morning?"

"I'm fine, thanks. What was that? It looked like an éclair, or maybe a Twinkie?"

"A cannoli, an old one, not fit to eat," she said, "and with my figure it's better that I didn't eat it," she said.

"You look fine," he said, smiling, "I don't think you have anything to worry about."

"That's kind of you, Mr. Foley. I hope Otto is treating you right," she said, changing the subject.

"Please, call me Foley, everybody does and yes, he is," he said, "and I guess I'm working for you, too," he added.

"Glad to have you on board, Foley. We've never had a robbery and Otto believed we never would, so I guess we made it easy for the crook, didn't we?"

"Doesn't look like it was too tough, but we'll find him."

"I hope you're right, Mr. Foley."

"Just Foley, please."

"Okay, Foley, you go and catch the bad guys and I'll see you later," she said, turning and leaving, breathing a sigh of relief. She had just disposed of Hogg's manhood stuffed in a cannoli.

She is an attractive woman, Foley thought. Too bad she's the boss.

JR LEON

HE WAS RUNNING LATE FOR HIS NOON MEETING WITH HEDY, a tactic he frequently used, but he had to be careful. This deal was different. Changing his style was frustrating him, and he had to keep reminding himself about it.

JR Leon had an enigmatic childhood. Although the clicking tongues of the caviar and crumpet crowd found his mysterious background a succulent subject, they didn't realize that he knew little more than they did. It bothered him, and over the years he tried to learn more about his background, but with little enthusiasm.

What he knew was what his father told him. He was born in northern Brazil of an American mother and Brazilian father, which provided him with dual citizenship. He was told that his mother died of fever a few months after his birth. He never saw a picture or image of his mother. They were all lost in a fire.

His father was a well-paid senior executive at the Ford Motor Company who traveled extensively, leaving little John Robert Leon in the care of nannies. His childhood was spent in a gated estate in Brazil, where he fell in love with two women—his nanny, a nurturing woman who returned his love—and an attentive American teacher, who tutored him.

The American teacher left first, and the boy snuggled into the loving arms of his nanny. But when she left a few months later, he felt abandoned and confused. As a retinue of shapeless figures droned through his life, little John became JR and surrounded himself with an emotional moat of distrust that nobody could cross.

JR's relationship with his father was tenuous. There always seemed to be an invisible barrier between them. Those rare times he saw his father were pleasant but restrained. His father gave him everything he wanted or needed, except love. JR envied the other kids with families but would never admit it, even to himself.

Just before World War Two, JR came to America where he lived in a tony home in Grosse Pointe, Michigan. Believing he would finally be with his father he rarely saw him. A housekeeper and nanny were his family. JR built even wider moats and higher walls around himself.

He attended Cranbrook, a private high school where he lived, isolating him even more. He was smart, but troubled, never making friends or taking part in after-school activities. He was a loner, and he preferred it that way. He was ambitious, and his private goal was to become extraordinarily rich. He believed that money replaced the need for friends and family.

Upon graduation from high school, JR was shipped off to Adrian University, a Methodist affiliated private college in Michigan, where he graduated with a business degree. JR was surprised that his father came to his graduation, and even more surprised by what his father told him.

His father was dying of cancer and didn't have long to live. He apologized to JR for not being a better father and that he was leaving everything to his son. He had no other family, and he hoped that this would give JR a good start in life. JR looked at the man he hardly knew and saw the sadness and guilt on his face, but it didn't move him. His father was just trying to buy his way out of his parental absence.

JR knew his father made an excellent living, but he never expected to be left a trust fund worth over ten million dollars.

He opened a venture capital firm, JRL Associates. Some good luck and wise investments, mostly in technology, soon had him up on the "richest lists." At some point, it's not clear when, he closed the business and left the U.S., moving back to Brazil where little is known of his activities.

Because of his accumulated wealth, he was fodder for the international gossipers, and rumors abounded. Some said he was a ruthless man, never getting enough, doing whatever he had to do to accomplish his goals; others claimed he was in business with the Sicilian Mafia, the rumor starting when he berthed his luxurious yacht in the Bay of Palermo for over a month. He established residence at one of Palermo's grand hotels, the Hotel des Palme's, a splendid old dame of a place that was known to have hosted some big Mafia meetings which probably spawned the Cosa Nostra gossip.

It was also public that JR Leon had a close relationship with a high-ranking member of the Al Maktoum royal family from Abu Dhabi, but little was known about that association.

Like many people of wealth, JR also believed that God had a hand in his success. Although he rarely attended church, he gave generously. It was easier to keep God on your side when you had a lot of money.

Now, JR was about to acquire a coveted asset, one that he had to have at any cost.

This deal was personal.

NEW YEAR'S DAY

HIS CAR WAS WAITING WHEN HE EXITED THE CONDO, THE ASTRINGENT air snapping at his face. He hated the cold, and here he was about to buy a ski resort. Roger, the blonde bodyguard, spotted him, jumped out of the Mercedes, and opened the back door. JR was in a navy-blue suit, white shirt, solid navy tie and gray cashmere topcoat, which was as casual as he got except when he golfed. The only time he wore shorts was when he played tennis, and he would occasionally slip into a bathing suit when he was cruising the southern Mediterranean.

He was a humorless man, always stiffly proper, contrary to what some women who slept with him suggested. Allegedly he was a rude, sexist in bed.

"Happy New Year, Mr. Leon," Roger said, taking JR's arm to guide him into the vehicle, but he shrugged it off.

"Same to you. What time is it?" he asked as he settled back on to the firm leather seat. Tim, the driver, quickly answered.

"12:10, sir."

JR didn't respond, thinking how fresh and bright everything looked, the new snow stretching a starched white sheet across the land. It was so different from the thick, dark greens of the hot and humid rainforest where he grew up.

Tim drove up the narrow snow-covered road to Pipa's main entrance. The valet hurried out from his cubby hole office, running up to the driver's side of the vehicle to open the door. Roger, who had jumped out of the car, waved him off.

"We'll park it ourselves," he said, "just tell us where." JR never allowed anybody to drive his vehicles. He ran a tight ship when it came to his personal safety. Some said he was overly paranoid, but he was certain there were people who wanted to harm him, if for no other reason than he was a wealthy man.

JR exited the car and was walking up the stairs to the entry when Roger caught up to him and opened the door.

He subtly scanned the room for Hedy as soon as he entered Pipa's. The place was jammed, but a woman like Hedy was easy to find. He wasn't surprised that he didn't see her. Under normal circumstances he would have left, but this situation wasn't normal. It was far from it. He saw the manager rushing his way.

"Good day, Mr. Leon. Miss Kasser is expecting you. Please, I'll take you to her table."

"I don't see her," JR said.

"But of course, sir. She will be here momentarily," he said as he led JR to a table snuggled between potted greenery in a corner near the water wall, JR noted that Hedy's table selection would have been his choice. Hedy was quite adept, and he had to watch her moves carefully.

"May I get you something to drink, perhaps a refreshing Bellini, one of our specialties," he said as he pulled out a chair for JR.

"Scotch, the Glenrothes, please. Neat, and keep that table over there open," he said waving to one just on the other side of one of the plants, "for my staff."

"But of course," the manager said. "Miss Kasser already arranged for it."

JR was annoyed. He traveled all over the world and no matter where he went, 'but of course' seemed to be the international language of maître-ds. It was their catch-all phrase that they always said confidently while saying nothing.

He had to handle this deal differently. It took him a long time to get here. His odyssey began years ago, but it was a chance meeting at Mar-A-Lago that really sped up the journey. JR wasn't a member at Trump's

Mar-A-Lago club in Palm Beach, but he was a welcome guest. JR didn't like Trump or most of the members. He found them a little too blaring about their money. He used the club only when necessary and it was at one of those times when he accidently heard something that grabbed his attention.

He was having lunch in the ornate dining room that reeked with crystal, gold, and frescos, when he overheard a man mention Stony Creek at a nearby table.

JR sent one of his men to invite the man for a drink. Dennis Reed, a new millionaire from North Central Pennsylvania, was surprised by the offer. He didn't know who JR was, but he quickly accepted. Only important people came to the club.

JR brought up Stony Creek. Dennis Reed said he knew the resort well. In fact, his daughter was close friends with one of the Kasser twins and owned a condo at the resort.

"I'll tell you, JR," Dennis said, "if you ever meet the twins, you'll be in the company of two of the most beautiful women I have ever seen."

"I would certainly like to meet them. Maybe you could arrange it?"

Dennis Reed said he would try. He became more enthusiastic after he found out who JR was. It became his mission, and after a few failed attempts, he pulled it together. Enlisting his daughter, Dennis had her plan a party at her condo. She was finally able to elicit a firm acceptance by Heidi and Hedy, and he let JR know the date and time.

A few months later, JR was one of the early guests to arrive for the party. Reed was tripping over himself to cater to JR's wishes and really became nervous when the party was well on its way and the twins were still not there. Reed was a nervous wreck. He was about to have his daughter call them when they arrived. Reed looked up and thanked the ceiling.

He introduced JR to them, but it was brief. Other guests were vying for their attention and they were being pulled in all directions.

When JR saw an opportunity to talk with one twin alone, he swung into action.

"I'm not sure you're Hedy or…"

"I'm Hedy."

"Thank you. I visited your resort the other day. It's quite a beautiful place. You should be proud of what you and your family have accomplished."

"We are. It's a labor of love."

"I understand your family is considering selling it," he said. He knew they weren't selling, but this was the fastest way to get the lay of the land.

That surprised Hedy. At first, she wondered whether he knew something that she didn't.

"No, there are no plans to sell. Where did you hear such a rumor?"

"I really don't remember. It could have been one of my bankers," JR said innocently, "but I'm sorry to hear that the information I have is unreliable. I would have been interested in bidding."

"That's quite flattering, but we have no intention of ever selling," Hedy said, "but thank you for your interest."

JR handed her his business card. There was hand-written number on it.

"I put my private number on there. If anything ever changes, I hope you'll call me."

"Nothing will change, Mr. Leon, but thank you," Hedy said, excusing herself.

JR was disappointed, but he had a Plan B. His people researched Stony Creek thoroughly, and his next move was Otto. He was the decision maker, and JR had compiled a dossier on the man and his operation. The one thing that stood out was his illegal gambling operation. That might be useful in negotiations.

Almost a year passed. JR had been trying to set up an "accidental" meeting with Otto when he got a surprise phone call from Hedy in December 2001.

She explained that the resort was not on the market, but that there was a bid, and it was the obligation of the board to hear it out. Since JR had mentioned his interest, she told them their by-laws required that she inform him of such and be given an equal opportunity if he was still interested. During the conversation, she learned that he was in Florida.

"I did have some interest at one time," JR said, "but right now my portfolio is fairly tight."

"I understand," Hedy said, "I was obligated to let you know. Thanks for talking with me."

"Ah, I'll tell you what. Since you were nice enough to call me, I owe you the courtesy of hearing you out. I'm going to be in Pittsburgh, ah, I believe Friday or Saturday. I'll get back to you in a few hours with a more definitive time and maybe we can get together if you'd like and we can chat. I owe you that."

"I understand, JR. Sure, why not?" Hedy said, letting a deep breath out slowly.

Hedy was under the gun. It was only a few weeks earlier that Otto informed everybody that a Swiss company wanted to present an offer. Otto was casual about it, saying that according to the by-laws he had to present it at the next meeting, which had been moved to January 2nd. He gave each board member a packet of information to review but indicated that it was nothing more than a parliamentary formality.

When she first heard about the Swiss deal, Hedy wasn't concerned. She didn't think anybody was interested in selling. But as she thought about it, doubt began to edge its way into her mind. Why was Otto even presenting the offer? Nobody wanted to sell, or did they? She was certain she had her mother and sister's votes, which would be enough, but she had to be sure.

She discussed it with her mother, who brushed the offer off, but Hedy wasn't convinced.

Heidi was a terrible liar and when Hedy questioned her about the voting it was obvious she was avoiding the truth. Hedy didn't like what she was hearing.

After contacting JR, a meeting was finally set up. JR suggested the Duquesne Club, Pittsburgh's baroque inner sanctum for old money, but Hedy was concerned that some of Otto's friends might see them. After some back-and-forth, Hedy offered a nice, but off the beaten path restaurant in the city's North Hills where she knew the owner.

Rico's was owned and operated by Rico Lorenzini, a Tuscan food aficionado who immigrated to the United States in the late fifties. He was a gifted restauranteur, a virtuoso of food and service, and a master of both the front and back of the house, but Rico's Restaurant was more of a clubby neighborhood establishment.

Hedy didn't tell Rico much other than she was bringing a wealthy South American business executive to lunch and wanted privacy. Rico didn't need to know anymore and planned to accommodate them in one of his private rooms that he adapted to meet Hedy's request.

When Hedy arrived, valet parking had been alerted to watch for them and Rico came out. Hedy saw him immediately as Rico, his thick gray hair combed back and wearing his usual white chef's coat graciously greeted her. He told Hedy that both she and her guest would be escorted through an employee's entrance. His son, who was now the maître d, would bring JR to her when he arrived.

Rico had just seated Hedy when JR arrived. JR waved his hand to signal Hedy not to get up, but she had no intention of doing so and gave him a big smile as he sat down.

"Hedy, so nice to see you," he said.

"Likewise, JR, hope your trip in was pleasant."

"As good as can be expected," he said as Rico, who had stayed in the background, came up to the table.

"May I get you refreshments," Rico said, "I have a wonderful Perrier Joulet that is quite expressive, yet it's light and elegant for such a sunny day and…"

"Iced Tea for me," JR said, interrupting and Hedy dittoed the request. Rico backed away and disappeared.

They both kept the conversation engaged in small talk, waiting for the server to bring their drinks. When she did, she asked if they wanted to order, but both declined.

"We'll find you if we need you, "JR said, taking charge. "I hope that's okay with you," he said to Hedy, who gave a cursory nod.

JR was mapping her face, his eyes roaming over her smooth milky skin, highlighted by a whisper of pink on her cheeks, her sharp blue eyes following his. From the report he read, she was a well-schooled woman who was as bright as she was beautiful. She was the type JR liked to have on his arm, but what bothered him was her ambition. Trying to control an ambitious woman, especially a beautiful one, was difficult.

There was always tension in negotiations, each party strategizing, looking for the opening that would give one of them an edge. Negotiating with a beautiful, smart woman added another tension—sexual—especially when it was an engaging woman such as Hedy. JR had to keep reminding himself that this negotiation was different.

Hedy had spent hours going over how she was going to deal with JR and decided on a "go for the jugular" approach, so before he got the chance to say anything else, she fired the first shot.

"Look JR, we both know why we're here, so let's get right to it."

JR smiled. He liked her spunk.

"Well, I know why you're here, so let's have at it," he said with a slight smile.

"I will assume you've done your due diligence," Hedy said watching his face for a reaction but saw none.

"I know a little," he said coyly "and I'm sure you'll provide me with everything I need to make an informed decision, but let's dispense with the usual stuff, and as you said, get down to it. If I could find room in my portfolio for such a deal, instead of you giving me a price that I counter, and we go back and forth, why don't we play it straight and cut out all the BS. I'm prepared, right now, to make an offer but I don't want to play games. Can we do that?"

Hedy recognized how quickly JR shifted to her approach and attempted to make it his, but that was no problem. She stayed the course.

"I'm sure you know we have an offer on the table from a European company," she said casually, watching his body language. He gave no tells, keeping his eyes locked onto hers, and then leaned back and took a sip of iced tea.

"All I know is what you told me on the phone," he said "That an offer was made, and it had to be presented. I got the feeling that telling me about it was a mere formality and…" JR said.

"Well, I wanted to be fair."

"Certainly. I understand. But let's play pretend. Let's pretend that your family takes the offer seriously and maybe even votes on it and it's accepted. That wouldn't be fair to me, would it?"

He didn't wait for an answer.

"So, here's what I propose. Whatever offer is put on the table, I will not only match it, but I'll also exceed it."

Hedy wasn't prepared for this. She expected a lot of negotiating. She recovered quickly.

"By how much?"

"Ten percent. But be forewarned. I'm not going to get into a bidding war. If your people go back for a higher bid, I'm out and believe me, I'll know if you're playing that game. My ten percent offer is valid only on the bid that you have on the table now. That is my best and final," JR said, his eyes never leaving hers.

"Don't you even want to know what their offer was?" she said with a cute smile. Hedy believed that JR already knew who made the offer and might even know what it was. He was well connected and banks share information when the price is right.

"You wouldn't tell me, nor should you," he said, crossing his arms on the table and moving closer towards her. "I believe you're an honest person who will negotiate in good faith. I'll do the same."

"You're right," she said, mimicking his physical actions, also leaning in. They sat there for a moment, nobody blinking. Hedy was thinking about the ten percent. That was a lot.

"So, I'm interested but there are some contingencies," Hedy said.

JR straightened up, the movement puncturing the tension, Hedy followed suit, and then they both left the moment. Hedy brushed back her hair and resettled her posture as he took a sip of iced tea.

"What contingencies?" JR said.

"I want a contract for five years, renewable of course if both parties agree, that gives me unrestricted freedom to run the resort as I see fit."

JR hadn't expected Hedy to throw herself into the deal, but it confirmed his beliefs about ambitious women. Under normal circumstances he would have rejected the suggestion immediately and inform her it was a deal-breaker, but he couldn't. He wanted this deal. He had to play it softer.

"That's asking a bit much," he said.

"JR," she said, leaning in again, her eyes flashing, fixed on his, "I promise you that I will be the best part of this deal."

JR didn't mind keeping Hedy on board in some capacity, but the "unrestricted freedom" caveat was something he didn't like. JR's philosophy was delegate but regulate, and he kept everybody in his employ on a short leash.

"I'm afraid I can't do that," JR said, watching Hedy's face very carefully.

Hedy thought he'd go for it, and his rejection threw her off. She had to re-group quickly.

"Why?'

"Because I have somebody else in mind."

"Nobody knows this place or can run it as well as I can. You have everything to gain."

"I understand that, but I like to do things my way, and you've made it clear that you want to do things your way," he said.

"I'm willing to work with you,"

"I don't know ..." JR said.

Hedy interrupted. "I do. We'll make a great team. Look, you draw up a contract that gives me operational freedom, but you hold the power of the veto. Let's make it for a year. If after a year we 're comfortable with our relationship you'll extend the contract into ten-year increments," she said, reaching her hand out to shake his.

JR hesitated just long enough to create doubt. She was quick. Although she settled for a one-year contract, she snuck in a ten-year renewal. She had a lot of confidence that the year would work in her favor. JR appreciated her confidence. He still didn't like the deal, but this was one he had to have at any cost. He smiled, extended his hand across the table and they shook on it.

"You said "contingencies?" JR said.

"Well, we covered the most important one in the event we sell, but as I told you on the phone, there is no indication we'll sell, so everything we've discussed here could be moot."

"I understand. Shall we have lunch?" JR said.

"Let's skip it," she said, sliding her chair back. "Who knows? We may have a lot of lunches in the future."

"We may," JR said.

HEDY & JR

JR WASN'T A MAN WHO TOLERATED WAITING, BUT HE RESTRAINED his impatience. He had to play Hedy's game. Pipa's was a beehive of activity as the New Year's Day crowd filled the air with ersatz chatter, sipping on mimosas and Bloody Mary's. JR had no desire to be part of this social scene. He still had some concerns about the Kasser meeting, and he hoped that the protection he purchased was effective. He was thinking about that when he heard the prattle in Pipa's soften.

Hedy Kasser arrived.

She was a portrait in silver and white, wearing a glistening après-ski body-hugging outfit. Heidi convinced her to get it last year, but she never wore it. The slim-cut, brushed fleece silvery pants clung to her body, and the white hoody laced with silver threads made her look cozy and comfortable. She radiated a rosy effervescence that added a glow to the room. Hedy chose the outfit with great care. She wanted to look as sparkling and confident as she could for her meeting with JR, even though she looked more like her sister in that ensemble.

She was impressive, but JR became quickly annoyed when she began stopping and chatting briefly as she made her way through the crowded room. She finally made it to his table, mumbling a quick "sorry" as he stood and pulled out a chair for her.

Before she was seated, a waiter was at her side.

"A nice tall, cold, cranberry juice and vodka, William, please. JR?" she said.

"I'm good, thank you."

"Happy New Year," she said with a big smile. "I hope you had a nice evening."

"It was okay, thank you."

"So sorry. You should have stayed here at the club. The place really rocked."

"I thought about it, but I had things to do."

"I'll bet," she said with a knowing smile.

"I wouldn't," he said with a serious frown.

Hedy moved on. JR wasn't one who engaged in light banter.

"Just joking, JR," she said.

Hedy liked JR. Although he had the sense of humor of a clam, and overdid the proper act, there was something intriguing about him.

"So, are we still good?" she said casually.

JR resented that question. He didn't like it when somebody questioned his integrity.

"You can go to any bank in the world on my word," he said, sitting up and leaning forward, "any bank, and you also have my signed signature on the agreement my lawyers sent over to you …"

"… and you have mine," Hedy interrupted quickly, "I didn't mean it the way it sounded. Just crossing the t's," she said, giving him a quick smile.

JR looked at her, gave her his version of a slight smile, and said, "I doubt that you'll miss anything. My purpose today was to see if there was anything more you need from me for your meeting?"

"No, I'm good to go," she said. "My attorneys looked it over and they're happy. I'm ready to present it at the meeting."

JR reiterated the details of his proposal, watching Hedy's face closely for any sign of doubt or confusion. She was clear and confident.

"Do you have the votes to get it approved?" JR asked, "if you decide to sell," he added.

"I'm prepared," she said. "Look, whether we sell or not I think you ought to meet Otto. Maybe a lunch?"

"Look forward to it. You'll make the arrangements?"

"Yes. I'll let you know."

"Good. How about some lunch?" he said, lightening up and looking less intense.

"JR, if you don't mind, I have a million things to do to get ready for this meeting, so please give me a rain check? I promise I'll make it up to you."

"Actually, it works better for me, too."

"Great. It works out for both of us," she said, getting up, grabbing her coat, and leaving as JR watched her.

She was a head-turner.

JOE DUCK

HE STAYED AT THE FOUR POINTS SHERATON IN GREENSBURG. THE hotel was off the main drag, tucked off to the side, so they didn't get the usual snowstorm walk-ins. Joe Duck knew it was there, and when they had a room for him, he thought that if God had a plan for him it was looking good.

He paid cash, making small talk about the storm and how happy he was that they had a vacancy. They didn't ask for an ID. He registered as Mike Scarcini.

The next morning, he awoke feeling good. He had more cash on him than he ever had in his life. He ordered room service, stuff that he didn't know, like Eggs Benedict. The only Benedict he knew was the guy who was a traitor or something, and he wondered why they named eggs after him, but they were pretty good. He watched the news from a Pittsburgh channel and there was nothing about the robbery, but he was sure the cops were on it by now.

So far, so good. Things were going his way.

The robbery was a piece of cake. Hell, he could have phoned it in. And then finding a place to stash the money, right under the cop's noses, actually right under the Sheriff's nose, was like hitting the lottery. He was feeling it.

He picked up the Gideon Bible that was setting on the nightstand next to his bed, wondering who the fuck Gideon was. Joe Duck was not a churchman, but how could anyone explain his good fortune? It had to be God, but why? Joe thought about his life, the botched surgery, the bad luck, the tough times, but he never gave up, and that's why God was helping him.

God helps those who help themselves. Shit, that's why.

But he needed confirmation. If God was truly on his side this time, he wanted a sign. He closed his eyes, opened the Gideon Bible to a random page, jammed his finger against the page, and held it there.

He opened his eyes and read the passage his finger was covering. It was Jeremiah 29:11.

"For I know the plans I have for you," says the Lord. "They are plans for good and not for disaster to give you a future and a hope."

Joe Duck slammed the bible shut, dropped it on the bed, stood up, and shaking his head in agreement, smacked his right fist into his open left hand and declared aloud, "Fuckin A, I knew God was with me!"

Joe wanted to get back to Pittsburgh and the safety of his apartment. He was enjoying the hot shower, thinking about what he was going to do, when his heart jumped.

Holy hell. I didn't change the license plate back!

He hurried out of the shower, dried himself, dressed and headed down to the lobby. It was almost 7 AM and a few stragglers were milling around drinking free coffee.

It was still gray out and more snow had fallen. He brushed off the snow and opened his car door and grabbed the license plate from the sun visor. He threw his Nike bag into the back.

Those stupid cops at Stony Creek didn't even notice the plate in the visor.

He checked and seeing nobody quickly changed the plate. He bent the stolen plate back and forth until it split in half and threw it in a trash can. He'd get rid of the other half somewhere else.

He climbed into his SUV, started the engine, and sat there until the heater kicked in as the wipers cleared the melting snow from the windshield.

His pockets were filled with packets of cash. He planned to count it last night, but after downing the booze he was too tired and fell asleep.

In a little over an hour, he'd be back in Pittsburgh. He'd tally it up then. It had to be fifteen or twenty grand.

When all this is over, I'll give some money to the church, maybe a hundred bucks, fuck it, I'll give a thousand.

Joe Duck was feeling good. He needed to call Ruby Begonia.

HOGG

IT WAS A BUMPY, BREEZY RIDE TO UNIONTOWN. THE KID DRIVING was nervous about having Hogg in his porous vehicle that seemed to have no springs. He tried driving slower than usual, but the Sherriff kept telling him to hurry. Hogg seemed to have a bad stomach-ache because he kept clutching at it, groaning at every bump, so the kid was happy when they finally got there.

"I've got him," the Doctor said, thanking the kid, taking Hogg's arm, and leading him into the big Victorian house where he had his offices. He led a mumbling, staggering Hogg into a small examination room.

"So, Bill, what's the problem?" he said as he helped Hogg up on to the exam table.

Here we go again.

"Jim, I have a problem."

"Okay?"

"It's not easy to talk about."

"No problem. I've seen everything and you know you can trust me," Doctor Jim said, thinking Hogg probably had an STD.

"Somebody cut off my cock."

"What do you mean 'cut off?'"

"Exactly what I said. Goddamn it, Jim. My cock is gone. Kaput. Understand?"

"You better lie back," he said, helping Hogg get his legs up, the exam table paper scrunching up under him. It took some doing, but he finally got Hogg's pants down.

"Damn, Bill. Duct tape? Really?" the doctor said.

"Just fix me up, Jim," Hogg said in a barely audible voice, burping out whiffs of regurgitated alcohol.

"Easy, Bill, easy," Doctor Jim said, gently removing the tape. "I've never seen anything, well, this is, ah, interesting," he mumbled.

The doctor removed the blood-soaked bandage. It was a mess, but it could have been worse. Whoever did this had taken precautions to prevent blood loss, which may have saved Hogg's ass. The doctor cleaned the wound, pumped anti-biotics and more painkiller into Hogg, and re-bandaged it.

"You need to get into the hospital," the Doc said. He was in his sixties, a white-haired man with a large, red alcoholic nose and narrow blue eyes.

Dr. Jim owed Hogg.

Doc was a gambler who once raised the ire of some stocky guys with short necks and bulging stomachs. Hogg helped, not because he liked Dr. Jim. A doctor was a good thing to have in your stack of due bills.

"No hospital," Hogg grunted.

"But Bill..."

"No buts, just fix me up so I don't die," Hogg said, "and give me a shot for this pain. I can't handle much more," Hogg said, gasping and clenching his teeth, scrunching his eyes tightly.

"The pain will ease up in a minute or so, but Bill, you can't..."

"Did you hear me?" Hogg said, his voice compressed, causing him to cough, trying to lift his head, only to collapse back onto the table.

"I'll help you, Bill, but I'd feel better if..."

Hogg was tired and desperate.

"Jim, I swear I'll personally blow your fucking head off if you don't help me and do what I ask. Patch me up, keep me alive, no hospital, nobody ever knows about this except you and me," Hogg said desperately, "or I'll kill you. I mean it and you know I'll do it."

"Take it easy, Bill. I'm going to take care of you. I already gave you a shot for the pain and it will be kicking in so stay cool," Doctor Jim said.

Hogg seemed to relax.

"I don't know who did this to you, Bill, but it looks like they did some homework. They took precautions to prevent you from bleeding to death, and they lucked out on the incision. I can see where they..."

A groggy Hogg interrupted. "Jim, just... just... patch me up. I don't need a blow by blow on what the fuck happened."

Dr. Jim cleansed the wound and fixed it as best he could as Hogg slept. Hogg needed a catheter and only a hospital would have it. He had to get Hogg out of his office and his life.

This wasn't the first time Hogg used him, and it wouldn't be the last. As Dr. Jim sat at his desk, he had an idea. He made a phone call.

He let Hogg sleep for a while and then woke him. It took a lot of shaking, but Hogg came out of his fog, flailing around as Dr. Jim calmed him down.

"Look, I have a friend that I went to medical school with. He runs a clinic in Costa Rica. I called him and he can take care of you properly. That way you can keep this thing quiet. If I do this for you, we're even. Okay?"

Hogg struggled to sit up, the Doc helping him. Hogg was barely conscious, and he struggled to talk.

"You'll go with me," Hogg said.

"What?"

"You go with me. Get me there. You owe me."

"Bill, I can't. I just can't. I have too many things that I have to..."

"Do it," Hogg said, somehow mustering up another burst of energy.

"But Bill, I…"

"No buts, Jim. Get that nurse you're fucking to make reservations on the next flight. I'll pay. Do it Jim and I'll never bother you again. You know my word is good."

"Okay, Bill, okay. Look, you rest while I get things in order?"

Hogg was groggy and he closed his eyes. That's when her face jumped out of the black. It was Heidi. He opened and shut his eyes a few times. He was close to remembering something and then came the flashbacks. Heidi. Something about snow. A snowmobile. Heidi.

Heidi was at his house. She made him a drink. Heidi? No way. But she was there.

Holy fucking Christ.

HEIDI

WHEN THE MORNING SUN SNUCK ITS WAY THROUGH THE SLIT between her drapes and washed over her face, waking Heidi up, she moaned her displeasure and pulled the covers over her head. She didn't want to get up, but the events of the night before burst into her mind and forced her out of bed.

She mechanically hobbled her way to the bathroom and leaned into the mirror, examining her haggard face. She was a mess.

She went back into the bedroom and sat on the edge of her bed. She didn't know how she was going to get through all the awful stuff that was happening.

How could Hedy do that? My God.

She rubbed her face and ran her hand through her rumpled hair, a nervous gesture she would repeat many times over. Everything was so weird.

She squeezed her eyes tightly when she thought of Bill Hogg. He was going to kill her. The thought sped up her heart. She hyperventilated. She stood up for a moment and then quickly sat back down. She was hot and cold at the same time. She lay back, burying her head into the feathery pillow, and tried to catch her breath. She couldn't, gasping irregularly, trying to get that one deep pull that would roll her breathing back into rhythm.

For the umpteenth time she replayed her relationship with Hogg. Their sex was good, but he was a mean-spirited person. She was certain she could change that, but she had to admit she liked the bad boy in him.

One thing was certain. Whatever existed between them was over. Of course, it was over—in every which way. She wasn't sure what to feel. It was so overwhelming.

One moment she wanted to call him and the next she wanted to get out of Stony Creek. What if he needed help? He could be dead or laying there bleeding to death. If she called and he answered she could hang up, but then he'd see the number—if he were alive. She could call from a pay phone and…and what? She had to stop thinking about calling him. Hedy would kill her.

Oh my God. Hedy.

Hedy didn't tell her much. Heidi was certain Hogg thought she cut off his penis.

He knows me. How could he believe I could do such a thing?

But the odds were that he did and that meant she was in deep trouble. Hogg would kill his mother if he thought she did him wrong. The more she thought about it, the more the more fearful she became.

But what could she do? Where could she go? Maybe she would move to the islands. She shook her head. He'd find her. She'd never be safe from Hogg.

Maybe it's better that he dies.

She felt light-headed, unable to move her arms and legs. She was shaking all over. She started hyperventilating again. She had to do something. Her hands wouldn't respond to her mind as she struggled to get the silver phone out of its cradle. In a daze, she dialed the number, her hands feeling like they were floating.

"I need to talk to you. (Pause) The sooner the better. Can you meet me at my place? Right now, please?"

As soon as she hung up, she knew she made a terrible mistake.

ROSIE

"HEDY, I'M SO SORRY," HEIDI SAID ON THE PHONE BETWEEN SOBS and gasps, "I just got scared and didn't know what to do and so I called and…"

Hedy didn't know what her sister was talking about. When she picked up the phone, Heidi started blurting out gibberish that wasn't making sense.

"Heidi, please honey, just calm down. Take a deep breath and talk slow," Hedy said, "Now who did you call?"

(Heavy breathing)

"Mom."

"What?"

"Mom. I called Mom."

"What did you tell her?"

"Nothing, well, nothing yet. She's on her way over here. What do I do, Hedy? I don't want to cause any problems and you know…"

"It's okay, honey. Don't worry, I'm coming over. If Mom gets there before me, tell her I'm on the way and I'll do the telling. Do not tell her a thing. Nothing," Hedy said.

"Please hurry. You know Mom and…"

"Just wait for me. I'm on the way. Don't say a word to Mom," Hedy said, hanging up.

Hedy didn't waste any time. If Heidi told her mother about Hogg, Rosie would pull out all stops to protect her daughter. She wouldn't hesitate to call every law enforcement contact she had, plus every lawyer and judge in her Rolodex. It would be like shooting off a confetti cannon in the legal system. The Hogg story would be scattered all over creation.

When Hedy opened the door to Heidi's condo, she saw her mother standing there, ubiquitous cigarette in hand as smoke swirled around her overly made-up face. She was still wearing her black wool blend Givenchy coat, which was a good sign. Heidi was leaning against the fridge. The word "guilty" tattooed across her forehead would have been less noticeable. Hedy took charge.

"What a surprise to see you here, Mom. What brings you up to the white palace?" Hedy said as casually as she could.

Rosie didn't know how to answer. She glanced at Heidi for help, who just stood there with a blank look.

"I hope I'm not interrupting anything private. Am I?" Hedy said, looking hard at Heidi.

"Ah, no, ah, I was going to…"

"It's okay, Heidi. I'll tell Mom," Hedy said, turning her attention to Rosie, who had a worried look on her face.

Hedy continued. "Mom, it's my fault. I swore Heidi to secrecy but, as you know, she's not the best in keeping secrets. It's nothing serious, so not to worry," she said, looking directly at her mother whose face was pallid as she kept licking her lips.

"Relax, Mom. This has turned into something it's not. It's a business thing, that's all, so please relax. Take off your coat," Hedy said, helping her mother remove it. "Let's go in the living room and I'll fill you in. Actually, I think its good news."

Hedy led Rosie into the living room and directed her to sit on the sofa while she sat in a matching white chair. Heidi remained motionless.

"Mom," Hedy said, "I need to tell you about another deal I'm going to present at the family meeting."

Rosie just sat there, waiting for some unseen ax to fall.

"Mom, did you hear me? I have another offer from somebody who wants to buy Stony Creek, and it's bigger and better than Otto's."

What Hedy was saying finally sunk in. Rosie's body relaxed, and she slumped. It was as if her muscles turned to jelly.

"A deal?" Rosie said giving her head a quick shake, "This is about some deal? I'm thinking somebody has cancer or worse, and you want to tell me about a deal?"

Rosie was a proud woman who had worked hard all her life, and in the last year she had shrugged off all the annoying details that came with working at Stony Creek. She began to do things she liked doing. Little nothing things that carried no responsibility, so she was annoyed as her two daughters danced around some sort of deal. She was sitting up straight, her blonde hair now gray, but perfectly coiffed, her eyes a piercing blue, a somewhat sharp nose, but a very pretty face. It wasn't hard to see where the twins got their beauty.

"Let me explain," Hedy said. "I have another proposal to present," Hedy said, moving in as close as possible as if she was revealing a big secret, "and I want you to consider it."

"Is that what this is all about?" Rosie asked, looking over at Heidi, who had moved to the island counter. Heidi nodded weakly.

"I think we need to look at alternatives, and I have a good one. This guy, very wealthy, JR Leon, has promised us at least 10% more than the Swiss offer. Ten percent, Mom," Hedy said, "so now we have two offers, and I didn't go looking for this one. It came to me."

"Well, I thought this was something serious," Rosie said, looking at Heidi, the frown leaving her face, "and I'm happy it's not." You could see the tension leaving her body as she relaxed and leaned back into the sofa.

"I'm glad you want to sell, and if you think your deal is good, of course I'll support you, darling. You are my daughter, after all. I do have to see the paperwork, but darling, I'm on your side. Does Otto know about this?"

"No, Mom, and please don't tell him. I'll get you the paperwork, and I'm sorry we tried to keep it from you, aren't we, Heidi?"

Heidi came into the living room. She nodded and mumbled out a "sorry." She marveled at how easily Hedy could lie, but she kind of admired it.

"I'm sorry, Mom," Heidi said, "Can I get you a drink?"

"No, darling. I must get back. I was in the middle of making a snack when Heidi called and I dropped everything," Rosie said getting up from the sofa.

Hedy gave Heidi a reassuring look. "I have to go, too," she said and then added, "I have one question, Mom."

Rosie stopped and turned. "Yes, darling."

"Were you going to vote to sell?" Hedy asked.

"Well, yes, darling. I knew you were against it and I didn't want to see you throw your life away working twenty hours a day in this place. I am so pleased that you've seen the light. All of us are going to be fine, aren't we darlings?"

Hedy made a mental note to bury her part of the deal with JR.

Everybody was smiling, but Hedy was concerned.

Heidi was a problem. A big one.

THE STATE POLICE

MAJOR ROBERT BUTLER HAD BEEN A STATE COP FOR TWENTY-SIX years. A tall man with steel gray hair, square rimless glasses, wide-set brown eyes, brown/gray eyebrows, and a quirky brief smile that put most people at ease, Butler knew the Chief from way back. In fact, he opened a file on him. The state police were investigating gambling in Pittsburgh, and the Chief's name came up.

His name appeared on a lot of lists, but that's as far as it went. He understood both sides of the street because he was on both sides. People would be surprised how many VIPs used both sides of the law to protect themselves. The Chief kept a "book" (a record) on every one of them and used it when needed. He knew where the bones were buried. It was a powerful tool. Like the slopes at Stony Creek the Chief was very slippery.

Butler was a straight-arrow cop, but not so anal that he didn't find the Chief a campy throwback from an era when both the crooks and cops respected style and enterprise. Butler admired the Chief for his entrepreneurship and cunning but kept a watchful eye on him. The cop that nails the Chief would make the Police Hall of Fame.

They met in Otto's sparse office. The Chief and Otto had met earlier and agreed that Otto would set the ground rules for the investigation with Butler and Foley. Butler began by giving an update.

They ran the license plates of everybody that left Stony Creek, and only one raised a red flag.

Although he said his name was Scarcini, the plate on his Explorer was registered to an Alexander Stevens, who worked for a Pittsburgh vehicle leasing company. The police learned that Stevens lived with his brother in Mt. Lebanon in the southern suburbs of Pittsburgh. After questioning the brother, they were told that Alex was skiing at Stony Creek for the weekend.

They found Stevens at the resort and questioned him. He was cooperative and his story checked out. Pittsburgh Police confirmed that the plate on Steven's vehicle was stolen. Since Scarcini had Steven's plate on his vehicle, the conclusion was that the plates were switched, maybe while his vehicle was parked at Stony Creek. An ASPB went out on the Steven's plate.

That rocketed Scarcini to the primary suspect. Certain that Scarcini was an alias, they still had to check it out. They sent two state cops to Herminie and found that he no longer lived there. He was a doctor working out of the Mayo Clinic in Minnesota, and a series of phone calls found him there. His story checked out and he couldn't identify anybody who might use his name. Yes, he went skiing at Stony Creek a long time ago but hadn't been near the place for at least fifteen years.

The other thing that jumped out to Butler was the robber's reference to Otto. Earlier Butler requested a list of ex-employees going back at least twenty-five years. Because Grandma Kasser was slow to move to computers, digging up the old stuff was going to be a massive chore. They were filed in boxes in one of the older buildings, and Otto assigned two people to retrieve them.

He asked Otto about the resort records.

"I've got people working on it now. I'm afraid it's going to be a mess, but we'll do what we can. I'll get an update as soon as we finish here," Otto said.

Butler nodded and looked at the Chief. "Your guys said they searched Scarcini's car, and it was clean. They gave us a description so we need to get your boys to either our Greensburg or Harrisburg barracks where they can look at mug shots. We'll also have our artist draw a portrait of this guy from their description. Come to think of it, Harrisburg would be better."

"Good luck on that," the Chief said sarcastically, "You'll be lucky if those two jimokes can identify themselves, but I'll make the arrangements."

"Okay, so we know that Scarcini is not the perp's real name, that he was driving a black 99 Ford Explorer, and that it was searched, and nothing was found. According to their report they checked the wheel well and underneath the vehicle," Foley said. "They did miss checking his ID."

"Yep, said it was clean," Butler said ignoring the ID comment.

"So, what do we think? That the money is still here on the premises?" Otto asked.

"Could be," Butler answered, "I think we have to consider that option, and that he may have had an accomplice, or accomplices, who still might be here on the property."

"Maybe the accomplice left before we even covered the gate. Looking at the timeline it's possible," The Chief said.

"Maybe, Chief, but my hunch is that it's still here on the property. If it turns out that our suspect is the thief, and things are beginning to look that way, where is the money? You can't hide, how much was its Otto?"

"So far, somewhere near $437,000 total," Otto quickly replied.

"That's a lot to hide," Butler continued, directing his response at the Chief.

"C'mon Bob. Maybe your guys can find it, but mine? Hell, they can't even find their dicks when they're trying to jack off," the Chief said.

"I understand, but a duffle bag full of money is hard to hide. The ground is too hard to dig and if it's buried under any snow a warm day will expose it. It could be stashed in one of your storage areas or in a condo, so we'll get the word out, but we want to be cautious about what we say. Letting people know we're looking for a duffle bag of cash can create a lot of unwanted partners, plus your money room employees did say that the perp told them he had an accomplice. And every guest has a suitcase or two so the money could be in any kind of bag."

Foley did more listening than talking. He was measuring what everybody was thinking. He was sure that the guy who left was one of the perps. The money room ladies said the robber claimed to have an accomplice outside the door, but they never saw him. Foley wasn't buying into that premise. Based on the lady's version of the robbery, it was a comedy of errors, and if they were correct, an accomplice would have come into the room to help. Because the perp mentioned Otto's name, Foley was considering it to be an inside job. That would mean that the perp knew his way around the resort.

Otto jumped in. "Let me make this clear. You are not, under any circumstances, going to disrupt my entire operation with cops running all over the place. In fact, Major," Otto said, "I don't want your uniformed men visible to my guests. If you need to investigate, do it with plainclothes men who look like skiers, and before any action is taken that could be a disruption, I want it run by me first. Can we agree on that?"

"It's your decision, sir. I understand and I'll do my best," Butler said.

Foley broke in, trying to ease any tension.

"I think it's possible that the money is still here. Why don't we call in all our department heads," he said watching Otto, "and give them a description of the perp, the bags and whatever else we think is pertinent and have them keep their eyes open?"

"I think it's a waste of time," the Chief said "and you'll be opening a panda's box. Them grifters that work here find that money, they'll bury it in places where the sun don't shine."

Foley wondered why the old man was being difficult. He understood that Otto didn't want any fuss and CB was sucking up to him, but an investigation had to be conducted.

"What do you think, Otto?" Foley asked.

"There's pros and cons on both sides. We have a lot of honest employees but there can always be a bad egg or two,"

"I agree," Foley said, "plus why not offer a generous reward and alert every employee that from now on their cars will be searched when they leave the property."

"That could work," Otto said. "What about a reward of $5000?"

Foley hesitated, and Otto caught it. "Hell, insurance will cover it. I'll make it $25,000."

"I think you're whistling uphill but them mountain hicks ain't ever seen that kind of bread and they'll go for it, but I think the perp and the money are long gone," the Chief said.

Foley believed CB was just trying to duck the investigation but maybe not. Maybe he had another angle. He was certainly brown-nosing Otto, but then Foley stood to make more money and CB wasn't helping him. That wasn't like him. Money never slipped through the Chief's fingers.

Butler spoke. "Look, I believe we have to consider that it could be an inside job and we need to look at that carefully. If it were an inside hit, you'd want to know that Otto, wouldn't you?"

"Of course, but…"

"Look, we'll be discreet as possible," Butler said, "but I need your help and I know you want this resolved quietly and quickly just as much as we do. Let's hold on to the reward idea for a while and let us follow the leads we have. I'm confident that we'll get it done for you."

"Gentlemen, I have things to attend to," Otto said, standing up, "Unless there's something else?"

Everybody mumbled agreement, and the meeting was over.

As Foley and his father were leaving, the Chief whispered to him, "I knew Otto wouldn't want to check out the rooms. It's no skin off his knees. The fuckin' insurance will pick up the tab. Otto ain't gonna lose a penny. Hell, he'll probably make out like a bandit, even better than the real bandit did."

"I don't know CB. I think the guy may have an accomplice. We need to look at all the employees, ex-employees, and…"

"You and whose army?" the Chief said.

"Yeah, I know," Foley said, thinking how much he could use Linda right now. I'm going to have to get some people up here."

Foley was in a bind. He needed to get more staff on board fast. Make assignments, organize the investigation, and set up a command post—all the things that Linda would usually do.

Thinking out loud he said, "I have to get Linda back up here," and as soon as the words slipped out of his mouth, he realized it was a mistake.

The Chief glanced at him but remained mum. As they neared the door, he finally spoke.

"Did you ever watch a cat go after a chipmunk? They'll sit by the chipmunk's hole for hours without moving a muscle, and when that little chipper sticks his head out, the cat claws him with a swipe so fast you don't even see it."

"And the moral of your story is?" Foley asked.

"Keep your head away from pussies."

THE FAMILY MEETING

OVERNIGHT A COLD FRONT MOVED IN, SWEEPING AWAY THE clouds to reveal a crisp blue morning sky and a lemony sun. Otto watched the queue of cars trying to leave Stony Creek, their exhausts sending up thick plumes of noxious fumes into the clear mountain air as the holiday crowd headed home.

"You tell Butler that I want his people to get out on the main road and control traffic. Tell them to do whatever they have to do to get this logjam straightened out, and under no circumstances are they to stop one single vehicle unless they can guarantee that it's the damn robber," Otto yelled into the phone as he looked out of the window of the Presidential Suite on the top floor of the newest building in Kasser Village.

The family meeting was usually held in the VIP Room at Pipa's, but Otto was going all out for this one. He decided that utilizing the most luxurious penthouse in the resort, the Presidential Suite, would create the importance that the meeting deserved.

It was an exquisite four-bedroom suite with nothing but high-end, custom designed furniture featuring rich, unique woods and marble. The dining room table, with seating for ten, was a magnificent two-tone zebrawood, which Otto covered with a powder blue tablecloth because he was concerned about somebody spilling a drink on the beautiful finish. The elegance of the table was even more disturbed by the customary yellow tablets, Number Two pencils, and brown insulated water pitchers.

There were other luxury suites, but the Presidential Suite was one of a kind. Otto was the only one who wanted it, the others saying it was too costly.

Otto's day came when the Secret Service contacted the resort. A President wanted to stay in the Presidential suite. It was an ex-President, but Otto was elated. Former President Gerald Ford was coming to ski at Stony Creek. Otto pulled out all stops to accommodate the coterie of bureaucrats and security in the former President's entourage.

It was a disruptive disaster that cost the resort a small fortune. The publicity was hardly worth the cost. Otto learned quickly that if the credit agencies rated the government, they wouldn't be able to borrow a dime from a loan shark. Nobody could figure out what in the hell they were doing, but a lot of physical damage occurred, and the resort was never paid. There was more red tape than at a red tape factory, and eventually Otto gave up.

Otto sat at the head of the table for the family meeting, his son Henry to his right, as they waited for the board members to arrive. Henry was a skinnier, sickly version of Otto, a fearful man who looked like he was modeled after a lowly clerk from eighteenth century England. All he needed was the green eye shade and sleeve garters, and he would have looked like he just stepped out of the pages of a Dickens' novel.

Otto, in a burst of seasonal goodwill, had room service bring up a tray of festive pastries, all of them leftovers from the holidays, but still a rare gesture. He believed that business meetings should be free of any diversionary amenities.

They were placed on the matching zebrawood buffet, also covered in a protective blue cloth, along with an assortment of hot and cold beverages.

"I need carbonation," Heidi said, clamoring into the room, causing Otto's heart to quiver. She spent New Year's Day mixing her jitters with too much alcohol, as she tried to exorcise the Hogg situation out of her overworked mind.

She went to the buffet, almost gagged when she saw the colorful holiday cookies, and moaned, "No Pellegrino. I need Pellegrino, the kind with gas. Uncle Otto?" she said, her face makeup free and looking a bit starchy. She had her hair pulled back tightly, and her eyes were watery, but she still looked beautiful.

Disgusted, Otto nodded his head and waved his hand, signaling his son Henry to take care of it.

"Really, Hedy…"

"Heidi," she blurted.

"Heidi, yes, you surprise me. I would expect your sister to come in here half in the bag, but you? We have an important meeting, and you need to understand just how…"

"Please, Uncle Otto. No lectures," she said as she plopped herself into the chair at the far end of the table, causing Otto to make a face as if he just swallowed a mouth full of cod liver oil.

Henry muttered that "the soda waters on the way," and sat down next to his father when there was another disturbance at the door. Rosie, who changed from a quiet accounting drone to a lively Auntie Mame, burst into the room with the flourish of a Broadway star entering from stage left.

Every movement she made, and every word she uttered, was draped in dramatic exaggeration. In the dead of winter, she dressed for a summer afternoon tea with Rose Kennedy on the back porch at Hyannis Port in 1937. She wore a wide-brimmed lavender hat, an oversized matching purse, and a much too flowery dress for the season. To Otto's dismay, she literally threw herself into a chair near Heidi, unburdening herself of the heavy bag by slapping it onto the zebrawood table with a bang. Otto cringed as the bag hit the table.

"Champagne, please," she said to no one in particular, "Ice cold, and top it with a light splash of fresh squeezed orange juice, which will make for a nice, refreshing drink on a sunny winter day, don't you think? Who's joining me?" she asked.

Henry looked at his father for approval. Otto, who abhorred alcohol at business meetings, didn't want any confrontations, especially today, and he gave his son a quick nod. He didn't understand what was happening to his sister. At one time, she was a well-contained woman, but a pipe burst somewhere in her system, flooding her with exaggeration and abstraction.

The champagne and Pellegrino arrived, Heidi deciding that alcohol would serve her better than sparkling water. She joined her mother and gulped down a well-filled tulip in one unbroken long slug, trying to hydrate her dehydrated body, which she knew wouldn't work. Otto didn't hide his displeasure.

"Will this meeting take long, Otto?"

"I hope not, Rose," Otto said with a disgusted shrug. He wondered why he took so much time to do things right.

"Well then, shall we start?"

"Hedy isn't here, Rose," Otto said with a weariness, just to let everybody know it annoyed him.

"Of course, she isn't, but I am in a rush. I am going to afternoon tea with those barge people in Pittsburgh, you know, the ones who were at the..." Rose was saying again to no one in particular, when Hedy came into the room, apologizing for being late.

"Sorry guys," Hedy said, "Got tied up with Mike," she added as she sat down in the chair to Otto's right. "Champagne? What are we celebrating?"

"Nothing, darling. Life. Let's get on with this meeting," Rosie said with dramatic impatience.

"Okay, Uncle Otto, you're on," Hedy said with a big smile.

Otto looked around the table and determined everybody was paying attention.

"I call this annual meeting of the Kasser family corporation to order," he said, following up with, "You all have a copy of the agenda, so we'll start with the minutes of the last meeting. Is there a motion to approve?"

Heidi, her head slumped in her hand, waved her right hand.

"Are you making the motion?" Otto asked.

"Otto darling, can we dispense with all this legal mumbo jumbo and get to the important stuff?" Rosie said, looking at everybody for approval. "After all, we're all family here."

"Well Rose, there are corporate procedures and I think we…"

"Of course, there are darling, and we all trust you, don't we?" Rosie interrupted, looking around and seeing affirmative nods, "you can handle those technical aspects anyway you see fit. Do we all agree?"

"Well, yes," Hedy said, "but we do have some important items…"

"Of course, darling, and let's be realistic. It's you and Otto who decide almost everything, and we all leave that to you," she said.

"Good then, Otto, I believe you have an important presentation. Please proceed," Rosie continued.

Otto usually had a stenographer at the meetings, but because a buy offer was going to be discussed, he thought it prudent to keep this to the family only. A decision was going to be made today to sell Stony Creek, and security was of the utmost importance.

"As you all know, by the proposal I sent to each of you last week, we have an offer to sell Stony Creek from a very reputable, and financially stable company, Wessleman-Alkcor, that the rules require that we should seriously consider. I hope each of you has studied the proposal and I will answer any questions, if I can, and if not, a Wessleman executive is standing by to take my phone call."

"I don't think we should sell," Hedy said, getting everybody's attention.

"But darling, I thought we agreed that it would be best …"

"I know mother, but Grandma wouldn't stand for it," Hedy said.

"Not if she saw how much was being offered," Otto said.

"As I understand it, Uncle Otto, once we accept this deal, we no longer have any say in the operation of Stony Creek." Hedy said.

"That's correct, but we do not have to vacate. Provisions have been made for each of us to select a condo or chalet for our use, and each of us will have a generous line of credit for any resort purchases. You and your family will be covered for life with comprehensive health insurance, and each of you will receive a consulting fee for two years. Of course, you will receive stock in the Swiss company along with your share of the sale price. I think it's an extremely good offer, and I have discussed it with each of you personally, and as I understand it, we're all pretty much in agreement. Is that correct?"

Rosie jumped in. "Of course, darling. Shall we vote?"

"Fine with me," Otto said.

"Mom, I have something to say," Hedy said, "Remember?"

"Oh my, yes. Otto, Hedy has a wonderful offer to present. Go ahead, darling."

Otto felt his body go rigid. He leaned back and crossed his arms, trying to look calm as his mind filled up with scenarios, none of which he could corner into a cohesive thought. Otto fought off the desire to reach over and strangle Hedy. He rubbed his neck, coughed, and sure his voice had jumped five octaves, said as casually as he could, "Of course, Hedy. By all means, have at it," he said, wondering what she was going to say.

"Uncle Otto, I apologize that I didn't get a copy of this proposal to you before the meeting, but I just got it and by the time I got through it, I had some changes I wanted to incorporate, mostly minor, so I didn't have the chance to get this to you and…"

"I will not vote on any proposal that I have not thoroughly read and that has not passed muster with legal," he scolded, puffing out his chest.

"I understand that, Uncle Otto and I wouldn't expect you to. Let me explain what I have."

Hedy stood up and took over the meeting, explaining how she accidently met JR Leon, and how, in a casual conversation, he expressed an interest in Stony Creek. When she learned the family was considering a sale, she called him.

"As you've told us time and time again, Uncle Otto, it is our duty as board members to present any and all issues that affect Stony Creek, and so when you informed us about the wonderful offer you received,

I did what you taught me to do. I called Leon to see if it was just idle chatter or whether he was truly serious, and I must admit, the man's answer totally surprised me."

Otto sat quietly, trying to look unconcerned, but his stomach was pouring out acid as if Hoover Dam had burst. Hedy continued.

"I was shocked," Hedy said staring directly into Otto's eyes, "but Mr. Leon was not only serious, he made an offer that is, well, just unbeatable."

"I'm anxious to hear," Otto said trying to look as unconcerned as he could, but he could feel the heat enveloping his face.

"I have paperwork, which I will pass around to each of you, but to sum it up quickly..."

"Yes, darling," Rosie said, "Quickly is good." Hedy shot her a wicked glance.

"I'll move as fast as I can, but I want Uncle Otto to have all the facts. After all, it will be his decision... mostly," she said, giving her uncle a quick smile. Otto didn't react, although the "strangle," thought re-entered his mind.

"Here's the gist of it. Mr. Leon will meet, or exceed every single item in the Alkcor offer, and exceed the sales dollar amount by 10%, but he does have one request."

Otto leaned back. Rosie sipped her mimosa and Heidi sat with her head slumped into her hands while Henry sat stiffly, afraid to move.

"He'd like to have lunch with you, Uncle Otto. He wants you both to get to know each other, and he'll answer any questions you might have. He told me that it's important that he personally meet the top people and I told him the only person he had to meet was you," she said looking around the table and adding, "No offense to you guys." There were no reactions.

"Who is this Leon?" Otto asked, stalling for time. He was fuming, but he kept himself in check.

"A man who can afford to buy us out and then some. There's a bio in his brief that you can read, and..."

Otto felt trapped. He made a quick decision.

"I make a motion that we suspend any actions in this meeting and close debate on the question of the sale, and postpone indefinitely the question..."

"Darling, we haven't debated anything," Rosie said.

"Reconsider," Hedy said.

"What is all this?" Otto said, somewhat taken aback.

"Yes darling," Rosie said, "Why can't we all meet back here in a week and consider both proposals without all this rule sh... ah, crap," she added, enjoying her wordplay, catching everybody off guard because she rarely used profane language.

"Look, Uncle Otto, Mom's right. Let's agree to do that. That way you'll have time to look over the proposal, check it out with legal, and meet with JR Leon. Then we'll come back and vote. I must warn you though. Mr. Leon said he will not engage in a bidding war and that this is his best and final. I would assume, Uncle Otto, that you used your excellent negotiating skills and squeezed the best you could out of the Swiss, so I doubt there will be a war," she said smiling at her Uncle, adding "Does that work for you?"

"Of course, Hedy," Rosie piped in, "That works, don't you agree, Otto?"

"Yes, but we have other issues and..."

"You can handle them. We trust you, Uncle Otto," Heidi said.

"Certainly," said Rosie as she stood up and said, "I make a motion that we adjourn.

"Second that," Heidi said, and everybody started moving.

As the family filed out, Otto was disgusted as he gathered up his papers. He was also pissed at himself. Hedy sucker-punched him.

"Henry," he whispered, turning to his son, "find the Chief and his son. He might be in his office. Have him meet me at my office as soon as possible, and Henry, I don't want to wait any longer than ten minutes."

Otto knew what he had to do. When you can't beat the deal, you beat the dealer. He had to discredit Leon, and he had to do it fast. The Chief's son could help, but Otto wasn't sure his company had the resources necessary to get the job done. He might have to bring in the big boys.

Otto believed that nobody got through life without getting a few ugly blisters, especially a guy like Leon, but the trick was finding those pustules and pricking them open.

OTTO

HEDY BLINDSIDED HIM. HE NEVER SAW IT COMING. HOW COULD he have been so lax? He knew Hedy was a problem, but how she found a buyer so fast was beyond him. His German mother would have called this "scheib machen," or a bloody mess. Hedy certainly pulled one out of her ass, and if he didn't discredit Leon immediately, he was in for a royal screwing.

"I need a comprehensive background report on a man named Leon, JR Leon. Here's what I have on him," Otto said, handing Foley and the Chief a manila file folder. Otto wasn't sure either one of them had the resources to handle the job, but it was all he had now.

"How much of a book?" the Chief asked.

Otto knew he had to be careful with the Chief.

"The usual, the good, the bad and the ugly," he said casually as if it were no big deal.

"How ugly?" the Chief pressed. Foley glanced at his father.

"What do you mean, Chief?"

"How ugly? Do you want us to just check the guy out or do you want to know if he leaves skid marks on his boxers?" the Chief said.

Otto was trying to be casual about his request. He didn't want anybody to know what took place in the family meeting, but he needed to impress them with the seriousness of the assignment.

"Look, I may be doing some important business with him so, yes, I want to know if there's anything I have to worry about. I want a thorough check. If there's even the tiniest speck on his boxers," he said, directing his attention to the Chief, "I want to know about it."

Turning to Foley he said, "Is this something your people can handle?"

"We can handle it," Foley said, thinking he'd break his ass to do it, but his company was hardly running smoothly with Linda's antics. "There will be additional costs incurred. Do you have a specific budget?"

"Foley," Otto said, standing up, "This is an extremely sensitive and important matter. I want everything on this guy that you can find—everything. Look over the bio and get back to me with some estimated costs, but understand, I want a first-class job done on this, nothing less."

"Yes, sir. I'll get on it right away."

The Chief liked the way Foley handled the extra costs.

"Chief, you have some excellent contacts within the mountain-climbing community, as you call them," Otto said, giving the Chief his full attention, "and I want you to use them to get what we need on Leon. You come up with some good stuff and I'll make it worth your while," Otto added, knowing that money lit a big fire under the Chief's ass.

"Okay, fellows, that's it. We good?" Otto said, standing up.

"Yes sir," Foley said, and they left.

As they walked down the hall, Foley was looking through the papers Otto gave him. As he read one of the documents, he realized it must have been given to him by mistake. It was a copy of a cover letter from JR Leon, and it showed that Leon wanted to buy Stony Creek.

"Holy hell," Foley said, muttering to himself.

"What are you mumbling about?" the Chief said.

"Nothing," Foley said.

Foley knew he had inadvertently become the recipient of prized information, and he didn't know what to do with it.

Whatever he did he couldn't give it to the Chief.

FOLEY

FOLEY SAT BEHIND HIS DESK LOOKING AT THE LEON LETTER. TALK
about a hot potato. What to do with it? He ran the choices through his
mind. Return it and let Otto deal with it; or say nothing and pretend he
thought he was supposed to have it.

If CB found out he'd jump on it like a rabbit in heat. God knows
what he'd do with it, but he'd be taking bids..

Right now, Foley's focus was the Leon project. He knew what had to
be done. His concern was having the staff to back him up.

With Linda in limbo, there was a sizeable gap in his operation.
Filling it required time, and he didn't have that luxury. He'd try to keep
Linda around if he could, but the prospects weren't promising. He faced
a difficult situation.

As much as he hated to do it, he called her cell phone.

"Look, I understand that you're going through a lot and I hate to
lay this on you, but I need your help." He explained the Leon situation
to her.

"I know the timing is lousy on this, but it is a big opportunity for the
company," he said, "and I really can use your research expertise."

Linda didn't respond. He waited. He jumped back in.

"Look, if you can't do it then that's it, but if you can help us on this,
I'd appreciate it greatly," he said, hoping she'd agree.

As she stood looking out of the large, double-layered tinted glass
window, watching a gentle snow falling, she didn't know how to respond.

"Linda, are you there? Linda?"

"I'm here."

"Well?"

"Let me see what I can do."

"I'll come and meet you in Pittsburgh, if that helps?" Foley said.

"Ah, no. Not necessary. I'll call you in a couple of hours. Okay?"

"Fine. Just let me know ASAP. Thanks."

She hung up and continued to stare out the window.

When she married Bobby, she gave him a few conditions. She told him she needed time to clean up the projects she was working on, and that she would stay until Foley found a replacement.

Now she was trying to straddle two lives in different worlds, keeping each of them viable until she could figure everything out. Nothing she had done on either end made sense anymore.

She called Bobby.

"Something came up and I have to leave for a few days," she said.

"What came up?"

"My mother, well, actually it's my Dad. He's not feeling well and refuses to go to the doctor. I talked with him on the phone, but he won't budge. My Mom wants me to come home and help her. I don't think it's serious, but I'm going to leave in a few hours. I'll call you later tonight and fill you in. I'm really sorry about this."

"Well, I understand. I was just hoping that we could get settled. The condo will be ready in a few days and…"

"I know how you feel, and I know I've been going back and forth, but this time it's my Dad, not work," she said.

"Yeah, well, okay. Call me later," he said.

"I will."

Linda hung up. She was still gazing aimlessly out of the window. Seven stories down she watched a few scattered people, looking like black insects, walking through snow-covered Rittenhouse Square. The park in center city Philadelphia was enveloped in white and garnished with colorful holiday lights that ribboned the twisted black tree limbs.

It was the postcard she didn't want to send.

She packed a few items in her Gucci overnighter, called her mother, and told her to cover for her. Despite her objections, her mother agreed. Linda ate a late breakfast and left the Rittenhouse Hotel around noon.

As she drove through the rolling hills of Pennsylvania, she knew she had to make a decision.

She had to end it. But which end?

HOGG

THE DOCTOR'S NURSE RUTH BOOKED THEM ON A FLIGHT TO COSTA Rica through Atlanta. They'd be in San Jose that evening. They had time before they left, so Dr. Jim let Hogg sleep while he got everything together. He packed a small carry-on with overnight essentials, but he wasn't planning on leaving the airport. He was returning on the earliest flight. He modified his medical bag so he could board with a minimum of problems. There would be an ambulance at the airport to take Hogg to the hospital.

Ruth drove them to the Pittsburgh airport with a stop at Hogg's house to get his passport and cash. Hogg's wife thought he was drunk and laid a heavy dose of grief on him as he staggered back out of the door. He didn't bother packing a bag. He'd get what he needed in Costa Rica.

The journey went better than Dr. Jim expected. He dosed Hogg with pain killers and managed to wheelchair him through the airport. Hogg slept most of the way, and Dr. Jim was feeling a little better. He was thanking himself for thinking of the Costa Rica idea.

Two nurses met them and rushed him through customs. Less than an hour later he was being attended to at the hospital.

The Clinica Santa Rosa was a small, upscale 75 bed facility that catered to high-end patients. The rooms were more like luxury hotel suites with amenities fit for those who wanted the best. Most of their patients were in for cosmetic fixes. Their staff included some of the best cosmetic surgeons in the world. The chief administrator was Dr. William Rhodes, an ex-pat from Chicago.

Dr. Rhodes, who graduated from Pitt Medical School with Dr. Jim, opted for the tropical climate of Costa Rica to the hustle and bustle of a big city practice and it paid off. Along with making a lot of money, he also wielded a great deal of power. He admitted Hogg under an assumed name and eliminated most of the usual paperwork. It was an all-cash deal.

Hogg slept for ten hours. When he woke up, he saw a distinguished-looking man smiling at him. Dr. Rhodes was tall and thin, a man whose bearing said he was somebody. He was dressed casually in a cream Brioni golf shirt and tan Zegna silk pants. He had a thick white brush mustache with matching hair and eyebrows. His lean face was deeply tanned, and his hazel eyes gleamed with confidence as he introduced himself to Hogg. He filled him in on his medical condition and assured him he was fine. He explained all the ramifications of his accident, including how he would have to urinate. Every statement was like a searing spike into Hogg's chest.

"There are surgical procedures you can explore. They might be able to build up some tissue to make it easier and I've heard that some researchers are experimenting with artificial devices, but that is much more complicated," Dr. Rhodes explained.

He also informed Hogg that it would feel like he still had a penis and that it would be possible for him to ejaculate. A new pain engulfed Hogg. He demanded more sleeping pills.

Hogg was feeling better physically, but mentally he was a mess. He just couldn't believe what Heidi did to him, and he replayed the vague scene repeatedly, trying to remember details, but he couldn't cut through the fog and get an unobstructed view.

Dr. Rhodes stopped by late in the afternoon of Hogg's second full day at the clinic.

"How are you feeling today?" he said, looking at his chart.

"Good enough to get back to the states," Hogg said.

"Everything's looking good. Let's see, you got here Tuesday evening," Dr. Rhodes said, looking at his chart, "and today is Thursday. I think we can get you out of here by Saturday..."

"Can we make it tomorrow, Friday?" Hogg interrupted.

"Well, I'd like another day, but if you feel up to it, sure. Let me have my assistant make all the arrangements and if we can get you on a flight, you're good to go."

"Good, Doc, good. I have a question."

"Shoot."

"Ah, is it possible I can get another, ah, a transplant, ah, one that works?" Hogg asked.

"I'm afraid not. There are doctors working on it, and there have been reports of some success, but nobody has officially done it yet, but I think it's possible. We've done it with other organs."

"Do you know anybody who's researching that kind of transplant?"

"I haven't heard about anybody in this country, but then I'm not up to date on that issue. I have a friend, a Chinese doctor that I did my residency with, and I heard he's working on it. I can check with him if you like?"

"I can't live this way," Hogg said, "In fact, it feels like I still have one. It's weird."

"That's normal. As I told you the other day, you'll continue to feel like you have a penis," Dr. Rhodes said.

"Well, if it's not too much trouble, could you check with your Chinese friend? See what's up? Any costs I'll pay."

"I will, but if he is open to doing something with you, you'd have to go to China. He's in Beijing."

"I don't give a shit if he's in Timbuktu. If he can get me a new tool, I'm all in. One thing I know for sure—I can't live this way."

"I'll see what I can do. Plan on tomorrow. I think we can get you out of here by then," Dr. Rhodes said.

"Thanks, Doc. I will."

Hogg felt like he could reach down and grab his dick, but he knew it wasn't there. He needed to do something, and the Chinese were smart. If anybody could do it, the Chinese could. Hell, every time he turned on TV there was another gook winning an award for brains. The problem was most of them were short, little guys.

He wondered if there were any Chinamen who had big dicks.

JOE DUCK

IF SOMEBODY HADN'T STUFFED THE TRIBUNE-REVIEW NEWSPAPER back into the rack upside down, Joe would have never seen it. It was nothing more than a small box on the front page. "Late Breaking. Stony Creek Robbed," was all it said. That pissed Joe. He wished they had put a dollar amount on how much was robbed. He had no idea what his take was.

He grabbed $25,000 of it and it was sizzling in his pocket like a brain on drugs, but Joe knew better. He had seen enough TV to know the first thing cops looked for was some guy flashing a lot of cash around, Joe wasn't about to fall into that trap, but he needed to get another car and get laid.

He parked his SUV on the narrow one-way side street near his walk-up, which got little traffic or police attention, but he guessed the cops had an Explorer on their radar and he had to unload it.

His first thought was to go back to the Cash-Man, a small-time mob guy out on 51 where he bought the Ford. The street people knew the lot was nothing more than a money Maytag where you could exchange cash for cars and then sell them back to the dealer laundering dirty money. Joe didn't trust them. If they thought he had some cash they'd come looking for it, so he went out to another guy in Monroeville.

He traded in the Explorer, plus some cash, for a low mileage 2000 silver Honda CR-V, and soon he was tooling down the Parkway East, heading into the city with the stereo blasting out the Red Hot Chili Peppers. The Honda was humming like a little kitty purring for more.

He couldn't believe how quick it was. Just a slight press of the pedal and the thing took off. It was like somebody put a rocket up Mario Andretti's ass.

All he needed now was a cold beer and a little action. He could feel his dick getting hard, and that's when Joe thought of Ruby.

Ruby Begonia was "a woman of size" as she referred to her nearly 250 pounds of rolling waves of fat. She had an attractive face, kind of like a black Betty Boop. She didn't know who tagged her with "Begonia," a reference to an old Amos & Andy radio character, but it stuck, and she didn't care as long as they paid.

Ruby claimed she wasn't a hooker, and it wasn't wise to refer to her as one. She called herself a charity volunteer who was helping those suffering with unfulfilled needs. What was wrong with accepting donations for her public service?

Nobody messed with Ruby. Cross her and you entered no-man's-land. She'd slice you with a razor as quickly as she could swat a fly in mid-air with her bare hand, which she did with amazing alacrity. Joe banged her before, and he loved immersing himself in her ocean of flesh and burying his face into her huge warm boobs. It was like rolling around in a pool of warm sponge rubber. He loved that feeling.

Ruby didn't get much pleasure from Joe. His penis matched his height-short and skinny. Because she was so obese, she was never sure if Joe got his "little white worm" into her or not.

"Ruby?" Joe said, fondling himself through his denim jeans as he talked on the telephone, "Joe Ducci, how ya doin, babe?"

"I'm doing just fine," Joe. "Whattya need?"

"I don't need a thing, honey, but how would you like to spend a couple of days up at Stony Creek, and everything's on me?"

"Did you rob a bank?"

"Funny, honey. Matter of fact, I did. Got myself a cool million. How about I buy you a mansion down on the ocean?"

"Sweet, Joe. Maybe I could be interested. I need a little time away. When did you want to go?" she said, thinking she could use a free trip and Joe was harmless. He popped his load faster than a hooker pulls her pants down for a drunken millionaire.

"I'm thinking we go up next Tuesday, when it's not so busy, and we'll stay a couple of days."

"Well, Joey, that sounds really nice. You lay two-fifty into my loving hands honey and I'll let you lay your head into my big, sweet pussy that right now is getting damp. How's that sound, honey-babe?"

"It sounds like you're upping your donation on me, Ruby. It was only fifty last time."

"Yes, my sweet baby, but that was down and dirty, this is long, slow and away we go my big man, so ante up and I'll pleasure you 'till you don't want no more," Ruby said exaggerating every breath and gasp, "unless you don't have the kind of donation Ruby needs to continue her work."

"Oh, don't you worry, honey. I have more than enough to get anybody I want, but I picked you, so you be nice to me and I'll be nice to you."

"How many days, darling?"

"Like I said, a couple. Two. We'll come back Friday morning."

"Well, darlin' I'm drippin' just thinking about it. I can't wait to feel your big throbbing monster slamming into me like a freight train, baby," she said slowly," but I'm thinkin' about the work and paycheck I'll miss, so I do believe another two hundred should cover it. I know you understand, baby."

Joe knew Ruby was negotiable, but this time he had the bread, so why hassle? He just needed some pussy to relieve the tension.

"You're on. Come by my place Tuesday morning, maybe about ten?"

"See you then, sweetie. Just make sure you have the donation, darling. You just don't want to tangle with Ruby. You understand?"

"I understand. I'll have what you want, baby. I always do."

If you know what's good for you, you will, Ruby thought as she hung up.

She liked the idea of going to Stony Creek. She would have cut her price if Joe had pushed, but he didn't, which meant he had more. She'd find a way to get some of it, but right now she was excited about going to Stony Creek. Ruby smiled at the thought of going to a fancy ski resort. Snow was for white people.

She imagined the look on those rich bitch's faces when they saw a woman of color and considerable size strutting her stuff with a white midget.

They'll be clucking like a bunch of hens in the Colonel's chicken coop.

THE CHIEF

BOB BUTLER BRIEFED THE CHIEF. HE WAS IN HIS GRAY UNIFORM, white shirt, black tie, and a black commando sweater they called a "wooly pully."

"Our forensic people went over the robbery scene and came up with more prints than we can count. We're running them all, but so far, we've got nothing. The hotel room was clean. Too clean, which meant somebody took the time to wipe the room down. I'd say that the guy that was in 420 is our number one suspect."

"I guessed that right off," the Chief said.

Butler ignored the remark. He continued his briefing.

"The real Scarcini is clean. Everything he told us checks out. Either our actor knew him or got his identity somewhere. We talked with Scarcini and he couldn't connect any of it up. He said the last time he was in Stony Creek was fifteen or twenty years ago. We contacted the Minnesota police and Scarcini agreed to look at mug shots to see if he recognizes anybody, but we're swimming upstream on this one."

"What about his 'Otto' comment and the liquor boxes?"

"That's a good lead. He could be an ex-employee. We asked management what kind of records they have, but it's like hunting for a needle in a haystack. Stony Creek has hundreds of ex-employees and they're not computerized. Just stacks of disorganized boxes. It's not impossible but close to it," he said.

"What's your thought on the money?" the Chief asked.

"Hard to say. If our suspect had an accomplice, and he left before your men closed off the exit, they're long gone. On the other hand, if there was or wasn't an accomplice, then it could still be hidden somewhere on the premises. If one, or both perps is an employee, or former employees, or there are a couple of them in cahoots, then we have our work cut out for us. We're checking current employees and their whereabouts that night. Hell, that money could be anyplace."

"Well, my experience with these piss-ants is that they don't get too far away from the scratch. My guess is that he had an accomplice who left with the take before we knew about the robbery. Them cough drops are probably sitting on the sand in Mexico sucking down tequilas, and dicking the Senoritas," the Chief said.

"That's as good a guess as any," Butler said, standing up, "I'll keep you posted, and you do the same."

"Right," the Chief said, walking Butler to the door.

The Chief went back to his desk and Hogg's face popped into his mind. He had to keep close tabs on him. He gave him a call.

Hogg was sitting in the Juan Santamaria International Airport, just outside of San Jose. He was looking at a sign, "Welcome to the happiest country in the world," thinking what bullshit, when his cell phone rang. He recognized the Chief's number.

"Yeah Carl, what's up?"

"Just wanted to see if you were alive," the Chief said.

"I'm alive."

"Good. Where are you?"

"You writing a book?"

"Just making conversation. How's the, ah… injury?"

"Better," Hogg said.

"Well, okay. Just wanted to check on you."

"You did. Thanks," Hogg said, and was about to hang up, when the Chief said he had one more question.

"When you coming up to Stony Creek?"

"Jesus, Chief, what's with all the questions?" Hogg asked, getting perturbed.

"Hey, you were the one that brought me into your fucked-up world. Since you did, I figure I ought to know how you're doing, so cut the crap."

"I'm doing fine. Thanks. I'll call you when I get up there, Okay?" Hogg said, putting a little nice into his voice.

"I forgot that my damn vehicle is still up there," Hogg added.

"Do you need it?"

"I will. I'll get somebody to drive me up and get it in the next few days," Hogg said.

"Well, call me when you come up. We'll have a drink," the Chief said.

"Yeah, I'll call you," Hogg said, hanging up. There was no doubt in his mind that the Chief was up to something. Asking me how I feel? He doesn't give a rat's ass about stuff like that.

The Chief wanted to make certain Hogg didn't pull him into his mess. He had to keep him close.

Hogg was so paranoid he'd have himself followed if he could figure out how to do it. That night somebody was lurking around Hogg's house. It could be the cutter or somebody else. And then there was the jagoff that robbed the money room.

A lot of crap was piling up, The Chief didn't want to step in any of it.

LINDA

LINDA CALLED FOLEY AND TOLD HIM SHE WAS ON HER WAY. THE turnpike was loaded with trucks and Linda didn't like it. Passing the big rigs on a sloppy wet road was a challenge. As she passed, their large, rolling wheels spun out gushers of dirty slush that splattered against her windshield. It was a safety hazard.

She vowed to start a protest group against their unshielded wheels. There had to be some way to add side panels or flaps that would direct the spray away from passing vehicles. Of course, the trucking lobby probably found it cheaper to add a little cash to the politician's pockets.

She had more on her mind than trucks. One moment she knew what she was going to do and the next she didn't. Talk about being between a rock and a hard place.

Foley was her thrill ride. A free-falling adventure while Bobby was like the kid's train at the mall—safe, slow, and steady. She loved free-falling with Foley, but Bobby fit better into her corporate future. She'd have to make a decision—one she didn't want to make.

She called Foley just before she got off the turnpike.

"I'll be there in about a half-hour," she said, "and Foley, don't take this the wrong way, but I'd prefer my own room." Foley agreed to make arrangements. Right now, he needed her expertise and operational skills, and he didn't want to rock the boat. She was also an excellent researcher who could find a flea in a sandstorm.

He suggested a dinner meeting, but she opted out. They agreed to meet in a small alcove off one of the less busy hallways.

Foley thought she had driven in from Pittsburgh and asked how the roads were. She hurried out an "okay" and moved to business.

"Okay, fill me in," she said.

Foley briefed her on the status of the robbery and Leon. He told her about the Leon letter.

"He's trying to buy the place," Foley said, "I think Otto mistakenly gave me a copy of his cover letter to what I assume was a proposal. From the way Otto talked, I don't think he wants to sell to Leon because he wants us to find some dirt on him."

"There's not a lot to work with here," Linda said, reading through the papers. He has a yacht somewhere, holds both South American and American passports, and has a lot of money," Linda said, looking at the brief resume.

"Well, we know he was born, so that's where you start. Follow the paper trail and I'm sure that even Brazil will have birth records. I have some contacts with the feds, so I'll track down the passport info," Foley said.

"It would be a lot easier if we had to search his history in this country, but South America?" she said, frowning and shaking her head. "I'm not sure how good their record-keeping is down there."

"Otto says he's willing to spend the money. Hell, maybe we can get a nice trip out of it. I've never been to Brazil," he said, with a nervous chuckle.

She gave Foley a quick smile and stood up.

That's the last thing I need.

THE SECURITY COMPANY

LINDA CALLED THE TV STATION AND HAD THEM SCHEDULE RERUNS of Foley's show, explaining he was out of town on business. The Chief set them up in an empty office near accounting and Carly brought up the company files on open cases.

Their Stony Creek office was open for business. Linda told Foley she planned to go to Pittsburgh for the weekend and would return the following Tuesday.

"I have a lot of loose ends I need to clear up for a meeting I have on Monday with an attorney," she told Foley. "I'll work at home, and if you need me, call me at my mothers."

Foley hated his dependency on Linda and was moving fast to find a replacement, but that wouldn't be easy.

He called an old friend, a retired cop, and cajoled him into helping temporarily. Fritzie Schmitt plowed his way up through the ranks, working in every division, retiring as one of the best homicide detectives the department ever had. His German heritage showed in his work; he was precise, dogged, and a no-bullshit cop who could find the guilty grain of sand in a giant dune. Linda also promised to bring in a college classmate of hers to help, but so far that hadn't happened.

He didn't miss Linda's "attorney meeting" comment, but his g was up. He wasn't sure about anything she said.

The phone rang. It was the Chief.

"You want to get together for coffee? I think I have a way for you to cover my little stipend without digging into your action."

"Geez, CB, is that all you're worried about?"

"No, it's you I'm worried about. That's why I'm thinking of ways for you to make a buck," the Chief said.

"Okay, okay. Anything new on the robbery from your end?"

"Nothing exciting. I think we can kiss that money goodbye. It's outta here."

"I disagree. Stony Creek is what? A couple thousand acres? That money could be anywhere on the property."

"Maybe, but I doubt it," the Chief said. "As big as Stony Creek is, Otto uses ever foot of it. And now that the employees know about the robbery, they're crawling all over the place looking for it. They're like cockroaches in a Chinese Restaurant. They'd of found it by now. I say that money's been turned into pesos and is buying pachingo and all the pussy you can eat."

Foley almost asked what "pachingo" was but caught himself in time.

"Could be. Aren't there some caves around here?"

"Forget them. The see-plunkers are creeping all over 'em. Otto don't care. Insurance will cover the loss. I say the money's long gone and we're wasting our time trying to find it."

"We're not trying to find the money. We're trying to catch a crook," Foley said.

"Yeah, well, you know what I mean," the Chief said.

Foley wasn't sure what anything the old man said meant. He was a master at double-talk.

"I assume the states are checking out motels along the way," Foley said.

"I'm sure they are."

"What about the ones on the back roads?"

"What back roads?"

"Suppose our suspect went to Bedford or Greensburg and holed up there?"

"Do you realize how many different ways they could've gone?" The Chief said.

"I do, but there aren't motels on all those roads. I think it's worth checking out some of them."

"I don't know, but that's a shitload of work," the Chief said, thinking he'd look at that option.

"Good police work always is," Foley said.

"Always is what?" the Chief asked.

"A shitload of work."

When he hung up, the Chief pulled out the Westmoreland County Yellow Pages. He guessed the perp might try to lose himself in Pittsburgh and a major airport was there. He looked at the Hotel/Motel listings. There was a bunch of them. He'd make a few calls himself, just in case. Better he finds the perp than anybody else.

And then there was Hogg's cock cutter. The Chief had a good idea who Jack, or better yet, Jackie the Ripper was, and that meant more problems for her. He had trouble buying into it, but the evidence was hard to ignore.

If he was right, it was going to be raining crap on a bunch of people.

It would look like Mother Nature OD'd on Ex-Lax.

THE TWINS

HEDY'S IMAGINATION KEPT REPEATING ONE IMAGE: SHE KEPT seeing Hogg's body decomposing in his plaid playroom. It was like an earworm. That one song that keeps playing in your head over and over again.

She had to find out if Hogg was alive. Against her better judgement, she drove by his house. She threw a hoodie over her head and wore oversized sunglasses, but she knew that wouldn't matter. If he were alive, he was probably sitting by his window with a shotgun or a bazooka waiting for her.

She wasn't sure what she was looking for, but she was hoping she'd see something that gave her a clue.

The house looked deserted. There were no lights or any sign of activity. She checked the chimney and there was no smoke, so the fireplace wasn't burning. As she got closer, she saw the front walk was still snow covered. The next thing she saw caused a nervous chill to run through her.

Parked on the upper side of the house, on the narrow driveway, she saw his vehicle. The snow covering it and no tracks told her it hadn't moved. Not good.

Her hands were clammy, and she felt the blood drain from her face. A wave of nausea ran through her stomach. Hogg was dead. She killed him. This changed everything. She didn't expect this. She thought of alternatives. She ran a bunch of scenarios through her mind, but no matter what she came up with none of them would work. She had to protect her sister. Heidi was like a porcelain doll on a bumpy road. She'd shatter at the first tiny quiver.

She started for her condo, changed her mind, and went to Heidi's.

Hedy said she stopped by to check on her and engaged in small talk trying to gage her sister's state of mind and quickly realized it wouldn't matter. Heidi would panic.

"It's possible that Hogg might be dead," Hedy said.

Heidi's face went whiter than her décor. She stiffened and leaned back against the kitchen counter, putting her hands on the cold marble for support.

Her voice was shaky as she asked, "What do you mean 'possible?'"

"I mean I don't know for sure, but it looks like it's… ah, possible that he's dead."

Heidi stiffened, stood up straight, moved away from the counter, and started pacing around the room. Walking in circles around the living room, she fought to stay calm. She knew Hedy worried about her. Realizing she was wringing her hands, she stopped, but she didn't know what to do with them. She had to act cool, think it all out. If he were dead, he couldn't hurt her. That part was good. But if he wasn't? It would be a nightmare. She couldn't believe that Hogg was dead. Men like Hogg don't die easy. Hedy said "possible."

"He's not dead," Heidi said in a soft, eerie voice.

She walked back into the kitchen where Hedy was standing and stood in front of her.

"He's not dead. I feel it, Hedy."

Heidi was in denial. That didn't surprise Hedy.

"I think he is," Hedy said, "and I was really careful although I'm not sure about the booze and drugs. I just don't understand it, but I knew there was a chance this could happen."

Heidi looked at her sister, wondering how she could be so unemotionally analytical.

"He's not dead," Heidi said again, as if she were hypnotized.

"His car is still there. It doesn't look like he moved it," Hedy said, thinking her sister might be in some sort of shock.

"He could have called somebody to come and get him," Heidi said, sounding mechanical and distant. "With his connections, he's probably in a hospital somewhere under an assumed name."

Hedy was concerned about her sister, but what she said was possible. The more she thought about it, the more she wanted it to be true. But a breathing Hogg was more dangerous than a dead one.

"He's alive. I just know it," Heidi said with more emotion as she crinkled her face and tears formed in her eyes.

"Heidi," Hedy said, choosing her words carefully, "I know you're worried, but there is nothing for you to worry about. Thinking about it, you could be right. Somebody came and got him," Hedy said, trying to calm her sister.

"I know you don't believe me, but I feel he's alive," Heidi said, her eyes glistening with tears, her face filled with fear.

Hedy thought this was a good time to bring up the trip.

"Look, why don't you go back to St. Bart's. Get far away from here. Don't tell anybody where you're going. Maybe take that girl you like, what's her name, the daughter of the woman who runs our housekeeping, ah…"

"Pam," Heidi whimpered.

"Yeah, take her, all expenses paid. She'll love it and she can keep you company."

"You don't know Bill like I do, he'll find me no matter what," Heidi said sobbing. "He'll find me, Hedy. I know he will," she cried.

Hedy put her arms around her sister. "I'll make sure you're safe, honey. You know that. If he's alive, he's busy taking care of his… his problem, so we have time. I think he'll stay away, at least for a while, and by then you'll be long gone."

"I think he's alive, and he's not calling me because he doesn't want any record of phone calls to me," she said.

Hedy stood up and walked over to the counter. She stared out of the kitchen window. She was thinking about the possibility that Heidi was right. Hogg was a shrewd son-of-a-bitch and he could be playing games. Maybe she was in denial of some sort, but she had to find out for sure.

"Heidi, honey, let's do this. You call him. If he answers, play dumb. Just ask when you can see him. If he attacks, act confused. You don't know what he's talking about. The truth is, you weren't there, and you did nothing to him, so just tell the truth. If he tells you what happened and blames you tell him you can prove you weren't there. Offer to take a lie detector test. You cannot waver or falter. You weren't there, and that's the truth. He thought he saw you there, but he was drunk. We can prove you were here."

"What if he doesn't answer?" Heidi said with mixed feelings. She was damned if he was alive and damned if he wasn't.

What had Hedy gotten her into?

"Better yet. Leave a message that you were calling because you hadn't seen him since…when's the last time you saw him?" Hedy said.

"Right before the holidays."

"Perfect. Remind him of that," Hedy said.

"What if he calls back and you're not here?"

"Just tell him that you miss him and want to see him, like we discussed, and then call me immediately and we'll go from there."

"I don't know, Hedy, I'm not good at lying," Heidi said.

Hedy wanted to say you did a rather good job of lying when you were screwing Hogg but knew better.

"That's just it, honey, you don't have to lie," Hedy said, "You didn't do a thing to Hogg. Just tell the truth. You were not there."

Heidi put her hand down for a moment, shook her head and said, "You're right. I didn't. Okay, I'll call him." She reached for the phone and ff.

o it."

"Look, if he answers, I doubt he'll say much to you. Hogg's a game player. He'll be watching to see how you react. Act normal, like you didn't do a thing, and honey you didn't. If it ever comes to that, a lie detector test will clear you. Of course, we'll only allow one question and that is, 'Did you cut off Hogg's penis?' and that will end it," Heidi said.

Heidi, still worried, agreed, and once again she reached for the phone.

She put the phone on speaker and dialed Hogg's cell. The phone rang. No answer. Hedy and Heidi looked at each other as it rang for the third time. Heidi gestured with the phone as if to say, "See, no answer," when Hogg's voice shattered the silence, the sound slicing through both like a sharp blade.

Heidi panicked, her blue eyes opening wide, looking for help.

Hedy paused, and then made the hand gesture for phone, bringing her thumb and index finger up to her mouth and ear, mouthing "TALK, TALK."

Heidi looked at the phone as Hogg said a gruff "Hello" again.

"Bill," she said, almost in a whisper, "this is Heidi."

"I know who it is."

"Ah, I've been calling you," Heidi said, looking for help from Hedy, who was relieved to hear Hogg's voice. Hedy waved her hand at Heidi, signaling her to keep talking.

"Are you okay?" she said, still weak voiced.

"Why wouldn't I be?"

"I don't know. I just didn't hear from you and I was worried," she said.

Hedy nodded, mouthing "good."

"About what?" Hogg said curtly.

"About you, because I haven't seen you for a while."

"Where in the fuck do you get off thinking I have to call you," he said, his voice rising, and then softening as he continued, "Sorry, just having a bad day. I'll call you later and we'll talk, okay?"

"Okay," Heidi said and hung up, looking up at her sister, "You heard?"

"Yeah. The good news is that he's alive. The bad news is that he's acting like nothing happened. He's trying to mind-fuck you," Hedy said.

"I told you," Heidi said, her face reddening, stalking off into the living room, wringing her hands, and repeating, "I told you, Hedy, I told you. He's going to kill me. I just know it," she said, sobbing.

Hedy caught up to her, grabbed her, and put her arms around her. Heidi was in tears, gasping and moaning between torrents of "I told you so's".

"Honey, don't worry," she soothed, "I promise you it will be alright."

Hedy took her sister's face in her hands, smiled, and said, "I know exactly what to do, and there's no way Hogg will get near you. If it's better that you leave Stony Creek for a nice vacation, then so be it, but I promise that you will be safe. Do you believe me?"

Heidi shook her head up and down, tears streaming down her pretty face, her mascara running, creating squiggly black lines on her rosy cheeks.

Houston, we have a problem.

STONY CREEK

THE CROWDED SLOPES LOOKED LIKE A NIGHT SKY THAT WAS TURNED inside out. Instead of bright stars against a dark sky it was the opposite. Minions of animated black figures scurried down the snowy slopes, leaving trails of scribbly lines behind them.

The holiday crowd poured in early Friday morning, planning to get as much slope time as they could with their weekend passes.

Hedy kept pushing Otto to meet with JR, but he stalled. He hoped to have an initial background check on Leon before they met but that wasn't happening. He finally relented and a meeting was set. They'd meet at Pipa's at 2 PM, after the lunch crowd left.

Hedy was pleased. Otto probably had a team of investigators on the case and if they found something the deal would be off. The quicker she locked up the Leon deal the better.

Then there was Hogg.

He was a dangerous psychotic. She believed his immediate focus was finding a doctor who could make him whole again if that was even possible. She joked to herself that he couldn't go to a used penis store, pick out a model, and have it reattached, so she had time. She didn't know if Hogg would have any memory of what happened. She was told the drugs she used could cause memory loss but there was no guarantee. The question was would Hogg link Heidi to the deed, and of that she wasn't certain. This wasn't going the way she originally planned but she had no choice. She had to manage Heidi and keep Hogg at bay.

Meanwhile, Foley planned on working the weekend with Linda, but she was back to her old tricks, saying she had to leave because her father was ill. He didn't try to change her mind. At least he got a few hours of work out of her.

Otto, eager to get something on Leon, kept pushing Foley. He finally told Foley the truth about the buy offer hoping that would get him to move faster. Foley was relieved. At least he didn't have to deal with that issue any longer. He explained that he was moving as fast as possible and had a team on it but digging out information from bureaucracies was a difficult process.

Another problem was CB. He was always looking for the money shot. Working with CB was like walking a tightrope with one leg. It was exhausting. He didn't doubt that CB probably knew about the proposed sale and that was troubling.

There were more things falling out of place than in and Foley was in the middle of it all.

Nobody had his back.

JOE DUCK

Joe Duck was slumped on his worn cloth sofa. When he bought it at Goodwill it was tan, but now it was freckled with dark stains. He was watching the noon news, drinking beer, and eating pork rinds, fretting over his hasty decision to take Ruby Begonia to Stony Creek.

Five minutes at Stony Creek and everybody within fifty miles would know who Ruby Begonia was. There was nothing subtle about Ruby. She'd roll into Stony Creek like the lead tank, her mouth firing out bombs that would blow up everybody in sight.

She'd be the black elephant in a white room. Joe wouldn't have a prayer.

But telling her the trip was off would be suicidal. Joe wasn't about to undergo that barrage. The trick was to find somewhere else to take her, maybe south, but first he had to get to Stony Creek. He'd leave immediately.

He'd get there by early evening, case the place, and if it were clear, go in and get the money and be back in Pittsburgh by midnight. Then he would handle Ruby.

He took a fast gulp of his beer and headed for the bathroom. He had to get rid of his beard. It was after four when a clean-shaven Joe Duck, wearing oversized shades, paid his twenty bucks to get through the toll booths at Stony Creek, bitching to himself about the entry fee.

Joe could make out some old tracks on the retention pond road, but the fresh snow hadn't been disturbed. Joe didn't like putting down the first tracks, but it would be dark soon. He drove back to the same spot.

He was about to get out but didn't like the direction his car was facing. He had to turn it around. He hurried, but the narrow road required a lot of short, jerky movements and Joe's blood pressure was soaring.

He wiped his sweaty hands on his pants as he quickly got out of his car.

Joe lifted his windshield wiper and put a piece of white paper under it.

"Went to get gas."

He strapped on his backpack. Inside was a pair of binoculars, crowbar, hammer, pliers, latex gloves, slim Jim, bump keys and lock picks.

Hogg's house looked quiet. He didn't see any lights yet. If there was anybody there, they'd be turning them on soon. He scanned the house with his binoculars. No movement.

It was a gloomy day, heavy gray clouds blocking any light, causing the day to fall faster towards darkness.

Joe watched and waited.

THE CHIEF

THE CHIEF CALLED SEVERAL MOTELS ALONG A POSSIBLE BACK route. Identifying himself, he asked if they registered a Scarcini. Most of the motels cooperated but a few refused saying they had no proof he was a cop. He came up empty. His hand was on the phone to make another call when it rang.

"This is the Chief. What do you want?"

"Is that the way a public servant greets a taxpayer," Hogg said.

Hogg was at his mountain house. He was discharged on Thursday, caught a flight that afternoon, and thanks to Dr. Jim's nurse Ruth, was at his Uniontown home by 10 PM. His wife wouldn't talk to him. Hogg was happy about that.

The next day he had one of his deputies drive him to Stony Creek.

"I'm not a public servant. Where are you?" the Chief said.

"I'm doing better. Thanks for asking," Hogg said sarcastically. "I'm in Stony Creek. You want to have a drink and I'll fill you in," Hogg said.

"It's Happy Hour at Augie's."

"Nah, I'm not in the mood to get involved with that crowd and I'm not staying here very long. Why don't you come over here, say in about a half-hour?"

The Chief's antenna shot up. He made the quick decision to play along.

"Sure, see you then," the Chief said.

Hogg didn't like bringing the Chief in on his problem, but at the time he had no choice. Now he had to watch him.

When Hogg got back to his mountain house, the cop in him said to check everything out and he did. He wasn't sure what he was looking for, but he'd know it if he saw it.

He started upstairs and everything looked exactly like it should. It didn't get much use and when he turned on the lights in the darkened bedrooms, he could see the dust on the bedside end tables. All the blinds were drawn. He thought he heard a noise downstairs, and thinking it was the Chief, went back down.

There was nobody there. He checked the back door and looked around. Everything looked normal although the fresh snow had covered everything with an extra coating.

He was sure he heard something and as he walked into the den, he realized what it was. The stack of burning logs in the fireplace had collapsed.

He checked out the rest of the downstairs area and saw nothing out of place. He stood in the den and studied his easy chair, his plaid blanket still crumbled up on the floor. He felt his face getting warm. He loved this room, but now it was filled with bad shit. He had to get new furniture, maybe cut down on the plaid. He was tired of the jokes.

He saw his old drink on the end table. It looked gross and as he reached for it, he stopped. He should have it tested for prints and drugs, but that would mean sending it to the crime lab in Pittsburgh, and he wasn't sure he wanted to create that kind of paper trail. He'd think about it. He picked it up carefully and carried it into the kitchen. He emptied it and put the glass in a baggie.

He poured himself a fresh scotch on the rocks and went back into the den.

He went over to the Rob Roy portrait and lifted it off the wall. He pressed on the edge of a wood panel and it swung open. He dialed in the numbers. Everything in the safe looked untouched. Inside were papers and four green vinyl bank bags from Mellon Bank, along with a.40 caliber Glock, and a 357 Magnum. The serial numbers were filed off both.

He held the .357 in his right hand, feeling the grip, thinking the kind of hole it would blow in Heidi's cunt, when he heard the knock on the back door. He quickly put the gun back into the safe and re-hung the portrait, checked to see if it looked straight, and yelled "come in" as he hurried to the back door.

"It's open," he called out.

As paranoid as Hogg was, he didn't always lock his door. There had never been any trouble at the resort, and he looked at it as a challenge. He was daring somebody, anybody, to break in.

"Chief, how are you?" Hogg said.

"I'm good. The question is how you are?"

"Well, I'm minus about twelve inches," Hogg said.

The Chief was careful with his response. "You wish. No, seriously, are you okay?"

"Don't stand there. You're letting cold air in. Let's go into the den. What do you want to drink?" Hogg asked as the Chief stepped in and closed the kitchen door.

"Whatever you're having," the Chief said, "except I don't want that buttermilk crap you use."

"No buttermilk tonight," Hogg said, pouring a scotch and handing it to the Chief.

They went into the den. Hogg started to sit in his leather chair but moved to the ottoman instead. The Chief sunk into the leather sofa.

"Slanj," Hogg said, raising his glass. The Chief figured Hogg was offering a Scottish toast, Hell, Hogg probably bled plaid when the chick sliced off his dick.

"Cheers," the Chief said and took a sip. "So, are you feeling okay?"

"As good as can be expected," Hogg answered.

"What do the doctor's say?"

"About what?"

"C'mon Bill, don't play games."

"The doctor said I'm okay, that's it?"

"Can they do anything like ah…"

"Maybe. They've had success reattaching one but I don't have one to reattach so I may get a transplant," Hogg said.

"They can do that?"

"Yeah, they're doing it in China and they're working on it here. Do you know that in Thailand, they have dozens of penises being cut off every year and they're getting them fixed so it's only a matter of time before I'm good as new," Hogg said? "Maybe even better," he added with a hasty smile.

"Why in the fuck they cutting off so many dicks in Thailand?"

"What the fuck do I know why," Hogg said. "They're nothing but barbarian gooks."

"Just curious," the Chief said, "so you think you're gonna get back to normal."

"I don't think it, I know it," Hogg said, "but enough about that shit."

"What can I do for you?" the Chief said.

"Nothing. I didn't call you because I wanted you to do something for me. I just wanted to thank you for what you already did."

"Glad to help," the Chief said, keeping a watchful eye on Hogg's face, looking for any clue what he was up to.

"I just don't want anybody to know what happened to me."

"I know, Bill, and you have my word. I won't say a thing to anybody, but you know, a crime was committed?"

"You could say that," Hogg said, taking another big slug of his scotch, "but there's nothing to report."

"I understand, but you're not the type to brush something like this off, and I would hate to see you get into a fuss over it," the Chief said.

"Well, Carl," Hogg said, "I didn't know you cared. That's downright sweet of you."

"C'mon Bill, you know what I mean."

"What is it you're looking for, Chief? The name of the person who did it, and if that's it, why?" Hogg said, leaning forward, burning his blue eyes directly into the Chief's.

The Chief never blinked. He leaned in towards Hogg, keeping his eyes lasered into Hogg's, and said, "It's your business, Bill, I just don't want to see anybody else get hurt."

"Who do you think will get hurt?" Hogg asked.

"I have no idea," the Chief said, still leaning in, their faces close.

Hogg leaned back and straightened up. He looked at the Chief and chuckled.

"Hell, Carl, what do you think I would do, shoot somebody?"

The Chief wanted to say yes.

"No, you're not that dumb, but you have to be pissed, and that's when everyone in range can get shit on," the Chief said.

"Where do you get these philosophies you spout?" Hogg said smiling. "Do you think I'd gamble my career on doing something stupid? Look, I'm pissed about it. Who wouldn't be, but I can't let it ruin my life?"

The Chief didn't believe a word Hogg was saying.

"That's good thinking. She didn't do any other damage, did she?"

"What are you talking about?" Hogg said, not taking the bait.

"Well, you know, a broad scorned is a broad on a rampage, and if she was willing to cut off your, ah, anyhow, she could've burned your place down or something like that. Place looks okay, though," the Chief said, standing and looking around.

"No damage. Everything's cool," Hogg said, now standing, "and who said it was a she? I know you're not going to believe me, but I don't know who did it. They doped me up."

It was possible he didn't know, but Hogg wasn't the type who let things go—especially not his dick.

They both knew their talk was over. Hogg began moving gingerly towards the back door and the Chief followed.

"Hey, thanks for the drink. You going back to Uniontown tonight?"

"Yep, I'm outta here as soon as you leave," Hogg said. "A lotta work backed up on me."

"Well, I ain't going to slow you up. You take care now," the Chief said and left.

Hogg closed the door. That conversation yielded little, but he knew he had to watch the Chief. The Chief was no fool, and he probably picked up some scuttlebutt on his affair with Heidi.

He spent a lot of time thinking about that night, and a lot of his memory had come back. No doubt that Heidi was there, but he had trouble seeing her as the cutter. She was such a meek bitch, but then you can never be sure what a broad will do when she flips out.

As for now, Heidi was his only possibility and the more he thought about it, the more he wanted to jam a sewer pipe up her pussy.

Whatever he did to that bitch, the Chief would know it was him. That's why it had to be something that she'd keep her mouth shut about.

Hogg was sure he'd find a way.

JOE DUCK

THE GLOOMY SKY WAS QUICKLY TURNING BLACK AS JOE DUCK stood in knee deep snow and watched Hogg's house, pissed because somebody just turned on the lights. He was shivering from the cold and his feet had gone numb. He was thinking that tonight was not going to be the night he'd get the money, but he was afraid to wait any longer. He didn't know what his next move was going to be, but it had to be fast. He had plans.

Once he got the money, he'd get out of the country. The hell with Ruby. He'd get all the scrunch he wanted in Mexico. He had his passport, but what he didn't know was how to get that much cash out of the country. He could've asked around, the dealers would know, but asking them would be like yelling nigger at an NAACP convention.

He heard that the Cayman Islands were a good spot to dump cash, but how does he get it there? He wasn't sure, but he thought that there was a ten grand carry-on limit. He'd be dead before he got it all out. He might have to hire one of them shysters that know how to do that kind of shit, but they're so crooked they'd steal the toilet paper right out from under a guy's ass.

But none of that mattered if he couldn't get the money out of Hogg's house and right now it looked like that wasn't going to happen. He was trying to think of a Plan B when the back door opened, and a guy came out. He looked bigger than Hogg, but Joe couldn't see him all that well. The lights were still on inside the house, so there was somebody still in there, probably Hogg, and Joe wasn't about to get into a pissing contest with the Sheriff. He thought the guy went around the corner of the house, but he wasn't sure.

Joe didn't know what to do. He was thinking of packing it in when the lights in the house went off. Another guy came out of the back door, but it was darker, and Joe couldn't get a bead on him. He thought the guy went around the corner of the house, but he wasn't sure when a beam of light lit up the far side of the yard.

Headlights. Hogg's in his car that he parks on the side of the house.

Joe's mouth went dry. He wanted to giggle. He was going to get that money tonight.

He was shivering, standing there trying to figure out his next move. The house was dark except for what Joe was sure was a nightlight. The headlights faded away and he watched the darkened house a little longer to make sure there was nobody in there. He could feel the excitement building. He was going to get his money tonight. He waited a few more minutes and decided to make his move.

He pushed through the snow, taking the same route he took that night, goose-stepping his way up to Hogg's back door. He peeked around the corner of the house just to make sure the car was gone.

He went to the back door and knocked. He'd use his "out of gas" story if somebody answered. He cupped his hand around his ear and listened. He knocked again, louder this time, and waited.

After what seemed like forever, he decided the place was empty. Remembering his luck the last time, he tried the doorknob, but it didn't budge. He took out his key chain penlight and looked at the lock. It was a single cylinder. Joe smiled. It was no contest. He brought his first class, stainless steel 20-piece lock pick set that would open just about anything, and he also had his bump keys. One way or another, he'd get in.

And the fucking guy is a sheriff?

It took Joe longer than he expected, but he finally got the door open. He slipped inside and quickly closed the door. He had to hurry. He stood for a moment listening for any sounds, and after hearing nothing moved quickly to the stairs.

He found the bench he used before, carried it out to the hall, climbed up and pulled the attic door down. This time he knew how to do it, and he got it open without falling on his ass. He was getting excited as he climbed the ladder.

A couple of steps from the top he felt around for the string, found it, and turned on the light.

He took another step up and could see the boxes stacked in the shadows. He aimed his penlight at them, looking for the ones marked "Xmas."

He didn't see them at first. He climbed up into the attic, and even as short as he was, he still had to hunch over because of the slanted roof. He saw the two boxes, but they didn't look right. It looked like they had been moved. Maybe not.

He lifted off the top box and set it to the side. He was getting excited as he hurriedly removed the cardboard cover. The top layer was the Christmas stuff. He pushed some of the garlands aside and felt for the money.

Maybe he hadn't gone deep enough.

He began digging, and then clawing, but he wasn't feeling any of the stacks of cash. He used his penlight to get a better look, pushing the loose decorations aside. There was no money.

I got the wrong box.

He went back to the other box and felt all around, his stomach doing flip-flops. He was about to throw up. The money was gone.

It must be here.

He frantically started looking in other boxes, knowing exactly where he hid the money, but hoping he somehow had made a mistake. He knew how this was going to end but he kept searching.

Somebody found the money.

His head was filled with static that was crackling everywhere. He couldn't hear his own thoughts as everything in his body was going haywire.

He was breathing like a stuck pig. He had to calm down before he had a heart attack.

He tried to think it out. Why would anybody think to look in Christmas boxes when the holiday was over? It didn't make sense. It had to be Hogg. But why? After grinding his mind through every possibility, Joe concluded that it was one of those once in a lifetime coincidences. Maybe Hogg had some decorations downstairs that he decided to put away, although Joe hadn't seen any. Who in the hell knows? Maybe his wife came up and started cleaning?

Maybe, maybe, maybe. What difference did it make? The money was gone.

He wanted to cry.

If Hogg found it the first thing he'd do is get it out of Stony Creek. Joe tried to conjure up Hogg finding the money. He must have thought he died and went to heaven. Hogg was a cop. He might not know how the money got there, but he'd sure 'n shit know from where it came.

Not for one moment did Joe think Hogg would return the money. Cops are worse than crooks.

What if Hogg didn't get it out of the house? Joe couldn't take the chance. Joe started searching upstairs, checking all the closets, looking under the beds, and found nothing. He headed downstairs and went room by room. He frantically checked all the closets. He didn't see the trapdoor in the hall closet that led to the crawl space. It was cluttered with ski junk.

Winded, his smoke-lined lungs were crying out for air, as Joe stood there perplexed. Joe finished up his search in the kitchen, checking all the cabinets, certain the money was gone. To hide that much money, you needed a space bigger than Ruby Begonia's snatch.

He even looked in the back to see if there were any tracks or disturbances to the snow. No luck.

That fucking crook stole it. It pissed Joe off, but he wasn't surprised. You can't trust cops. They're trained to lie, cheat and steal.

So, where would he take it? You just can't hide a stash like that so easy. Nobody would ever suspect Hogg of having the money. Hell, Joe didn't even know he was going to hide it there. The best bet was that Hogg took it to his house in Uniontown. That way he could keep it close. That made sense to Joe.

Joe Duck knew where Hogg lived, well, not exactly the street and stuff, but he'd find him. Joe was sure he lived in Uniontown or somewhere in Fayette County, but he'd get a line on him quick. He'd get a hold of Key, he couldn't remember his last name, a long Slovak one, but he'd know. Key got his name from robbing houses with some sort of key he made, but he wasn't as good as Joe. Joe Duck could pick any lock there was, and his next stop was Fayette County.

That was Joe Duck's money, and he was going to get it back, sheriff or no sheriff.

Cops will steal the shoes right off your feet.

HEDY'S CONDO

HEDY WAS RUNNING LATE. SHE HAD FIFTEEN MINUTES TO FINISH dressing. She kept changing her mind about what to wear. She wanted to dress sexy, showing cleavage and leg, but thought better of it and went for a "snow bunny" look.

She put on a light gray V-neck cashmere sweater, form-fitting black fleece leggings, and a pair of gray knee-high boots. A simple silver strand necklace with a solitaire round cut black diamond and matching earrings completed her look. It was casual, but business-like, with enough cleavage and body accents to satisfy her intentions. Hedy could make a nun's habit look provocative.

As she finished fixing her face, she thought about how much she and Heidi looked alike, and yet how different they were. She was going to put her paperwork in a gray leather shoulder bag but changed her mind.

She decided on a thin camel leather briefcase with gray piping that she bought in Milan. It was a nice color match.

She gave herself the once over in the full-length mirror and was satisfied she was ready to go. She leaned into the mirror and took a closer look at her face. As she made eye contact with herself, she thought about Hogg.

She had to protect Heidi, and herself, because Hogg was sure to come after them. She ran several scenarios through her mind, but nothing clicked until the word "defense" pushed itself to the front of her mind. "Defense," she said to herself, "Self-defense. That's it."

She had the idea. Now she had to find a way to make it work. She gave a quick wave of her head and threw back her shoulders. There was no way she was going to let Hogg ruin their lives.

She switched off the light, opened the door and stepped out. The cold mountain air snapped at her face.

Good ideas are a dime a dozen she thought. You only get a gold medal when it works.

THE NOON MEETING

THE CHESS GAME BEGAN BEFORE THE MEETING STARTED. OTTO arrived early, but not early enough. JR, breaking his own rules, arrived ten minutes sooner. Hedy was the last to arrive.

After the salutations, Otto quickly began the conversation.

"So, Mr. Leon, I understand you live on a boat. Is that so?" Otto said, leaning back in his chair.

"My yacht is quite comfortable with all the amenities of home," JR said.

"How big is it?"

"Almost 55 meters." he said.

"How big is that in feet?" Otto asked. "I'm not a math whiz," he smiled.

"About 180 feet."

"Nice size," Otto said. "Must take a big staff to operate such a vessel."

"Crew. We call them crew. Not really. Find a good Captain and Chief Engineer to run the ship and the rest is smooth sailing."

"I know little about boats. Never had an interest in them. Hard to use them up here in the mountains," Otto said with a grin.

"They weren't built for the mountains, Mr. Kasser," JR replied.

Hedy didn't like the verbal dance that was taking place.

"Enough about boats and yachts," Hedy said, "Let's talk about Stony Creek. JR, why don't you give us a brief overview of your interest and your offer."

"Why don't we do this?" JR said, "You've seen copies of my proposal. If you have questions, let's get them out of the way."

Otto asked a few meaningless questions, just to respond, but the proposal was detailed and covered everything of importance. Otto had to be careful because he didn't want to get into any kind of serious discussion yet. Leon's offer was clear. It would better the Swiss offer by at least 10% and right now he didn't want to open that door. He went back to the personal.

"When you're not on your boat, Mr. Leon," Otto said, "where do you call home?"

"Wherever I am," JR said.

"I mean, where is your permanent home?" Otto said with a forced smile.

"I have many places throughout the world and I'm not sure I can call any of them permanent. I travel a lot. Each one of them is home to me."

"I see," Otto said, not believing him.

JR went back to his proposal, explaining he wouldn't get into a bidding war with the Swiss company. That threw Otto off. Had Hedy told him it was the Swiss? He glanced at her, but her face revealed nothing.

"Ah, yes. The Swiss. They are a long-established worldwide company with tremendous resources," Otto said, implying that JR didn't have those same credentials.

"Yes, they are. I once considered buying them, but I thought their corporate structure was unwieldy and carried too much overhead to be an effective operation," he said.

That verbal volley had Otto reeling. "When was that?" Otto asked, trying to regain his footing.

"About a year ago. I assume you're dealing with either Claus or Friedrich," he said, mentioning only their first names.

Otto felt his stomach jump. He didn't want to acknowledge that JR was correct. He couldn't be sure whether JR was name-dropping as a ploy or that he really knew them. He changed the subject, but Hedy raised her eyebrows. Score another one for Leon.

There was discussion about the contract, nothing of substance, and some operational issues, again relatively unimportant, when JR suggested they wrap it up. Otto quickly agreed. He wanted the meeting to end.

"Look, I'm sure your folks here have a lot of due diligence to do regarding my offer, and I understand it will take some time. I would guess ten days will be sufficient," he said, looking for any dissent. "Does that work, Otto, Hedy?

Otto was flustered at JR's aggressiveness but mumbled out a "certainly" and Hedy nodded in the affirmative. JR stood up. The meeting was over.

"You'll stay for lunch, JR? We can eat right here, of course," Otto said immediately regretting the stupid statement. He had to admit he was nervous.

"I hope you don't mind, but I'd like to skip lunch. I have a few phone calls I must make, but thank you," JR said, standing and extending his hand to Otto and nodding at Hedy. They shook hands and all three headed for the door when Foley walked in. Otto was taken aback but chose to introduce Foley. He wanted to let Leon know he had a security operation.

"Ah, Mr. Leon..." Otto began.

"JR, please."

"Yes. JR, meet Foley, Christian Foley, but he prefers just Foley. He heads up one of our security teams," Otto said, grabbing Foley's arm and pulling him closer.

"Nice to meet, you Mr. Foley. For a man in my position, I recognize how vital quality security is. It's a tough, demanding profession, but

I'm telling you something you already know. Good luck to you. Now if you'll excuse me, I'm running late for a meeting."

"Good meeting you, Sir," Foley said.

"I have to get going, too," Hedy said. "Thanks Otto, you did good," Hedy said as she walked away.

He stood there thinking it had all been a waste of time and then Hedy thanks him and says he "did good." That pissed him off.

At least he knew what Leon looked like.

JOE DUCK

HOGG LIVED ON THE EDGE OF UNIONTOWN AND JOE GOT LOST looking for his house. He pulled over to study the map. After a few wrong turns, he finally got on the right road. There was a strip of about eight homes that lined the two-lane blacktop road on the one side. Across the road was a wooded area. Hogg's nondescript ranch was in the middle of the eight homes, most of them built at the same time by the same contractor. Joe thought the Sheriff would have a fancier home, but those guys knew how to hide their take.

On Joe's first drive by, he found Hogg's house to his right. He went up the road a piece, turned around and came back down. That put Hogg's house on his left and the wooded area on his right. All the houses had driveways and integral garages, and there were cars parked in front of a few of the houses.

Joe was uncertain where to park. If he parked on the wooded side, his vehicle would look out of place and could draw attention. Parking on the right, in front of a house, was also risky, but those were his only choices. He didn't want to keep driving up and down the road, so he pulled off to the right side, about twenty yards before Hogg's house. There was enough room to get his car off the asphalt. He went into his "lost" routine.

Pretending to study a map, Joe studied the houses. Most of the people kept their vehicles in the driveway or in the garage. He noted one mailbox, about two doors up from Hogg's, marked "The Kelleys". He locked that one into his mind.

Hogg's house was an unpretentious three-bedroom ranch, something befitting a public servant. It sat on the top of a spacious lot that sloped down to the road. The lot was at least a half-acre, with stands of trees on both sides, providing privacy. There weren't many trees or bushes around the front of the house, which made it tougher to get close because there wasn't any cover. It was a lot of lawn with a couple of waist-high evergreens near the front door. To the left was a long gravel driveway to the integral garage. The buff brick structure had a picture window on the right side of the house, probably the living room. The driveway and garage were on the left side. Above the white wooden garage door there was a small picture window. Joe figured that would be a bedroom. Joe couldn't see what was around back, but he thought it was a wooded area because he didn't see a street on his map.

Joe saw enough, and after a few minutes he folded up the map and left. Hogg was a cop, and cops suspected everybody. To them, the fucking Pope was a suspect. On the way back to Pittsburgh, Joe came up with his plan.

He'd return Monday morning and get his money. He didn't want to tangle with the Sheriff, so he'd wait until he went to work. That left only his wife, and he could handle her. He'd work on his plan over the weekend.

Monday was another typical winter day. A heavy dark curtain of iron gray clouds hovered over Pittsburgh. Sunshine was rationed during the winter months. Joe Duck left East Liberty at 4:30 AM, stopping for coffee on the way, and was at Hogg's house as daylight was breaking. He wanted to be there to see Hogg leave for work. When he arrived, he saw a white Toyota parked on the street. The garage door was closed. He knew Hogg didn't drive a Toyota, so it must be his wife's. His first thought was that Hogg had already left, and he chewed himself out for stopping for coffee. On the other hand, Hogg's car could be in the garage. He'd do a couple more drive-bys.

As he drove by the third time, he saw a thin, slight, dark-haired woman come out the front door. He slowed and saw her get in the Toyota and leave. He'd kill some time for the next ten or fifteen minutes and then make another run. His guess was that Hogg left, but he was going to be patient. He'd make sure. If Hogg left, and the house was empty, Joe would read that as God was still with him.

About twenty minutes later, he drove by again. He didn't see any lights. The house looked deserted. Joe wasn't going to jump the gun on this one. As much as he wanted to get into the house, find the money, and get out. He wouldn't rush it. He'd drive around for another ten minutes and then come back and take another look.

After another five minutes his impatience kicked in and he decided it was time to make his move. He reached over and felt for the package on his right front seat. It was a small box, wrapped in brown paper addressed to "The Kelleys."

He continued down the street and parked on the right side of the road, just a little before Hogg's house. His plan was to knock on Hogg's door, and if somebody answered, he'd say he was delivering a package for the Kelley's. He didn't expect anybody to be in the house, but if there were, he'd do his Kelley thing and get the hell out of there fast.

He rang the bell on the front door. No answer. He held the package in his left hand, keeping his right free so he could get to his 22 tucked under his belt. He rang again. Waited. Listened. Nothing. After three rings, and he knew it was working because he could hear it, he banged on the door. It relaxed him when there was no answer.

He checked the street and seeing nothing, walked off to his right onto the lawn and around to the back. Heading for the back door, he glanced into a window, and everything was dark. In the rear there was a stone patio with a barbecue grill and a stack of logs near a door. Joe passed a large window right before the door and it was dark. He peered in. It was the kitchen.

He knocked and waited. He didn't expect an answer. He didn't get one, and he went to work. He put his package down on the patio and began picking the lock. It didn't feel right, so he turned the doorknob. The damn thing was unlocked.

The dumb fucks.

Joe was no fool. It could be a trap. He knocked again. Still no answer. He pulled his gun from his belt and stuck it in his coat pocket so he could get to it faster.

He slowly pushed open the door but didn't go in. He stood there for a moment and listened, but everything was quiet. He leaned in a little farther and saw an empty kitchen.

"Anybody home," he cried out.

No answer. He yelled again. All he heard was the furnace running.

He cautiously took a few steps into the kitchen. He stopped and listened. He didn't hear a sound. The next room was through an archway. He crept to the archway, and standing on one side, peered into the darkened room that he figured was the dining room or living room. He didn't see or hear a thing. He kept his right hand on his pistol in his jacket pocket.

"Anybody home," he yelled again. No response.

He slowly stepped into the unlit room, noticing a sliver of light coming from the closed drapes. He figured the bedrooms were off to the right. He was feeling comfortable that there wasn't anybody home. He had to hurry. Trying to think like Hogg, which was a stretch for Joe, he concluded that because the money took up a lot of space, he would have to hide it somewhere where his wife wouldn't find it. Cops trust nobody.

Joe stood there, thinking, and decided it had to be in the basement.

The door to the basement is usually in the kitchen.

Joe turned and was about to go back into the kitchen when a man's voice cut through the darkness like a razor.

"What can I do for you, motherfucker?"

Joe spun around, looking for the voice. His hand was still holding the pistol in his pocket when the voice slashed through the darkness again.

"Down on the floor now. Hands away from your body where I can see them. NOW, MOTHER FUCKER OR I SHOOT!"

It scared Joe shitless and his hand came out of his pocket empty as he belly flopped on the floor flapping like a fish out of water. He stretched his arms out in front of him as far as they would go. His heart was beating like a drummer on cocaine, and the static in his head was back.

Joe sensed somebody standing over him, but he was afraid to open his eyes. He was just waiting for the bullet.

"What are you doing here?" Hogg said, moving around Joe's outstretched body until he was behind him.

"Nuthin, nuthin. I was lookin' for the … the," Joe forgot their name.

"Looking for who, asshole?" Hogg said.

It came to him and Joe took a fast breath. "The Kelley's. I got a package to deliver to them and I thought this was their house."

"I don't see a package."

"Yeah, yeah. I have one. I left it outside by the door and…"

"Which Kelley?"

"The Kelley's, the ones that live down the street," Joe said before he could stop the words from coming out of his mouth.

"I meant… I wasn't sure what house, ah, they ah," he stuttered.

"Get your ass up slowly and I want to see your hands trying to grab that ceiling as you do. Do you understand?"

For a moment Joe didn't understand. "I need my hands to git up off…"

"Just get up, punk, and then put your hands up as high as you can."

Joe got up, his eyes fixed on the archway to the kitchen, wondering if he could make a run for it, dismissing that idea quickly.

"This is a misunderstanding, Sheriff, please, I can explain," and once again Joe's tongue jumped ahead of his brain. .

"Ah, I didn't mean," and he let the words fade off. He was toast. His arms were aching from keeping them stretched up so high.

Hogg wasn't sure what this punk was up to, but he knew he wasn't the usual B&E asshole.

Standing behind him Hogg said, "Take three or four steps forward to the wall and keep your hands up high where I can see them," Hogg said, jamming the, 357 into Joe's back.

Joe took three steps. He hadn't reached the wall.

"To the wall, asshole. Then put your hands up against the wall and spread them. You know the drill."

"I won't cause you no trouble, sir," Joe gurgled as he assumed the position.

Hogg kicked Joe's legs farther apart. Joe almost fell but regained his balance. Hogg patted him down. Joe was about to crap himself, when the Sheriff said, "Now, turn around slowly, keeping your hands out in front where I can see them, and press your back against that wall like you were holding it up."

He missed the gun. God is with me.

"Open your jacket. No, just with your left hand," Hogg ordered. "Unless you want to die, don't touch that pistol," Hogg said. He hadn't missed it.

Joe wasn't about to do anything except follow Hogg's orders.

"Yes sir." The static in Joe's head had turned into Niagara Falls.

"Okay, punk. I'm going to ask you a question and you better give me the right answer, or I'll blow you in half. What are you doing in my house?"

"Nothing, nothing sir. I was jist… jist, ah …" Joe couldn't even muster up a brain fart. Shit filled his entire head.

"Did you not understand me?" Hogg said jamming his gun harder into Joe's back. "You knew whose house this was. One more time. What do you want?" Hogg said bringing the.357 Magnum up to his face, the cold metal touching Joe's cheek.

"Okay, okay sir," Joe said, "I knew you was the Sheriff, and I was looking for guns. I can sell them and make some good money. That's the truth, sir. I just wanted to steal your guns. You can put me in jail for that, sir. I deserve it."

Hogg looked at the short, chunky, frightened man.

"I don't believe you, asshole, and I'm going to blow your brains out, if I don't get the truth."

"Sir, I'm telling the truth," Joe pleaded, "I just wanted to steal your guns. Sheriff's always have a lot of guns and…"

Hogg studied the guy's face. He didn't remember any warrants coming through on him. The bastard looked dumb enough to try to pull something stupid like robbing a Sheriff's house. Luck was with him earlier when he glanced out of his window and saw the idiot casing his home. This guy was a stupid lowlife.

"I want you to reach into your right jacket pocket and pull out your gun very slowly and very carefully, or I'll put a hole in you big enough to drive a truck through."

Joe Duck nodded.

"Good, that's it, nice and easy, and I want you to hold it at your side, pointing it towards the floor, with your finger off the trigger."

Joe was scared, his hand shaking, as he pulled the pistol from his pocket, holding it between his thumb and first two fingers, showing Hogg that he wasn't holding it in firing position.

"I told you to hold the fuckin' gun like you're going to shoot it asshole, your finger near, but not on the trigger, and hold it down at your side, the gun pointing at the floor. One funny move and you'll make my day," Hogg said. "Understand?"

Joe did as Hogg asked, keeping his finger off the trigger, his face feeling hot and flushed.

"Now, put your finger on the trigger," Hogg said.

Joe Duck shot a fearful look at Hogg. Something wasn't right.

"I don't want this gun, sir and…"

"Freeze," Hogg yelled. "Do not let go of that gun until I tell you."

"I'm sorry, sir," Joe Duck said, "What do you want me to do?"

"I want you to stand there. Don't move a muscle. Now, put your hand with the gun down to your side, making sure you point the gun at the floor, that's it, gently, and now put your finger on the trigger. I'm going to show you how to empty that pistol with one hand, and then I'm going to kick your ass out of here."

"You'll let me go?"

"Why would I want to bother with a punk like you? Our jails are filled with gutless weasels, and we have to pay to keep them. I have no intention of having the state feed and house you. You'll get yours on the street."

"I won't ever bother you, or nobody, ever again. I promise," Joe said, his voice breaking up, almost sobbing.

"No you won't," Hogg said.

Those were the last words Joe Duck heard.

Hogg shot him in the heart with his .357 Magnum, blowing an ugly hole in his chest. Joe Duck flew back against the wall, and then slumped to the floor. He was still holding his gun.

Blood sprayed out of the hole in Joe's chest as Hogg looked at him, thinking of the mess it was making in his house. He pulled his police radio out of his jacket pocket.

"This is Hogg. I just shot somebody who broke into my house. I don't know if he was trying to rob me or kill me, but he tried to shoot me. I had no choice. Send an ambulance and backup immediately."

Hogg stared at the son-of-bitch crumpled up on the floor, his head twisted against the wall, his mouth agape, and his empty eyes wide open. He was bleeding all over his floor. Hogg would be redecorating, courtesy of the county and his insurance company. They'll trip over themselves to accommodate him when they read in the Herald-Standard how their brave sheriff shot a killer, probably sent by organized crime, and how Hogg risked his life to protect his home and family. That will play well in Fayette County, where they love their guns and have redder necks than an albino in a sun storm.

"Too bad my warning shot hit the bastard," Hogg said to no one, laughing at his own joke.

He felt exhilarated, the adrenalin pumping through him, pushing him into a new high. This was the first time he could take out an asshole so up close and personal, and he was feeling the surge. It was almost better than sex. He shuddered at the thought, but he felt something down there.

That's one less asshole to suck off the taxpayer's tit. Nobody fucks with Bill Hogg and gets away with it. Nobody.

HEDY

HEDY WAS SATISFIED WITH THE LEON MEETING. SO FAR, OTTO HAD nothing. She wasn't sure where Foley fit in with the Leon thing, if at all. She caught him before he left Pipa's.

"Foley, I need to talk with you about a security matter. Can we meet later?" she said.

"We can meet now, if you have the time," he said.

"Okay. Why don't you grab a quiet table in the back, and I'll get us drinks? What will you have?" Hedy said with a big smile on her face.

"You know, a tall, cold Bloody Mary, real spicy, would hit the spot," Foley said, feeling his mouth moisten.

"You got it," Hedy said and headed for the bar. Foley watched her walk away, staring at her legs, when he caught himself. He didn't want to be seen leering, but she was certainly something to leer at.

Foley found a corner table in the half-filled room and chose the chair that would put his back to the wall. It was a habit he picked up a long time ago.

He watched Hedy as she made her way to the table with his Bloody Mary and what appeared to be a Mimosa.

As she neared, he rose and pulled out a chair as she placed the drinks on the beige tablecloth.

She sat down, raised her drink, and said, "Cheers," and he responded as they tapped glasses. They both took a sip of their drinks, their eyes locking on each other for a long moment, too long for Foley, and he feigned a cough breaking the mood.

"How can I help you, Miss Kasser?" Foley asked, returning to the business at hand.

"Hedy, please."

"OK, Hedy it is."

"As you know, we've not been big on security here, especially Otto, but with recent events I think we need to take a hard look at that issue," she said, "particularly our personal security. Heidi never locks her door, and my mother probably doesn't either. I do, but I'm kind of sloppy and I think it's time to pay attention to it."

"What do you have in mind?"

"I think we need to secure everything, our personal condos, our offices, the money room," she said, "that is if you have the time. I hope Otto's not keeping you too busy?"

"Not at all," Foley said. He knew she was fishing. He wasn't sure what she knew or what she should know, and he didn't want to go down that road.

"I agree and my team is putting together a proposal on how we can best do that," Foley said.

"Will you be including video surveillance in your proposal?"

"Of course. Certainly in the money room and in high-traffic areas and…"

Hedy interrupted. "I'm certain it will be thorough and extensive, Foley, and I'll leave that to you and Otto to work out the details. What I was wondering about was the personal safety of our key employees and, of course, the family."

"Well, our first objective was to secure the business side of Stony Creek, but you bring up a good point," Foley said, thinking the additional work will put more money in his pocket.

"I have concern for the safety of my family," Hedy said.

"As well you should, Hedy. In fact, I'm glad to hear you say that. Too many times businesspeople put all their focus on the business and forget about themselves, but statistics show that business owners and their families are at risk because the criminal element thinks they have a lot of money and valuables in their homes and …"

"I get it. Here's what I'd like to do, maybe kind of like a trial run to give us an idea of how this all works. I'd like you to install a top-of-the-line surveillance system in Heidi's condo. I want cameras everywhere it makes sense and I want them hidden so nobody knows they're there. You just can't trust anybody anymore. She's the biggest worrywart and this would make her feel better. Ever since the robbery she's been beside herself with fear. How soon can you begin?"

"Well, I can get you a proposal with costs and installation options to you in about …"

"No need for that. I trust that you'll provide the best there is out there. I'll clear it with Otto. I'd like a cost estimate, but don't hold up the installation. Get the ball rolling immediately and I'll see that the estimate is approved, if acceptable."

"Well, it will take a few days to survey the property and determine the best equipment."

"Foley, I have a sister that's having anxiety attacks. I want this done immediately, and even faster if that's possible. Do you understand?"

"Okay, I'll start as soon as I leave you."

"Great, and when we complete Heidi's installation we'll work on mine. Okay?"

"Okay. Just so you know it will take a couple of days to get the equipment in and …"

"I'm sure you'll do whatever is necessary to expedite this project, Foley, and don't worry about any rush charges. I understand and you'll be covered."

"Got it," Foley said.

"I'm counting on you," she said, getting up from the table. She extended her hand. Foley shook it gently and was surprised by her overly firm grip.

As she walked away, Foley watched her. Suddenly she stopped and swung around. Startled, he quickly dropped his eyes and looked at his drink. She caught him looking but pretended she hadn't as she walked back to the table and handed him her business card.

"Call me on my cell when you're ready to install at Heidi's. I'd like to be there when you start."

She gave him another quick smile and turned and left.

Foley was impressed. She was one smart lady.

HEIDI

"PLEASE COME UP HERE NOW. HURRY, PLEASE HURRY," HEIDI SAID frantically into the phone.

"Are you okay? What's happening?" Hedy said.

"You need to come here now, Hedy. I need you."

"Okay, calm down. Just answer one question and I'll be there in a few minutes. Okay? Are you safe?"

"Yes, now come quick, please."

She threw on her ski jacket and was at Heidi's in seven minutes. The door was unlocked, pissing Hedy off. She stormed through the door, yelling at Heidi, who was curled up on the sofa under a white blanket. Hedy didn't see her until she got up.

Heidi was waving some sort of card, muttering things that Hedy couldn't hear. Fear possessed her face.

"What's wrong?" Hedy said, walking over to the sofa.

Heidi handed her a large card with a picture on it, trying to answer, but the words garbled up in her throat. All that came out were gasps and sobs.

"What's this?"

"It's... it's a... ah, the death card," Heidi said, whimpering the words out.

"Take it easy, honey. Get your breath and then you can tell me about this card. Breathe baby, that's it," Hedy said as Heidi settled down.

"That's death riding on the white horse," Heidi said so quietly that Hedy had to ask her to speak up.

She did, almost yelling. "It's the death card, damn it. He's going to kill me. I knew it. I knew it," she said, jumping up from the sofa.

"Hold it, Heidi. Please, sit, take a breath, and tell me about this card… from the beginning. Take a deep breath, honey. I'll help you, so don't worry," Hedy said, delicately guiding Heidi back to the sofa, and sitting down next to her. Hedy put her arm around Heidi, gently caressing her shoulder and neck.

"Okay," Heidi said between gasps, "It came in the mail today. It's a tarot card that means death," she said, her voice rising again, "and I know it's from him, I just know it."

"Easy baby, easy. You're talking about Hogg?"

Heidi nodded her head up and down vigorously.

"He doesn't seem like the Tarot card type," Hedy said.

"He isn't. I am, and he knows it. He made fun of me because of it," she said, her words running together.

"Okay, just relax. We'll get this all straightened out," Hedy said, looking at the card, "Do you have the envelope?"

Heidi pointed to the coffee table. Hedy picked up the envelope and looked at the postmark. It was a Pittsburgh postmark.

Hogg wasn't stupid. He knew they'd look at the postmark. He also had to know that it wouldn't fool Heidi, so what was he trying to accomplish?

Hedy's cell phone rang. It was Foley.

"Yes, Foley."

"The security equipment came in. The guy who will install it can be here in a day or two. When do you want to do it?"

"As soon as you can. Just call me with a heads up."

"Will do."

"Thanks, Foley," Hedy said, hanging up and turning to Heidi, "Honey, that was the security people and they're going to wire this place so nobody will get near you."

"He'll find a way."

"And we'll find a way to stop him."

FOLEY

LINDA WAS CAUSING SERIOUS PROBLEMS. HER CONSTANT SHUFFLING back and forth was disruptive.

It was late as Foley stared out of the window, sipping on his drink, watching a few hearty skiers got their money's worth as they zigged and zagged down the nearly empty slopes. His mind was on Linda. He believed her explanations at first but now they were wearing thin. What made sense had turned into nonsense.

Why would she play both ends against the middle? There was nothing to be gained. It was obvious she was confused, but about what? Foley wondered if he put too much importance on her as an employee and not enough as his lover.

He tried to get into her mind. He understood the family pressure, and the panic attacks, but was that enough to push a person into marriage? It could be, but it was radical. He had to stop thinking about it and get some sleep. You're bound to lose when you argue with yourself.

He looked at his drink and realized that wouldn't ease the pain. He put it down and went to bed. Enough was enough.

Somewhere a telephone rang. He slowly opened his eyes, trying to get his bearings, and realized that it was the resort phone, He managed to pick up the receiver, dropping it on the nightstand once, before he finally mumbled "hello."

It was CB.

"What in the hell are you doing? It's after eight. Otto called me looking for you and wait 'till I tell you what happened," the Chief blared into the earpiece, Foley holding it away from his aching head.

"Meet me in my office," the Chief continued, "and hurry, because the shit is piling up and the commode ain't working."

The shower didn't help much. He still had a headache; his stomach was at war, and no calls from Linda.

It wasn't going to be a good day.

The cold air snaked around the face mask, hitting Foley in the neck as he snowmobiled his way up to Pipa's. He went up to the old man's office and banged on his locked door.

"Take it easy," the Chief said as he let Foley in.

Foley was relieved to see that CB had a pot of hot coffee on the burner and he grabbed a cup, its ceramic inside brown with coffee stains, causing him to grimace as he poured. The hot coffee helped.

"You look like shit," the Chief said. "Is your friend coming?"

"She got tied up in Pittsburgh. She'll be up later."

The Chief looked at his son for a moment. The broad was causing problems.

"Look at this," he said, sliding a newspaper across his desk.

Foley picked it up. He wasn't sure what he was looking for, and then he spotted it.

Fayette County Sheriff kills intruder

He quietly read the story. When he finished, he remained quiet for a moment. He didn't know the Sheriff, but something else in the story caught his attention. He almost mentioned it but caught himself.

"Whattya think?"

"What am I supposed to think? I really didn't know the guy that well."

"Typical Hogg, though. He infers that the punk might have been sent by the boys. They ain't that dumb to send somebody to his house to whack him, but Hogg'll milk the shit out of this. He'll suck it drier than a withered old witch's tit."

"Well, I agree with you. This isn't a Mafia hit. From what I read it looks like it's a stupid punk who picked the wrong place to rob."

"Yeah, I thought the same thing. Them cough drops ain't the smartest pencils in the sharpener."

"You're right there," Foley said, almost whispering.

"You okay?"

"Yeah, just put a few too many away last night."

"Maybe you ought to drink what Hogg drinks. That somabitch could drink a distillery dry and not get a hangover."

"What does he drink?"

"How about scotch and buttermilk. He claims the buttermilk coats his stomach. Who knows?"

"Yeah, well good for him. Hey, CB, I've gotta go."

"It's that broad, isn't it? She's wringing out your head."

"Things are okay, CB. Nothing to worry about," Foley said, shrugging off the question.

"Do you love her?"

Foley was surprised at the question. His father was as sensitive as a tornado hitting a double-wide, but he decided to answer him honestly.

"Yeah, I think so. I'm like you in that respect. I've never been good at love or understanding it, but I think I'm in love with her." Foley waited for one of the old man's smart-ass answers.

"I understand how you feel. It's like you're on a treadmill that keeps going faster and is getting you nowhere even faster. Have you heard from her?"

"No."

"How long?

"The last time I talked with her was when she left the Leon meeting. She said she'd be back Tuesday."

"Foley, I don't think you're gonna hear any of this, but I'm going to try. You need to step back and take a hard look. You're a cop. Look at the evidence, follow the leads, go with your gut."

"CB, there's a lot you don't know."

"I'm sure there is. Is she pushing you to marry her?"

Foley sat silent, thinking about the question, finally deciding to tell his father the whole story. When he finished, he waited for the old man to launch into him.

"I'm truly sorry, Foley. You must be going through hell."

"I'll survive," Foley said, a little taken aback by his father's concern.

"I know you will. Have you ever heard of *The Rubaiyat*?"

"Yeah, I have. I'm surprised you know it."

"I'm full of surprises. There's a verse in it that goes something like this; *Ah, come fill the cup that clears, of past regrets and future fears, tomorrow, why tomorrow I may be myself with yesterday's seven thousand years,* or something like that. See, what it says…"

"I know what it says," Foley said, looking at his father, puzzled by his foray into poetry.

"I'm here to support you. Just let me know if I can help. Until you ask, I'll stay out of it," he said, pulling out a thin book from a drawer in his desk. He handed it to Foley.

"Read this when you can. It'll only take you a few minutes. I loved this guy's cartoons in Playboy," he said with a quick smile, and then returned to his old self adding, "I bought Playboy because of their cartoons. Funny stuff."

"Yeah, me too," Foley said, taking the book.

"I warned you about them pussy peddlers, the Chief said, getting up from behind his desk.

"I gotta git to work. Leave yourself out when you're ready. Make sure the door locks. Talk to you later," he said as he left the room.

Foley sat there for a moment and then looked at the book his father had given him.

It was Shel Silverstein's, *"The Giving Tree"*.

LINDA & FOLEY

LINDA SENT FOLEY AN E-MAIL. IT TOOK HER LONGER TO COMPOSE the message than it did the attached Leon report.

Foley,

I'm sorry I didn't call you, but things got a little crazy here, and until I can fully resolve them, I think it's better that I stay here and get this thing done with. You probably won't agree, but I think it's the best way to handle the situation. I hope you'll bear with me for the next week or so.

I've attached a copy of my Leon investigation, most of it gathered via telephone and computer searches. As you know, there's little out there on him, but I found some interesting things that could lead you to more.

Thanks for understanding. I'll be in touch.

Linda

He printed out a copy of the e-mail and the attachment. He re-read her e-mail. He analyzed it sentence by sentence. She never says where "here" is, nor does she suggest that he call her. She indicates that she will stay wherever she is until "I get this thing done with". What does that mean? She says, "bear with me for the next week or so." What does "or so" mean? Another week? A month?

And were things so "crazy" she couldn't make a phone call? Was she really expecting him to stand by while she figured her life out? He had become very well defended against thinking badly of her, but his gut was sending him warning signals.

Sometimes he was angrier about what she was doing to the company than what she was doing to him. She loved the company as much as he did. It wasn't only his company, it was theirs, and the unspoken truth of the matter was that they would build it together.

He picked up the report Linda attached to her e-mail.

CONFIDENTIAL*CONFIDENTIAL*CONFIDENTIAL

SB Status Report: JR LEON

JR Leon was born in Santarem, Brazil, a river town in the Amazon jungle on Feb. 15, 1932, but there is no record of his birth that I could find, which is strange. (This is the info. on his American passport) His full name is Joao (John) Roberto Leon. There are a lot of de Leon's, but Leon, by itself, is not a common name in Brazil, which should help our investigation. Origin of Leon derives from Lyon, a habitational name from either Lyon in south central France or from Lyons-in-Foret in Normandy, so his parents could be of French descent. Since he has an American passport my research indicates that an American parent(s) had to register the birth in person at the American Embassy. (Consular Report of Birth Abroad). You might want to check your contacts in the State Department.

His yacht, the Bonito Estacia, is registered in Panama to an offshore company, the JK Corporation. According to the purchase agreement that's on file, he paid $13,000,000 in 1997 to the VS, Inc., a corporation registered in Brazil. (Brazilian Ministry of Maritime Defence). It is a super-yacht that can handle up to 10 guests with a crew of 9 to 12. The yacht was built in 1995 by a Dutch company. Here's where it gets a little slippery. I thought that Bonito Estacio was the name of a fish or maybe somebody famous in history, but after digging a lot (I won't waste time telling you how and where) I found that it was two surnames and that it was the name of a well-connected law firm in Rio, Bonito, Estacio, and Armando. I don't know why Armando got cut out-space maybe? I checked a list of their clients and didn't see Leon listed but that doesn't mean anything.

He could have numerous dummy corporations, but the law firm is worth checking. What got my attention was that they did have a KI, Inc. and a ER Corp. listed as clients which I thought could be somehow related to Leon because he used the JK Corp. for his yacht, and I understand that his proposal to buy Stony Creek is from the MB Corp.

That's what I've come up with so far. I'll keep working on it.

Foley was disappointed. She hadn't come up with as much as he wanted, but it was a start. She spoiled him, doing so many things for the company that he didn't like doing. He found research tedious and boring but now that she left him hanging high and dry, he had to pick up the ball.

He'd deal with it later. It was the story about the Hogg shooting that had his attention, more importantly the guy they called Joe Duck.

Foley recognized his name.

Earlier he put out the word to his contacts in the Pittsburgh police department to give him a heads-up if anybody was flashing money around and one report came back naming a Joe "Duck" Ducci. A street cop in East Liberty reported that Duck bought a Honda SUV. Another said that a street hustler, one Ruby Darkins, was mouthing off at the local eatery where she worked, telling everybody who would listen, that Joe Duck was taking her to an expensive resort.

When Foley first got the info, he didn't think that much about it. He couldn't connect any of the dots until he read the newspaper story that put Hogg and Duck in the same space. That set off an alarm.

Why would a street punk in Pittsburgh, who is suddenly flush with cash, take a side trip to Uniontown and then break into the sheriff's home? The same sheriff who also has a home in Stony Creek, the place somebody robbed.

It could be a coincidence, but Foley doubted it. It was worth checking out.

He had to get more on Ducci.

The first order of business was to check him out and see what the cops had on him. If he had a record, and Foley was sure he did, there should be a mug shot.

He was betting somebody at Stony Creek would recognize him.

THE CHIEF

"**YEAH, YOUR SON CALLED WITH THE SAME QUESTION LAST WEEK.**
We didn't come up with much except a bottom feeder named Joe Ducci,
aka Joe Duck. He scored a used Honda, and the guy was lucky if he
ever had enough for bus fare. Here's the funny thing. The asshole tries
to break into the Sheriff's house in Fayette County and gets a trip to the
Promised Land. Now consider that the punk never worked too far from
home, so what he was doing in Uniontown is beyond me. Your son
calls, you call, and the punk getting whacked in the Sheriff's house says
to me that maybe this Joe Duck character was climbing up the charts.
You got anything more on him?"

The Chief was talking to a Pittsburgh police Inspector out of Zone 5.

"Nah, I'm just running down some petty stuff that I'd like to close
the files on," the Chief said, talking louder than usual because he was on
speakerphone.

"Is your kid working for you now?"

"He's doing security consulting for Stony Creek, and he's giving me
a hand cleaning up the junk. If I get anything for you Freddy, I'll pass it
on, I promise," the Chief said.

"You owe me, Chief, so don't forget your friends downtown,"
Freddy said, "and if I pick anything else up, I'll let you know, and you
do the same."

"Will do, Freddy," the Chief said, hanging up.

He leaned back, his old chair creaking with age, and stared at the small bulletin board on the wall. It was an accumulation of years of willy-nilly postings, mostly things the Chief didn't know where to file.

Since he read the Hogg/Duck story, things were falling into place. He ticked off what he knew. Duck may have robbed the money room; Hogg was in on it, probably the brains; Duck dumps the money and gets out of Stony Creek clean as a whistle. It was the tracks in the snow by Hogg's window that the Chief saw that puzzled him. They could belong to the pecker perp or maybe Duck, but why? Hogg could have planted them in case something went astray, and say somebody broke into his house?

Duck breaks into Hogg's house in Uniontown, probably hunting for the money. What happens is almost too perfect. Duck, the petty thief, breaks into Hogg's house; the sheriff confronts the thief; the good sheriff does his duty to serve and protect and makes a large lead deposit into the asshole's chest

The sheriff is a hero, and a lot richer. The bad guy is dodging pitchforks while his ass burns in hell. All's well that ends well.

It's a sweet package, all wrapped up nicely with a big red bow, except for one thing that doesn't fit. All this shit happens at the same time the sheriff is getting his dick chopped off. Einstein couldn't get that to add up. The other thing is why would Hogg hook up with such a loser unless he did it intentionally, and if so, why?

So why does Hogg call me? I ain't a snot nosed kid on his first Kennywood ride.

The Chief was left with a couple of possibilities. Hogg had no choice, or it was a setup.

Foley was another problem. He was close to putting a lot of it together. When he read the story about Duck and Hogg, he clammed up. That meant he knows more than he's letting on.

The phone rang.

"Yeah," the Chief said.

"Didn't mean to upset you, Chief. This is Butler, (pause) you know, the state cop that's trying to help you catch your robber."

"Sorry, Bob. I was thinking about something else. What's up?"

"Not a helluva lot. As you know, Scarcini's out. The perp used his name. We've had anybody and everybody who might have met him look at mug shots and we're coming up dry. We did get an APB out on his description. I'm sure we'll smoke something out. You got anything new?"

The Chief paused. He was debating about throwing a bone Butler's way, but he wasn't ready.

"Did you hear me, Chief?"

"Yeah, just thinkin' things out. Ah, no, we haven't come up with anything yet. I'll keep you posted."

"Do that. I'm sure you saw the story about Hogg shooting that punk trying to break into his house."

"I did. The idiot broke into the wrong home."

"Yeah, you could say that. Makes you wonder, though," Butler said.

"Hey Bob, I gotta run. Got a meeting. Talk to you later," the Chief said, hanging up.

Butler was fishing around. That wasn't good. Too many people fishing in the same pond scares the fish away. While he was talking on the phone, he thought of something the ladies from the money room told him. He had to run it down fast because Foley would be just a few steps behind.

He couldn't let Foley beat him to the punch.

HEIDI'S CONDO

HEDY WAS AT HER SISTER'S CONDO WHEN FOLEY AND HIS SECURITY installer arrived. Foley introduced the man with him as Eli and said he would do the installation.

"I'm sure Foley explained to you that whatever you do in this condo will be replicated in others, so make this one really good and we'll do a lot more business," Hedy said.

"Yes, of course," Eli said.

"Look, I want a system that nobody, not even the best spy, can detect."

"This is top of the line equipment," Foley said. "Eli here," he said taking the installer's arm "is one of the best, if not the best in the business."

The installer, a former Israeli agent, was a handsome young man. He was a sturdy six feet, well built with an angular face, a very black two-day beard, and dark eyes. His shaved head left nothing but dark stubble. He smiled and nodded at Hedy.

"If somebody want to find cameras," Eli said, "they can find."

Foley jumped in. "Eli doesn't like me to say this, but Hedy, you can be assured you're getting not only the best equipment but one of the best security guys anywhere. Eli was an agent for Shabak, like our CIA, except they were Israel's internal security agency. We can conceal the cameras, but if a professional has the time to hunt for them, he'll find them. For example, there's a device that can detect hidden cameras. You scan the room with it, and if there's a camera, the unit will pick up the lens and cause it to reflect, showing the exact location. There are also instruments that will pick up wireless cameras. It scans frequencies and zeroes in on the camera's signal and will show exactly what the camera is seeing."

"Isn't there something to counteract that?"

"It's a back-and-forth game. Of course, we'll also install alarms on all possible entrances and that will be a deterrent. Do you really think you're going to have professionals casing your place?"

"No, but I want the best," she said, thinking she damn well might.

Foley glanced over at Heidi, who was lying on the white sofa reading a book. He thought that for a woman who was really frightened, she wasn't much interested in what they were doing.

"As you requested, this is the best that's out there right now. As new stuff comes on to the market, and it does just about every day, we'll monitor and keep you informed so that if you want to upgrade, we'll be able to do it quickly and easily.

"I understand. Now, will there be enough cameras that if one doesn't work, the others will? I don't want just one camera in a room. I want enough back-up so that in case one fails, the others will work so there's no chance of some sort of technical glitch."

"I understand what you want, and we'll have back-ups. We plan on utilizing pin-hole cameras, cone shaped, sprinkler, smoke detector cameras and probably screw button cameras. There will be numerous cameras in each room, and back-ups so you, well, Heidi, will be well covered."

"Make sure they work in the dark," Hedy said.

Foley looked at Hedy. "They will."

"Good," Hedy said, "and run the bill by me before you submit it to Otto. Okay?"

"Done. What about your place and the offices?" Foley said, "We haven't even looked at them yet, so maybe we should do that while we're at it."

"Let's get this one done first so I can see how it works, kind of like a test place, then we'll look at the others, okay?"

"Works for me," Foley said.

"Oh, I'm sorry. I didn't offer you guys a drink. Do you want something?" Hedy said.

Eli waved his hand, signaling no when Hedy's cell rang. She glanced at her phone, and excused herself, saying to Foley, "There's drinks in the fridge. Help yourself," she said, walking over to the corner of the room to take the call.

"Thanks. I'll take you up on that," Foley said. He opened the fridge and looked around for a soft drink. Foley noted that Heidi kept plenty of champagne. She had at least three bottles on call. Behind the milk Foley saw Pepsi and Pellegrino, torn between the two, finally going with the cola.

"I hope you found something to drink," Hedy yelled.

Foley turned. "Yeah, a Pepsi," he said, holding up the can, and closed the refrigerator door.

Heidi got up from the sofa and went upstairs.

FOLEY

THE HOT COFFEE HIT THE SPOT AS FOLEY WATCHED THE TODAY Show and thought about the things he had to do. The Leon project was a priority and Otto was in a rush to meet on it. Foley hadn't come up with the silver bullet that would do Leon in, and that wouldn't make Otto happy.

Foley had a lot of people working on Leon but getting information from foreign government bureaus was extremely slow and difficult. The phone rang.

It was Linda. She was calling from her car.

"I'm on the turnpike. I'll be there in a few hours," she said.

Foley felt better. Maybe she'll come up with something before the Otto meeting. As soon as that thought crossed his mind, he criticized himself for being hopeful. With the irrational way she's been acting, she'd probably not show. He had to stop counting on her.

He was pleased with the new information he dug up on Duck. He might be able to use it to appease Otto a little, but it was Leon who Otto wanted to shut down.

Foley went to Stony Creek's Human Resource Director and found that a Joe Ducci had worked for the resort back in the late eighties. His file included a head shot and showed that he was fired for theft. He was pilfering prime steaks from the freezer. Foley planned to show the photo to Williams and LaVella and see if that jogged anything.

So how does this guy Duck end up getting killed in Hogg's house? If it turns out Duck is the money room robber, and Foley was certain that's how it was going to fall, then Hogg had his hands in it somewhere. He could be the brains, or he may have stumbled on something that led him to Duck. Foley winced at the thought of a cop being involved in a robbery.

The phrase, "one rotten apple spoils the whole bunch" seems to always fit police officers more than any other group. If a firefighter or doctor makes a mistake, the public doesn't come down on the entire industry like they do with cops. There was a chance Hogg wasn't involved, but the Hogg-Duck encounter would require a tremendous amount of justification to eliminate it.

As far as Foley was concerned, he'd have to stretch his imagination into never-never land to consider it a coincidence. Hogg killing Duck was the clincher that did it for Foley.

The big question in Foley's mind was CB. Was he somehow involved? The odds were high that he could be and that not only threw a wrench into the works it threw the whole damn toolbox into it.

At some point soon, he'll have to report his suspicions to the state cops, and they'll put it together. It angered him that he was being hampered by his uncertainty about CB. He had to get that resolved.

There was something else bothering him. It was minor, and probably a coincidence, and he wished he hadn't seen it, but he did, and that meant he had to follow up. It was the old man who told him about his CCC theory. Coincidence, clue, conviction. Many things are coincidences, but every single one must be checked out because it can be a clue—and clues get convictions.

The coincidence was in Heidi's refrigerator. When he went to get the Pepsi during the security installation, he saw a quart of buttermilk. No big deal except that CB just mentioned how Hogg drank scotch and buttermilk. It was probably nothing but a coincidence. That's why Foley had to check it out.

He remembered a quote he read somewhere. "Where some people see coincidence, I see conspiracy."

Foley believed that coincidences were like compasses. They'll point you in the right direction.

HOGG

A COLUMNIST FOR A CLEVELAND NEWSPAPER, STEALING A LINE from a comedian and applying it to the Sheriff, pointed out the difference between Bill Hogg and God.

"God," he wrote, "doesn't walk around pretending he's Bill Hogg."

Hogg embraced that description, joking about it, but now his ego was under siege. He was doing everything to maintain his balance. His inquisitorial mind was having trouble separating fact from fantasy. He tried to reconstruct that night, but each time ended up in ftrustration.

Sporadically he pulled up ghostlike images that disappeared as quickly as smoke in a windstorm. There were moments but it was like trying to make a snowball out of water. He never blacked out like he did that night. Heidi must have spiked his drink, but it didn't add up. That wasn't her MO. She wasn't capable of doing it, but Hogg remembered that she was there. Maybe she snapped but why? Did somebody help her? Who? And why? Nothing was adding up, but she was his only lead. If he had to live in hell, she was moving in with him.

His life was a wide-awake nightmare, constantly tormenting him with the weirdest kind of agony. He'd feel like he was getting an erection, which he knew was impossible, and yet he continually checked. He couldn't live this way. His hope was the Chinese doctor. Even if they could sew another dick on him, his life would never be the same, but it would be better.

Hogg's cell buzzed. It was Dr. Rhodes.

"I talked with Dr. Chen, the Chinese doctor, and he is making progress in penile transplantation, but it's still in the early stages. I discussed your situation with him and he's not promising anything but if you're willing to travel to Beijing, he'll examine you and see if he can help," Dr. Rhodes said, "but remember, it's all experimental and there are no guarantees. He won't charge you for the exam. Anything after that is between you and him."

"Thanks. I'm willing to do anything because I know I can't live this way," Hogg said.

"He makes no promises and I want to alert you, that even if Dr. Chen can do something for you, the psychological impact on the patient is enormous and difficult and …"

"I don't give a fuck about that psychology shit. I can handle myself," Hogg said, catching himself. "I'm sorry for the foul language, Doc."

"I understand. I believe you will have to undergo counseling before he attempts any procedures, so think about it, and if you decide you want to pursue it, call me and we'll begin to work out timetables," Dr. Rhodes said quickly adding, "And it will all be contingent on finding a donor."

Hogg had no doubt that he was going to do two things; go to China, and if he had to kill a chink with a big dick, so be it; and the other was to fuck up Heidi Kasser, and she was first on his list.

He regretted sending her the tarot card. He had to control his anger. Things were going on in his mind that he didn't understand. He had to make peace with her. He hated to apologize, but he'd do it. He'd do whatever it took to get that bitch.

Anger burned through his body again. He spent hours thinking of ways to hurt Heidi. She didn't have a dick that he could cut off and sewing her pussy shut wasn't an option. Killing her was too easy. She had to suffer like him.

How do you destroy a hole? You fill it in, but with what?

He had to calm down. Stay cool. Get a read on her. He took a deep breath.

He dialed her cell phone. The phone clicked and he could hear background noise.

"Heidi, this is Bill."

Silence.

"Heidi, are you there? I'm not angry with you anymore. Just talk to me and I'll explain," Hogg said.

"What do you want?" she said timidly.

"I don't want anything. I want to apologize, and I want us to be friends. I know you don't believe me, but I realized I love you more than I thought. I miss you," he said.

Silence.

"That's just it. I'm going to be fine. I found a doctor in China who is going to fix me up as good as new, so everything's going to be okay," he said.

"What are they going to fix up? I don't understand," she said in an exaggerated childlike voice.

"Okay. I see. We'll talk about it later," he said.

"It was you who sent me the Death card, wasn't it? Why would you do that?" she said more firmly.

"Yeah. I'm sorry about that. I was drinking and feeling sorry for myself, just not thinking. It was stupid. But I'm over all that now, because I'm going to be like new, maybe even better," he said, laughing, "and I don't want to lose you. I know you didn't mean to do what you did. You were like me when I sent the card. I just snapped and so did you, so I understand what you must have been ..."

"I really don't know what you mean. I didn't snap or anything else," she interrupted. "You're confusing me."

"It's okay, honey. We'll work it out," Hogg said his jaw tight. The bitch was really pissing him with her innocent act.

"But I really didn't do anything."

What's with her? Is she that stupid to try and con me?

He had to give her credit. She was playing this one better than he thought, but he'd crack her. She was no match. Let her think she was winning.

"Honey, I'm sorry. I just haven't been myself. Didn't mean to talk in riddles. Everything's cool."

"I don't understand what you're talking about," she said. "Are you sure you're okay?"

Hogg wanted to reach through the phone and grab that bitch's neck and twist it right off, but he calmed himself. He had to gain control and if it meant acting like a puny asshole, he'd do it.

"I'm okay. I didn't mean to sound so confusing. I've had a rough time and you're the only person I can talk to. I really need your help right now. Just to talk. That's not asking too much, is it?"

He hated saying this shit to her.

"I don't know what to think," she said.

She was weakening.

"Heidi, you know me. We had a good thing. I just need a friend right now. If nothing else, just to talk. You owe me that at least."

"I don't know, Bill."

He went in for the kill.

"Look, at least have a drink with me. We can meet somewhere out of Stony Creek, maybe in Bedford or Somerset? We can meet at that little bar that you like," he said, figuring that she would be more receptive if it was a public place.

There was a long pause. Her answer shocked him.

"No, maybe we can just meet at my condo."

"Of course, honey. If you're more comfortable with that. When can we meet?" he said.

"I'll call you back, later tonight or tomorrow."

"Make it tomorrow. I'll be in my Uniontown office all day cleaning up some work. Okay?" he said, not wanting to sound too anxious.

"Okay," she said, still whimpering like a little lost soul.

As soon as he hung up, he felt a new surge of energy. He was back.

He had to get to work.

HEDY

As soon as Heidi hung up, she called Hedy.

"I just talked with him," Heidi said.

"Hogg?"

"Yes, Hogg."

"What did he say?"

"That he wanted to be friends with me and that he understood and stuff like that," Heidi said.

"Did you do what I told you to do?"

"I did. I pretended I didn't know anything."

"Are you sure?"

"Yes, Hedy, I'm sure. I did exactly what you told me."

"So, he didn't question you?"

"Not really. He just wanted to meet somewhere," she said, "in public, and I…"

"You didn't agree with that?"

"No, but I almost did. I didn't see anything wrong with that. It would be safer than what you want me to do and …"

"What did you say to him, honey. Exact words."

"I told him we could meet in my condo."

"When?"

"I didn't give him a time. I said I'd call him tomorrow."

"That's good, honey. Don't do anything until we talk."

"He did say he found a doctor in China that will fix him up. Maybe he really does want to make up," Heidi said.

The last few days Heidi seemed to be out of it, moving mechanically, disinterested, and distant.

"Sometimes I feel like I'm watching a movie and you are all in it," she said one afternoon.

Hedy studied psychology in college. Heidi could be suffering from dissociation, causing her to feel disconnected from her body. She'd think she was having an out-of-body experience.

"Everything will be fine, darling. If he calls back, don't agree to anything until you and I talk. I think you're right. I think everything's going to be okay. And don't forget, you have that security system in now, so you'll be safe. Tell you what? I'll be over and we'll talk and work everything out, okay?"

Hedy hung up and looked out of her window at the night sky. It was a cloudless night, and the black sky was teeming with twinkling stars.

Hedy wished she could fly away to one of those stars and watch the world from up there. She thought that's how Heidi must feel, so far away from it all.

But neither one of them were floating around in space. This was the real world and they lived in it.

So did Hogg.

STONY CREEK

THE STONEY CREEK ACCOUNT WAS BECOMING A FULL-TIME JOB stretching Foley's resources. Coincidences were turning into major projects and his key employee was in Neverland. Foley had to jump off Linda's unmerry-go-round and get clinical. The problem was he had no replacement for her. Right now, he had to take care of business the best he could.

Foley showed the dated employee picture of Joe Duck to the two cops who were at the gate the night of the robbery. La Vella thought it could be him, but the beard made it difficult to be 100% certain. William's was "pretty sure it's the perp." Foley hoped he'd get a more recent mug shot that would make the ID solid to satisfy the D.A.

Foley was juggling the Leon investigation, the robbery, and now the Hogg, Duck, and CB connection. He checked his e-mail and two more problems appeared.

Foley,

I'm so sorry I didn't make it, but I was on the turnpike when I began to feel sick to my stomach. I had to turn around. Maybe it's a 24-hour virus because I'm feeling a little better. I'll call you later.

I did more research on Leon and I accidently stumbled on something.

In my report, I mentioned Leon's "initial corporations" i.e., KI, Inc. and MB, Inc. etc. Because Leon wants to buy Stony Creek, I decided to look at the original paperwork filed on the resort, figuring we might need that info. We all know the rumors that Greta got the

land from Jacob Kimberly for a song to bury their affair, but what caught my attention was the deed transfer. Greta bought the land from the KI Corporation and when I double checked, Leon had his yacht registered to a KI, a Panama offshore corporation. It could be a coincidence, but I think that's a stretch. I'll keep digging.

At least Linda's e-mail wasn't a total loss. The one from the Pittsburgh Police was. They had no current mug shots of Joe Duck. He was picked up numerous times for petty crap but never charged or booked. They attached a photo from juvenile that looked like it was taken around the same time as the one Foley had, so it was no help.

Foley was a bit intrigued by the K-1 connection.

What were the odds of Leon naming one of his shell companies K-1 and the land that Stony Creek sets on today coming from a K-1 corporation way back in the early thirties?

Coincidence?

HEDY

HEDY WAS ANNOYED FOR NOT PUTTING ON HER FACE MASK AS SHE maneuvered the snowmobile up the back trail to Heidi's. She was going slower than usual, but that didn't stop the cold air from frosting her already reddened cheeks.

Hedy had a plan to deal with Hogg, but she didn't know whether she could pull it off. She needed Heidi and she was questionable. As she neared Heidi's door, she looked for the camera. She knew approximately where it was, but she couldn't see it. That was positive.

She stood in front of the ivory paneled door for a moment, afraid to turn the knob for fear of what would happen. She turned it slowly, and as she expected, it opened.

"Damn Heidi," she said as she entered, "You have to keep this damn door locked."

She was wasting her breath. She yelled out again and from upstairs came a "be right down."

Hedy got a Pellegrino from the fridge as. Heidi came down the steps. She was dressed in a powder blue après ski outfit, her blonde hair dripping down around her shoulders, looking as if she was in a trance.

"Oh, Hedy. How are you?" she said, her voice soft and childlike.

"I'm fine. Heidi. Are you okay?"

"I'm good."

"Well, you're quite the fashion show. Are you going somewhere?"

"Oh, this old thing. Maybe. I don't know," Heidi said.

"Are you up to calling Hogg?"

"If that's what you want?" she answered mechanically.

"Come, let's sit for a moment," Hedy said leading her to the sofa.

"Are you sure you're okay, Heidi?"

"I'm doing fine, Hedy. Why?"

"Well, you seem to be in a fog," Hedy said, "you haven't been sipping champagne, have you?" she said, moving closer to Heidi, and giving her a hug, sniffing for the scent of alcohol. All she smelled was a hint of Patou's Joy.

"Drinking, no. Dreaming, yes. Remember when we went on that sailboat in St. Barth's? It was wonderful?" Heidi said, as she snuggled up against Hedy's shoulder.

"It was baby. It really was." Hedy said, feeling the warmth of her sister's breath on her neck, "and do you know what? We're going to do it again, real soon."

"Oh, I would like that. When?" Heidi asked.

"Soon, real soon," Hedy said, hugging her tighter, and then quickly releasing her and holding Heidi's shoulders with her hands, leaning back, and looking directly into her eyes.

"We'll get it all worked out, but right now darling I need to make a call. Can I borrow your cell phone? I forgot mine," Hedy said.

THE CHIEF

THE CHIEF EXPECTED TO HEAR FROM FOLEY. FOLEY WAS CLOSING in on the money room robber, and he figured that he made the Hogg/Duck connection. The Chief was thinking about how to handle the situation when he heard banging at his office door.

"It's me, Foley."

The Chief wasn't sure who was going to be the cat and who was going to be the mouse, but it was game time.

"There's coffee on the thing over there," the Chief said, waving his arm in the direction of the coffee maker. Foley poured a cup, added a dash of half and half, and took a seat in front of the Chief's desk. The Chief got his coffee, cream, sugar, and sweeteners from Pipa's, so he was always fully stocked. A small fridge kept his drinks cold.

"So," Foley said, "bring me up to date."

"On what?"

"Well, let's start with the robbery. Anything new?"

"Nah, nuthin. I heard from The Greek, you know Inspector Copetas down at Zone 5. Said Duck was flashing some cash, but these punks do that on a regular basis," the Chief said.

Foley guessed CB knew he talked with the two cops even though it was only an hour ago. He warned them not to call the Chief saying, "I'd like to be the one to tell my father," but he doubted they listened. The Chief kept his men on a short leash.

"Yeah, I checked Duck out, too, The Hogg connection is interesting. What do you make of it?" Foley said.

"I dunno. Maybe coincidence, maybe something else," the Chief said, drumming his finger on the desk.

"You don't think there's a connection to the robbery?"

"Do you?" the Chief said.

"I'm asking you," Foley said.

The Chief looked at his son, not answering for a few seconds.

"Okay, let me have it, and no more snipe hunting," The Chief said, leaning forward.

Foley stared back at his father.

"You never took me snipe hunting, or anywhere else. If you had, I would have caught a snipe for sure," Foley said smiling, "but as you always say CB, you can't bullshit a bullshitter, so stop bullshitting me."

"If you have something, spill it," The Chief said.

"I have something. In fact, I have the guy who robbed the money room, and it was Joe Duck. So, I ask again, what does Joe Duck have to do with Hogg?"

"How do you know it was Duck?"

"I got his graduation photo from the morgue, showed it to your two boys, and they made a positive on Duck," Foley said.

"Well, I thought he might be our perp, but I didn't want to nail the scumbag before I had all the facts, and I see you picked up a few more than me, Dick Tracy. What's your next move with this?

"Like what?"

"Like calling Butler and telling him what you have," the Chief asked, staring at his awards hanging on the wall.

Foley noted CB was avoiding eye contact. He was surprised because he knew he was better than this at lying.

"No, I didn't call him. I wanted to hear what you had to say first," Foley said.

"I don't have nothing to say," the Chief said, now eyeballing Foley head on.

"I think you do, CB, and I don't want to do anything that might cause you grief," Foley said, standing up and walking over to get another coffee. He really didn't want coffee, but he was stalling for time, trying to figure out how far he was going to go with this.

"It's the Hogg thing that concerns me," Foley added. "He's in this somewhere," Foley continued, walking back, and sitting down, "and I think you know something about it."

"I do, sonny boy. You got that right. I know Hogg shot Duck. That's what I know," the Chief said, standing up. "Foley don't waste your time trying to get blood out of a stone. I have no idea what Hogg's involvement was, if any, in the robbery. Just keep me in the loop and I'll do the same and I guarantee you you'll come out of this smelling like a rose."

Foley knew the CB wouldn't give an inch, so he ended it for now. He wasn't sure what he was up to, but he didn't want to push too fast. He didn't think he'd intentionally try to screw him, but mistakes happen, and with CB, you could never tell. The problem was the two cops. Now they knew who committed the robbery.

"Look, CB, maybe we should keep this under wraps until we can piece it all together. Like you said, get all the facts. The problem is your two cops. We don't need them going around blabbing about this. I only talked with them an hour ago, so I doubt they've had much chance to spread the word, but I think it would be in your best interest if you kept them quiet," Foley said.

"In the interest of good police work, I agree. I'll take care of it," the Chief said, walking around his desk. He was standing directly in front of his son, who stood up. They looked at each other for a long moment, both knowing this wasn't over, each wondering how this was going to end. The Chief broke the silence.

"Foley, you're a good cop, and you want to do right, and you will, but I think you need to stay cool until you get all the facts," the Chief said, putting his hand on Foley's shoulder, "and I'll see that you do, when I get them all."

"I'm sure you will CB. I'm sure you will."

JR LEON

JR RAN A THOROUGH BACKGROUND CHECK ON FOLEY. WHAT HE was about to do was risky, but JR saw some flexibility. Based on the background report, JR had to walk an ethical tightrope with Foley, but he believed he could do it causing no serious breaches.

Foley's resume was impressive, but his father was a weak spot. The Chief was a bottom feeder, but he was well connected to very important people. JR was certain he could be handled.

He told one of his men to call Foley.

"Mr. Foley. My name is Roger Collins, and I work for JR Leon. He would have called you himself, but he didn't want to put you in an uncomfortable position since you are doing due diligence on him. He thought it would speed things up if he met with you, and you could question him directly. Nothing is off the table. Mr. Leon is anxious to close this deal, and he has nothing to hide. Feel free to tell your employer and any others you deem necessary about this contact. Mr. Leon wants everything legitimate. If you can meet with him, call me at this number, and I'll arrange it. If not, just let me know and that will be fine."

The yellow caution flag went up. Foley thought it could be legitimate, but he'd run it by Otto.

On his way to Otto's, he ran into Hedy. After the usual greeting, Foley told Hedy about JR's phone call. She didn't seem concerned about it and thought he should meet. He had nothing to lose, and a one on one might give him a better feel for Leon.

After a brief discussion with Otto, they came to the same conclusion. Foley called, and the meeting was set up. They met at JR's VIP chalet.

"Good to see you, Foley."

"Mr. Leon," Foley said, shaking his hand.

"Please, I prefer JR," he said.

"These chalets are nice. I hope you're comfortable here," Foley said, walking around, trying to see as much as he could without looking like he was snooping.

"It's very comfortable, thanks. Can I get you a drink? I have a nice single malt scotch I think you'll like."

"Well, if you're having one, I'll join you."

"I am having one," he said, and went over to the bar and poured two Glenrothes and dropped one ice cube in each.

"I think you'll like this," JR said, handing him the drink.

"Thanks," Foley said.

Foley took a sip. "You're right, this is a nice scotch."

"It's one of my favorites," JR said, walking over to a gleaming dark cherry desk and retrieving a manila folder.

"Please, Foley, have a seat," JR said, gesturing to a heavy looking dark burgundy leather chair. JR sat on the matching sofa and set the folder on the cherry coffee table with matching leather piping.

"Are you ready to begin?" Foley said, opening his briefcase and pulling out a file folder along with a yellow tablet and pen.

"I don't think you'll need that," JR said, reaching for the manila folder. "I've had my people prepare a complete dossier, which should save you a lot of time… and money. Of course, I don't want to cause you to lose any income because of this, so I'll say nothing about it," JR said with a slight smile, sliding the folder towards Foley.

Foley was taken aback. He didn't expect this. He picked up the folder and took a quick glance inside.

"My financials are in there, and I had my people include all lawsuits that have been filed against me and the results. You'll quickly see that there were many frivolous suits, but of course that's one burden of being a rich man. You may find this hard to believe but I included some negatives that have been said about me. I want a clean deal that benefits all parties."

"Well, JR, I appreciate this, but I thought I would have the opportunity to question you and..."

"No need for that now," JR interrupted. "Why don't you take that file with you, look it over, and if you think there's more information you wish, contact me. That'll save us both a lot of time."

Foley realized he was boxed in. Until he went through the file, there was little wiggle room.

"Let me freshen up that scotch," JR said taking the glass from Foley's hand before he had a chance to respond.

"Ah, just a little, please. I've got a busy day today and..."

"Just a little," JR said, "and you can be on your way."

"Cheers," JR said after handing Foley his drink. JR leaned in and clinked Foley's glass. JR's dark eyes fixed on Foley's. "To a long and profitable relationship."

"I have some other scotches that I think you'll like. We'll have to get you and your wife (pause) are you married?" JR said.

"Not yet," he said, certain that JR knew what kind of toothpaste Foley used.

"Nor am I," JR said. "Maybe somewhere down the road we can get together for a real scotch tasting. I have a man from Scotland who knows every scotch ever distilled. He puts on quite a show."

Foley wasn't sure where JR was heading but his caution flag was up.

"Let me ask you a question," JR said putting his drink down on the coffee table and leaning in towards Foley. "If you think it's out of line, just say so—or maybe it's out of line, but I want to be honest with you."

Foley felt his senses sharpen. He leaned back, trying to appear relaxed, but he was tense.

"I'm assuming I will close this deal with Otto," JR said, "and I've checked you and your firm out and I like what I see. Let's be hypothetical here. If I close the deal, would you be open to an offer from me to handle my security—not just here at Stony Creek, but my personal security and for all of my interests?" JR said.

Foley was a bit addled. This was totally unexpected. He felt both a positive rush and a red warning signal. He stalled for time.

"I can't believe a man of your caliber doesn't have somebody doing that for you already," Foley said.

"I do, an ex-FBI Assistant Director, but he's retiring as soon as I find a replacement. I've been hearing good things about you, and I wanted to look into the possibility of you coming on board. Not now, of course, but when this is all over. You have the background and experience that meets my needs."

JR was shopping. Foley wasn't about to let JR buy him. Although if Foley was tempted to find out more about the offer, he had to get off the shelf immediately.

"Mr. Leon," Foley said as he gathered up his papers and put them in his briefcase, "I know you understand that this is improper and that I must inform my employer."

Foley closed his briefcase and stood up. "I am under contract to Stony Creek and my loyalty and any actions I take are on their behalf and I cannot be part of this kind of conversation, so I thank you for the…"

"That is exactly the response I wanted," JR interrupted. "I knew you were a man of integrity and I hope you'll excuse my inappropriate actions, but I found out what I wanted to. I apologize for my somewhat unorthodox tactics, but it helps me determine the quality of the people I'm dealing with," JR said.

Foley smiled, thanked him, and left.

As he closed the door, JR was pleased. Things were falling into place.

HEDY

THE PHONE CALL FROM HER MOTHER COULDN'T HAVE COME AT A better time for Hedy. Rosie was off to New York City and wanted the twins to join her for shopping and theater. It was exactly what Hedy needed to get her sister out of town.

She went to Heidi's condo to give her the good news.

Hedy was surprised by her response. It was a dull, mechanical "okay." Hedy tried to pump her up with all the great things about the trip, but Heidi's reaction was a humdrum monotone, resigned, robotic, and distant. Hedy saw these signs earlier, and now she was even more concerned.

She wanted Heidi to call Hogg, but in her current state Hedy wasn't sure she could do it.

"Honey, you know you have to call Hogg today, right?"

"Yes."

"Do you feel up to it?"

"Yes."

Hedy was worried, but the call had to be made. Hedy went over every likely scenario with Heidi and the answer she should give. It wasn't complicated, but the way Heidi was acting was concerning.

"You sure you're okay with this," Hedy said.

"Yes," she answered, picking up the phone and dialing.

Hedy leaned in close to her sister, their breaths intermingling as she could hear Hogg's phone ringing. After the fourth ring, Hogg's voice came on.

"I'm not here. Leave your name, number, the time you called, and why you called. Thanks."

Heidi moved the phone away from her ear and held in front of them both.

"Message. Leave the message," Hedy mouthed her chin almost bumping Heidi's cheek as she grabbed Heidi's wrist and moved the phone back up to her ear.

For a moment Heidi gave Hedy a dead-eye stare and then seemed to come out of it.

"This is Heidi, Bill," she said in a weary drone, "I am going out-of-town shopping and will be gone for a while… ah, I should be back for the weekend. I'll call you. Bye."

She handed the phone to Hedy and went and sat down on the sofa and picked up a magazine.

Heidi was not right. Hedy would have a doctor in New York examine her. She pecked her sister on the cheek and left, telling her she'd be back to help her pack.

Hedy called the Chief. She wanted 24-hour surveillance on Heidi's condo, but she couldn't tell him the real reason. No matter what she told him he'd be suspicious.

"Listen, Chief. I have a little police problem, which stays between you and me. I don't think it's serious but let me run it by you and get your input. My mother, Heidi, and me are going to New York City for a few days. We need to get Heidi out of town. She met a guy, and he's become a bit of a problem. He comes from a prominent Pittsburgh family, and we want to keep this quiet, but the guy appears to be a little unstable. He's been stalking Heidi, and that's why we're going out of town. I'd like you to stake out her condo. We think he may come nosing around, might even try to break in, and that's why we put in a security system, but I'd still like you to monitor the place. I recognize that putting men on 24-hour surveillance is a drain on your resources and I promise I'll make it up to you when budget time comes around. Can you do this very special favor for me? If you catch anybody snooping around her condo call me immediately on my cell. I know it's a lot to ask, but can you do that for me, Chief?"

More alarms went off in the Chief's head than at a prison break in Sing-Sing. What Hedy was saying could be true, but twenty-four-hour surveillance?

"Twenty-four-hour surveillance is a lot, Hedy. Who's the asshole that's bothering our little girl?"

"I'd rather not say. It will be for only three days at the most. I know it's overkill, but we need to find out if this guy is going to be a real problem or just another love-struck jerk."

"You know I'll do what you want, but…"

"Look, Chief. When I get back, we'll talk. I know this is a big ask and I won't forget it, but it stays between us, and only us."

Something wasn't quite Kosher, but the Chief saw an easy quid pro quo.

"You're asking a lot, Hedy, and it's going to put a real strain on me and my resources, and I want to help you…"

"Chief, I understand, and I won't forget it."

"I know you won't, Hedy. You can count on me to take care of it," the Chief said thinking about what he could get in return as he hung up.

Otto would get buggy about it if he found out, but the Chief could finagle his way out of it. He'd just say he thought Otto knew all about it, family, and all that.

He also had to stay a step ahead of his son who was moving fast.

Foley was close to sorting things out on the robbery, and the Chief wanted to be the one to control that.

He sent Williams and LaVella to Panama to run down leads on JR, and those two ji-mokes were happier than pigs in a mud hole. When he found out Otto would fuss about it, but that would be it.

The phone rang. It was Hogg.

"I was just thinking about you," the Chief said.

"I'm sure you were," Hogg answered with a forced chuckle, "but if you can find a minute will you stop down at my house? I have something to talk to you about?" Hogg said.

"Can't we discuss it on the phone?"

"You know better," Hogg said. Here we go, the Chief thought.

"When did you want to do this?" the Chief asked, letting Hogg know by his tone that he wasn't happy about it.

"How about later today, maybe around five? We can have our own happy hour," Hogg said, with a brief chuckle. "Seriously, I have some important information that may help you."

Hogg could have information, but the Chief was betting it was more disinformation. He had to play it out.

"Okay, see you at five."

"Great, I'll leave the light on for you," Hogg said with a slight chuckle. Hogg had the sense of humor of a dead man walking.

The phone call had the Chief running down the moves Hogg might make. He wasn't sure of any of them.

He decided to carry. He holstered his Glock and he brought along his police radio. He didn't think Hogg was crazy enough to do something to him in his own house, but the bastard was a dick shy, which was one too many, and who knew what that would do to a man's head? He told one of his men to call him on the police radio at 6:00 PM and say he was needed back at headquarters for an emergency. It was an old police trick, and the officer gave the Chief a knowing smile. Cops used it to get out of the house at night, and it really came in handy when you wanted to ditch the broad you just screwed. Police work had its advantages.

At five, he drove down to Hogg's, parking out front. Remembering Hogg's bitch about using the front door, The Chief walked around to the back door, passing the spot where Hogg usually parked. It was empty.

He banged on the door. No answer. He pounded again. He turned the knob and was about to push the door open when somebody pulled it out of his hands. He stepped back, and as the door opened, he saw a young girl, well, young to him, guessing she was in her late thirties, standing there with a big smile on her face. She had red hair, blue eyes and a face filled with freckles. The Chief's first thought was that she was an over the hill Orphan Annie.

"Oh, you must be the Chief. C'mon in," she said pleasantly, "I'm Tammy, a friend of the Sheriff. Alarms began ringing.

She extended her hand and the Chief shook it gently. She gave him a quick smile and asked if he wanted a drink as she headed for the kitchen counter.

"Scotch okay? she said, "without the buttermilk."

"Yeah, sure the Chief said looking over her body.

"Bill waited for you, but he had to leave. You probably passed him on the road. He got a call. Said to tell you it was important, and he'd be back in fifteen or twenty minutes. Go on into the den and make yourself comfortable."

"After you," he said as she handed him his scotch and he followed her into Hogg's den.

Walking behind her he thought she looked like a Sottish cheerleader in the short, plaid skirt she was wearing.

"You gotta be careful wearing plaid in this place. You'll disappear and Hogg'll have trouble finding you," the Chief said.

She turned and looked at him, silent for a moment, and then broke into a big smile, her breasts bouncing under the baby blue cashmere sweater.

"Oh, you mean this old thing," she said pulling her plaid skirt up a smidgen, giving the Chief a glimpse of her thigh.

She sat on the sofa. Ella was singing "Someone to watch over me" on the stereo and the fireplace was blazing. The Chief was thinking setup. He was about to sit in Hogg's chair but, remembering what happened there, sat on the ottoman.

Could she be the cutter?

She gave him a toothy smile, raised her glass in a toast, and took a sip. The Chief followed suit and said, "How long have you known Bill?"

"Actually, not long. I just met him a few nights ago at the bar in Uniontown and he seemed like a nice guy, and here I am," she said with a lilt in her voice.

"What do you do?" the Chief asked.

"You mean for a living?"

"Let's start there."

"I'm a dancer."

"What kind of dancer?" the Chief asked certain he knew the answer.

"Guess," she said.

"Ballet?" the Chief said.

"C'mon Chief, you know exactly what kind of dancing I do," she said, standing up, and moving her body back and forth slowly to Ella as she sang.

"I can guess," he said.

"It's a good living. I hope you aren't an old fuddy-duddy who doesn't approve of that kind of dancing."

"No. I appreciate the finer things in life, and you look fine."

She continued to sway to the music her eyes closed. The Chief thought she was a pretty woman, but her face revealed she had been around for a few years.

"I love Ella, don't you," she said, with a little slur in her words.

"One of the best," the Chief said. "When's Bill coming back?" he asked, trying to get out of the mood he was falling into.

"He promised to call as soon as he was done," she said dreamily. "He'll yell at me if you leave. He said I had to keep you here no matter what," she added with a brief smile.

The Chief was sure something fishy was going on.

"Well, you're very nice, but I've got things to do," the Chief said, taking a big hit of the scotch and getting up from the ottoman.

"He's married, isn't he?" she said.

"Who's married?"

"Our Sheriff," she said stumbling, grabbing the Chief's arm.

He held her up but kept his distance.

"I think I'm a little tipsy," she said.

The Chief led her back over to the sofa. He wasn't buying her amateurish act. She was overplaying her big scene.

He couldn't understand what Hogg's angle was.

Was Hogg trying to get him in a compromising situation, take pictures, blackmail him somehow? He was single, maybe the girl wasn't, but she's in Hogg's house. He'd have to explain that.

Underage? No way. This woman has more mileage on her than a '57 Chevy. She's gotta be in her forties.

He couldn't understand why Hogg had this twinkie waving her pussy at him. It didn't make sense.

As she started to sit on the sofa, she seemed to lose her balance and grabbed the Chief's hand, pulling him down with her. He guarded his scotch as he spun and plopped down next to her.

She ain't going to get the part she's trying out for, the Chief thought.

"He's married," she said again.

"Who's married?" the Chief said. He played along.

She was leaning into him. "I knew he was married, but he lied. I don't like lying, do you? I hope you don't," she said, snuggling her face up against his chest, seeming to get drunker by the second.

"I don't know where you're headed, and I like where you're going, but I ain't about to get caught up in some menagerie or whatever," the Chief said, trying to extricate himself from her snuggling.

"I'm not his girlfriend. I never even touched him," she said, and then pulled back, sitting up straight, "You're not married, are you?"

"No, I'm not, but this is…"

"I knew it. I don't go with married men. Too much trouble," she said, snuggling even closer.

"I'm getting tipsy," she said again, "and that's bad for me, good for you though, maybe." She suddenly sat up, took another hefty swallow of her drink, her face so close that he could see the heavy lipstick ridges on her bright red lips, and said, "I think I had a little too much, and when I drink, I get silly. I just feel all loose and happy."

He got up from the sofa to put some distance between them. No question she was coming on to him and he'd like to have sex with her, but he had to be careful.

"Did I say something wrong?" she said with an exaggerated pout.

"No, I just need to freshen up my drink," he said, heading for the kitchen as she slumped back on the sofa.

As he splashed a little more scotch into his glass, he couldn't come up with why this chick was coming on to him unless the booze turned her on. Booze did that with women. The question was did Hogg put her up to this and why? There was just nothing to be gained by Hogg if he screwed her. In fact, that's what he ought to do and see where it all goes.

He went back into the plaid room, and as he neared the back of the sofa, he said, "So, where were we?"

She didn't answer, and he saw why when he walked around to the front of the sofa. She was out, curled up into a little plaid ball, her hands under her face, sound asleep.

He laughed at himself for thinking she wanted to lay him. So much for that thought. He took another drink of his scotch and decided to leave. He didn't like the smell of this thing anyhow although she was tempting.

He took another robust gulp of the scotch, nearly draining the glass, the burn in his throat almost making him choke, but he cleared it with a series of little coughs. He wasn't a big drinker, and he could feel the booze getting to him. He put his glass on the end table and headed for the kitchen door.

As he walked through the kitchen, he was woozier than he thought, staggering a bit, finding the kitchen counter to lean on for a moment as he tried to regain his balance. The Chief stood there for a few seconds, took a deep breath, and went to the kitchen door when he heard her calling out.

"Oh, please Chief, don't leave. Bill will kill me. He said I shouldn't let you leave because it was important that he meet with you. Please don't get me in trouble," she said pleading as she came into the kitchen.

"I ain't about to hang around for Hogg. If it was so important, he'd be here," the Chief said reaching for the doorknob. He was feeling the booze.

"Chief, if you leave," she said, losing her little girl's pleading voice, "my ass is back in the slammer. You know how he is. If you don't do what he wants, you get your ass kicked, and he told me that he had to see you and I was to do whatever was necessary to keep you here until he got back."

"You out on bail?"

"No, I was picked up at the club I danced at. Cocaine. Hogg got me out and invited me to come up here with him."

"Well," (pause) I can help you out, but then you have to help me out. What did Hogg want you to do with me?"

"I told you. Just keep you here 'till he got back. He said you might leave if he wasn't here."

"C'mon, there's more. You tell me and I'll get Hogg off your back and maybe even get your record cleared up."

"I'm telling you the truth. I thought he brought me up her to have sex, but he hasn't touched me. I wasn't lying to you. When I get a few drinks, I get horny and I had a few with Hogg and got a little squirmy," she said her hand moving over her vagina area, "and the bastard left me hanging. I was horny when you walked in. Still am. I don't know why Bill didn't make a move on me… I mean I'm…"

"Yeah, well I can understand, (pause), what in the hell is your name?"

"Tammy"

"Okay, Tammy. Maybe some other time."

"Let me call him. I have his cell phone number. Please," she said.

The chief hesitated, thought out the pros and cons again, and let the redhead call. Maybe she was telling the truth. He couldn't see anything she could do that would cause him trouble. He gave her the okay.

She called Hogg.

"Bill, he has to leave. You need to get back here right away. Oh, well how long? Fifteen minutes? No later, please," she said ending the call. "Well, you heard. He'll be here in fifteen minutes. Please stay so I don't have aggravation from him."

The Chief was still feeling a little woozy. He tried to keep his eyes zeroed in on hers, looking for any uncertainty, but she never wavered, returning his penetrating gaze.

"Look, let's have another drink and by that time he'll be here," she said, taking the Chief's arm and leading him back to the den.

"You go in and relax, and I'll fix you a fresh drink," she said.

The Chief didn't see the harm, so he went back to the leather sofa in the den. It felt good to sit down. He leaned his head back and closed his eyes.

"Here you go," she said leaning over and handing him his drink. Her hanging white breasts were inches away and he could smell her perfume. He felt the rise in his pants.

He shook his head, trying to clear out the cobwebs. "Thank you, Tammy," he said loudly, almost too loud.

She stood there for a moment. "Do you mind if I sit here," she said gesturing to the sofa.

"Hey, sit where you like," he said, downing more scotch.

She sat down with a thump and her plaid skirt slid up above her knees. He couldn't help but notice.

She turned to him, raised her drink into a toast and said, "Thanks. You're a good, decent man to help out a damsel in distress," she said her thick red lips opening to a quick smile.

"Cheers," he said.

"Can you really help me?" she said not looking at him.

"Depends."

"On what?"

"On nothing. You call me in the next few days, and we'll talk," the Chief said.

She was so close to him he could hear her breathing, smell her perfume, and feel her soft breasts up against his arm. He was thinking that maybe he ought to screw this Orphan Annie when she moved closer to him.

"Thanks," she said suddenly giving him a kiss on the neck. "Sorry," she said, pulling back.

He turned and looked at her. She leaned back into him a little closer. He took the drink out of her hand and put them on the end table. He pulled her towards him and kissed her full on the lips, grinding up against her as she willingly lay back. She guided his hand to her vagina, pressing it up tightly against her silk panties, as he tried to slip his fingers under the edge.

The Chief had a sliver of caution creep from his brain, but it was too thin to stop anything. His dick was already hard, and this sweet, young thing was moaning and moving in ways he hadn't seen in a while. He tossed that slice of caution out, grabbing her shoulders, pulling her to him, and kissing her full on the mouth, feeling her tongue dart between his lips.

As she pulled and he wiggled, finally getting his pants down, the weight of his pistol and radio banging on the floor, he struggled to stand up and said, "You sure you wanna do this?"

She answered by pulling down his boxers and taking his cock into her mouth. The warmth of her wet mouth caused him to moan.

She was gentle, careful not to do too much back and forth, but using her tongue like a soft artist's brush, sweeping, caressing, and feeling his pulsations. She had him ready to jump on her.

He grabbed her hair and gently pulled her head back. She stared up at him, his dick stiffly pointing at her face, her mouth slightly open. Her eyes were open wide as she looked up at him.

"Are you sure this is what you want?" He said again, hoping she might stop him somehow.

She nodded her head as much as she could, his hand still holding her long red hair.

"Wait," she said, sliding out of his grip and grabbing her purse from the coffee table. She pulled out a rubber, tore open the foil pack, and rolled it down his cock. She did it in such a slow, teasing way he was worried that he might come, and he coughed trying to break the spell.

"There," she said, her sexy blue eyes looking up at him.

Damn, he hadn't thought of a rubber.

He wasted no more time, pushing her back on to the sofa, plunging his dick into her, she thrusting, him pumping, intense and fast, and then it was over quickly. He lay there for a moment, took a deep breath, pulled out, and stood up.

"Wait one second," she said, sitting up, his drooping dick hanging loosely in front of her face.

"I want to take this off," she said, slowly rolling the rubber off, making a ritual out of it, her fingers grazing his cock, flicking against his skin, causing it to stir.

"There," she said, "I needed that. Thanks." She stood up, gave him a peck on the cheek. "I will call you. I need to go to the bathroom," she said as she walked away.

He hurriedly put on his clothes, not sure how much time had passed, grabbed her clothes and went to the bathroom door that was in the hallway between the den and living room and said," I have your clothes. Do you want them?"

She opened the door, smiled, and took the clothes, closing the door.

The Chief was still feeling a little loose. He tightened himself up and started looking around the room for a camera. He enjoyed the sex, but he was still uneasy. He checked the usual places where an audio device or camera could be hidden, but he couldn't find a thing.

Where in the hell is Hogg?

After about five minutes she came out looking as fresh as she did when he walked in.

"I liked that," she said, "We'll have to do that again." She went into the kitchen and yelled, "Do you want another drink? I'm having one."

Just then the Chief's radio cackled startling him. He answered quickly.

"Yeah. I got it, Thanks, I'll call back in a few minutes," he said cutting off any conversation.

The Chief was sated. His brains returned to their original location, and now he was using them to think out things rationally. It was amazing how quickly men lost their feelings once they ejaculated. He quickly reviewed the events that just took place, trying to find any weaknesses in what he had done. Of course, he shouldn't have screwed her, but then that's always the reaction when a man lets his dick do the thinking. The question was, did he leave himself vulnerable to Hogg? If he did, he'd soon find out.

"No darlin', I'm outta here. If Hogg wants to see me, he knows how to find me… and Tammy, if you want to do the same, you'll find me," he said, still feeling a little shaky but more in control.

"You sure? Maybe we could …"

"Oh, we could, but we're not. I just used up my entire week's supply," he said, grabbing his coat from the kitchen chair and pushing by her, going out the way he came in.

"Toodle-oo," she said with a smile in her voice

He closed the door behind him. It was dark and a few flakes hovered around in the quiet, cold air. He stood there for a moment, wondering if he made a mistake. Too late now.

Toodle-oo? That's all I need.

FOLEY

FOLEY WAS TIRED OF LINDA'S DRAMATIC, SELF-IMPOSED TUG OF war. The situation was way beyond his pay grade. It was costing him too much capital in time, money, and emotions. He didn't know what her end game was, and he didn't think she did either. It was time to cut her loose.

Carly surprised him by picking up the ball. She was doing a good job trying to fill the huge gap left by Linda. She also introduced Foley to two of her friends, both Carnegie-Mellon graduates and experienced researchers. They were in graduate school and agreed to work part-time on the Leon project.

Foley pulled out all stops. His first step was his contact list, and it was extensive. His background in both in law enforcement and the judicial/legal system was an invaluable resource, and he put it to work. A lot of information trading goes on in those professions, but it doesn't come easy. Nothing is for nothing, and Foley called in due bills while also creating some new debts. Persistence and promises paid off, and Foley collected more information on Leon than he expected.

Carly's team added to the dossier, and Foley spent hours trying to connect the dots. He checked and cross-checked all the information that everybody had amassed, and he wasn't finding anything negative enough that would help Otto.

Foley didn't sleep easy. He was a light sleeper who woke up at the slightest sound. Most times it didn't even take a sound. It was normal for him to wake up at three or four in the morning and once awake, he'd start thinking and then couldn't get back to sleep so he'd go to the office. One morning he woke, glanced up at the ceiling and saw that it was 3:05, (he had one of those projection clocks) groaned and tried to go back to sleep but his mind started running before he could doze off. He started reworking the Leon info and when he couldn't remember the name of one of Leon's law firms, he went back to an old trick he learned in a psychology class. Run through the alphabet, beginning with A, and see if that triggers your memory. It was when he hit K that caused a small spark. K-A, K-B and so it went and just as quickly the dam broke.

He went to the office and started back through the Leon files and found what he was looking for. Talk about connecting the dots. This connection was a bombshell. It was adding up, but there were loose ends.

He was sitting on a keg of dynamite and the fuse was lit.

As much as he hated it, he needed CB's input. The old man didn't start his day until around eight. For the next few hours, he double-checked, thought out all the potential scenarios, went through the pros and cons, and was happy to see the clock hit 8:00 am. He gave it a five-minute cushion and called CB.

"CB, I need to meet with you ASAP."

"I haven't even had my coffee yet and you're calling. You okay?"

"I'm fine, but I need to talk with you. How safe is your office?"

"Safe from what?" the Chief said.

"Thin walls," Foley said.

At first the Chief didn't get it. When the phone rang, he was standing. He sat down and put his elbow on his desk.

"It's safe," he said. "I sweep it every few months, mostly because I know Otto's always trying to track me."

"I'm on my way."

Just before he left, he took another quick look at his e-mail. There was one from Linda.

Sorry about everything. Doing my best. I can get up there on Thursday. I'll call you when I'm on the way.

Pressed for time, and his mind overweight with unexpected information, he had no more room for Linda. All the spaces were taken. He pecked out a quick reply.

Thanks, but no thanks. You can't live two lives, nor can I. Fix your problems permanently and I'll be glad to talk. Until then, I'm moving on.

He left the door open for her with his "until then" comment. He held his cursor over "Send," re-read his e-mail, pressed the button, and instantly it disappeared into cyberspace. He grabbed his notes, stuffed them into his worn leather shoulder bag, and headed to CB's office.

On the way, he went over the pros and cons of bringing the old man into it. Before he could come to a conclusion, he was climbing the back stairs to CB's office.

"So, what's this hot stuff you have?" the Chief said, leaning back in his creaking chair and propping his feet up on his desk.

"It's a long, complicated story, so I don't want you interrupting until I get through it," Foley said, pulling out his notepad.

"Sounds serious. Okay, you got my attention."

"It is serious and it's going to really stir things up."

"Fire away."

"I'd appreciate it if you would hold any questions or comments until I finish. In fact, grab a pad and write down any questions and we'll talk about them when I'm done."

"Jeez, this better be good, teach" the Chief said picking up a pen.

"I'm not sure whether it's good or bad, and that's why I'm telling you about it."

"I'm ready to go."

Foley pulled his chair up closer to the Chief's desk.

"Can you clear a little space for me? I don't want to disturb anything from your haphazard filing system," Foley said, pulling files from his leather bag.

The Chief moved papers to the side and Foley set his files on the desk along with his note pad.

"Okay, I'm going to start way back. I'm not going to go into every detail on how I tracked this down, but I can assure you the info is valid," Foley said.

"It was Linda, no comments please," Foley said, "who put me on the trail. She learned Leon bought his fancy yacht with a company named the K-1 Corporation, which was probably one of his cover companies. Linda thought there was something familiar about it, but she couldn't remember where, so she went back through her files. She dug up the paperwork on the deed transfer of the Stony Creek property to Greta Kasser. The property was sold to Greta by the K-1 corporation. She tracked that back to a Jacob Kimberly, the one who founded JK Steel back in the day. Now it could have been coincidence, but I tried to see if there was a connection. I tracked some of other Kimberly companies and found a pattern. There was a JK, AI, CM. OB, and BE. A little stupid luck and I found that if you take Kimberly's first name and his last and match them vertically, you get how he came up with the names. For example, J is the first initial of Jacob and K is the first of Kimberly, JK, A, the second letter of Jacob, and I the second of Kimberly, AI, and so on. Not fancy, but a simple way for an ego-centric rich man to remember all the names of his money's hiding places. But that wasn't anything," Foley said, standing up and walking around, "until I started looking at Leon's corporations and found a similar pattern. Here's the strange part. Leon didn't use the initials of his name, but those of Kimberly. That one puzzled me. I looked for a connection but couldn't find one."

The Chief, still leaning back in his chair looking at the ceiling muttered, "Coincidence?"

"Yeah, coincidence. I considered that possibility until my contact at the State Department plugged me into a source at the American Embassy in Brazil. They started digging, and they had to go way back, but damn if they didn't find a Leon, One Jacques Ronaldo Leon…"

"JR Leon?" the Chief said.

"No, Jacques was JR's father. It took a lot of digging but here's what we think happened. Our JR Leon was born in Santarem in 1932, which is one of the larger cities in the Para region. It's in the middle of the Amazon Rainforest. It's located on the confluence of a river called the Rio Tap-a-hos, whatever that means, and it's …"

"I don't need a geography lesson," the Chief complained.

"CB just stay with me because the location becomes important. Jacques Leon, the father had dual citizenship, Brazil and the U.S. and worked for Ford Motor in Detroit as one of their senior managers."

"Why would he go back to the jungles?" the Chief said.

"You know CB, every once in a while, you ask a good question. In 1928 Henry Ford built a town in the middle of the rainforest, down along the Tap-a hos river. He called it Fordlandia, and he sent Leon down there to run it. They were going to grow a lot of rubber trees to make tires. It was a grand idea and Ford spent a fortune, but the damn thing bombed. Something about the trees not growing and … but that isn't the important part. When Leon left the U.S., he didn't have a wife, but in 1932, he ends up with an American wife, and here's the kicker, Ford didn't allow women in Fordlandia."

"Those poor sons-of-bitches must have been walking around the jungle with terminal hard-ons," the Chief said.

"Yeah, it was bad from what I read. Anyhow, there is a woman listed as his mother on the birth certificate, and this one will get your attention."

"She had to be a pro, because if they didn't have broads in Fordland, or whatever they called it, the hookers would move in fast, jungle or no jungle," the Chief said. "Shit, that would be a gold mine," he said with a faraway look in his eyes.

"Actually, the hookers did, but she wasn't one of them. No, this was an American woman from Pittsburgh, Pennsylvania named Greta Kasser."

The Chief sat up, his feet coming off the desk, causing him to stumble as he stood up.

"You gotta be shittin' me?" he said, looking at Foley.

"Nope. The info is solid, and as they say in the infomercials, but wait, there's more," Foley said, enjoying his father's excitement.

"Go for it," the Chief said, his eyes riveted on Foley.

"So, I tried to track Greta from the U.S. and where do I find her name?" Foley said, teasing the Chief.

"Don't play," the Chief said, as he sat back down in his chair.

Foley riffled through his notes.

"Here it is. *The Mooremack News.* Another lucky find."

"I'm all ears."

"When I tell you, you'll see just how lucky we got," Foley said.

"Tell me."

"In the late twenties and early thirties there was a shipping line called Moore-McCormack and when I dug around, I found that one of their ships was the SS Brazil and it ran between the U.S., and well, the obvious. They published a newsletter for their passengers, printing gossipy things, like shipboard events and stuff like that. Believe it or not," Foley said proudly, "I found somebody who collected those newsletters. Not only did he collect them, but he also put them on the internet. As I was going through some of the old issues, a name I recognize pops up. According to the story a drunken passenger almost fell overboard but was saved by a lady, and that lady was, I think we need a drum roll here, Greta Kasser."

"You gotta be shittin' me?" said the Chief.

"That's twice you said that, but I'm not finished. Then I found the manifest and about 7 months before JR Leon is born, Greta sails to Brazil, takes riverboats through the jungles, finally ending up in Santarem. There, I think, Jacques Leon comes up the river from Fordlandia, gets her set up in Santarem, and 6 months later or so, out pops our JR."

"The numbers aren't adding up." The Chief said.

"You're right,"

"So, who's the real daddy?"

"I don't know..." Foley said, but the Chief interrupted.

"You don't know?"

"CB, what I do know is where my sentence was going, so if you'll stay quiet and not interrupt, I'll tell you what I think, okay?"

The Chief just looked at Foley, not an angry stare, just a look.

"Okay. You know what the rumor is, that Greta Kasser had an affair with Kimberly, and he gave her the land to keep quiet, so it starts to add..."

"Shit, that's it," the Chief said.

"Damn CB, let me finish." CB went silent again. "Kimberly could be the father. I can't establish that factually yet, but if so, I think Kimberly forced her to go far away to have the baby, and she agrees. Kimberly sold steel to Ford. He goes to some top dog, or maybe even Ford himself, and they come up with this scheme. What better place to hide from the prying eyes of the press? It can't get much better than the Amazon jungle. Ford makes one of his employees take the fall and everybody walks away happy, But I still wonder why she would put herself through all that?"

"A good question, what's the answer?" the Chief said.

"I don't have one. From what I learned, she traveled to Brazil by herself, so she chose to do it. Kimberly was a powerful man. Maybe he threatened her or had something on her. We know he gave her the land for practically nothing, so maybe that was it. She had the hots for the land, and she was willing to go through hell to get it," Foley said, leaning forward and putting his elbows on the Chief's desk.

"Maybe, but what's Leon's angle?" the Chief said

"Which Leon?".

"The one we're dealing with now. JR."

"I've been thinking about that one a lot. I've narrowed it down to two choices. Revenge and revenge. He wants to get even with the mother who abandoned him and what better way than to take away the one thing she loved. What he'll do with it when he gets it is something I haven't figured out." Foley said.

"I dunno," the Chief said, shaking his head, "Wouldn't he figure that somebody was going to dig up his history and put it all together, which is what you did?"

"You know, I don't think he did. It was pretty well buried and if it wasn't for the K-I corporation thing, which was pure luck on our part, I think it never shows up. It appears that he must have known something about his background, but maybe he didn't have the entire story."

The Chief was thinking. He leaned back, his hands across his gut, and stared at the ceiling again. Finally, he sat up, his chair squeaking even more in the quiet room, and looked directly at Foley.

"You are sitting on a gold mine with this information. We just have to find a way to dig a bunch of it out for ourselves," the Chief said.

"Damn, CB, is that all you can think about? We're not digging any gold out. Just think about what this is going to do. JR Leon is the Kasser's stepbrother. We have to deal with this," Foley said, raising his voice and then catching himself.

"I'm warning you," Foley said, walking around the desk and standing directly over the Chief, "You will not do a thing, nothing, unless I tell you, and this time I mean it."

"Foley, Foley," the Chief said in a pleading voice, "I'm just a kid from the country trying to make it big in the city. You can't blame me for taking a shot. I'll do whatever you say, don't worry."

Foley gathered up his papers and put them in his worn leather shoulder bag while the Chief just sat there gazing at nothing, thinking about everything he just heard.

"I'm not worried CB," Foley said as he headed for the door, "You make one funny move and I'll spill my guts to Otto and Leon about things you don't want them to know, and your cushy ride here will be over. I don't want to do that CB, so don't force me."

The Chief, still leaning back in his chair, just smiled.

HOGG

HEIDI SAID SHE WAS GOING TO NEW YORK FOR A FEW DAYS, BUT Hogg didn't like the smell of it. She could be making a run for it, using New York as a jumping off point. His airport contacts confirmed that Heidi, and her mother and sister, were on a flight to LaGuardia, but their return tickets were open. Following their trail from Manhattan was just about impossible. With all the airports, big and small, plus trains, busses and cars, there was no way he could follow their next moves.

Heidi didn't have the smarts to skip by herself, but that slutty sister of hers did. He should have gotten rid of that bitch a long time ago. He had a contact check out Teterboro in Jersey. A lot of private aircraft flew out of there and those rich bitches like to go first class, but they came up empty. There wasn't much else he could do but wait it out, which pissed him off more.

Heidi said she'd be back for the weekend, but she didn't sound right, talking like she was reading from a script. He kept running that night through his mind, trying to get a picture of what happened, but it was like trying to drive through a heavy rainstorm without windshield wipers.

He could make out blurred colors and vague forms. Everything melted into a blob. Fuzzy filmy figures and flickering images spun his mind into a vortex. It was like trying to climb a spinning greased pole.

As stoic a man as Hogg was, he was beginning to break. He couldn't imagine living as a man without his manhood. It wasn't something that bothered him—it was destroying him. As much as he tried to stay calm and reasoned, he couldn't. Nobody, no human can do this to another human and be allowed to get away with it. It wasn't long before his every thought was getting even with Heidi.

He hated her. He had to settle her before he could settle himself. No man worth his salt would let anyone do such a vicious thing without retaliating.

He had to find some way to castrate her like she did to him.

As soon as she got back, if she came back, he had to be ready to make his move.

First, he needed to establish an alibi. Pauline "Pauli" McConnell, a senior VP at one of Pittsburgh's biggest commercial real estate companies, and a well-connected Democratic fund raiser, would fit the bill. She and Hogg had a sporadic relationship, one with no illusions of romance. Laugh lines were pushing Pauli to be less cautious in her choice of males, and she and Hogg hooked up for the first time after too much alcohol at a party for the Mayor.

She was a pretty woman, a blonde with flashing green eyes that sponged men into them. She was petite, with a slim, but well-formed body that was designed for clingy summer dresses. They fit her like they were painted on.

She was wary of Hogg. Although they had been together only three or four times, and he was always polite, she sensed a streak of harshness in him when he drank, so when he asked her to come to Stony Creek for the following weekend, she wasn't quick to accept. It took some pleading on his part and she finally agreed, adding a backup provision that she might have to return to Pittsburgh for an important business meeting on Saturday. If Hogg got out of hand, she'd leave.

He knew he was rolling the dice about Heidi's return, but he had to be ready. He wanted to do it Friday, but he had a backup plan if he had to move it to Saturday.

The internet is the shopping center of the world. Whatever it is that you want, the internet has it. It just takes a little time to dig it out and that's where Hogg found an answer. He needed to hurt Heidi like she hurt him, and he thought he found a way.

It was an ad on a porn site that got his attention.

"Kinky Sex—10 freaky ways to excite your mate."

Kinky sex. It was perfect. An accident during kinky sex was ideal. If she gets hurt getting her freak on and ends up in the hospital, it's not a crime. It's an accident. He knew what strings to pull to keep her in line. Heid feared him and the last thing she needed was to go public about her affair with a married man. Kinky sex could be the answer.

He searched the internet and found a possibility on a web site that discussed atrocities committed in Africa. He learned that rebels in Uganda, after raping women, inserted wooden stakes into their rears causing a fistula which tore the wall between the vagina and the rectum, causing them to excrete through their vaginas. Hogg's uncontrollable bitterness toward Heidi had no boundaries. In his sick mind this was the ideal revenge. The search for the right tool began.

He ordered it from Thailand. To cover his tracks, he rented a mail forwarding service, using the name of a street punk that he knew when he was in Cleveland. He had the package forwarded to another mailbox service in Altoona, PA, that he secured using the name of a gay male hooker from that area. Disguising himself with a fake beard, sunglasses, and a tousle cap, he gave a homeless Iraqi war vet $20 and the fake ID so he could pick up the package. It went off without a hitch, and he anxiously opened the box to get a look at it.

It was a 14-inch strap-on wooden dildo.

Hogg was just short of being a madman. Sometimes even he didn't recognize himself. He couldn't control his rage, and he suppressed the whispers in his mind that tried to warn him.

He'd use "roofies" the date rape drug and sleeping pills to immobilize her. Although it wasn't a necessary part of his plan, he wanted to keep the Chief in line. He needed to get the Chief to call Heidi on Friday. That was the tricky part, but he had an idea.

He was ready to even the score. It was his turn to stick it to her.

He almost laughed out loud.

THE CHIEF

HOGG CALLED THE CHIEF AND APOLOGIZED FOR NOT MEETING him the other night. He never mentioned the girl, and the Chief played along.

"I got tied up and I'm sorry," Hogg said, "but I wanted to tell you about Heidi Kasser, and I wanted to do it privately."

"What about Heidi?" the Chief said.

"I'm not sure I want to do this over the phone," Hogg said.

"My phones are clean."

"Are you alone?"

"What the hell? Is Heidi a terrorist or something?" the Chief said, raising his voice.

"She has a thing for you?" Hogg said, waiting for a reaction.

The Chief took the phone away from his ear and looked at it.

What in the hell is Hogg trying to pull off?

"You gotta be shittin," the Chief said, "What the fuck you up to, Hogg?"

"I'm not kidding. Look, I just wanted to warn you. She's a little flaky as you know and she…"

"Why are you telling me this?"

"Well, I owe you and you have to admit, getting a little of that would be like hitting the lottery and…"

"How do you know this?" the Chief said, now standing wondering where Hogg was headed.

"She told me."

"Hold it. Start at the beginning," the Chief said.

"I think you know I've been banging that," Hogg said, "but we've been done for a while. We're still friends, and no, she wasn't the one who cut me. If I told you it was one of the hookers, I wrangled you wouldn't believe me, but it was. A cheap slut did this to me," he said, "and that's why I won't say anything about it. Believe me, if it was Heidi, I'd break her bank account before I'd break her back. Anyhow, Heidi has a thing for cops, and I'm having a drink with her and she tells me she likes you, and I say what do you mean like, and she says, I think he's a nice man, and I ask if she might have a thing for cops and she just looks at me and smiles, and then says could be. Just like that. She doesn't even blink. I say to her, call him. I'm sure he'd reciprocate, but she says she wouldn't do that, and that's where I leave it."

"I don't know what you're up to, Hogg, but you're full of shit," the Chief said. Ever since he saw the buttermilk in Heidi's refrigerator, he suspected she and Hogg were a thing, but this crap that Hogg is spouting was crazy. Ever since he had his dick cut off the man has turned into a Loony Tune.

"Believe what you want to believe. I don't give a shit one way or the other. I'm not a fucking dating service. I just think it's there if you want it, and let me tell you, she is a wild thing in the sack, but do what you want," Hogg said.

"Is this why you wanted to meet with me, and I sure 'n hell hope it wasn't?" the Chief said.

"It wasn't. I wanted to talk with you about Leon?"

The Chief could feel his heart jitter. His mind kicked into gear as he tried to figure out how Hogg might be connected. Otto had to be the link.

"Ah, what about him?" The Chief said.

"I think that has to be a private conversation," Hogg said. "Let me know when you want to have it." Hogg hung up.

The Chief sat rocking in his squeaking chair wondering what in the hell was going on. He figured Otto must have talked to Hogg about Leon. That wouldn't be out of the question, but the Heidi thing? Hogg knew how easy it would be for the Chief to check out Heidi. Hell, all he had to do was engage her in some sort of business thing, drop a few crumbs, and he'd know in a minute if she was hot for him. No, Hogg was up to something, but what?

The Chief was convinced that Hogg lost his mind when he lost his dick.

FOLEY

LINDA RESPONDED TO FOLEY'S E-MAIL.

I understand your anger and you're right. I am getting it together, so don't be surprised if I show up.

Foley just shook his head. He didn't want to be pulled back into her nebulous world, yet he found it difficult to stay out.

He looked at his fingernails. They were longer than he liked. He searched in the desk for his nail clippers. He couldn't find them, forgetting he was using a temporary desk. The phone on his credenza rang.

"Foley."

"Foley, Hedy Kasser. I'm in New York with my mother and we'll be here a few more days. Heidi was with us but had to get back. She has some sort of fundraising event in Pittsburgh that she must attend on Sunday, so she should be getting in late this morning. Do me a favor. Double check the security cameras in her condo and make sure they're all working."

"I'm sure they are. but I'll double check," Foley assured her.

Heidi was another issue, albeit a minor one. When he was installing the security cameras, he saw the buttermilk. The old man told him about Hogg and his buttermilk drink, and as much as Foley wanted to ignore it, and call it another coincidence, he knew he couldn't. Buttermilk drinkers were few and far between.

Although he had a shocker to report to Otto about Leon, there were still a lot of unanswered questions.

What was his Leon's motive in buying Stony Creek? Why keep his family connection under wraps? Why did he offer Foley a job?

And then there was the Hogg/Duck connection. Foley still hadn't come up with how he was going to handle that with Otto. It was a sensitive issue, but it had to be addressed.

He ran a couple of errands, bought nail clippers, and had a hot dog at the food court. He enjoyed the hot dogs at Stony Creek. They sold the ones with skin and he liked them better than the skinless, especially with mustard and onions. As he was leaving, he ran into the old man.

"Where ya headed?" the Chief said.

"I have to go up to Heidi's condo to check her security system."

"You just put that in. Is it messed up already?"

"No, she just wants it checked to make sure it's working," Foley said.

"Jesus. Hedy called and told me they were in New York and wanted me to watch the condo. Claimed there was some rich guy from Pittsburgh stalking her."

"There you go," Foley said although he was feeling some doubt.

"Well, I'll go with you," the Chief said, "It looks like we're going to have a busy weekend."

"I know I am. I'm going to get that Leon report cleaned up and give it to Otto Monday," Foley said.

The Chief didn't respond.

They drove up to Heidi's condo in the Chief's Jeep.

"Did Heidi ever come on to you?" the Chief said.

Foley looked at his father. What was he thinking?

"What in the hell are you talking about?"

"A simple question. Did Heidi ever come on to you?"

"Geez, CB. No. Why would you even ask that question?"

"Just curious. That's all," the Chief said.

Foley knew better. The old man didn't ask frivolous questions.

They were almost at Heidi's, so he let it go for the time being.

HOGG

ONE PART OF HOGG'S PLAN WAS FALLING INTO PLACE. PAULI would be in Stony Creek late Friday afternoon. Now all Heidi had to do was show up back in Stony Creek.

Hogg was thinking about his backup plan when his phone rang. He looked at the number. He recognized Heidi's condo phone. She was back. He was elated.

"I just wanted to tell you I'm back," she said, her voice echoing into his ear as Hogg tried to restrain himself from jumping with joy.

"I'm glad you called. I've been thinking about everything and I think it's important that we sit down, maybe only for fifteen minutes, just to clear the air."

"That's just it. I don't know what air we have to clear," she said.

"You sound like you're talking in a barrel. What phone are you using?"

"My condo's. I'm using the speakerphone. I'm unpacking while I talk to you. Is that okay?" she said.

Hogg wanted to reach through the phone and choke the bitch. Her innocent act was irritating him. Somebody was coaching her, probably that whore of a sister. She's the smart one. He might have to adjust her way of thinking, too.

"I'm sorry everything sounds confusing. You're right. Some things have happened that I need to tell you about. The sooner the better. Can you meet me tonight—just for fifteen minutes?" Hogg said in his best caring voice.

"I can't. I just got back from New York and I'm tired and I have too many things to do," she said.

"Just fifteen minutes, honey?" he said. He could feel his anger surging.

"No, not tonight," she said firmly.

"Goddamn, Heidi, I need to see you," he shouted, and then catching himself quickly softened his tone.

"Sorry," he said. "Just anxious to talk to you. I need your advice and help." He hoped his needy act would appeal to her.

Heidi was silent for a moment, finally saying, "I understand. How about tomorrow around 6 PM?"

He wouldn't get what he wanted. Now he had to manipulate her into a meeting place where he could do what he had to do. He was sure she'd suspect just about anything he suggested, so he had to work it slowly and patiently. To throw her off, he'd make it a public place, one he was sure she'd reject.

"How about Augie's?" he said.

"Too noisy and busy," she said.

"Well, I'd invite you to my house, but I have one of my deputies and his wife staying here. How about one of those bars in Bedford?" Again, he hoped for a rejection, but if she agreed he would ask her to drive, explaining he didn't have his car. It wasn't the best idea for what he had to do, but he could make it work.

"Why don't you just come to my place?" she said. Hogg almost jumped up and cheered. It couldn't have gone any better.

He didn't answer right away. Every nerve in his body was sizzling, but he stayed cool.

"Well, okay, if that's what you prefer," he said hesitantly.

"Fine. See you at six."

He hung up the phone and stood there. He restrained his excitement but smacked his fist into his open palm and grunted out a "Yeah."

He didn't like the change of days. He had a lot of manipulating to do, including a way to keep Pauli in Stony Creek until Sunday.

She hung up the phone and began pacing around the condo, thinking about everything she had to get done. She kept looking at the white walls, trying to spot the cameras. She couldn't see them, but Hogg was a pro. She didn't think Hogg would try and harm her here. Committing a crime in the condo would be stupid and Hogg wasn't stupid. She was sure he was going to try and get even with her, but it would be where he couldn't be connected to it. Maybe she'd learn what's in his head but probably not. It was worth a try.

No matter what she had to be ready for anything.

She hoped she was.

HEIDI'S CONDO

IT WAS LESS THAN TWENTY MINUTES AFTER TALKING TO HOGG on the phone that she heard noises at her front door. Somebody was fiddling with the lock. Her first thought was that it was Hogg. Her mind raced. She looked for something to use as a weapon or a place to hide. Her instinct was to run upstairs to the bedroom, lock the door, and call the cops.

Before she had the time to act, she heard the lock click, and the door opened. The blood drained from her face as every nerve in her body sputtered. She frantically looked around, pulling a knife out of the wooden block on the kitchen counter.

The door opened. She raised the knife, and Foley came in, the Chief right behind him. It took a moment for her to realize who it was. Foley froze when he saw her standing there with a knife raised in a stabbing position.

"Whoa," he said, the Chief bumping into him muttering, "What the hell..."

"Oh, my God. It's you," she said dropping her arm down quickly. "I thought..."

"It's okay. It's okay. Didn't mean to scare you. We didn't think you were home," Foley said as she put the knife down on the counter.

"I am so sorry," she said.

"No problem, Heidi," Foley said as the Chief pushed around him.

"Well, I'm glad you didn't have a gun, but then you would've gotten Foley first," the Chief said with a chuckle. "Why don't we have a drink and cool down?"

"Sorry about the surprise. I got an earlier flight, Ah, yeah, a drink would be nice," she said.

"No thanks, we just wanted to check the security system," Foley said. "Hedy called and asked us to," he added quickly.

"I'm just along for the ride, so I'll have something. Hell, it's almost happy hour," the Chief said.

Foley gave his old man a quick glare and a head shake.

"It will take me just a minute," Foley said, heading for the closet where the guts of the system were hidden in a false wall. Hedy insisted on it. It was as if she expected somebody to case the house to see what security was in place.

"Chief, what would you like," she said, heading for the kitchen and feeling a little better. She could sense the tension draining out of her body. She was pleased that the Chief wanted a drink because she needed one.

Beer and whiskey were his usual choice, but he knew Heidi drank wine.

"I'll have a glass of wine."

"I'm sure there's something good here," she said, pulling a bottle of red from the small wine rack on the kitchen counter.

"Sounds good. Join me," the Chief said.

"Well, okay, I think I will," she said, getting two Riedel glasses and pouring the wine. She handed one to the Chief who raised it in a toast. She noticed the Chief was looking at her with some intensity and it disarmed her.

"Do I have wine on me?" she said, wiping her hand across her mouth and chin.

For a moment, the Chief didn't respond, and then caught himself.

"Ah, no, I don't see anything," he said, leaning in to look and then quickly backing away.

"I thought you saw something the way you were looking at me," she said.

"Sorry," then quickly changing the subject, "This is pretty good wine. What is it?" the Chief said.

"A 1990 Caymus cabernet, one of their better vintages," she said.

The Chief had no idea what wine etiquette said you say about a 1990 Caymus, so he diverted the conversation to something he had planned.

"I know we've budgeted money for new uniforms, and I thought we might want to change the design, get something a little dressier, you know, for around a resort. Maybe you could work with me on the design," he said watching her face closely.

"Did Uncle Otto authorize the change? I didn't hear anything about it," she said.

"Well, no, it's just a rough idea right now, but when we do, I thought you might like to be involved in that project," the Chief said.

"Chief, no disrespect, but I really don't care what you guys wear as long as it's clean and neat," she said.

"Oh, I'm sorry. I thought maybe that was something you might be interested in," the Chief said, trying to figure out why Hogg told him she had the hots for cops. She was about as interested in him as he was in learning Latin.

"I'm into fashion a little, but police uniforms are not my idea of haute couture," she said smiling as Foley came back down the stairs.

"Everything good with the system?" she said walking over to Foley.

"All good," he said.

"Thanks guys, I appreciate it," she said, taking the wineglass from the Chief's hand as she led them to the door.

FOLEY

OTTO CALLED FOLEY EARLY SATURDAY MORNING. HE WANTED AN update on Leon.

"I have a preliminary report," Foley said, "and I was going to go over it with you on Monday. I was hoping to get a few more details before we met."

"Time is of the essence. This is important. How soon can we get together?" Otto asked.

Foley had hoped to delay Otto until Monday. He wanted to talk with CB again and clean up some loose ends, but that was out of the question now. He caught himself drumming his fingers on the old oak desk and stopped, trying to decide on a time for Otto.

"How about later today or early this evening? I'm still waiting for a call from a contact in the State Department and I should hear from them sometime today," Foley said.

"Okay, let's make it around five at the VIP suite at Pipa's. Will that work for you?"

"I'll make it work, Otto. See you at five," Foley said.

Should he bring CB to the meeting? The old man knew Otto better, and with the news Foley had, he might need him there.

It was the robbery that bothered Foley. Hogg was somehow involved, and Foley was sure CB knew something about it. He also had to be careful since Otto and Hogg were friends. He didn't like the Hobson's choice he was facing.

He took one last crack at CB.

"CB, I'm meeting Otto at 5 at the VIP suite. I need to see you before then and I think you ought to be in the meeting when I give him the Leon report," Foley said, choosing his words carefully.

"Whatever you need, kid," the Chief said cheerfully, "I'm at your service, but you better clear it with Otto that I'm coming."

"I'll be at your office in ten," Foley said, hanging up before the Chief could respond.

The Chief wasn't ready for a confrontation with Foley, but he suspected one was coming. Foley was putting the Hogg thing together and that could blow things wide open. He had to head him off at the pass.

He was also troubled by Hogg's comments about Heidi. The Chief knew Heidi was about as interested in him as Ellen DeGeneres would be. He couldn't figure out what Hogg's angle was. He was sure there was one, or maybe Hogg had slipped over the edge. The guy was acting crazy.

But then, who wouldn't act crazy if they had their dick cut off?

FOLEY & THE CHIEF

FOLEY WASN'T ABOUT TO PLAY ANY MORE GAMES. HE HAD TO GRAB all the loose ends and put them in a cohesive package. His first stop was with CB. The double talk had to end.

The bitterly frigid January air chipped away at Foley's exposed skin and the snow squeaked underfoot as he walked to the snowmobile. It was glazed with a coating of frost, a solitary machine in a sea of white, mirroring the way Foley felt at that moment. These feelings of isolation would wrap over Foley from time to time. He felt heavy and weary, and the craziness with Linda was siphoning away his energy. He had to drive it out of his system. He believed he had the self-discipline to face the facts and put his willpower to work.

He was about to provide a family with information which would alter the course of their lives. He had to be sharp, strong, and focused. He could feel his resolve, the frigid air now edging him on. He turned the key, released the choke, and the engine growled with power. He could feel the fuel pouring energy into the machine as the rubber tracks clawed at the snow and leaped forward. He gunned the engine as the machine tore up the snow and the cold air bounced off his face.

He was ready.

He wasn't sure what he'd get out of CB, but he was going to get something. There just wasn't any more time to keep circling the wagons.

When he got to Pipa's the lot was almost empty, save for a few snow-covered vehicles that looked like they had been there overnight. Foley navigated his snowmobile around the building, cutting through a small stand of pines, parking in the rear.

He took the steep staircase two steps at a time as he psyched himself into the task ahead, knocking louder than usual on the CB's door.

He heard the muffled voice of CB curtly grumbling, "Take it easy" as he heard the locks being disengaged.

Foley pushed open the door, stepped inside, and without saying a word grabbed one of the wooden chairs and pulled it closer to CB's desk as he removed files from his leather bag. The Chief read the situation quickly. His son was fired up. The Chief wasn't going to get sucked into a pissing contest.

Without a word, he went over and freshened up his coffee. With his back to Foley he asked, "You want a coffee?"

"No thanks. I'm good," Foley said.

The Chief went to his desk and sat down. Foley was still standing, his files on the desk.

"You gonna sit or you doing whatever you're doing standing?"

Foley paused for a moment and sat down. He grabbed one file and looked in it.

The Chief waited him out. Foley knew it was his move. The old man's skin was like rusted iron-you didn't get under it easily, and if you did, you'd most likely get cut up and infected. Yet Foley had sensed some soft spots. The old man never gave up much, but Foley realized CB was grudgingly proud of him. It seeped through no matter how hard CB tried to hide it.

Foley used it.

"I need to wrap things up and I have loose ends all over the place. I need you to step up and give me what you know without any bullshit. Otherwise, I'm going to go down with the ship and neither one of us want that," Foley said.

The Chief leaned back in his chair, the squeaking the loudest noise in the room. He was naturally wary.

"It happens to all of us. Cases can wear you down, but I don't see anything that should have you in a dither. You're on a roll. Hell, the shit you have on Leon is a big payoff… for both of us."

"Yeah, but I don't have that packaged up. I still don't know motive and I think this guy has some angles we haven't figured out yet," Foley said and then added, almost as if it were an afterthought, "and then there's the robbery? I'm sure Duck is our boy, but Hogg is in there somewhere and if we don't wrap that one up right, we're all headed for the unemployment line."

The Chief didn't respond, and Foley fiddled with his papers. He pretended he was studying a paper, stalling for time, hoping to get a response from CB but he wasn't taking the bait.

The quiet was noisy for both of them. The Chief broke it. "What do you want from me?"

"What you have that I don't."

The Chief wasn't ready to give up any more yet.

"There's nothing to worry about. You're doing good. Otto likes you"

"Think about it CB," Foley said, "We know Joe Duck did it, and we've kept it under wraps trying to make the Hogg connection so we can alert Otto with hard evidence and save him from getting embarrassed."

The Chief decided on diversion.

"It's that female who's doing this to you," he said.

"No. CB. I'm over that. She's history," he said, sitting up and leaning forward to show that he meant what he said, his voice louder and firmer.

"Well, I think she's the crunch," he said.

"That's your problem, CB. You always look for somebody else to blame when you know it's you," Foley said.

"Me?"

"Yeah, you know what went down with Hogg, but you're willing to screw me to take care of your buddy," Foley said.

"That's bullshit. I don't know what went down. I know as much as you. And he sure 'n hell ain't my buddy," the Chief said, standing to show his discontent.

"I don't believe you," Foley said, "and so I guess I lose this one." He buckled up his leather bag.

"Foley, I'm telling you, I don't know. The only thing I know is that Hogg got his wiener cut off."

"CB, all our wieners are going to be cut off if we don't get this right," Foley said.

"No, I'm serious. Hogg got his dick cut off. For real. He doesn't have a dick anymore," the Chief said, as he looked at Foley, extending his hands, palms up, as if he were begging for something.

Foley looked at his father's face for some sign that this was a joke, but the Chief raised his eyebrows and nodded in the affirmative.

"It's absolutely true," the Chief said.

"What do you mean he got his dick cut off?"

"Well, let me walk you through it," the Chief said sarcastically, "What in the hell do you think I mean? Somebody chopped off his dick, Period. End of sentence."

"His whole dick?"

"Hey, I didn't look at it, but that's what he said."

"How do you know this?"

The Chief told Foley about getting the 5 AM phone call, going to his house and hearing what happened, and then arranging for the kid to drive Hogg to Uniontown.

"Jesus. It would have been better if he lost an arm or a leg, but your dick?"

"It's a major loss," the Chief said.

"Who would cut off his dick?" Foley said still incredulous.

"Who wouldn't?" the Chief replied quickly.

"Joe Duck?" Foley said hesitantly.

"No way. Duck would've just shot him. What man would cut another guy's dick off, even in a mad rage? It's not what men do. Now maybe a bubble blower, but not a guy who likes women," the Chief said.

Foley sat there for a moment trying to put it all together, but nothing was making sense. He went through the timelines with the Chief, agreeing that Duck probably wasn't the cutter.

"I agree. It had to be a woman," Foley said, and then they looked at each other knowing exactly what the other was thinking. Foley spoke first.

"She's not the type."

"Who."

"C'mon CB, you know who I'm talking about," Foley said.

"I don't."

"I heard the rumors and then when I saw the buttermilk in her refrigerator…"

"You saw it, too," the Chief said.

"Yeah, but I don't see her doing something like that," Foley said.

"Hogg made it a point to say it wasn't her. Said it was some hooker he was banging," the Chief said.

"When did he say that?"

"Maybe a week ago. He called."

"Just to tell you that?" Foley said.

The Chief realized that he just stepped into it and had to find a believable way out.

"Nah," he said as casually as he could, "He wanted to meet for a drink and I couldn't, and in the conversation he said that it was a hooker who did the dirty deed," the Chief said.

"Do you believe him?" Foley asked, now standing, and moving around.

"Made sense to me. Why protect Heidi if she did it?" the Chief asked. "Hogg could sue the shit outta her and become a rich man."

"Yeah, I can see that," Foley said hesitantly, "he could, or maybe he's saying it was somebody else to fake you out."

"What's that get him?"

"I don't know, but if I were you, I'd watch myself." Foley said.

"I'm not worried," he answered getting up from his chair and stretching.

The Chief was trying to filter what he would tell Foley and what he wouldn't. He decided not to discuss the little redhead he screwed at Hogg's house. At first, he didn't see any connection, but now he was concerned.

Foley stood up. "C'mon CB, give me a little more."

"Well, there was this thing with Heidi that…"

"What about Heidi?"

The Chief told Foley what Hogg said about Heidi and how she had the hots for him.

"Hell, CB, how could you believe that crap?" Foley said wondering why Hogg would even suggest that to the Chief.

"I didn't, but checking it out was fun," the Chief said.

Foley looked at him, shaking his head. He had to admit that the twins were hard to ignore, and he really didn't blame CB, but he wasn't about to tell him that.

"It was stupid, CB. You're a cop who always told me you don't shit where you eat," Foley said.

"I didn't shit, maybe I farted, but that's all, and listen to who's calling the pot black," the Chief said.

Foley realized he wasn't going to get anything more out of him, and he recognized CB threw him a couple of unimportant bones. Foley moved on.

He went over what he wanted to do at the meeting. They discussed bringing Hogg into it, but they had no actual evidence. They agreed to bring up Duck and his association with Hogg and let Otto wonder about it.

Everything CB knew wasn't being shared with Foley. Foley was certain there was more to it, but the old man was a big boy. Foley just didn't want to get caught up in any of CB's shenanigans.

He just hoped that CB wouldn't become collateral damage when the cops put all this crap together.

When he thought about it, he smiled.

If there was one thing CB knew how to do, it was how to dodge a bullet.

OTTO

OTTO HAD TO GIVE HER CREDIT. HEDY HAD HIM OVER THE proverbial barrel. She finessed him beautifully with Leon. He was hoping the security people would come up with something. Rosie was the swing vote. All she wanted to do was sell to the highest bidder, and Leon took care of that with his bid guaranteeing at least 10% more than the Swiss.

He wasn't sure how good Foley was, and now he wondered whether he had been hasty in giving him the Leon assignment. He was a small operator, and Otto needed the big boys with the heavy resources. If Foley and his people didn't come up with something Otto was hiring a well-connected New York firm, expensive as hell, but one he was sure would find something. It was now clear to Otto that Hedy was his foil, and she wouldn't give up easily, so he had to nullify the Leon deal. He wouldn't be surprised if Hedy didn't have a side deal with Leon.

Foley wanted the Chief to come to the meeting. At first Otto opposed the idea, but when he thought about it, he relented. Otto didn't want the Chief on the outside, nibbling at the edges. He wasn't certain about what Foley might be telling him. Better to have him attend.

As he sat in the VIP room waiting, Otto made a vow to himself. There was no way Leon was going to get Stony Creek, even if they had to tie this up in the courts for the next ten years. Otto was going to make this call, not Hedy, and that was that.

"Hey Otto, how they hangin,'" the Chief said, startling Otto, causing his body to jerk. He swung around in the swivel chair to see the Chief followed by Foley who muttered out a "hello."

"Gentlemen," Otto said, standing up, "Have a seat."

"Thank you," Foley said, hooking his saddlebag over the back of the chair only to have it slide off and fall to the floor. Foley picked it up quickly, annoyed that he started out with a clumsy move.

"Is your assistant coming?" Otto asked.

"No, it'll be just be us," Foley said as they all sat down at one end of the long, polished table. Otto winced, thinking he should have put a tablecloth over the gleaming table.

"Okay, give me something good," Otto said as Foley removed files from his bag.

"Let me preface my report by saying that this is an ongoing investigation and information continues to come in, so it is a work in progress," Foley said, "and I must warn you we have found some, well, interesting information."

"I'm ready. Let's have it," Otto said. He liked what Foley was saying, overlooking the word "warn."

"I want to start with the robbery," Foley said.

"I'm not worried about the robbery. It's Leon that I want to…"

The Chief interrupted. "Otto, I think you better listen to all of this."

Otto slumped back into his chair, impatiently tapping his pencil on the table, saying nothing but making sure they both knew he was unhappy.

"We're pretty certain an ex-employee of yours, a Joe 'Duck' Ducci was the actor who robbed the money room. We've told nobody of our suspicions, except you.

"Where is this 'Duck' guy now," Otto said, not recognizing his name.

"He's dead," Foley said, and then explained what happened at Hogg's Uniontown house, "and that brings us to our suspicion that Hogg is somehow involved, but we can't prove it."

"You're kidding? Hogg wouldn't be involved in a robbery, especially here at Stony Creek," Otto said, shaking his head in disgust, "No way."

"We think he was. We wanted to inform you so that you wouldn't be caught flat-footed if Hogg turns out to be one of the bad guys."

"Well, I just don't believe it."

"We didn't think you would. We just wanted to warn you of the possibility. Otto, it's just too much of a coincidence that Duck ends up trying to rob Hogg's house. We think he went there to get his share of the money."

"There ain't no coincidences," the Chief added as Otto sat there, a stunned look on his face, "with assholes like Duck."

"I still can't believe it," Otto said looking down and shaking his head. He could feel the sweat forming under his armpits.

"Now, let's get to Leon," Foley said as he stood up, hoping to change the momentum. He moved to the side of the white dry erase board on the easel that he had requested. He wrote "Leon" on it in big letters.

Otto was rattled by the Hogg revelation, but he fought it and focused on Leon.

Foley rehearsed how he would present his information and took Otto through the investigation step by step, holding the results until the end. He wouldn't bring in Greta Kasser until he outlined everything else. He was sure that Otto would question Leon's heritage, so he had to build a case for it.

He put it into story form, beginning with JR Leon's date and place of birth, identifying the father but keeping the mother's name out of it. Otto didn't even notice, which made Foley think how unconsciously prejudiced men really were. As Foley worked his way through, occasionally writing an important point on the board, Otto fidgeted, leaned back, sat forward, rubbed his head, and tapped his pencil. He was looking for dirt on Leon and all he was getting was a fairy tale.

Otto was about to interrupt when Foley said, "What I'm about to tell you, Otto, has been thoroughly checked out and we're sure the information is correct, but nothing is ever 100%. There's always a chance that something may not jive, but this is what the record shows."

Otto sat up straighter and pulled the yellow tablet closer as if he were going to write something down. He waited for Foley to continue. Foley was milking the climatic end to his story, clearing his throat, and moving the white board a few inches closer to the table.

"After an exhaustive investigation by our team, and using reliable contacts, some of whom hold high positions within our government, we have learned that JR Leon is the son of," Foley said, looking hard into Otto's eyes, "Greta Kasser, your mother, therefore JR Leon is your half-brother."

Otto looked dumfounded, glanced at the Chief, sure this was some sort of ugly joke, or maybe he just didn't hear right. He stood up, and in a threatening voice and said, "What did you say?"

"JR Leon is your mother's son, making him your half-brother, born in 1932 in a jungle town in Brazil," Foley said, going into the detail of her journey to South America and placing all the documents he had on the table.

Otto looked at Foley and then back to the Chief. He was stunned, unable to get words out of his mouth. He picked up the top document, which was a copy of the Brazilian birth certificate showing Greta Kasser as the mother. He just stared at it, looking for the mistake that must be there somewhere.

"You're saying my mother went to South America and had a baby?" Otto said throwing the birth certificate down on the table. "That's crazy."

"Otto, I know this is a shock, but we have traced her movements. Look at the ship's manifest," Foley said, "and this newsletter from the ship. He picked up the documents and handed them to Otto who read them, his face going white.

He sat there stunned. Picked up the documents again and studied the birth certificate. He looked at the ships manifest and reread the newsletter article about his mother. Shaking his head, he stood up and walked over to the large picture window and gazed out at the traffic filled slopes of Stony Creek. He was trying to compose his thoughts, which were in pieces.

The Chief stood and was about to head for the fridge for a cold drink when Foley hand-signaled him to stop, giving him the "quiet" sign by putting his forefinger to his lips.

Otto stood at the window for a long, quiet minute. His mind was numb. If they were right?

Without turning around Otto said, "You're absolutely sure?"

"We're sure," Foley replied quietly. "No doubt."

Otto stared out of the window for another thirty seconds, but it was a tense thirty.

Finally, he turned and said, "I want all of your backup."

"I have copies of everything for you," he said, as he pulled out a white three-ring binder from his bag. Otto walked back and took it from Foley mumbling a quiet "thank you."

"Everything is in there," Foley said.

"Nothing that has happened here today leaves this room—not to Rosie, the twins—nobody. If one word of this slips out without my approval, I promise you I'll destroy you. Who on your staff knows this?"

"Nobody. I discovered the connection by myself," Foley said.

"Don't do or say anything to anybody until you hear from me," Otto said, his eyes locking into Foley's. He gathered up his papers and left the room.

"What do you think?" Foley said, looking at his father.

"Not my ball," the Chief said.

HOGG

HOGG WAS ON HIS BEST BEHAVIOR FRIDAY EVENING, TAKING PAULI out to dinner at Pipa's, making sure he was highly visible by greeting everybody he knew and some he didn't. He limited his drinking, watched his language, and ignored bothersome things that he usually didn't ignore. He also kept an eye out for any Kassers but saw no one. Inside, he was seething but he held it in.

After dinner they returned home. Hogg couldn't afford to get into an intimate encounter with Pauli. Although she was hesitant, Hogg talked her into a nightcap which he had spiked with a heavy dose of temazepam. Combined with the alcohol, that should do the job. As she started to lose it, he led her to a bed in the guest room. She was drugged enough not to ask any questions.

He had one scotch before he turned in, dozing off thinking about what he was going to do to Heidi Kasser, and when he awoke the next day, it was his first thought.

His morning routine had changed from pleasant to horrible. He used to love to take a shower, washing off the crap from the night before, the hot water soothing him. He loved feeling the slippery soap on his body, especially around his groin, as he lathered his dick, pubic hair, and testicles. He'd feel his penis lengthen as he caressed himself with the warm soapy mixture.

But now a shower was nothing more than an ugly reminder of his shattered life. He saw the carnage she had done to his body; the scar tissue; the totally ugly, unnatural hole that she left in his body, and in his life. He couldn't bear looking at it. There were times he felt overwhelmed. He felt like his mind was breaking into pieces. That bitch stripped him of his life. She peeled him like a raw potato and then poured boiling acid over him. Sometimes he thought he was losing his mind. It was too much.

Hogg felt like he was back in the jungles of Vietnam, wearing camouflage, mud on his face, an M-16 in his hands, lying in wait to put hot slugs into those little yellow bodies. He loved the idea that the 5.56-millimeter spitzer boat-tail bullet was designed to only wound the NV's. The military used it because it required more enemy personnel and resources to take care of the wounded. Hogg liked it because it caused pain and suffering.

He slapped himself in the face. He had to keep his thinking straight. Soon he was going to get that bitch. He had to stay cool.

His good behavior towards Pauli was working. He had to keep it up. She was still sleeping, which for no reason pissed him off, but he had to be nice. He made scrambled eggs, toast, and hot coffee, put it on a tray and took it to Pauli's room. He hated every minute of it.

Pauli was flabbergasted. The Hogg she knew was die-cut from Attila the Hun who believed raping and pillaging was a saintly act. She didn't know what to make of it, but she liked it. She figured as soon as she was finished eating Hogg would make moves, but he politely sat on the side of the bed as she sipped her coffee.

When she finished, he gently took her cup, placed it on the tray, and lifted it from her lap. She was ready for sex, but he sat there with the tray now on his lap.

"I have an idea," Hogg said, brushing a wisp of hair back from her eyes, "Instead of going back to noisy Pipa's, why don't we eat in tonight? I'll grill a couple of thick, juicy steaks, open a bottle of champagne, rev up the fireplace, and we'll have a nice, quiet evening. Sound good?"

She was confused. She didn't know where this Hogg was coming from. Her head was still cloudy. She was trying to figure out why she zonked out the night before. She apologized to him for falling asleep, but he brushed it off and that surprised her.

"Sounds good," she said, still baffled.

"Great," Hogg said standing up, "You do the shopping and I'll do the cooking. Deal?" he said, extending his hand.

She lay there, still somewhat bleary-eyed, reached her hand up to Hogg's, and gave him a cautious shake, "Deal."

"How about this? Relax this morning, then we'll go to lunch. Afterwards, you go shopping and I'll get things ready at the house. You in?" Hogg said.

"I'm in, now get out of here so I can shower and get my face on," she said.

They had lunch, and then Pauli went shopping for dinner, as Hogg got ready for his meeting with Heidi.

Hogg never carried a briefcase. Thought it was a sissy thing. If he had files to carry, he stuck them in a cheap vinyl notepad. But he had to find something to put the dildo in, and he settled on a shopping bag he saved from Saks.

He went to the fridge and retrieved the plastic container. He threw out the grapes that hid a baggie. Inside the baggie was the seamen filled rubber. He didn't want to leave it in the fridge for fear that Pauli would find it, so he put it in the dildo bag. He placed three "roofies" in a plain brown plastic medicine bottle and put it, along with a pair of latex gloves, into his pocket.

He took everything out to the car, his wife's Toyota. He told his wife that he had a mechanic friend at Stony Creek who would service the car and do any repairs it needed at no charge. She could use his SUV. The car was excellent cover, and if Heidi changed plans on him, the Toyota would give him the reason for her to drive.

He built a fire in the fireplace, straightened up the house, went outside and cleared the snow off the gas grill. Pauli came back around 4 PM with the groceries and they put them away. Although Pauli wanted to help make dinner, Hogg insisted that this was his deal, and he wanted to do it alone.

"Tonight, it is my treat all the way," a cheerful Hogg said.

This was a different Bill Hogg than she was used to.

"Look, let's have a drink, then you go and make yourself pretty for dinner, although that won't require much work, and while you're showering, I'll get dinner ready. If you want to take a nap, feel free because I'm not serving until around 8, cocktails at 7:30. Sound good?"

"Sounds good," Pauli said taking a sip of the drink Hogg made for her. She wasn't sure just what was going on with Hogg. He was laying it on thick, but what the hell? Since he was being nice, she'd enjoy it, but she'd be ready if he went back to his old ways.

They chatted for a while, Hogg hurrying her along because he had things to do, and Pauli went upstairs to her room. She was feeling a little woozy, surprised how just one drink was having such an effect, and lay down for a moment since she had the time.

Hogg laced her drink again. If she woke up before he returned, he was ready with an excuse. He'd leave Pauli a note that he had to run out to get a few things. He allocated thirty minutes to get it all done, but if it went longer, he'd tell Pauli he ran into an old friend.

He'd light the gas grill before he left. That way it would be ready when he returned. Earlier in the day, he baked a couple of potatoes wrapped in foil. He also made the salad and put it into a baggie.

As soon as he took care of Heidi, he'd come back to the house. If she was still asleep, he'd get the food started and then wake her up.

It was after dinner that concerned him. She'd expect sex. He'd have to knock her out again, maybe add he wasn't feeling good, and call it a night. The anger rose in him again.

As soon as this was all over, he was heading for China.

Every time he thought about getting a new dick, even if it worked just like the old one, he couldn't erase a line that many men have uttered.

"I wouldn't fuck her with somebody else's dick."

HEIDI'S CONDO

SHE DIDN'T WANT TO DO IT AND SHE DIDN'T KNOW IF SHE COULD but something inside of her pushed her into it. She wasn't sure how she mustered up the courage, and she wasn't sure she could pull it off, but she felt she had to do it. She had no choice. It was risky, even crazy, and she couldn't believe what she was about to attempt.

She told no one about it, so she was totally on her own. She left the others in New York, telling them she had an important engagement in Pittsburgh, but she couldn't be sure her sister bought it.

She thought of asking the Chief to post a man outside her condo using the excuse that she was still being stalked, but that would cause more problems than it would solve. She couldn't tell the cop what was really going on and Hogg would spot him in seconds and that could make it worse.

Her plan, if you could call it a plan, was to get Hogg to incriminate himself on camera and then use that to keep him in line. It was risky but she felt she could have some control using sex as her weapon. Hogg claimed he was coming in peace, but she wasn't buying it, although for him to pull something radical off in her condo didn't seem like his style. Hogg wouldn't do anything that might cost him jail time, but she couldn't count on that. She tried to cover all contingencies but couldn't. She was shaking, and she knew that taking the valium, even a low dose, was stupid, but there was no way she could continue without it. She took a deep breath and hoped she had it in her because she was going for it.

The valium was already kicking in and she relaxed a bit. Before she went downstairs, she looked in the full-length, silver framed mirror. She knew she was attractive, but she didn't own up to the "beautiful" that people pinned on her. She liked her eyes. They were a vivid blue green, but she thought they were too far apart. Her eyebrows were thicker than she liked and required a lot of maintenance. Her smile was okay, but she didn't like the little crooked hitch it had. For a moment she wondered if she was saying goodbye to herself.

She stepped away from the mirror. She promised herself she wouldn't panic, but it was taking all she had, including the valium, to keep going. She tried to think of other things.

She read somewhere that the average woman spends almost 3300 hours of her lifetime primping. She was sure she would exceed that and then some. It angered her that somewhere along the evolutionary chain, women were sold a bill of goods on makeup and cover-ups, and now they were trapped in an endless battle of dissimulation. They masked their natural beauty with polishing, plucking, moisturizing, exfoliating, straightening, brushing, and glossing every day before they stepped out of the sanctity of their mirrors. Such a waste.

As brave as she was trying to be, she couldn't bury her fear. She kept going over every possibility and what she would do if it happened, but she was rattled. She didn't know where she got the strength to get this far—too far to turn back—and now she had to go through with it.

She moved her face close to the mirror and stared herself down— eye to eye—defying herself. She pursed her lips, backed away from the mirror and said out loud, "Let's do it."

From that moment on, she became a soldier about to enter a firefight. She dressed in camouflage-the short, plaid schoolgirl skirt he liked, a tight, white silk blouse, and no panties. She pulled her hair back into a ponytail, but worried that it gave him something to grab. She had to take that chance.

She said goodbye to the person in the mirror, and before she turned off the light, she took one last look at the white walls, the silver and white furniture, and the stainless-steel light fixtures. Everything was twinkling and sparkly. She wondered if she would ever see it again.

She took a deep breath, firmed up her jaw, wiped back a few strands of her lush blonde hair, and went downstairs. She had to make sure everything was in its place. She was surprised at herself. She was going to do it.

It was 5:53 PM.

Otto looked at his watch. They had been in the VIP room for a half-hour. He couldn't believe what he just heard about Leon. He couldn't show any emotion or fear, but his stomach was churning, and he had to get out of there, to be alone, to think.

Foley headed back to his suite. He was looking forward to an ice-cold vodka martini, dinner in the room, and as much mindless TV that he could find. He wanted a night of pure escape

The Chief went back to his office. He made a few calls to take care of his normal police duties and then remembered he had his cell phone turned off. He checked it for messages. There was only one. He punched in Star 86, and then his code, and listened to the one unread message.

"Chief. I'm a friend of Heidi Kasser's and she asked me to call you. Please call her at her condo, 814-555-4545. She's okay but needs to talk with you. Thanks," the female voice said.

It made little sense. If Heidi wanted the Chief, she'd call him. He reviewed all the possibilities. Hogg was one of them. But why? He checked his directory, and the number was good.

He tried to flesh out all the possibilities but couldn't see any danger in calling Heidi. He had the message on his phone, so he could prove he had a reason to call. Could the crap Hogg told him about Heidi liking cops be true? Nah, no way. Maybe she needed to talk to him about the Pittsburgh guy that was harassing her. That seemed logical.

He called.

The phone rang just as she came down the stairs. It startled her. She had no time for phone calls right now. What if it was Hogg canceling? She couldn't bear that. It took everything she had to build up her confidence, and if he copped out, she'd collapse. She looked at the screen on the phone. It was the Chief. Why would he be calling? She almost answered it but thought better of it and let it ring until the answering machine took over. After the beep, she heard the Chief's voice.

"This is Chief Bayer returning your call. I'm at my office."

What the hell?

She didn't call him, so who did? She had to find out. Then it struck her. The Chief called the condo. Like most people, the Chief would have just tapped the return call feature. She was sure nobody had used the condo phone, yet the Chief said he was returning her call. Something wasn't right. But what if her sister had called on her cell and left a message to call the condo? That made no sense. Maybe he was responding to an old voice mail.

I don't have time for this!

She debated about calling him back when she saw the clock on the kitchen stove.

It was 5:58 PM.

There was no time. She was scared. This was much too risky. Too many uncertainties. Maybe she should call it off. Then again, maybe Hogg wouldn't do a thing. She kept the light over the stove on and dimmed the corner lamp in the living room. She wanted a lot of shadows in the room.

Hogg got to Heidi's condo early and cased the place, going around back and checking all possibilities. Everything looked clean. For the last ten minutes he was parked in the shadow of a large blue spruce, away from the lights, but with an unrestricted view of the front window and door. He saw nothing suspicious. He worked out a timeline, and he had little breathing room. He left Pauli sound asleep, but his time was limited. He looked at his watch.

Inside her condo, she was pacing and clock watching. She was almost ready to call it off when she heard the knock at the door. Her heart jumped. She looked around quickly as if something or somebody was going to come out of nowhere and help her decide. She looked at the stove clock. It was six on the nose.

The knock was louder this time.

She ran over to the sofa and checked it one more time, plumped up the pillow and yelled, "Coming." There was no way out now.

She opened the door to see Hogg smiling at her. He had a shopping bag in his left hand. She glanced at it.

"Oh this," he said, lifting the bag towards her. "It's a surprise for you, (pause) for later."

"My, don't you look cute," he said, eyeing her outfit. She stood there, speechless, trying to get her fear under control.

They both stood there.

"Ah, oh, here I'll take it and put it on the kitchen counter," she said, reaching down for the bag, Hogg pulling it back.

"Better yet, how about I put it on the coffee table," he said, shutting the door, hoping it would automatically lock. "It's a little present for later." he said walking over and putting the bag on the white glass coffee table.

"You didn't spare any expense wrapping it," she said, and then wished she hadn't said it.

"Scotch and milk?" she asked, pulling out two glasses from the cabinet above the kitchen counter.

"I don't know," he said walking into the kitchen and standing close to her, "Why don't I make the drinks and you go and relax. Are you having wine?" he said, taking her arm and walking her a few steps out of the kitchen.

She didn't want to do it, but she had no choice. She was sure he was going to do something to her drink, and she didn't want to make him suspicious.

"Okay, I'll have the cabernet. There's an open bottle over by the wine rack. I think it still should be okay," she said and went to the sofa where she sat down on the far right side, leaning up against the overstuffed arm. She tried to see him making the drinks, but she couldn't.

She wondered if she had just made a mistake—a big one. Her mind was whirring, trying to find an escape route out of drinking the wine because she was sure he spiked it.

He turned, drinks in hand, and sauntered to the sofa.

She saw him scanning the room, and then he glanced at her. He caught her watching him even though she looked away. She felt her face flush. She hoped he didn't notice.

"You do keep it white in here," he said as he handed her the wine. He had a scotch on the rocks, no milk.

He sat down next to her and raised his scotch in a toast. "Cheers" he said reaching over to bump her wine glass. He took a big sip, mumbling "good scotch."

The first moment of truth was here. He watched her as she gave him a quick smile, gave the wine a swirl, and brought the glass to her lips. Hogg never took his eyes off her.

She sniffed it, gave it another swirl, and sniffed it again.

"Oh, that's oxidized," she said. "It's gone bad. I'll open a fresh bottle."

"What's wrong with it?" Hogg asked with a curious look on his face.

"Here, try it yourself. You can smell the oxidation," she said handing him the glass.

"Nah, I believe you," he said wanting to smash the glass in this stupid cunt's face. He was doing his best not to lose it. Was she fucking with him?

She got up to get another glass of wine, breathing a sigh of relief that she got through that one.

"Give me a minute," he said, putting his drink down on the coffee table, and almost running towards the stairs, "I gotta go to the bathroom. I'll be right back."

"Hey, there's a powder room down here," but he was halfway up the stairs.

He stopped, looked over his shoulder and said, "Hell, I'm almost there. You don't mind, do you?"

"No, go ahead," she said knowing full well he was checking out the upstairs. She was going to take a quick look in the shopping bag, but it had interlocking handles. It would take too much time. She had to get another bottle of wine open.

She poured only a small amount of wine in the glass, so she'd have an excuse to get more if he somehow managed to get something into her drink.

Hogg checked out the upstairs and saw nothing out of place.

As he came back down the stairs, she pretended she had just taken a big sip of wine.

"Now, that's so much better. '98 Stags Leap. Nice," she said as he came over and sat next to her.

"I took a taste of the other one and it was gone. Loose cork, probably."

"I want to apologize," he said looking at her. "I'm sorry I yelled at you and I didn't mean to scare you. I know you must have snapped, and that you weren't yourself, and I'll admit I was angry and hurt at first, but now I'm okay. I'm going to China in about a month and they think they can fix me up like new. I hope you like Chinese food," he said with a lecherous grin that disturbed her.

He couldn't help but be who he really was.

"Bill, I really don't understand what you're talking about. What's this China stuff?"

He gave her a disgusted look but caught himself. "I'm sorry. I thought you knew. I'm going to have to have some highly specialized surgery, which will make everything right for me, but let's not discuss it right now. Okay?"

"Oh, Bill, I'm so sorry. What's…"

"I said I didn't want to discuss it right now," he said with a burst of anger, his voice rising, and then gaining control mumbled out a "sorry."

"I'm sorry. We won't talk about it," he added with a cloying tone in his voice that made her shiver.

"No, I'm sorry. We'll talk when you want to talk," she said in her most submissive voice.

She saw he was watching her closely, his face inches away from hers.

"Good wine, huh?" he said, his eyes searching her face. "I'll get you some more."

She looked into his eyes. It was as if they both knew what was going on.

"You look tired, honey. Relax. We have plenty of time," he said.

"I'm okay," she said wondering if the valium and the wine might be too much. She was feeling a little lightheaded. She leaned up against him. He put his arm around her.

"Looks like you can use a little more wine," he said.

"No thanks," she said, putting her wineglass on the coffee table and leaning back deeper into the sofa. She closed her eyes for a moment, opened them, and closed them again.

"That's it, baby," he said soothingly, brushing the hair from her forehead, "Just relax." He wasn't sure what was going on. She said she drank some of the wine before she threw it out. He laced it with a good dose, so maybe she got enough in her, or maybe she was faking. He didn't care. He'd play along.

She closed her eyes, her breathing getting deeper. She was more frightened than she had ever been in her life, and she fought to keep her eyelids from springing open. She never felt so helpless. All she had were her ears, and she was using them to their fullest.

"You okay, baby?" he asked. She didn't move. He thought she might be faking, but why? He looked around the room again. Nothing unusual.

She fought her fear, trying to breathe deep and normal.

"You awake?" he said again.

No answer. Just heavy, even breathing. He looked around the room again, this time more carefully. He didn't see anything. He studied her closed eyes.

She had taken a self-hypnosis course, and she was using everything she learned about relaxation. She forced herself to go limp and let all the tension flow out of her extremities.

She felt him get up from the sofa. She heard him pick up the shopping bag and take something from it. She prayed it wasn't a gun. She didn't think that's what he would do, and she hoped she was right.

This entire escapade was dangerous. She knew that. She wanted to catch him on camera. She didn't think he'd try to kill her, but what if she were wrong? She realized now that this whole thing was stupid. She heard some rustling noises. Hogg was doing something. She felt him moving around. She couldn't stand it any longer. It had only been seconds, but fear overwhelmed her, and she reacted, jumping up from the sofa, blindly grasping at anything she could get her hands on.

"What the fuck," he yelled, as she felt her hands grabbing at him. Her eyes open now she saw she had her arms around his knee, causing him to fall backwards. Something hard hit her on the head.

Hanging on to his leg, Hogg fell back, just missing the coffee table, landing on his back, yanking her off the sofa. She was lying on his legs, her face pressed into the floor, her adrenalin taking over as something hard kept hitting her on the side of her head.

Using his legs, he pushed upwards and to the side, pushing her off him. Her back hit the coffee table. He was too strong for her. She saw a club or a bat swinging by her face as he rolled over and pinned her against the white carpet. She was about to scream when he clamped his hand over her mouth. He rolled her over on to her stomach, pulling her right arm behind her back. Something kept hitting her as pain shot through her shoulder.

"What is it with you? I'm not going to hurt you so why are you attacking me. Maybe you want it a little rough tonight and I can give that to you, baby. Now, calm down and let's have a good time. Okay, baby?"

She nodded her head, barely moving it.

"Good. No more screaming. One sound and I'm going to put my hands around that pretty neck of yours and squeeze until your face turns red, then blue, and your eyes pop out," he said his voice firm and then getting softer, "and you don't want that baby, do you?"

She shook her head, and he loosened his hand from her mouth. She was trying to keep it together.

"No more screaming, baby. Just sex like you never had before. You up for it?"

"Please," she sobbed, "please don't hurt me. I'll do whatever you want … anything. Please." she mumbled her voice cracking.

"Baby, I just want to make love to you. Like we always did."

She lay on the floor face down, afraid to move, and she heard him doing something, but she couldn't see what. She was frightened and had to get him to the sofa but how, and that's when her prayer was answered.

"I want you to get up, slowly, very slowly, and walk over to the sofa because I'm going to fuck you like I never fucked you before. Just do what I say and enjoy."

She began to get up and he moved around her, so he was always behind her.

"You know I wouldn't hurt you, baby. I just want to make love to you, like the old days, okay baby? You'll do that for me, won't you?"

She nodded. "Yes, but please don't hurt me," she whimpered her eyes on the sofa. She had to get to the sofa. She hoped the camera was catching all of it because this was rape.

She walked quickly, made her way around the coffee table, and was almost at the sofa when he yelled.

"Stop."

He came up behind her, something bumping her rear.

"Take off your panties before you lie down and spread your legs for me."

"I'm not wearing panties."

"Oh, baby. That's so good. You want it, don't you. Well, you just lay down on the sofa and spread those beautiful legs for me because I'm going to give you the fuck of your life."

She lay down on the sofa and that's when she saw it.

She gasped.

It looked ridiculous, but it wasn't funny. He had a big fake wooden cock strapped on with some sort of belt. The thing was huge, and it was drooping downward, probably because of its weight. It looked like a scene from a Tarantino movie. She was frightened but her head was clear. She was on the sofa. She wanted to appease him, keep him off guard.

"I didn't wear panties, baby. just like you like," she said in a baby doll voice, "so just take that fake thing off and give me the real you. I want it inside of me now, baby," she said breathlessly, "now, hurry."

He wondered what this bitch was up to trying to pretend she didn't know what she did to him. He'd piss on her face if he could.

She lay there, legs hanging over the side of the sofa; arms drooping at her side, her neck hurting because it was scrunched up against her chest. She saw the look in his eyes. They were devoid of any emotion, empty and distant. It was like they weren't even part of him.

"You don't move unless I tell you to move," he said standing over her. Because the dildo was so heavy, he used his left hand to hold up the tip and the other in the middle of the heavy dark brown wooden dildo.

She was frightened but now she felt some control. A cold calm had come over her.

"I just want to get into a better position so I can spread my legs better for you honey because your ah, you are so huge and hard and I want all of it," she said in a sexy and submissive voice.

"Take everything off. Everything. I want you naked."

She sat up and struggled out of her clothes as quickly as she could dropping them on the floor.

She lay down with her back up against the right side of the sofa, her feet still touching the floor. He had trouble keeping the strap-on upright, and he had to keep holding it up. That kept his hands busy.

"This one's for you, bitch," he growled and began to pull her one leg to the side.

"I have to go to the bathroom," she said.

"You think I'm going to let you go to the bathroom, bitch? Do you think I'm that stupid? Turn over baby because I'm going to fuck you in the ass. DO IT NOW," he said loudly, grabbing her arms and forcing her to turn. She hadn't expected this and as she lay on her stomach, her head jammed against the sofa arm, she grabbed at the sofa pillow as if she were trying to get something to hang on to.

This was the moment he had been waiting for. He was literally going to cut her a new asshole. Without warning he pressed down on her, pushing her into the sofa, trying to insert the huge wooden dildo into her ass. He was clumsy and out of control, mumbling and grunting, and the entire scene would have been hilarious if it hadn't been so real.

"I'm going to fuck you in the ass baby, and I don't want to hear a sound," he said, pulling her head back as he covered her mouth with his hand. "I'm going to ram this thing right through you," he said with venom in his voice that sounded almost supernatural.

"Stop. Please stop. Please don't hurt me," she pleaded, but she knew he wouldn't quit.

She had to stop him before he plunged that huge wooden thing into her. He was having trouble managing the oversized dildo. It was heavy and cumbersome and as he tried to get it under control, she managed to get her left hand under the sofa seat. Her right hand was unusable because it was jammed under her body.

She could feel the cold wood up against her rear and she screamed again for him to stop, but he was in an uncontrollable rage, growling unintelligible words as he struggled to maneuver the immense dildo into her rectum.

Using her left hand, she frantically searched under the pillow seat and found it, pulling out the Glock and firing wildly over her shoulder at Hogg, the sound echoing into her ear.

That's the last thing she remembers.

She fired three times, two bullets missing their mark. She had to twist her left hand and fire right past her ear at a slight upward angle, one .40 caliber bullet ripping into the left side of Hogg's neck, blasting a hole through his carotid artery. Blood spurted out like a geyser as Hogg's face went calm for an instant, then contorted into confusion, and finally realization. He looked as if he wanted to say something, his lips moving, but nothing coming out.

Right before he collapsed, his body stiffened, and a funny gurgling sound came out of his stomach and he fell forward, trapping her underneath him.

She struggled to free herself, wiggling out from under his dead weight and finally falling off the sofa to the floor, the gun still in her hand. She scrambled to a standing position and stepped away from the sofa. Hogg wasn't moving, and Heidi's silver and white condo was splattered by bright red blood.

She didn't remember any of that. She didn't remember phoning the police or throwing up. She didn't even remember shooting him.

She remembered hands putting a blanket around her because she was cold and shaking.

Somebody said she had to go with them. She thought she saw Otto and a lot of people in gray uniforms, but she wasn't sure.

People were chattering, all talking at once, faces drifting in and out through the fog, bright lights, funny noises, and then nothing.

THE HOSPITAL

SHE WOKE UP AND SAW A PALE CREAM CEILING. SHE DIDN'T KNOW where she was. She looked to the side and saw her arm connected to an IV. She must be in the hospital. She tried to think, but her mind wasn't working.

She thought she saw a nurse, maybe not, and then she dozed off until she saw another face. A man. She was so nauseated. She heard Otto's voice telling her everything was going to be all right, and then things came into focus. A nurse asked her how she was feeling. She mumbled "okay."

There were people in the room, but they were all blurry, like she was looking at them through plastic wrap.

"How are you?" Foley breathed, leaning down close to her face, and then things went hazy again.

She closed her eyes, hoping that shutting them would help clear them. When she opened them again, she saw people, men, around her bed.

A strange face leaned over her and spoke.

"I'm Bob Butler with the state police. When you feel well enough, we'll talk. You just let us know when you feel ready," he said with a soothing voice that sounded like he had done this many times before.

She tried to compose herself, remember what happened, but everything was so surreal. It was all like a dream. She rubbed her eyes and tried to sit up. She wanted to sit up so she could get control. The nurse jumped in and pushed some buttons bringing the bed up to a sitting position, asking her when she should stop.

Once she was sitting up, she saw what was going on around her. At first, she had trouble focusing, but finally she could see clearly. She looked around the room. There were some she didn't recognize, finally seeing the Chief and his son. She settled on Foley.

"May I talk to Mr. Foley, please," she said, "alone," she added weakly, as everybody fidgeted and shuffled around, mumbling and then they began to leave the room.

Foley nodded for his father to stay as the room cleared and somebody shut the door.

"I asked the Chief to stay, if that's okay with you?" he said.

"Fine. It's okay. Did you check the security video?" she asked, her voice stronger.

"Don't worry about that now, just rest," he said.

"Please, I need to know. Did you check the tapes?"

"Yeah. We have it all on tape and we've talked to the prosecutor. Here's what's going to happen. Technically, you're under custody right now. There's a police guard at the door. Once you're released from the hospital, there will be a Coroner's hearing. Everybody agrees it will be a mere formality. The tape exonerates you and it will be ruled attempted rape and self-defense. It will all be over in a few days," Foley explained.

"Hogg. Is he... what happened to him?"

Foley paused for a moment. "He's gone."

"Gone?"

"Dead."

"Oh, my God. He's... I, I killed him?"

"It's all over, Heidi. You did the right thing, the only thing you could do. It was self-defense."

"Has anybody heard from my mother?"

"She's on her way. Seems Hedy had some medical problems, nothing serious, and had to stay in New York for a few more days," Foley said.

"Is she okay?"

"She's fine," She'll be back here in a few days and you'll see for yourself.

"Your mother will be here in an hour or so. She's taking a chopper from the Pittsburgh airport," the Chief said.

"Thanks," she said.

"Look, you rest right now. You've been through a lot. When you're able, the police want to question you so just let the nurse know when you feel up to it. Lucky Hedy put that security system in when she did, or who knows how this would have all turned out," Foley said.

"Yeah," she said, "Who knows?"

EPILOGUE

AFTER VIEWING THE VIDEOTAPES, THE COUNTY AUTHORITIES agreed to release Heidi Kasser on her own recognizance the day after the shooting. A few days later, a Coroner's Inquest was held, and the court ruled that Hogg died from "lawful causes" and the case was closed. The dildo was entered as evidence. Not entered was a semen-filled rubber found in Hogg's brown paper bag. Authorities concluded Hogg was going to leave the semen at the scene of the crime to divert the police. It was agreed that it had no relevancy and trying to determine whose semen served no purpose, so it was discarded.

Joe Ducci's unclaimed body lay in the Fayette County Morgue for weeks. Officials tried to get Allegheny County to take the body but had no luck, and eventually he was buried in a pauper's grave in a rural part of Fayette County.

Because the latex gloves that he wore during the robbery were thin, police lifted two prints off the doorknob and a palm print from the table in the money room that matched Duck's.

The money was never recovered, and the case file remains open.

The insurance company covered the loss for Stony Creek.

When Joe Duck didn't contact Ruby Begonia about the trip to Stony Creek, she went looking for him. When he didn't answer the door, she jimmied the lock and went in, finding $3695 hidden in a fake hardback book. It only took her a few minutes to spot it in his bedroom. She knew that Joe Duck never read a book in his life. Ruby Begonia went on a shopping spree at Lane-Bryant and took a trip to Haiti.

The police executed search warrants for both of Hogg's homes and Duck's walk-up but found nothing significant. No evidence was ever found that implicated Hogg in the robbery. There was $14,000 cash found in a safe in Hogg's Stony Creek house, but it couldn't be tied to the robbery and the money was turned over to his wife.

When the authorities released his body, his wife had him cremated immediately. There were no burial services. A month later, she applied for permits to remodel both the Stony Creek property and their Uniontown home. Her brother was the contractor who worked on both houses. The gossip was that she wasn't remodeling, but tearing things apart looking for the money. Six months later, both houses were sold, and she moved to Florida.

Rumors spread, mostly among county morgue employees, that Hogg didn't have a penis. The rumors circulated in law enforcement entities across Pennsylvania and beyond. Along with the rumors, a pirated video tape of Hogg's crazy attack was making the rounds of police stations, although the authorities claimed they were never able to intercept a copy.

After weeks of family meetings and intense negotiations, an agreement was reached with JR Leon and he became the owner of Stony Creek. In the process, Leon told the Kasser family what he knew about his heritage. Originally, he was told that his mother died in childbirth. He said he was raised by nannies and rarely saw his surrogate father. JR said he never questioned his heritage, and when he received his trust fund, he spent his time building it into a fortune. It was only a few years ago, while cleaning out some family files, that he stumbled across some old documents. He found correspondence from lawyers to his surrogate father that caused him to investigate. He hired a Brazilian law firm to do the job, and they uncovered much of the truth.

He learned that his mother, Greta Kasser, had demanded that both she and Kimberly's name appear on the Brazilian birth certificate because "every child deserves to know where they came from." Kimberly refused, and after a fierce battle, Greta agreed to a settlement. Only her name would go on the birth certificate, and she signed an agreement that she would never reveal who the father was. In return, Kimberly set up a $500,000 trust fund for the boy payable to him on his 21st birthday. Kimberly's law firm provided Greta with a copy of a Brazilian birth certificate with her name on it. What she didn't know was that it was fake, and what Kimberly didn't know was that Greta had filed the birth with the American Embassy.

By the time he reached legal age the trust fund, much of it Ford stock, had grown to over ten million dollars which JR Leon then parlayed into billions.

When he learned the truth about his actual family, he was angry. As time passed, his attitude softened, and he wanted to meet his birth mother. His legal team advised caution and JR listened to them. When Greta died, he realized he had made a mistake in not contacting her. His guilt and anger drove him to his plan to buy Stony Creek. It was his way of validating his life.

As he learned more about the family, his feelings became mixed. When the opportunity came up to buy them out, he moved quickly. He wasn't sure what he'd do when he bought Stony Creek, but he pushed ahead. It was during this period that he wanted a family more than revenge. Once he purchased Stony Creek, he planned to tell them the truth.

In the end, it all worked out. JR confessed he hired Hogg to secure Heidi's vote, and hopefully Otto's confidence.

As soon as the deal was closed, he appointed Otto Kasser to the Board of Directors and Hedy Kasser was named CEO.

Rosamunde Kasser retired with a substantial financial package of cash and stock and bought a beachfront home in Manalapan, in Palm Beach County, Florida. She became involved in local social activities and was an active member of Donald Trump's exclusive Mar-a-Lago Club.

Heidi Kasser continues to live in Stony Creek where she has had an on-and-off relationship with Mike Barron, who is now head of operations. She is a major stockholder but plays no active role in the day-to-day operation. There were rumors, now silenced, that she had spent time in Western Psych in Pittsburgh, but it has never been confirmed.

Linda Nexton continued to tell Foley that she was coming back to work, but time and distance took over. Foley learned she was living in Philadelphia with her husband, Bobby Wagner. She was a Vice President of a large multi-national corporation and was moving up the ranks. She called Foley a few times, usually when she had too much to drink, but that soon dwindled into nothing.

It took a while, but Foley finally let his love for Linda Nexton go and moved on.

Unfortunately, when she left the company, The Security Bureau struggled to fill the hole she created. He kept the Stony Creek account but could not follow-up on JR Leon's interest because of staffing problems. He had to rebuild the company and financing it was a problem when money came from an unexpected source. The Chief offered to fund a rebuilding program with $250,000 cash for a piece of the action. Foley knew his father was a cash stasher, usually burying it in various places around his home, but a quarter of a million dollars stunned him. With all the old man's nefarious deals, Foley couldn't see him accumulating that much money, but with the Chief, you just never knew. After refusing the money at first, Foley finally accepted, and his company is now growing into a prosperous security company that is branching out in other cities. The Chief receives a monthly expense check and has a consulting agreement with the firm.

The Chief retired from Stony Creek and hangs out with a bunch of his cronies, playing cards, and watching for what he calls "opportunities." He still gets up to Stony Creek monthly, where he runs a private card game in one of the hotel suites. Nobody has bothered him about it.

Hedy and Foley struck up a friendship and are dating. Their relationship is casual. Time and distance have been a deterrent, but they do get together when they can.

It was at one of their weekend get-togethers that Foley caught Hedy off guard, making a statement that startled her.

"I know who shot Hogg," he said.

"So do I," she said flippantly, wondering why this had come up.

"I know," he said confidently. It was his inflection on the word "know" that made Hedy realize he was getting into something that was never discussed before.

"Everybody knows," she said, "It's on the videotape. Why are you bringing this up?"

"You can't always believe what you see," he said.

"Are you sure you want to go down this road?" she said, smiling.

She hoped that would end the conversation, but Foley persisted. She was getting annoyed.

"Foley, this is no joke. I have no idea what you're talking about," she said, a defensive edge in her voice.

"Pull up your blouse," Foley said, looking directly at her and smiling.

"Foley, be serious."

"I am being serious. Just do this for me. Pull up your blouse, please, just so I can see your tummy."

She was puzzled, and her face showed it. Keeping her eyes locked on his she gently pulled up her white silk blouse, exposing her stomach.

He bent down and kissed her on her belly button, stood back up and said, "I do like you."

He could see the confusion in her face and when she was about to speak, he put his finger to her lips.

"Nobody can really tell you and Heidi apart. You are so much alike in looks, but not in personalities. But you can hide a personality," he said still smiling, "and I noticed something the night Hogg was shot. It took me awhile to realize what it was. Remember Valentine's Day when we all went down to the indoor pool for a swim? There was me, you, Heidi and Mike Barron."

Hedy nodded, still trying to figure out where he was going with this.

"I was looking at your beautiful flat belly, and I must admit with lust, when it struck me. I immediately looked at your lovely sister in her bikini and that confirmed it for me. The night Hogg was shot, Heidi was a mess. She had somehow tried to get some clothes on, but she was in a daze. Me and the old man were the first people to get there, and I tried to get some clothes on Heidi. That's when I saw it. I saw that Heidi had an 'outtie,'" he said putting his finger on Hedy's belly button, "and the person who shot Hogg had an 'innie,' and you, my darling, have an 'innie,'" he said smiling.

Hedy was taken aback for a moment, pulled herself together, smiled cutely at him, and said coyly, "and you have an overactive imagination. I think we should leave it at that. It could be a very slippery slope and I don't think you want to go down it."

She rose on her toes and gave him a peck on the lips, and with a big grin added, "Do you?"

He nodded and gave her a gentle kiss.

"Only on skis, darlin'. Only on skis."

ACKNOWLEDGEMENTS

If you want to read great poetry check out Leslie Anne McIlroy.